THE EMPRESS SWORD

Wonderful things said about
The Empress Sword

⚬⚬⚬

The Empress Sword is a wonderfully vivid tale with a most intriguing twist. Just the right mix of light humor and quirky characters that kept the pages turning and left me wanting more... What a delightful tale!

> – Chris A. Jackson, author of *Scimitar Moon*, 2009
> *ForeWord* Book of the Year Gold Medal Winner

The Empress Sword carries the reader on an unexpected journey full of excitement, mystery, and new perspectives.

> – Christiana Ellis, award-winning writer and podcaster

The Empress Sword is a charming tale of dragons and magic, of trust and betrayal, of bravery and vulnerability. Her crisp vision and poignant story telling conspire to take the reader along as a young prince learns that all is not exactly what it seems. Highly recommended.

> – Nathan Lowell, creator of the
> *Golden Age of the Solar Clipper*

With The Empress Sword, Paulette Jaxton follows in the footsteps of great story-tellers by delivering a fabulous tale in a fantasy world we all remember from our childhood. A giant dragon, a 13-year-old prince and a quest for a magical item – classic fantasy, so far. But there is more: strong girls and independent women as well as characters that do not fit into standard black and white categories of this genre and force the listeners to re-consider their first impressions or completely change perspectives in the course of the book. All in all, it is a fast paced ride for younger and older listeners.

> – Alexander HTN, iTunes reviewer

Paulette Jaxton has written an intriguing story with a classic fantasy background. I'm not normally a fan of the swords and sorcery type stories, but the turns this story takes are unexpected, and certainly drive the character development. Seeing the changes that Prince Aster goes through with his search for the sword, it causes a reader to think about his or her own identity.

– sjg1978, iTunes reviewer

Far from the usual fare in fantasy fiction, *The Empress Sword* shakes things up and invites us to re-examine standard archetypes from a new perspective. Ms. Jaxton not only spins a fine yarn, she does so with both authority and accessibility, using the fantasy genre to express complex ideas in clear, engaging language. Throughout the novel, the author resists the temptation to resort to clichés, except as a precursor to breaking them. Instead, she focuses on the internal challenges of a lead character faced with extraordinary circumstances. The fantasy elements...[provide] a vehicle in which the author explores a variety of human issues, sometimes with surprising clarity. Insightful, intelligent, and playful...a pleasant, if unorthodox, journey through the world of *The Empress Sword*.

– Heather Hibbs, iTunes reviewer

Jaxton leads you easily into a story of magic, growing up and consequences. The Empress Sword takes the well-known young prince slays dragon story and tips it upside down and inside out in the most delightful ways.

–Philippa Ballantine, author of *Geist* and *Spectyr*

THE EMPRESS SWORD

Paulette Jaxton

The Empress Sword

ISBN 13 978-1-897492-24-6

Printed and bound in the United States

www.dragonmoonpress.com

Acknowledgements

In spite of what I may have once believed, great books do not spring forth, fully formed, from the foreheads of authors like Athena sprang from Zeus. Instead they are hammered out over long months of hard work with lots of help from a whole bunch of people.

First and foremost I would like to thank Gwen Gades of Dragon Moon Press for giving this book a chance. In these days of dwindling sales and changing markets, it takes a special kind of publisher to give a new and untested writer her first chance.

Then there is my editor, Gabrielle Harbowy, who took the time to hold my hand and make this strange new process of turning a good story into an awesome book as painless and educational as I could have ever hoped.

I would like to thank all my first readers, second readers, rereaders and rerereaders for helping me turn this crazy idea into a coherent readable tale. Barbara Haass, Heather Haze, Nathan Lowell, Linda Bradley, Allison Duncan, Beq Vyper, R. Taylor, Heather Welliver and Marc Bailey all helped me to put the finishing touches on this story and along the way also helped me to become a better writer.

I'd also like to thank the one literary agent who took the time to send me something other than a form letter rejection. She let me know what she found lacking in my story and thus gave me the chance to make it better. I only wish she'd stayed with me for the duration.

And finally I'd like to send out a huge thank you to all of my loyal podcast listeners for keeping the dream of this book one day seeing print alive. Without their support and understanding, I'm sure this book would not be the treasure it has become.

Dedication

This book is dedicated to my mom, who has always supported my crazy dreams. The ones that worked out and even the ones that didn't.

The Dragon and the Prince

The cave was small, damp and confining. It was also remote, and provided the kind of protection a lone male needed if he ever hoped to get any rest. It was so narrow he could barely extend his wings to half their span, and right now he had a cramp in his left wingtip. Mandrake needed to stretch, he needed to fly, and he wanted revenge.

"A mountain!" His voice rumbled down the cave like a sounder of wild boars. His dam had taught him how to speak the human tongue—it was difficult, and some dragons never got the hang of it—but she'd thought it important and it was one of the things that had brought him this far. She'd also taught him about the humans' fascination with magic.

He moved to the mouth of the cave and stared out into the grey morning fog. A light rain splattered the muddy ground outside and the sound of the drops echoed off the cave walls around him.

"It should be clearer out near the coast." He spoke aloud in the noble and more powerful dragon tongue this time. *"Out past the human farms, where they till their pathetic fields, build their tiny houses and work their damned magic."*

Extending his sore wing into the drizzle, he stretched the tip until the cramp began to ease. Breathing in the cold damp air, he tried to gauge how much gas was in his chest sack. The gas made him lighter, allowing him to fly higher and farther if he so chose, but it was the destruction the gas could wreak upon the humans when ignited that interested him more today.

Stepping fully into the rain, he was able to straighten out his other wing. He flexed them both a few times to stretch the muscles in his back, and then leapt into the air. Rising quickly above the rain-soaked walls of the little ravine, he turned north and headed for the river.

The humans called this land Caledon. Mandrake desired to call it home, but before he could do that and awaken the others from their long slumber, he intended to drive every last human from these green rolling hills.

He turned westward when the river came into view. The valley it cut through the surrounding hills widened quickly into fields of tall grass. Wild cattle, grazing in the fields, broke into panicked stampedes as he glided above them. The remains of a farmhouse appeared, its scorched and broken walls covered with vines. It looked ancient, but he'd only burned it out a few years ago. Its former occupants obligingly fled the valley, never to return.

His thoughts drifted back to the mountain the humans had somehow conjured into existence while he slept. It was a massive and unnatural thing, with sheer rock walls rising higher than any dragon could fly. A thick blanket of fog that never seemed to change always obscured its base, completely covering the gap between the northern and southern ridges of the Eastern Mountains, right where the pass leading to the Valley of Wind had once been.

It could only have been put there by magic. The humans denied any knowledge of it, claiming the mountain had always been there, but he knew better.

For a thousand years he had slept in the frozen caves of the Slumberlands, dreaming of one day returning to the beautiful valley where he and his kind were born. He was the chosen one, the first to awaken, the pathfinder, and the one responsible for reclaiming their homeland. Now, thanks to the humans, there was a mountain in his way and he couldn't fulfill that destiny. Rather than disappoint the others, who still slept in the cold hills far to the north, he'd set himself the task of making a new homeland here in Caledon; one that was safe from humans and their magic.

Human settlements began appearing to either side of the river. Just a few farms huddled together at first, but these were soon replaced by villages and larger towns. Most showed signs of his previous attacks: burned out buildings, ruined orchards, cemeteries filled with fresh mounds. And yet the damnable humans clung to these places like lichen to a rock. He fought the temptation to attack each one over again, and quickened his pace.

Soon the salty tang of the ocean reached out to tickle his nostrils and he turned south. He'd long since driven the humans from the mouth of the river, and to the north lay the city of Castlekeep, where the king of Caledon had armies and sorcerers aplenty to challenge a lone dragon.

The humans were only truly dangerous in large numbers. Mandrake had defeated many a worthy knight in single combat and even held his own against two or three at a time. But an army could surround him, come at him from all sides, find his weak spots and maybe even hurt him.

Sorcerers were another matter altogether. They wouldn't face him openly. Instead, they set traps. They used spells to hide braces of archers or tried to capture him in webs of magic so pitifully weak he barely felt them. Still, it was those same sorcerers who had conjured up a mountain between him and his home. Yes, Castlekeep was best avoided for the time being.

In the distance he could make out the collection of buildings the humans called Merrifield. A small trading port, it acted as a collection point for food and goods destined for the city to the north. Its granaries and warehouses should be full with the summer's first harvest and would burn nicely.

Mandrake circled the town once, picking out his targets and assuring himself there were no hidden dangers. Nothing appeared amiss, no soldiers were lurking in the morning shadows and, more importantly, there were no signs of magic. Predictably, the humans panicked at the sight of him, running wildly in every direction except the one direction he wanted them to run in—away.

Banking to the east, out from the center of town, he began to slow his breathing. A dragon's fire was his most fearsome weapon; one that could do almost as much damage to the dragon himself if he wasn't careful. He finished his turn and leveled out, then filled his lungs with air and held it.

As he lined up on his first target—a storehouse for grain, by the looks of it—a lone figure appeared in the street before him. Unlike the others, this one did not run. Calmly and deliberately it raised a longbow and let fly a shaft directly at him.

The arrow struck Mandrake squarely in the chest, bouncing ineffectually off his scales. He glanced down as its shattered remains fell to the ground. There had been considerable power behind the shot, but not nearly enough to do him any real harm.

He regarded the figure standing in the street, already nocking a second arrow. *Some of them never give up,* he thought, letting gas seep into his throat. *And why is the first one to get in my way always a female?*

Mandrake opened his mouth slightly and began to exhale. In an instant the woman with the longbow, as well as the granary she so foolishly tried to protect, disappeared in a cloud of blue-white fire.

Prince Aster flattened himself against the stone wall of the bailey, looking quickly from side to side for any sign of his adversary. When he thought the coast was clear he made a dash for the staircase leading up to the wall walk. He sprinted up the stairs and crouched behind the low inner parapet.

He was pretty certain he hadn't been seen, until he turned around and saw the man in the chain mail armor and dark blue tunic of the royal guard, standing less than three yards away. The man raised his crossbow and looked as if he were about to speak. Aster quickly raised a finger to his lips and the guard relaxed.

The guardsman bowed his head ever so slightly to his prince while discreetly pointing down into the bailey. Aster saluted the man and then carefully peeked over the parapet. Standing in the middle of the bailey, looking about in every direction, was his enemy: the evil Lord Paul.

Aster grinned. Paul wasn't looking up and obviously had no idea where Aster was hiding. Now would be the perfect time to launch a surprise attack. He edged his way along the parapet until he reached the small wooden platform that could be used to haul supplies up to the wall walk during a siege. A siege, Aster mused, that had never come in his or his father's lifetimes.

A rope was tied to the platform's railing; its other end ran to a block and tackle suspended high overhead from a boom attached to the northeast tower. He slipped the knot and pulled on the rope until the block came tight to the boom, then wrapped the rope twice around his left arm and drew his sword. Standing at the platform's edge, he laughed loud enough to be heard throughout the courtyard.

"So Lord Paul, we meet at last!"

The boy standing below spun around and gazed up at the prince in wonder. "What are you doing up there, your High...Uh...So, there you are, Prince Aster! Did you think you could hide from me up there?"

"Hide? Never! I was merely seeking the high ground."

"That's pretty high ground." Paul looked nervous. "Don't you think you ought to come down from there so we can fight like men?"

"Why don't you come up here and fight? Oh, that's right, you don't like heights." Aster smiled. As far as he knew Paul had never even been up on the wall walk. "In that case, maybe I will come down there."

Aster took a step backwards and tugged on the rope. Down on the ground, Paul gasped. "No! Your Highness, don't!"

"Don't call your enemy 'your Highness'!" Aster launched himself off the platform. He swung out across the bailey, heading right for Paul. The young "lord" quickly drew his practice sword and managed to parry Aster's blow in mid-strike. Aster twisted away from the parry and started to swing upward again.

He laughed. This was his idea of fun, and he kept on laughing right up until he realized he'd held on too long. He was now quite high off the ground and rising quickly toward the bailey's inner wall. The prince managed to turn around and plant his feet on the wall instead of smashing into it. His knees took the impact, but the recoil sent him flying off in the direction of the tower. With no real goal other than to avoid hitting another wall, Aster let go of the rope.

He fell right on top of the stack of hay bales the guardsmen used for archery practice, utterly destroying the target in the process. As he fought to push aside the mounds of damp hay surrounding him, Aster heard the sound of running feet nearby and the clapping and cheering of grownups in the distance. Soon a hand appeared out of the hay and he grabbed for it.

Paul hauled the prince out of the pile and to his feet. "Are you all right, your Highness?"

Aster laughed. "You're not supposed to ask me if I'm all right. You're supposed to stand over my fallen body and gloat. You make a terrible evil sorcerer."

"I'm not playing now, your Highness. You scared me half to death. Please don't do that again. What if you'd been hurt?"

"Listen to the groomsman, your Highness."

Aster looked up at the sound of a husky voice and saw Captain Landings walking toward them from the garrison house. A large crowd of guardsmen had gathered on the porch to watch the boys playing and many were still clapping and laughing at what they'd just seen. Aster noted that Captain Landings was not laughing.

"That was very foolish. If you'd fallen a few yards to the left you could have skewered yourself on the practice dummies. As it is, I'm still out an archery target."

Aster glanced at the row of straw dummies tied to tall, pointy-topped poles, and flinched. Falling on one of those probably would have hurt more than falling on the hay, but since he hadn't fallen over there, what was the problem? He turned back to face the captain and forced a smile. "I was aiming for the archery target all along."

"Of course you were, your Highness." The big man came up behind Paul and clapped him on the shoulder. "That was a very nice move, Master Fisher. Your sword work is improving. One day soon I'll talk to the stable master about having you start guard training."

"Thank you, sir." Paul's face reddened as he stared at his feet, but Aster could tell the captain's words had lifted the boy's spirits. Paul, at twelve, was a year younger than the prince, but was already just as tall. People often said the two boys looked alike, except that the prince had the royal family's yellow hair where the stable boy's was brown. They'd been playmates as long as Aster could remember and Paul was his only real friend.

"So what have you boys been playing at this time? Storming the castle? Catching thieves? Rescuing pretty young maidens?"

Aster wrinkled his nose at that last one. "No, Paul's an evil sorcerer and I'm the brave prince come to defeat his evil schemes. It's from a new book I'm reading."

"I turned his princess into a goat." Paul raised his eyebrows and looked at Aster. They immediately broke into laughter.

Captain Landings chuckled. "Well, in that case we'll have to be careful which goat we roast for dinner. Aster, weren't you supposed to be at some sort of party this afternoon? Was that canceled?"

It was Aster's turn to look embarrassed. He kicked at his boots a few times, studying the grass that was now mostly covered in hay. "Well, actually..."

"There you are, your Highness. What in the world are you doing out here and why aren't you dressed yet?"

All three of them turned to see a tall man come marching through the gate that led to the palace courtyard. His immaculate white tunic had gold trim, and the crest of the royal household was emblazoned across the chest. In his arms, the man carried a stack of neatly folded clothing. It was Aster's valet, Louis, and the man looked furious.

"You are supposed to arrive at Lady Penelope's within the hour, and here you are rough-housing with the guardsmen again. Just look at you, you're a mess!"

Captain Landings edged his way towards the garrison house, suddenly preoccupied with studying the clouds. Paul looked longingly at the pile of hay, as though he wished to crawl inside it and disappear. That left Aster alone to face his valet. He decided to try an evasive maneuver first. "Is it that late? I was just on my way to my room. You go ahead, and I'll meet you there..."

"Please, your Highness, we don't have time for this." Louis held the bundle of clothing out to Aster. "Here are your clothes. Put them on and please be quick about it. Queen Constance is already in her carriage waiting on you."

Aster poked through the stack of clothes and frowned. There were an awful lot of ruffles and pleats on the shirt and the pants didn't seem to have a flap in the front. It was going to be a long, uncomfortable afternoon if he had to be dressed up like some prissy girl's doll the whole time.

"Can't I wear my new armor instead?"

Aster had received a handsome suit of armor just a month ago for his thirteenth birthday. It was made of hardened white leather and encrusted with bright gold fastenings. The epaulets were made of the deepest blue velvet and the buttons were studded with rare gemstones. He thought he looked pretty dashing in it.

"No you may not. This is a garden party, your Highness, not an affair of state. Besides, girls don't want to dance with young men dressed in battle armor."

Evasion hadn't worked, so he tried deception next. "I don't think I can go. I'm not feeling well. I fell and hurt my arm." Aster began massaging his arm. He winced in fake pain even as his eyebrows arched in expectation. Not that he really expected to get away with such a simple ploy.

"Then your Highness will simply have to suffer in the name of his people. Please, go get dressed!"

Aster's shoulders drooped as he took the bundle of clothing. He marched slowly toward the garrison house. Its porch was now empty, not a guardsman in sight. To a man, the royal guard would lay down their lives to defend their prince in battle, but apparently none were brave enough to face a member of the palace staff for him. He glanced over his shoulder at the tall valet and couldn't blame them.

"I think I'm old enough to dress myself. Go tell my mother I'll be right there."

Louis glanced at the gate, then took a step closer to the prince and crossed his arms. "Her Majesty's orders were to find you and make certain you were properly dressed and in her carriage in no more than ten minutes. Please be quick about it, your Highness."

Aster sighed and looked past his valet to where Paul stood by the ruined hay bales. His friend looked sympathetic, but also very relieved to not have been noticed. Louis followed Aster's gaze and turned on the stable boy.

"As for you, young man, the stable master is looking for you. While you were out here playing games, he had to make ready the queen's carriage all by himself. When I last saw him, he didn't look at all pleased."

Paul's face lost all its color and he dashed off through the gate without uttering a word. Louis looked back at Aster with a satisfied grin on his face, but the smile turned into a frown as he caught the prince glaring back at him. He pointed a long thin finger at the garrison house. "Now, your Highness."

Aster fought the temptation to stick out his tongue. He didn't want to go to Penelope's and he didn't understand why his mother wanted him to attend all these stupid parties anyway. They were never any fun. He was usually the only boy his age in attendance, and all he did, from the moment he showed up until the time he left, was dance with stupid girls and listen to them gossip about their stupid friends.

2

The Garden Party

Aster finished dressing, then followed his valet to the waiting carriage. His mother was already inside, but rather than being upset with her tardy son, she gushed about him.

"Oh Aster, you look so handsome in that outfit. The girls are going to eat you up today!"

Aster arched an eyebrow as he seated himself across from the queen. "Really, Mother? If they're so hungry, maybe I should bring along some table scraps."

"Don't be contrary. Social functions are an important part of ruling a kingdom. You'll find more political disputes are settled in the salon than on the battlefield."

The prince's shoulders drooped. "And what sort of treaty do you expect me to sign with Penelope?"

Lady Penelope Winthrop was Aster's cousin. She was a year older than the prince and her parents made no secret of their desire for her to become the next queen of Caledon.

"That's between you and Penelope, dear, but might I suggest you begin with a peace treaty? It's most unseemly to have the guest of honor arm wrestling the hostess."

"She started it!" Aster tried to stand, but the carriage set off and he was thrown backwards into the seat. He crossed his arms and pouted. "Anyway, it was more fun than talking to her. All she ever does is go on about the other girls and how ugly they are. If she doesn't like them, why does she keep inviting them to her parties?"

"It's called etiquette. You can't just invite anyone you want. There's an order to these things." The queen smiled, then turned to gaze out the window as if looking for a way to explain the intricacies of court life to her dim son. She was always making social politics sound so mysterious. Aster much preferred discussing politics with his father. The king didn't mince words about anything when talking to his son and only heir.

Aster sighed. "I suppose you'll want me to dance with her, too."

"The hostess gets the first and last dance, as is customary. In between, you will be dancing with eight other young ladies."

Aster jerked forward as if someone had punched him in the stomach. "Eight?"

"Well, it's only a garden party. We had to pare down the list from the sixteen girls who petitioned. We'll hold a ball at the castle soon to make it up to those who didn't get on the list."

Aster groaned. He stared out the window as the streets of Castlekeep gave way to the manicured pastures of the estate lands northeast of town. Soon the stately roof of Winthrop Manor appeared over a hill.

The Winthrop family had only been elevated to the nobility a few generations ago, but with their wealth and ambitious nature they had risen quickly in the ranks of Caledon's noble families. Now they stood just one marriage away from royalty, a marriage Aster would prefer to avoid if at all possible.

To Aster's dismay, his cousin was waiting for him when the carriage rolled to a stop. Penelope stood before the grand entrance flanked by what appeared to be all of Caledon's eligible noble daughters. Dressed in every imaginable hue not found in nature, the gaggle of girls looked like a field of tall flowers enchanted by a colorblind wizard.

He helped his mother down from the carriage and then turned to face a mass curtsy. Penelope was the last to rise and the first to speak. She blatantly ignored Aster and bowed her head to the queen.

"Your Majesty, you honor my father's house with your most gracious presence. Thank you for accepting our humble invitation."

"Humble?" Aster made a grunting noise and rolled his eyes upward, glancing across the overly ornate façade of the manor. Its walls were covered in blazing white stucco with hundreds of little gold-leafed decorations. There was probably more glass in the windows of this one wall than in any other two noble estates combined. "Humble is hardly the word I would use."

Penelope's head snapped up and she glared at him, eyes flashing with anger. "I'm certain your Highness knows many fine words. Perhaps later you can entertain us with some of the ones you've learned while spending all that time at the garrison house."

The collection of young women behind her tittered and blushed. Aster's hours spent in the company of the royal guardsmen were often the subject of court gossip. The time he addressed the assemblage at the age of seven using some of the more colorful language he'd heard from them was still a favorite topic.

He considered giving his cousin a few prime examples, but his mother held up her hand. "Hold your tongue, Aster. This is a party. Try to have some fun for a change. Penelope, we're most happy to have accepted your invitation. Where is your mother?"

Penelope bowed her head again and answered in a demure voice. "She awaits your Majesty in the salon, with tea."

"Excellent. Then I shall join my sister there and leave the festivities in your capable hands. Aster, escort these lovely young ladies to the garden and try to remember what I told you before."

"Yes, your Majesty." Aster bowed formally as his mother ascended the steps, followed by her attendants. This was not going to be anything like fun. And he didn't care how diplomatic it might be. He and Penelope simply didn't like one another, so being civil to her was little more than a joke. Reluctantly, he held out his arm for his cousin to take.

The anger still in her eyes betrayed the smile on Penelope's face. "Come along, your Highness. Wait until you see what Mother has done with the gardens."

Aster couldn't remember what the gardens had looked like the last time he was here, because they had never been the same on any two consecutive visits. Duchess Winifred Winthrop played with her gardens the way some people played chess: always trying something new, and never repeating even the moves that worked well.

He greatly preferred his mother's approach. She loved roses and they grew well in the poor soil and harsh conditions of the castle's few green areas. She tended them with loving care and the only change from year to year was the ever-increasing size and number of the blooms.

The Winthrop manor gardens turned out to be every bit as garish as the various girls' outfits. Bright colors exploded everywhere, seemingly placed so as not to complement one another at all. A great dance floor had been erected over a small pond Aster thought he remembered from before, and at the far end of the platform some musicians were tuning their instruments.

"I claim the first dance with His Royal Highness, Prince Aster." Penelope said it loudly enough for everyone in the garden to hear. Aster looked around and, as he feared, he was the only boy present. He sighed and led his cousin to the center of the dance floor as the other girls paired off around them.

He placed his right hand on Penelope's shoulder and raised his left for her to grasp. Despite his cousin's attempts to get closer, Aster used this grip to hold the girl off and make sure no other part of their bodies touched. They stood frozen in that position, poised for the music to begin, and Aster let his mind drift. *Two hours. No, three at least. Mother should be satisfied with that, and then we can leave.*

The music started and Aster began moving around the dance floor with Penelope in tow. He didn't bother trying to follow the other dancers. He knew they would follow his every move no matter what. He let his mind drift to other things while his feet moved in well practiced patterns. He tried to ignore his cousin as they glided in big lazy circles around the other girls, but Penelope wouldn't stay quiet for long.

"Can you believe that Mildred Hepplewhite? I swear she has spies who do nothing but sneak into my wardrobe and tell her what colors I'm wearing this season. The fat cow has the audacity to come to my party wearing the same color dress as me."

Aster glanced around, unsure just which girl Penelope was complaining about. "There are a lot of girls wearing pink."

"This isn't pink! Honestly, do you ever pay any attention to what I'm wearing? What do I have to do? Wear battle armor before you'll even notice..."

A commotion from the direction of the manor house drew everyone's attention. The dance continued for a few seconds more, but then the musicians faltered and everyone stopped dancing when Aster did. Soldiers of the royal guard, armed with crossbows, poured into the garden from the side gates. Aster recognized Lieutenant Maxwell of his mother's bodyguard and waved him over.

"What is it, Lieutenant? What's going on here?"

The guardsman dropped briefly to one knee, then rose and spoke hurriedly. "The dragon, your Highness, has attacked and destroyed Merrifield to the south. We must get the queen to safety."

Aster stiffened. Merrifield was less than a day's ride away, and the dragon could easily fly that distance in a matter of minutes. "Right! Mother is in the salon with Duchess Winthrop. Assign a detail to get these girls inside the manor, then reassemble at the front entrance. We'll make for the castle."

Turning to Penelope, he found her not at all frightened, as he'd expected, but rather with a furious look on her face. She hissed at him through clenched teeth. "That horrid dragon will not ruin my party. You can't leave yet!"

He couldn't help grinning as the lieutenant looped a sheathed broadsword over Aster's shoulder. He shrugged it comfortably into place across his back. Soon he'd be tall enough to wear one on his hip. He could already wear a short sword that way, but he still preferred the broadsword in a fight.

"Sorry, Penny, but duty calls."

Fury turned to steely determination in the girl's eyes. "Then I'm coming with you. I can wield a broadsword every bit as well as you can."

Aster tried not to laugh. The very idea of his cousin in that absurdly colorful, frilly dress, donning a broadsword and riding into battle against the dragon was just about the funniest thing he could imagine.

"Lieutenant, please escort Lady Penelope to the manor and make certain she remains there after we leave. You have the crown's permission to use force if necessary."

"Yes, your Highness." The lieutenant held a gloved hand to his lips to hide his grin.

"Aster!" Penelope screamed at him, but he held up a finger and looked at her with his best imitation of his father's most reproachful look. She took the hint and curtsied. "As you wish, *your Highness.*"

Aster turned toward the house with a self-satisfied smirk, only to find a dozen pairs of adoring eyes staring back at him. He sauntered through the crowd of insipid girls to the edge of the garden where the soldiers stood waiting. After selecting six guardsmen to accompany him, Aster entered the manor to find his mother.

As expected, Queen Constance was in the main salon sipping tea with her sister. Both women smiled as he entered, but their smiles faded quickly as the guardsmen tromped in after him. He crossed the room and knelt at his mother's knee.

"Your Majesty, we must return to the safety of the castle immediately."

Duchess Winthrop glared at him while the queen sedately set down her teacup and reached out to touch his shoulder. "Good heavens, Aster, don't be so dramatic. Just tell me what's happened."

"There's been another dragon attack. Merrifield's been destroyed."

The duchess gasped and all the color drained from her face. The queen turned and touched her sister's arm gently. "I'm sorry, but I really must go. Cosmos will need me. It's a shame, too, Penelope's party was only just starting. We'll do something at the castle soon."

"Of course. Of course. But Merrifield is less than a day's ride from here. Is it safe to travel?"

Aster stood quickly to attention and repeated something he had overheard in his father's council chambers. "So far, the dragon has never attacked armed riders. The queen will be quite safe."

His mother gave him that *you don't understand at all* look, then turned back to her sister. "Would you and Penelope like to come back to the castle with us?"

Duchess Winthrop was silent for a long moment, then shook her head. "Heavens, no. I have a house full of guests, and what sort of hostess would I be if I abandoned them at a time like this?"

Aster thought it was a brave gesture. The manor was built mainly for show and had no real defenses to speak of, especially not against a dragon attack. Still, he was just as glad not to have Penelope riding back to the castle with them.

"You know best." The queen patted her sister's knee and then stood. "All right, let's go. We don't want the king to worry."

If he even knows about it yet, Aster thought. He suspected the royal advisers would wait until the queen and prince were safely within the castle walls before breaking such news to his father.

Outside, he helped his mother into the waiting carriage and then mounted a horse offered to him by one of the guardsman. As he prepared to ride off he looked back up at the manor. Each of its many large windows contained one brightly clad girl, each with a silly doe-eyed look on her face.

Stupid girls! The dragon could see a display like that from leagues away!

The Adventure Begins

"Speak!"

King Cosmos stared down at the young page with cold, expectant eyes. Mandoline, his chief advisor and court sorcerer, leaned over the king's left shoulder, glaring at the boy as well. Still breathless from his run through the castle, the page shook visibly.

"The dragon has attacked again, your Majesty! The village of Merrifield has been all but burned to the ground. Many of the villagers were injured and those who are still missing...well, the dragon probably took them."

The king leaned heavily on the arm of his throne and pulled at his beard. "These attacks are becoming more and more frequent. At this rate there won't be a single village left untouched by summer's end. There must be some way to stop it, but how?"

He stared at the floor for a long uncomfortable moment, then noticed the page was still standing there shaking his head, a perplexed and anxious look on his young face. With a wave of his hand, the king dismissed the page. "Go to the garrison house and tell Captain Landings to send troops to aid the survivors."

"At once, your Majesty!"

The page hurried off, leaving the king alone with the sorcerer. Not completely alone, as it turned out. Aster used the distraction to sneak up behind a pillar closer to the throne.

"What am I going to do, old man? Merrifield is a little too close to ignore. The beast will surely attack Castlekeep soon."

Mandoline stepped from behind the throne to stand at his sovereign's side. "The dragon is clever. He avoids the seat of your power, while cutting off your supplies of food and trade. He steers clear of your armies by day and hides in the foothills by night."

"This dragon's been a thorn in my side for ten years. Haven't the people suffered enough? There must be something we can do!"

"You've done all that can be done, sire. The beast avoids large gatherings of soldiers, and all attempts to catch it by surprise have failed. Your bravest knights sacrificed themselves attempting to slay the dragon, and it only appears to have grown stronger as a result."

"Is there no magic which can rid us of this monster?"

"We've tried every spell known to have any effect on dragons, but either the ancient sorcerers exaggerated the power of their spells or we're simply too weak to make them work properly. Perhaps if we could combine our talents we might catch the beast off guard, but so far it's managed to avoid any such gathering of mages."

"What about all that research you've been telling me about? It's been years. What have you discovered?"

"Very little, I'm afraid. My research has taken me back over thousands of years of our history and many dragon cycles—all the way back to the great dragon wars of old, when the dragons were thought to have been wiped out. They disappeared entirely, only to return *en masse* a thousand years later. Every appearance since then has ended in chaos and ruin."

"And what of the last cycle? Are the legends of the old empire and a magic sword true?"

"True? That's debatable. There are many tales of ancient talismans with the power to defeat the dragons. The sword is said to have belonged to the ruler of the Eastern Empire. Unfortunately, any trace of the sword disappeared with the empire itself. If it existed at all, it is now beyond our grasp."

"Then what are we to do?"

The sorcerer bowed his head. "I fear we may simply have to suffer until the dragon is ready to slumber again."

"And how long will that be?"

"Another century or two, I should think."

The king paused and then shook his head. "Every now and then you can just tell me you don't know something. It might cheer me up. Now, leave me. I need to think."

"As your Majesty commands." Mandoline bowed and backed away, but then he paused for a moment, scanning the great hall with a scrutinizing gaze. He seemed to sniff the air like a wolf in search of prey, but then walked to the side door and faded from view.

Aster breathed a sigh of relief. He'd always taken his role as the future king seriously and could often be found eavesdropping like this on the affairs of court, sneaking a peak at forbidden texts in the royal library or pestering the castle guard for more fencing lessons.

Suddenly stepping from the shadows, Mandoline reached out and grabbed Aster by the ear. The prince began to protest, but the old wizard held a finger to his lips. In silence he dragged Aster from the great hall and out into the corridor.

"The king values his privacy, which includes having confidential discussions with his advisors beyond the prying ears of his upstart heir. How can you expect your father to discuss these troubled times freely, when you might be hiding behind the nearest tapestry?"

"I wasn't hiding behind a tapestry and I didn't hear anything that isn't already common knowledge. That page wasn't the only visitor to Castlekeep today with news from Merrifield, you know. Is what you said in there true, that there's a sword powerful enough to defeat the dragon?"

"Forget you ever heard us speak of that."

The prince smiled up at the old sorcerer. "Oh, come on. You know I'll just go to the library and look it up."

The old man sighed and stared down his nose at the prince. "What do you know of the Eastern Empire?"

"That it existed long ago and ruled over all the Four Kingdoms.

The Emperor was said to control dragons somehow and make them do his bidding. When the dragons took to the north to sleep for a thousand years, the Empire fell to the combined armies of the Four Kingdoms. The passage through the Eastern Mountains leading to the Empire and all traces of its people suddenly vanished and its location has been forgotten."

Mandoline paused, regarding the prince the way a gardener might look upon a weed. Then he shook his head. "I really must speak to the royal historian about changing the locks on the library doors. Sometimes you know far too much for your own good."

"I'm the crown prince. Would you have me unprepared to take my father's place?" Aster grinned. "How'd I do?"

"You were correct, for the most part, but missed two important facts. Firstly, there was no emperor. A woman named Afanasia ruled the Great Eastern Empire. As you said, she ruled by controlling dragons and she did so using the sword your father mentioned. Its magic was great, and many of the beasts were slain by it before they made peace with the empress. She used her alliance with the dragons to threaten the Four Kingdoms into joining her, and she ruled over them for decades."

Aster's eyebrows knitted together as he thought that over. "So when the dragons went away, the empress lost the power to rule over the other kingdoms. Why didn't she just use the sword to defeat the armies sent against her?"

"Perhaps the sword only has power over dragons. Or the empress may have simply chosen not to use it against our people. We shall probably never know."

"What's the other thing I got wrong?"

The corners of the old man's lips curled into something akin to a grin. "The location of the Eastern Empire may be hidden, but it has not been forgotten."

"You know where it is?" Aster's eyes grew wide. "We can go there and get the sword and use it to destroy the dragon!"

"No, we can not!" Mandoline's expression turned grim. "You don't understand the power behind such a weapon. Magic like that always requires a grave sacrifice from those who seek to use it. Do you know why most wizards are old men? It's because the ones stupid enough to fool with such things die young."

"But..."

"Enough! We've already lost our best knights fighting this dragon. We are not sending the precious remaining few out on a dangerous quest which will most likely cost them their lives or worse. I've made my decision and its final, so just let it go."

The old sorcerer turned on his heel and stomped off down the corridor, leaving the young prince seething in silence.

"I didn't say we should send the knights, you old fool," Aster whispered to himself. "And I never use the doors to get into the library."

The cliffs of Drakenshold provided the perfect spot upon which to build a castle. The sheer wall of rock rising out of the sea was unassailable. The dark stone towers and thick walls of the castle were equally formidable. The lush green fields beyond them provided the perfect setting upon which the city of Castlekeep had grown.

In all of Drakenshold's five hundred year history no enemy had scaled its walls. Luckily for the kingdom of Caledon, Prince Aster was not her enemy.

Aster had first climbed the rugged stone sea wall when he was only seven years old and he'd been using it as his private playground and access route ever since. Who needed secret passageways when nearly every room in the palace had a window looking out to sea? The long drop to the rocky coastline below posed no particular problem for a boy whose well-earned nickname was Prince Aster the Daring.

He worked his way up, carefully climbing from one huge stone block to the next, until he came to the three large windows of the royal library. Perched comfortably in the deep inset of the middle window, he peered through the glass at the darkened room beyond. By the dim light of the setting sun he saw the shiny new brass locks the librarian had hastily installed at Mandoline's order.

The prince smiled at that. It was a shame really, they'd even gone to the trouble of locking the windows, but the library wasn't his destination. He leaned back and looked up the face of the castle wall to where he knew a tiny window hid amongst the stone blocks several floors above.

He zigzagged up the wall, avoiding the pools of light spilling from his parents' rooms, until he arrived at a tiny slit of a window, barely visible in the growing twilight. The opening looked smaller than the last time he'd been here, but of course he'd grown some since then. It was a tight fit, but Aster managed to squeeze through the opening and emerge into a small room.

It smelled of old parchment, dusty tomes and stale mead. The walls were lined with shelves of old books, stacks of yellowing maps and hundreds of crumbling scrolls. There appeared to be no order to their placement, in stark contrast to the extreme tidiness of the main library below.

A single large table with one chair took up the center of the room. The table was covered completely with more books, maps and opened scrolls. A large inkwell with many ragged quills sticking out of its open top sat precariously close to the edge. A huge black stain on the floor attested to the many times it had been knocked over.

The only light in the room came from a small brass lamp suspended from the ceiling by a chain. The faint blue light it cast on the table below gave the final clue to the room's purpose. It was a sorcerer's lamp, the kind that never needed oil, which meant this was Mandoline's private study chamber.

Aster crossed to the room's only door. Not surprisingly, it was unlocked. He knew from previous visits that the secret door to the library at the bottom of the long circular staircase beyond was always kept locked. It was also guarded by spells he was sure would leave a lasting impression on anyone foolhardy enough to challenge them.

He turned to the table full of papers, looking for the information he felt sure would be found there. Among the stacks of books he found a history of the Kingdoms that he'd never seen before. He carefully removed it from the pile and laid it on the table. A bright green ribbon had been used as a place marker, so he opened the old tome to that spot.

He grinned when he read the first few lines. "So, the old wizard has been researching the sword, after all."

He pulled the chair closer to the table and began reading.

The weapon destined to become the Empress Sword was forged in the forty-seventh year of the reign of King Grayval, son of Exeter, for his daughter, Princess Afanasia. By royal decree the sword was made smaller and lighter so the Princess could handle it better in battle...

"Typical," Aster muttered. "Girls are always making those excuses: 'It's too heavy,' or 'I can't reach that.'"

Shortly after the sword's presentation on the Princess's thirteenth birthday, both she and the sword disappeared and were not seen again for two years. It is believed that during this time the sword acquired its magical powers. All that is known for certain is that the Princess went alone into the Eastern Mountains looking for a way to end the dragon menace...

"She went into the mountains alone when she was my age? Pretty gutsy for a girl!"

The nature of the sword's magic is not well understood. Although Afanasia slew many dragons with it, more often than not the sword was used to subjugate them. Whether it held some power over them, or they chose to swear fealty to the Empress rather than face the awesome power of the sword, is not known.

"All that matters to me is that it has the power to kill the beast. Now, where was this Empire located?"

Aster closed the book and returned it to the stack where he'd found it. He foraged though the piles of old maps and scrolls until he turned up an ancient map drawn on yellowed parchment and another made more recently. Aside from the obvious differences in script and place names they looked pretty much the same.

However, when Aster closely examined the range of mountains along the eastern edge of each map, he found a small pass drawn on the older one that did not appear on any contemporary charts.

"That must be where it is, but how do I find something that doesn't exist according to any court cartographer for the last thousand years?"

He searched through the scrolls looking for Mandoline's distinctive scrawl. He didn't know whether the wizard had the worst penmanship in the Four Kingdoms or if he did it on purpose to make his writings harder to decipher. But Aster could not mistake the old man's notes for anything else when he finally found them underneath an old book.

He scanned the parchment carefully, picking out a few of the less garbled passages to read until he finally found something unusual. He recognized the ancient symbol representing a spell book and determined that the badly drawn characters just before it were probably the title. There were also two numbers that looked like they might refer to a page or paragraph.

He looked around the small room at all the bookcases. Anything Mandoline kept here permanently on those shelves was most likely a spell book. It would take him hours to search through them all. He looked hopefully at the stacks of books on the table, but they all seemed to be textbooks brought up from the main library.

His hand came to rest on the old book under which he'd found Mandoline's notes. He glanced at its ancient spine, but if there had ever been a title there it had succumbed to the ravages of time long ago. He carefully lifted the fragile cover and glanced idly at the first page. The archaic symbols he saw there matched those from the old sorcerer's notes perfectly.

Aster carefully turned the brittle pages one by one until he came to the one referred to in Mandoline's notes. As with most books of this type the spells themselves were written in the arcane symbols of the sorcerer's art, but the description was in the common tongue.

The young prince's forehead wrinkled as he struggled to read the ancient text. *Shrouded in Mist: A spell to call upon the forces of wind and water to hide anything from a hut to a whole city within a cloud of dense fog.*

"What's that possibly got to do with…wait just a minute."

He pulled out the maps again and placed them side by side, aligning the Eastern Ridge on the ancient map with the contemporary one. Where the older map showed a narrow pass through the mountains, the newer one showed a high mountain peak. He scrambled to find an atlas among the stacks on the table and quickly looked up its name.

"The Misty Mountain…" A smile broke across his young face. "The mountain doesn't really exist! It's just an illusion hidden inside a magical cloud. If you know there's nothing actually there, you can probably ride right through it!" And somewhere beyond the pass lay the Eastern Empire and the Empress Sword.

Aster quickly put everything back the way he'd found it. The Misty Mountain was a well known landmark about ten days' ride from Castlekeep. He shouldn't have any problem finding his way, and with any luck he'd get there and back again before his father sent the army out looking for him. He squeezed back out the narrow slit and scaled down the wall again to the window of his own room.

Escaping the Castle

Aster crawled through his bedroom window and went right to the big wardrobe. Opening both doors, he looked longingly at the handsome new armor hanging on a dressing dummy inside. He might need heavy armor on this quest—he had no idea what dangers he would face—but he also knew that anyone seeing him in the gleaming white leathers would recognize him instantly. So he let the armor be and turned to the drawers on the other side of the wardrobe.

Crouching down, he pulled the bottom drawer completely out and set it aside. Then, reaching as far back into the wardrobe as he could, he grabbed the old haversack hidden there. This was followed by a pair of well worn riding boots, a bundle of simple linen riding clothes, and his most prized possession: a tarnished chain mail shirt.

Paul had one just like it. The boys had made the shirts the year before, from an old suit of armor Captain Landings had given them. They'd worn them all summer, storming troll caves, battling sea monsters, and parading victoriously through the castle. But they'd both grown over the winter and now the shirts were too tight.

Aster found his belt knife in the haversack and used it to cut the leather bindings down both sides of the shirt. He could replace them later with longer ones, but for now this would allow him to drape the chain mail over his riding clothes. His sides might be open to attack, but even a little protection was better than none.

He changed into the riding clothes, packed the mail shirt into the haversack and added a few books and a couple of extra undershirts. At the last minute he also packed one of his fine silk coats, as well. He had no idea if there were people still living in the Eastern Empire, but it might be a good idea to show up looking like the Prince of Caledon if there were.

He slung the pack over his shoulder and leapt up onto the windowsill. With a grin he pulled the windows closed behind him and started climbing down the sea wall. A few minutes later he crawled through one of the windows of the palace kitchen. It wasn't the real kitchen—that was in a separate building out back where the great hearths were tended all night long. This area was used for plating the food before carrying it up to the various dining rooms on the palace's main floor.

As he'd expected, it was deserted. He was able to walk casually over to the small larder and take what he needed. He filled a sack with dried meats, fruit, and some of the hard crackers the cooks made to feed the goats. From past experience he knew they tasted all right and wouldn't crumble up in his pack.

He worked his way quietly down the corridor, past the sleeping quarters of the house staff, and exited the palace through the service door. He was surprised to find the baker's cart sitting in the middle of the small courtyard. The baker's horse made some noise as he ran by, but not enough to awaken anyone. He wondered why the baker's cart was there so late. Everyone in the castle should already be in bed.

The royal stables were just on the other side of the courtyard, and Aster slipped silently through the gate and into the paddock. Twenty minutes later, he'd found his favorite horse, Troy, and was in the process of saddling him when he heard a noise from inside the stable.

"Your Highness?"

A light appeared at the doorway and Aster spied a short figure in a night gown, staring out at him from behind a lamp.

"Paul?"

"What are you doing, your Highness? It's late."

"I know it's late. I'm saddling my horse."

Paul walked across the paddock and held the lamp up to Troy's saddle. "Well, you're doing it all wrong. That's not how you tie off the saddle strap. You won't get half a league before that slips and you go flying off. Why are you out here trying to do this in the dark anyway?"

"Obviously, because I didn't want to wake everyone up by doing it inside. Did I wake the stable master, too?" This was not a part of Aster's plan. If any adults found him out here, or his friend raised an alarm, his quest would end very quickly.

"No, Old Ben could sleep through a dragon attack. It usually takes two guardsmen to wake him any time before dawn. What in the world are you up to? It's the middle of the night."

"Can you think of a better time to sneak out of the castle?"

"Why are you sneaking out? Are you going hunting by yourself again?" Paul paused and tipped his head to one side. Then a smile broke across his face. "You're going on an adventure, aren't you?"

Aster grinned. "Listen, there's a magic sword with the power to defeat the dragon hidden away in the eastern mountains. Mandoline told me about it."

"The Lord Sorcerer told you where to find a magic sword? Why didn't he send the army to go get it?"

"Because he thinks it's too dangerous. Besides, the army is busy taking care of the people from Merrifield."

"But he thinks it's not too dangerous for you to go off and find it by yourself? That doesn't make sense, your Highness."

"Mandoline doesn't know anything about this. I snuck into his study and found out where the sword is; it's in the mountains somewhere east of the Misty Mountain. You can't tell anyone where I'm going. You have to promise me."

Paul tipped his head to the side again and stared at the prince. His smile faded into a frown, then he shook his head and crossed his arms. "I don't know about this, your Highness. It's just not right, you going off like this." Then he grinned. "You can't go on a proper adventure without supplies. You go back inside and get what you need. I'll finish saddling your horse."

Aster grinned and shook his finger at the stable boy. "One of these days I'm going to throw you in the dungeon for scaring me like that." He punched Paul in the arm, took the lantern and headed for the stable.

When he returned, his arms full of gear, Paul was standing there fully clothed, and holding the reins of two saddled horses.

"And just what do you think you're doing?" Aster stalked up to other boy and stood staring at him, unable to do anything else with his hands full.

"I'm going with you, of course. You want everyone to think you've gone hunting, right? Would you have gone hunting without me, your Highness?" Paul took the bedroll from under Aster's arm and went to tie it to Troy's saddle. Aster's only choice was to follow him.

"But this isn't a hunting trip. This is going to be dangerous." Without even thinking, Aster began handing over the rest of his gear for the stable boy to tie to the saddle as well.

"All the more reason you need me along. A knight doesn't ride into battle without his squire there to help him."

"Sometimes the battle doesn't wait for the knight. Sometimes the battle comes to the squire. What are you going to do if that happens?"

Paul turned and smiled. "Then my prince will be there to save me. Look, you have to take me with you. If you leave me behind, Old Ben will just beat me until I tell him where you've gone."

"He wouldn't dare!" The thought of his friend having Aster's whereabouts beaten out of him angered the prince, but he knew that was exactly what might happen; if not by the stable master then by someone even worse, like Mandoline. They would force Paul to tell them everything he knew, and then they would come looking for him. "Oh, all right, but I'll have to go back to the armory and get more equipment."

"Don't bother, your Highness. I'm all packed." Paul finished attaching the last of the gear to Aster's saddle and then turned to the other horse. It was a grey mare about the same height as Troy and her saddle was already laden with two large packs.

"Where did those come from?"

Paul handed Troy's reins to Aster and then stroked the grey mare's nose. "We keep a few packs loaded to outfit the king's messengers with, and some for the huntsmen too. Wendy here was supposed to be a messenger's horse, but she came up a hand and a half too short for them. She'll just end up pulling a wagon someday, so no one's likely to miss her for the next couple of weeks. How were you planning to get out of the castle, your Highness?"

Aster sighed. So much for striking off on his own. "I hadn't gotten that far yet. I suppose some sort of diversion, or maybe a disguise... Wait, did you say your horse can pull a wagon?"

"Sure, they can both pull wagons. How's that going to help us get out of the castle?"

Aster grinned, then tapped his head with a finger. "I've got an idea."

A little past midnight, a baker's wagon pulled off the King's Road just outside the city gates of Castlekeep. The cloaked driver secured the reins to the running board and stood, revealing the saddle he'd been sitting on to make him look taller.

"Is this where you wanted me to stop, your Highness?"

Aster stood inside the wagon and peeked out between the front curtains. It irked him that he was the one hiding inside while Paul got to drive the wagon out of the castle and through the city streets. The prince had always been so anxious to ride horses that he'd never paid much attention to how they were driven when hitched to a carriage.

"Yes, that's the roadhouse over there, where all the castle messengers change horses. I've heard the guardsmen talk about it lots of times. If we leave the wagon here, out of the way, it won't be discovered for a while."

"What if the baker needs it?" Paul swept the hood of the oversized cloak off his head. By the dim moonlight Aster could see the worry in the stable boy's eyes.

"It'll be fine. We're not stealing the wagon if we leave it somewhere he can find it. Besides, when they figure out who took it, my father will pay him for all his trouble. Now, go unhitch the horses and bring them around back."

Aster bent down and lifted the saddle off the seat while Paul shrugged the cloak off his shoulders and jumped to the ground. Aster carried the saddle to the back of the wagon and set it down next to the other one. Then he pulled apart the back curtains and waited for Paul.

His stomach rumbled, and he pressed on his tummy to quiet it. He shouldn't be hungry this late at night, but the baker's wagon smelled strongly of bread and yeast. He'd had to endure that smell for nearly an hour, and now he was starving. However, a thorough search of the interior had turned up nothing but a few empty flour sacks and some crumbs. He was about to go searching through his haversack for a cracker when Paul appeared with the horses in tow.

Aster laid his saddle gently on Troy's back from inside the wagon. "You know what I don't understand...why was the baker even at the castle tonight?"

"You don't know?" Paul looked up from between the horse's legs as he grabbed for the saddle strap. "He's sweet on Agnes."

"Agnes? The fat cook, Agnes?"

Paul straightened up on the other side of the horse and began tightening the straps. "They've been seeing each other since before your birthday party. He comes by the castle more and more and stays later every time. Henrietta thinks they're going to get married soon."

"So what have Fat Agnes and the baker been doing at the castle until all hours of the night?" The two boys stared at one another for a long silent moment before each screwed up his face and shook his shoulders like he'd just seen something disgusting. "I suddenly don't feel so bad about taking the wagon."

"Me neither, your Highness."

Aster leaned out of the wagon, placing his hands palm down on Troy's saddle and stretching out over his horse to get a better look at his friend. "Now, that's got to stop right now. If we're going to have any chance of reaching the Misty Mountain, no one must find out I'm the prince. It's bad enough they stamped my picture on all the sovereigns, but if *you* go around calling me *your Highness* all the time we'll wind up back in Drakenshold before the week's out."

Paul finished tying down the straps and let the stirrup drop down over top of them. He looked up at Aster. "I suppose you're right, your Highness."

Aster reached down and playfully bopped the stable boy on the head. "I said, stop that."

"All right then, what should I call you?"

Aster picked up Paul's heavier saddle and packs with a grunt and put it down on Wendy's back. "Take your pick, I've got enough names to fill a book. William, Fenrick, Harcort, Nicolas, Elgin, something else with an ick on the end, I forget the rest. Call me anything you like as long as it's not your Highness!"

"How about Aster?"

The prince leaned back and stroked his chin the way the king often did while contemplating matters of grave importance. His father had once told him it was all an act, that he only did this when he'd already made up his mind and just wanted everyone at court to sweat a little. "I deem your proposal acceptable to the crown, Master Fisher. It is so decreed, henceforth you shall call me Aster and I shall call you Alowishus."

"Oh no you don't!" Paul pulled the saddle strap tight and Wendy snorted. "Not the court herald, anything but that, your... your Aster-ness."

Aster started laughing as he hopped down from the wagon. He walked over to Troy, gathered up the reins and mounted his horse. "How about Louis?"

Paul mounted his own horse and moved her up next to Aster.

"Your valet? That's even worse."

Aster kicked lightly at Troy's sides and moved off, Paul following suit. "Then I shall call you Fat Agnes and you shall do all the cooking!"

"Aye, I know I'll do the cooking, otherwise we'll starve to death, but that's all I'm going to do for you. I'm saving myself for the baker."

They both dissolved into laughter as they headed down the road, into the darkness, riding east toward the mountains and adventure.

5

The New Boys in Town

ster, I think I can see the Misty Mountain from here!"

Aster looked up the hill to where Paul sat astride his mount, pointing at something in the distance. He turned back to the thorn-filled thicket covering the valley floor and scowled. Wiping his forehead on his sleeve, he turned Troy around and headed back to the top of the ridge.

They'd been traveling for nine days and Aster was generally pleased with the progress they had made. The Eastern Ridge was within sight now, a jagged line of blue peaks capped in white stretching from north to south ahead of them. Sometimes, like today, the going had been tough, but he was seeing more of the kingdom from astride his horse than he'd ever seen from inside his mother's carriage.

They met farmers along the way who graciously offered them food without ever suspecting they were feeding their prince. In the mornings he and Paul hunted small game in the fog-shrouded forests, they swam in cool ponds and streams during the heat of the day, and spent the warm quiet evenings sleeping out under the bright summer sky. Up until now, this adventure had been a lot of fun.

He reached the spot where Paul was sitting and stretched, standing in his stirrups and craning his neck to look back down at the bramble-choked valley. "I've got no idea where that stupid trail is now. I can't even see it anymore."

"Look." Paul was pointing again. His finger stretched out towards the line of the Eastern Ridge to the south. It was a beautiful day without a sign of a cloud. The Ridge stood out as a sharp white line against a deep blue sky. Except where Paul was pointing. There a fuzzy white ball obscured the line and from its midst a tiny solid peak wafted in and out of sight.

"I think you're right. That's got to be the Misty Mountain, and we're definitely going the wrong way." Aster looked from the mountain in the southeast to the line of ridges that were leading them further north. "We've got to find some way to turn south."

"We haven't seen any signs that anyone is out looking for you yet, and no one has recognized you. Why don't we head back to that dried out riverbed we crossed this morning? That looked like it might take us far enough south."

Aster took a deep breath and let it out slowly. "I suppose the King's Road can't be more than a few leagues away, and we're days east of Maybrook where the garrison post is. How are our supplies holding up?"

Paul scratched his head and looked skyward for a moment. "All the dried meat's gone. We've got a little of the cheese the Baileys gave us. Two apples, three potatoes and a cabbage root from the Gamblins. That's about it, except for all those goat crackers you swiped from the castle kitchen, but they're not even edible."

"I didn't swipe them. You can't steal something from your own kitchen. Besides, they're not so bad if you soak them in water." Aster grinned. "For a day or two. So you're telling me we need to stop for supplies."

"I don't fancy our chances hunting game down in those brambles. Finding a place to camp isn't going to be easy either." Paul had a way of looking like a puppy begging for table scraps when he really wanted Aster to change his mind.

Aster looked back the way they'd come, then into the distance ahead. "The chart I saw in Mandoline's study showed a trading village where the King's Road meets the Great Road. I suppose we could stop there for a little while."

Paul smiled, no longer the begging puppy. "We should get some oats for the horses too. And a stew pot, about the only thing you can do with a cabbage root is boil it. Then maybe we could..."

"I don't want to spend all day traipsing about some little town. There's bound to be a garrison there and we might be recognized." Aster turned his horse around and noticed Paul had already done so.

"You mean you might be recognized, your Highness. Even hundreds of leagues from Castlekeep, where no one has ever seen a member of the royal family, everyone is just waiting around for Prince Aster to show up and buy a stew pot."

"Well..." It did sound kind of silly, put that way.

"But nobody expects poor Paul Fisher the stable boy; he can move silently through the streets and buy anything he wants. Don't worry, your Highness, I'm sure we can find a nice cave for you to hide in while I ride into town to buy you cakes and pies."

Aster glared at the other boy now, who stared back defiantly. They stayed that way for several minutes, neither boy blinking, until Aster thought his eyeballs were about to pop out of his head. When he felt the corners of his mouth twitching into a smile, he took a deep breath.

"Race you to the riverbed!"

Aster kicked Troy in the sides and rose in the stirrups as the horse bolted into a gallop. Paul followed, racing across the hilltops, laughing all the way.

The race ended long before they reached the riverbed. It was too hot and the horses were carrying too much weight to gallop for long. Troy and Wendy slowed to a trot and then a walk despite their riders' insistent urgings. Even so, they arrived at the dried-out wash much sooner than Aster expected.

He rode down the hill into the gully first and headed out across the dusty rock strewn surface. Paul followed a bit more cautiously.

"Maybe we should ride along the riverbank? It might get muddy in places."

"There hasn't been water running in this gully for weeks. All the mud's dried hard as cobblestone. Why ride through the weeds when we have a perfectly good highway right here?"

They worked their way slowly down the riverbed as it twisted and turned through the little hills. Sometimes they were turned completely around, heading back the way they came, but eventually the river always took them further south. Aster thought they'd come about a league, as the crow flies, when they spotted a stone bridge in the distance.

Paul stood in his stirrups to get a better look. "That must be the King's Road already. I had no idea it was this close."

"We must have been closing the distance between for the last couple of days without knowing it. No sense looking a gift horse in the mouth, let's go." Aster kicked at Troy's sides and moved ahead at a trot. He listened to the sound of Troy's hooves clopping on the hard dried mud, occasionally hearing a pop or snap as a stone was crushed under their combined weight.

Then suddenly Troy stumbled and Aster was almost thrown off. The horse slowed to a walk and then stopped altogether. As Aster dismounted, Paul rode up beside them.

"I think he picked up a stone, your Highness." Despite Aster's repeated warnings, Paul still fell back on the honorific when he was nervous about something. "You could have fallen. Are you all right?"

"I'm fine, but I'm worried about Troy. Look how he's trying not to stand on that leg."

Troy was definitely favoring his right foreleg, holding the hoof off the ground whenever he could. Paul got down and positioned himself under Troy's shoulder. With some difficulty, Aster managed to lift up the hoof with both hands. There, wedged tightly between the iron shoe and the pad was a dense black rock with sharp looking edges.

"We've got to get that out, your Highness. Do you have a hoof pick?"

"What's a hoof pick?"

"It's what farriers use to clean the hoof before putting on a shoe."

Aster looked over his shoulder and stared at the stable boy. "Why on earth would I have brought something like that?"

Paul shrugged as best he could while supporting the horse's weight. "I don't know, but it's what we need to get that stone out."

Aster looked back at Troy's hoof and the little rock. He was having a hard time holding the heavy leg between his legs and he knew Paul wouldn't be able to balance the horse forever. "Well, we don't have one, whatever it is, so we'll just have to improvise."

Aster took out his belt knife and began to pry the rock loose.

"Be careful, your Highness."

"Stop calling me that!"

Troy grunted several times as Aster worked unsuccessfully to dislodge the stone. Finally he wedged the knife between the rock and the shoe and gave one swift yank. The rock flew out, but not before Aster's knife broke in two.

Aster swore under his breath. He'd had that belt knife for years. A guardsman gave it to him and showed him how to oil and hone the blade. It was about the only thing he owned that wasn't covered in jewels. With a sigh he slipped the remains of the knife into its sheath and started to examine Troy's hoof.

"There's a gash on the pad, probably from when the knife broke."

"If it's not bleeding, your... If it's not bleeding, he can walk on it."

Aster rolled his eyes and then poked at the horseshoe with his finger. "The worse thing is, the shoe's loose now."

"He'll need to be stabled and have someone fix that."

Aster dropped Troy's leg and stood up. "Like it or not, looks like we'll be spending the night in that little town, after all. I hope it's not too far away."

He moved out of the way as Paul crawled out from underneath the horse. When he began untying his haversack from the saddle, Paul tried to stop him.

"What are you doing?"

Aster pulled the haversack off the horse and away from the stable boy, then slung it over his shoulder. "I'm not making him carry any extra weight on that hoof. Especially when it's my fault it's hurting him."

"Then let me carry your pack. You can ride Wendy."

"You think a prince is too good to carry his own pack or walk his own horse? Don't be silly."

"Then at least let me put your pack on Wendy and I'll walk along with you. It wouldn't be right for me to ride while you're walking. Please, Aster?"

The prince looked his friend up and down, then smiled. He handed over his haversack and took up Troy's reins. "All right, you win. Now let's get out of this wash before somebody steps on another of these stupid rocks."

By mid-afternoon they'd come to the bridge and the main road. Turning east to follow it towards the mountains Aster quickened their pace. Soon crops began to replace grass on many of the hillsides, and on the others cattle grazed in silence. They met a farmer who told them the town wasn't much further and suggested a good stable. Finally they crested the last hill and got their first look at Traders Run.

Built at the crossing of the big north-south trade route and the King's Road from the west, Traders Run was just that: a town founded by and for the tradesmen carrying goods in and out of Caledon. As such there was no sign of a manor house or castle, just one church steeple and a large open market at the center of the town. The brightly colored tents of the market gave the village a carnival feel.

The stable was right where the farmer said it would be. It looked decent enough, but there was no sign of a farrier's shop or blacksmith. The doors were wide open, so they led the horses inside and found a man dressed in simple clothes grooming a horse. When the man didn't stop what he was doing or even glance in their direction, Aster cleared his throat. "Excuse me. My horse needs his shoe fixed."

The man set down his brush and then walked up to the boys, wiping his hands on the sides of his pants legs. He looked directly at Aster. "Of course, young master. What's wrong with the shoe?"

"It's loose. He picked up a stone outside of town. I'm afraid I may have cut him prying it free."

"Well, let's have a look at it then." The man stood regarding Troy for a moment and then without asking went straight for the leg with the loose shoe. He positioned himself under the horse's shoulder and expertly lifted the hoof between his legs with one hand. "Well now, this ain't so bad. This cut's not deep enough to worry about and I can have the blacksmith come look at it tomorrow."

"Tomorrow?"

The man dropped Troy's hoof and then began patting the horse down as he talked. "The blacksmith's shop is across town and he's usually busy this time of day. Not enough daylight left to fetch him and him get set up in time to work on your horse today. Don't worry, I can have him over first thing in the morning."

"Oh, that'll do, I guess."

Paul cleared his throat. "How much will that cost?"

The stable master glanced at Paul for a moment and then back to Aster. "We can take care of that in the morning, young master, after I settle up with the blacksmith. This is a fine animal you've got here. Where are you staying, so I can send your boy for you in the morning?"

"Staying? I don't really know. I've never been to Traders Run before."

"Really? What brings a young gentleman such as yourself to these parts?"

Aster hadn't considered what to tell people about his quest. Of course he was dying to tell everyone they met all about it, but he couldn't even say who he was. If he left a trail too easy to follow, his father would find him and stop him long before he found the Empress Sword. He'd never been good at lying, but in this situation there seemed to be no other choice.

"We're on our way to visit relatives." The man's eyes narrowed; he didn't look convinced. "In the south...a few days ride from here... uh...up in the mountains..."

"Oh, you must be Lord Evington's boy! You should have said so, lad. Everyone hereabouts knows of Lord Evington's hunting estate. You're a good bit closer than you think. Ain't more than a good day's ride from Traders Run. You'll be wanting to spend the night at the Five Crowns Inn then, best place in town."

"Thank you." Aster was relieved, but also a little confused by how easily he'd just taken on a whole new identity. Now he just had to hope Lord Evington's real son didn't show up in town as well.

"And your boy here can sleep with the horses. No extra charge." The stable master jerked his thumb at Paul.

"What do you mean sleep with the horses? He's sleeping at the inn with me."

"It's all right, Aster." Paul spoke softly even though the stable master, standing right in front of them, could hear every word. "I can sleep here."

"William at the Five Crowns don't take kindly to servants staying at his place."

Paul tugged at Aster's sleeve, but the prince brushed him away and took a step towards the stable master. "Paul happens to be a very good friend of mine. We've been traveling together for over a week and he sleeps where I sleep. What makes you think he's my servant?"

"Pardon my saying so, young master, but he is a bit scruffy looking."

"Scruffy looking?" Aster glanced over his shoulder at Paul who just nodded, looking sheepish. Aster turned back to the stable master. "We've been on the road and sleeping rough for nine days, how do you expect us to look? Of course we look scruffy. That's no reason to make assumptions about a person's station. Now, will you stable these horses and tell us where the Five Crowns Inn can be found, or not?"

The stable master actually cringed and Aster was worried he'd laid on the royal presence a bit too much, but the man's head bobbed up and down as he reached for Troy's reins. "Oh yes, young master. No problem at all. The inn is just a bit south of the market square along the main road. You can't miss it. Shall I send a boy around with your bags?"

"No, we'll take them ourselves." Aster turned to Paul and grinned. "Get our packs. We'll leave the rest of the supplies here."

Paul shook his head and then untied the packs from Wendy's saddle. When he'd done, the stable master led both horses to their stalls and the boys walked back out into the street.

Aster fidgeted with the buttons on his jerkin. It was the plainest one he had, soft leather with only a little embroidery down the front. He'd picked it out because he thought it would make him look like a commoner. "Do I look...scruffy?"

"Heavens no, but you did look an awful lot like a prince in there just now. " Paul chuckled. "But you shouldn't have. He was right. I do look like your servant."

"My clothes are every bit as dirty as yours Why would he assume I was some minor noble's son?"

"Well they're very nice clothes. Even dirty, they're obviously a lot nicer than what Ben gives me to wear. I'm not upset. He's right. If he thought you were a nobleman, it stands to reason I'd be your manservant."

"Oh." Aster looked back inside the stable, then grinned. "Hand me my haversack. I want to get something out of it before we go to the inn."

The Shopkeeper

The Five Crowns Inn was hard to miss. While most of the buildings in town were only a single story, the Five Crowns stood an impressive three stories tall. Well, impressive for Traders Run—buildings that tall were common in Castlekeep. There was also nothing lavish about the place, the windows were small, the walls hadn't been painted in some time and there was little in the way of decoration save the sign swinging above the door. Still, it stood out among its surroundings.

So did Paul, who looked very uncomfortable dressed in Aster's bright silk coat.

"I don't feel right wearing this. What if I tear it or something?"

"Then we'll find a tailor and get it fixed. Stop acting like I asked you to wear my crown. It's just a coat, and not a very fancy one at that."

"It's the fanciest thing I've ever had on, that's for sure."

The coat was made of a bright blue silk and had gold piping down the front and around the collar. There was little else in the way of decoration save some gold embroidery on the cuffs and the collar itself. The best thing about the coat, as far as Aster was concerned, were the pockets. There were two large ones, one on either side, with openings cleverly hidden by the side seams. There was also a special pocket just inside the left panel for a hidden dagger. Aster had never actually put a dagger in there, but he thought it was a great feature.

"Look, when we get inside, don't fidget with the coat. Just stand around looking important and I'll do all the talking. Maybe the innkeeper will think I'm your manservant." Aster grinned, but Paul's expression paled.

"Oh no, I wouldn't want anyone to think that, your high..."

"Shush! None of that your highness stuff, remember? Now come on, your lordship."

Aster winked and hurried through the door. Paul's shoulders drooped as he followed after the Prince. Inside, the first floor was one large room. Tables and chairs filled most of the space. There was a big hearth off to one side and at the back of the room a round faced man in spectacles stood behind a tall desk. Aster approached the man, who appeared to be busy writing something into a large book.

"Excuse me."

The man looked up and stared at him for a moment, then he glanced up at Paul standing by the door and a big smile spread across his face. "Hello there. How may I help you?"

"We need a place to sleep for the night. The man at stable said this was the best place in town. Would you have a room available?"

"The man at the stable was quite right, the Five Crowns is the finest inn east of Maybrook. My name's William Harrison and I'm the proprietor. We have several nice rooms available at the moment. How much were you looking to spend, young sir?"

Aster had no idea how much inns charged for a night's lodging and he glanced nervously over his shoulder at Paul. To be honest, he had no idea what anything cost. Subjects of the crown weren't in the habit of demanding payment from the people whose images were stamped on the money. He'd brought plenty of coins with him, so he turned back to the innkeeper and shrugged. "We'd like your best room, please."

The man hesitated for a moment, looking back and forth from Aster to Paul several times before responding. "Our best rooms are quite expensive, young man. They go for the equivalent of one gold sovereign a night."

"When you say the equivalent of a gold sovereign, would you accept an actual sovereign?" Aster reached into his belt pouch and pulled out several of the brightly polished coins.

Mr. Harrison's eyes widened. He slowly rounded the desk, never taking his eyes off the gold. When he was close enough to see that the coins were real, he smiled again. "I think you'll find room number three much to your liking, milord."

The room was actually a good bit smaller than his bedroom at the castle, but considering the size of the inn as a whole it was positively grand. The furnishings were an oddly mismatched collection of well crafted pieces, lending the room more the feeling of a second hand shop than the best lodgings in town. However, the only thing that really mattered was that the bed felt soft and the linens smelled clean.

When he asked Mr. Harrison where they might buy supplies, the man began rattling off the names of shops all over town. However, when Aster mentioned that he also needed a new belt knife, the innkeeper suggested he check with the traders in the central marketplace. The boys headed out to the street after a short argument over which side of the bed each would sleep on.

"You go find the shops he was talking about. Have them send all the supplies we need to the stable." Aster dumped a handful of coins into Paul's hand. The younger boy winced.

"I don't know, this is an awful lot of money. Maybe we should do this together."

"We don't have time. It'll be getting dark soon. You know what we need better than I do and I want to go looking for a knife. You don't have to spend all those coins, just give the shopkeepers whatever seems fair and hang on to the rest. Meet me at the marketplace when you're done."

Paul didn't look too happy, but he stuffed the coins into one of the pockets of the silk coat. He trudged off up the street, looking from side to side like a frightened animal in a wolf's den.

Aster felt sorry for his friend and almost went after him, but he really wanted to explore the village on his own. He'd never actually seen the working side of a town, except from inside his mother's carriage, and everything he saw fascinated him. Stopping to watch a wheelwright fit a new wheel to a wagon or a potter shaping clay into a bowl was like visiting a land of strange new wonders.

One part of town life he'd never missed while riding in a carriage was the smell, but actually seeing the animals and people those odors belonged to made them seem less fetid. The fouler smells soon gave way to more pleasant ones as he neared the market.

Following his nose, and the innkeeper's directions, he soon found the large plaza at the center of town. All four sides and most of the central area were crowded with multi-colored tents and wagons of every imaginable design. The smells of cooking meats and exotic spices assailed his senses. There seemed to be no order to the market; someone selling fine lace might be set up right next to someone selling salted pork. With no real idea where to begin, he just started wandering around, taking it all in.

At first he was reluctant to look too closely at any one table, preferring instead to walk down the center of the lanes running between the wagons. He wasn't certain what the proper protocol was for actually buying something, but after watching other people pawing at the goods he was soon walking right up to the tables and marveling at everything on display.

Under a canopy of bright orange stripes he found an array of blades. There was a rack with two fine long swords, a broadsword, and a wicked looking cutlass. Laid out on the table were several kinds of knives. Aster stopped to look over the small collection of belt knives. They all looked well made if not especially ornate. One in particular had a mottled grey blade that looked sturdy enough to pick a stone out of a horseshoe without breaking.

He glanced around for the merchant, but only saw a girl a bit shorter than himself with long brown hair, smiling at him from the next stall. He smiled back and nodded politely. He thought she might know where the merchant was, but with that silly grin on her face he didn't want to ask.

Turning back to the table, he picked up the knife and examined it more closely. He turned it over in his hands a couple of times, looking for imperfections. It would do him quite nicely, assuming he could find someone to buy it from.

"That's a good one. Are you looking for a new knife?"

Aster turned around to find the same girl, with the same silly smile on her face, now standing right next to him.

"Uh...well, yes. I broke my belt knife earlier today. Would you know where the owner of this stall might be found?"

"How did you break your belt knife?" The girl seemed to be ignoring the fact that Aster had asked her a question first.

"I was digging a stone out of my horse's hoof with it when it snapped in two."

"Well of course it snapped in two. Good knives aren't made to be used that way. Why didn't you use a hoof pick?"

"I don't have a hoof pick."

"You went riding out in the country without a hoof pick?"

"I didn't say I was riding out in the country."

"Where else would your horse pick up a stone?" The girl bent down and rooted around inside a chest lying beneath the table. When she stood up again, she handed Aster a small tool shaped like a question mark. "Locally made. It'll cost you six shillings at the blacksmith's shop. You can have it for four if you're still interested in the knife."

Aster looked dumbly at the knife in his other hand. He'd forgotten all about it for some reason. "Knife?"

"Finest blade I've got. It came from the famous forges of Keldon in the south. That blade has nearly a thousand folds; can you believe it? If you look closely you can just see the layering right there. Only three florins, a steal really, and I'll even throw in a sheath and the hoof pick for that price. What do you say?"

"Wait, wait, wait." Aster's head was reeling. "Who are you?"

"Maggie Griffin, merchant at your service, milord." She curtsied in a mocking sort of way.

"You expect me to believe these are your goods?"

"Ask anyone on the square. They'll tell you Maggie sells only the best quality goods at the lowest prices." She reached out and took the pick and the knife away from him.

"Hey!" Aster's voice cracked, shifting suddenly into falsetto. "I was going to buy those."

The girl giggled. "Well maybe I don't want to sell them to a total stranger. I've told you my name, but I still don't know yours, now do I?"

Aster had to blink away the confusion in his eyes. He wasn't used to meeting people who didn't already know who he was. "Aster. My name's Aster."

"Is that your first name or your family name? In polite society, it's customary to introduce yourself using your full name."

Now, Aster's full name could take a court herald more than twenty minutes to read aloud. He couldn't remember more than the first ten or so names himself, and he usually got those in the wrong order. He probably shouldn't risk using any of them, but what was he to call himself? The girl was staring at him impatiently, so he blurted out the first thing that came to mind. "Prince. My name's Aster Prince."

"Well now, I always wanted to meet a real live Prince." Maggie winked at him and then laughed. "It's a pleasure making your acquaintance, Mr. Prince. Will that be cash or were you planning to barter for the knife?"

Maggie shoved the knife and hoof pick back into his hands and stepped to the other side of the table. She searched around for a moment and then handed him a new leather sheath as well.

"Um...I can pay for them." He fumbled to take the sheath from her with one already full hand while trying to remove his belt pouch with the other.

"Easy there, you're going to stab yourself and I'm fresh out of lavender oil." Maggie reached across the table and took Aster's hand.

Her touch was warm and her grip surprisingly firm for a girl. She held his hand steady as she plucked the knife from it and slid the blade into the sheath.

Aster looked up from their clasped hands to find her smiling at him again. Only, this was a different smile from before. This one lit up her whole face and made her green eyes sparkle. He was barely able to croak out a whispered, "Thank you."

"Can't let the customers go around hurting themselves with the wares." She let go of his hand and grinned. "At least not until they're paid for."

She twisted around and went to the wagon. Aster noticed the fluid way she moved—quickly but not abruptly, so that the silky brown hair reaching nearly to her waist barely moved as she turned. She brought out a wooden box and opened it to reveal a small collection of coins.

Aster frowned when he saw them, they were all old and tarnished, some were even bent, and none of them were gold. He opened his pouch and looked in at his own collection of mirror bright coins fresh from the royal mint. He avoided the gold sovereigns—the ones with his picture on them—and selected three silver florins. These he dropped into Maggie's waiting palm.

She gave a whistle and eyed the shiny new coins dubiously. "Now there's something you don't see in Traders Run every day. Just where'd you come by these fancy things?"

"Um...Castlekeep, I just came from there a few days ago and all the coins look like that. I guess they just made a new batch or something."

Maggie took one of the coins and held it up to the light. She looked it over front and back and then bit down on it with her teeth. "No offense, but a girl can't take chances. Thank you for your custom, Mr. Prince. Enjoy your new knife and try not to use it like a pry bar, okay?"

"I'll try to remember that." Aster grinned. Up close she was really quite attractive and not at all like the girls he'd known at court. They were all soft and silly, but Maggie was...well, more like a boy. He suddenly wanted to get to know her better. "Would you do me the honor of joining me for dinner?"

"What?" For the first time Maggie looked as though she wasn't sure what to say next. She stared at him for a long awkward moment, but then cocked her head to one side. "You're joking with me now, aren't you?"

"No, I really mean it. I'm staying at this place called the Five Crowns. We could eat there if you'd care to join me..."

Maggie laughed. "The Five Crowns, you say?" She turned away for a second, her shoulders tensing like a cat preparing to strike. Then they sagged and she turned back to face him. "I'm terribly sorry, but I already have a dinner engagement with *Mister* Griffin."

"Mister..." Aster's jaw dropped. He'd guessed Maggie to be about his own age, but she was already married? "I'm sorry, I didn't realize. I'll take my leave then. Thank you for the knife. Give my regards to Mr. Griffin."

As he walked away he heard her giggling. She waited until he was several yards off before calling out after him. "I'll do that. My *father* will be pleased to know we have another satisfied customer."

The Huntsman

Aster felt his face redden as he hurried away from the sound of the girl's giggling. While Penelope often made sport out of baiting and embarrassing him, his cousin's attacks never hurt as much as this simple shopkeeper's laughter. What did he do wrong? Why didn't she want to eat a nice meal with him at the best inn in town?

He stared at the knife and hoof pick in his hands. He slipped the sheathed knife under his belt, but had no idea what to do with the other thing. He guessed Paul would know, hadn't he been going on about hoof picks when Troy first picked up the stone? And speaking of Paul, wasn't that his voice shouting in the distance?

Aster looked around and found that he'd wandered into a part of the marketplace populated by potion and talisman sellers. The darker color of the tents and the row upon row of glass jars filling the tables were a dead giveaway. He knew from Mandoline's constant warnings about secondhand magic that most of these traders were dealing in fake elixirs and useless trinkets.

He followed the sound and found Paul standing in front of a potion dealer's wagon. An old woman dressed in far too many layers of robes for a warm summer evening was standing over the stable boy, wagging a finger in his face and shouting at the top of her lungs. Paul, for his part, repeatedly tried to say something, but was cut off by the woman each time.

"How dare you come here just to make fun of common people! Someone needs to tan your hide before you get too big for your fancy silk britches, that's what! Well, what do you have to say for yourself?"

"Ma'am, I was only asking..."

"Don't ma'am me, you little lordling. You come around here, flashing your shiny coins and expect people to bow down to you, is that what you think?"

Aster put his hands behind his back, trying to hide the hoof pick. He didn't want to threaten this old woman, at least not yet. He cleared his throat and stepped forward. "Excuse me, are you having a problem, Paul?"

The old woman twisted around and stared down at Aster. He returned her gaze with a steady, calm look he'd learned from his mother. He made sure to blink once or twice before smiling at the woman.

"Who are you?" The old woman was no longer shouting.

"I didn't do nothing, I just asked a question and she started shouting at me." Paul took a step back from the woman, as if he'd been unable to do so before.

Aster's smile never wavered as he tipped his head ever so slightly to the side. "Is that so? Tell me, my good woman, what exactly did my friend ask that upset you so?"

"It weren't what he asked, but how he said it." By now the woman was facing Aster, her hands coming together in a wringing motion. "A noble lad, such as him, shouldn't make fun of us common folk."

"But I didn't..." Aster held up his hand to silence his friend.

"I'm sure he meant no disrespect, Paul's just not experienced in dealing with people below his station."

Behind the woman's back, Paul stuck out his tongue.

Aster had to fake a cough so as not to laugh. "If I may, what was the question?"

"I asked her if her healing potions worked on horses. I was going to get some for Troy's hoof."

Aster nodded and returned his wide-eyed gaze to the potion peddler. "Well, do your potions work on domestic animals?"

"Of course they do. There ain't much difference between a man and a horse anyways, they both have heads too big for their brains."

Aster turned so she wouldn't see him snort and ended up looking at a rack full of dark bottles. It was surprisingly neat compared to the old woman herself.

"Do you make all these yourself?"

"Don't be silly. Do I look like a sorcerer? I get most of my stock from up north in the Greylands, where they know a thing or two about healing potions. The rest are glamours from Igalia."

"Are the potions still potent? We're a long way from the Greylands."

The woman stiffened. "You think I'd sell old stock? I brung them down not three weeks ago. You ask anyone, they'll tell you, I only sell good potions."

Paul took that moment to pipe up. "Maybe you ought to show us how good they are?"

Aster sighed and frowned at him. He'd just about had the old woman in the palm of his hand, but now she glanced over her shoulder, obviously agitated again.

"Show you? Show you what?" She turned to glare at Aster again. "And you? I suppose you'd like to see something too?"

"Well, it might settle any question about the quality and potency of your wares." Aster thought if he batted his eyelids any faster they might fall off.

She turned on Paul again, jabbing her thumb back over her shoulder as she spoke. "You ought to be more like your friend here. He's a nice lad, but you..."

Paul stiffened as the old woman locked gazes with him. Aster began to suspect the woman had more magical ability than she let on.

"Yes, that's the ticket. You need to be more like your friend." The peddler went to the table on the far side of her stall and rummaged through a stack of small bottles. Presently she held one aloft, jiggled it a few times in the light from a nearby torch, and then came back to the boys. She shoved the little bottle at Paul.

"Drink this."

"What?" Paul nearly shrieked and held up his hands to ward off the bottle as if it were a wasp. "I'm not drinking that."

"It won't hurt you. Besides, you think my potions don't work anyway. Go on, drink it."

Paul looked beseechingly at Aster. It stood to reason the old woman wouldn't do anything to harm them. If she did have some magical ability, it wouldn't do her any good to raise suspicions. Mandoline had once told him some gruesome tales of what sorcerers did to their own when they went bad.

"Go ahead, let's see what happens." He smiled and winked.

Paul took the little bottle and the old woman pulled out the tiny cork. With a shaky hand Paul held it to his nose and sniffed. His eyebrows arched and he sniffed at it again. "Don't smell so bad." He put the bottle to his lips and took a sip. "Tastes sweet."

"Drink all of it, fool." The peddler reached over and pushed up on Paul's wrist to upend the bottle into his mouth. He swallowed. The old woman smiled, crossed her arms and leaned back. She reminded Aster of a cook who'd just put something savory in the oven.

"That wasn't so bad, left a funny taste in my mouth. What's supposed to happen?"

"Just wait, it shouldn't take long."

As Aster watched, Paul's dark hair began to lighten. In a matter of moments it had changed from brown to tan and then to yellow. He tried not to laugh, he really did, but he couldn't hold it for long.

"What? What are you laughing at?" Paul grabbed at his face, feeling for his nose and the outline of his mouth. "What did she do to me?"

Aster turned to the peddler. She wasn't laughing out loud, but the mirth showed in her old eyes. Aster took a deep breath and tried to keep a straight face. "We'll take a healing potion for my horse's hoof and I would also like to pay you for that excellent glamour you gave my friend."

The old woman reached past Aster and took two small bottles from the table behind him. "Two florins. Apply one of these directly to the wound and put a few drops of the other in its water for the next two days. Your horse should do fine, young master, and the glamour is on the house."

They both looked at Paul who was now examining his arms and feeling at his backside for a tail. He saw them grinning at him and whipped around to face them; his bright blond ponytail glistening in the torch light.

"What did she do to me?"

At breakfast the next morning, Paul was still fingering the hank of yellow hair draped over his shoulder. Aster looked up from his bowl of rather excellent porridge and tapped his spoon against his friend's tankard of apple juice.

"It won't rub off you know. It's not dyed, it's magic."

"I know, but how long do I have to look like this? It's weird."

Aster grinned. "You think looking like the prince of Caledon is weird?"

Paul's head snapped up and Aster nearly spit out the mouth full of oats he'd just tucked in. Last night, in the darkening marketplace, he'd failed to notice the old peddler had also changed Paul's eyes to blue. That was going to take more getting used to than the yellow hair.

"No disrespect, but yeah."

"You should try being the prince all the time. If she used an illusion spell, that should fade away in a few days..."

"But?"

"But, if it was a transmutation spell it'll probably stay that way. I guess we should have asked about that last night. We can go back and find the potion peddler before we leave, if you really want to know."

"No thanks, I'd rather look like you than face that scary old lady again."

They finished breakfast and paid the innkeeper, who looked disappointed that his best guests were leaving so soon. When they arrived at the stables, they found the blacksmith's wagon already outside and the sounds of metal striking metal ringing in the cool morning air.

"You go out back and see if the blacksmith is working on Troy. I'll go inside and see if the supplies showed up." Paul headed around the building towards the clanking sounds and Aster strolled through the open doors.

Inside he found a young man saddling a large black horse. Standing next to the stallion, dressed in bright huntsman's greens and with a long feather stuck in his cap, he looked for all the world like the hero from one of Aster's adventure books.

Aster saw his own saddle sitting on a rail near the paddock door. Below it sat two large bundles wrapped in canvas. He walked over and began examining the supplies.

"That your colt they're shoeing out back?" The young man didn't look up from tightening the saddle strap on his horse. "Fine looking animal, better than most of the nags you see around this place. Except for Nightstorm here, of course."

"Thank you. Troy's my favorite."

The young man looked up from what he was doing to stare at Aster. "Your favorite? Must be nice to have more than one horse to choose from. You're not from around here, are you?"

"Uh...no, I'm from Castlekeep. I'm here to do some...uh, hunting."

"Hunting, you say?" The young man suddenly seemed more interested. He stopped saddling his horse and turned to face Aster. "Then this could be your lucky day. My name's Eric Buckingham and I just happen to be the best huntsman in the whole east country. What sort of game are you looking for?"

Aster really should have given more thought to what he was going to say to people. The lies about what he was doing here were becoming more complex and harder to keep track of every time he talked to someone new. "Well, I don't really know. I was just going to head up into the mountains and see what I can find."

Eric raised his eyebrows at that. "Into the mountains? Only thing you're going to find up there are goats and maybe an elk if you're lucky. Not exactly the best game to go after alone. I could put together a hunting party for you by the end of the week. Wouldn't cost more than a sovereign a man and I'd guarantee you a nice big trophy to take back home."

Aster looked the boy over more carefully. He was tall, broad shouldered, dark haired and perhaps sixteen or seventeen years old. All the huntsmen he'd met on royal hunting parties were much older men with greying manes and years of experience. "With you leading the party, I suppose. Aren't you a little young?"

"Look who's talking—what are you, eleven? I'll have you know I supply the meat for half the inns in town. One day I'm going to catch the eye of a nobleman and become the youngest hunt master in the realm. So what do you say, you want me to take you into the hills so you can bring back a rack of antlers to impress mom and dad, or are you willing to show up empty-handed?"

"I'm thirteen, I can hunt very well on my own, thank you, and I can't wait around here for a whole week." For all Aster knew, a garrison of soldiers was marching from Castlekeep this very minute to bring him home. In another week he hoped to have the Empress Sword and be well on his way to killing the dragon.

"Then can I at least give you some advice? If you're really heading into the mountains, that kit of yours won't do." Eric pointed to the saddle and bundles at Aster's feet. "You're going to freeze to death unless you get some heavier blankets and you'd better take along some sapwood to start your fires. The scrub brush up there don't burn easy. Oh, and if you really expect to bag an ibex or elk, better take a longbow. You'll never get close enough to one for a crossbow shot."

Aster looked at the gear. The huntsman had a point. He'd forgotten it was colder up in the mountains, even in summer. The snow on the peaks should have reminded him of that. "Thank you. I'll stop by the marketplace on my way out of town."

"The marketplace? You should look for a wagon with an orange canopy. A girl named Maggie runs it with her father."

Aster groaned remembering the insufferable girl who'd sold him the knife. "Yes, I think I know the one. Long brown hair, likes to tease boys?"

"You've met Maggie? Isn't she a little firebrand? She and her father only started coming to Traders Run a couple of years ago, but she's already a fixture in the market. Tell her I sent you over and she'll get you everything you need."

"Is she your girlfriend?"

"My girlfriend?" Eric started laughing. "Heck no, Maggie's not my type. She's too much of a tomboy for me."

Aster wondered how anyone could not like a girl as pretty as Maggie who had the personality of a boy. "So what's your type?"

"My type?" Eric stopped laughing and started scratching his chin. "I like noble ladies, those who'd rather attend a fancy dress ball than stand around in the market all day selling cheap trinkets. Real ladies secretly prefer the rugged outdoors types like me, you know. One day, when I'm a famous hunt master, I'll have to beat the ladies off with a stick. You know what I'd really like to find? A princess in distress."

Aster chuckled, a bit too loudly. "Last time I looked, Caledon didn't have a princess. And I hear the prince isn't the type who needs rescuing."

Eric gave him a hard look and then turned back to saddling his horse. "No princesses? There are princesses out there, mark my word, and someday one of them is going to need someone like me to come along and rescue her. After that we'll be wed and I can settle down and do as I please for the rest of my days. Happens all the time in books."

Aster frowned. The books he liked usually did have a girl in them and at some point the hero always ended up saving her. More often than not the hero married the girl and they lived happily ever after. That had always sounded like a realistic outcome to him, until he heard Eric say it with such naive conviction.

"So, what sort of girls do you like?" Eric was looking at him with a crooked grin now and for some reason Aster blushed.

"I don't much like girls at all." Then he thought about the girl in the marketplace. "At least none of the girls where I come from."

Eric laughed. He finished with the saddle strap and pulled down the stirrup. Then in one quick fluid motion he put his foot in the stirrup and swung up onto his horse. He turned towards the stable doors then looked down at Aster.

"Then where do you come from? Good luck, kid. Happy hunting and if you change your mind about the hunting party, remember the name is Eric Buckingham, the finest huntsman in the east country."

Aster watched the cocky young man ride out of the stable and disappear down the street. "Does he always begin everything he says with a question?"

"Aye, that he does!" Aster jerked around, startled by the stable master, who was walking through the paddock door with Paul and the horses in tow. "Eric's a fine lad and almost as good a huntsman as he claims, but he's still young and foolish. The blacksmith's finished with your horse and that potion closed up the cut right away."

"How much do we owe you?" He took Troy's reins from Paul and stroked the horse's nose.

"Lord Evington usually settles up with me at the end of hunting season. I can just put it on his ledger."

"No, no, I want to pay now if you please. I...I don't really want Lord...er...father to know about this."

"Aye, lads. I think I understand. A sovereign should cover it all. I've already settled up with the blacksmith."

Aster dug one of the gold coins from his pouch and handed it to the man face down. The stable master smiled warmly and stuck it in a pocket without even looking at it. He watched them as they saddled their horses and tied the supply bundles in place. They were walking the horses out of the stable when he called after them.

"You know, I never realized Lord Evington had twins."

They rode through the foothills east of Traders Run for two more days and set camp within sight of the fog bank. The potion they'd put on Troy's hoof had worked its magic and the horse showed no sign of going lame. The potion the old woman had given Paul was still doing its work as well and Aster insisted he continue to wear the silk coat.

"I'm getting used to seeing you like that. Maybe when we get back to Castlekeep I'll let you be the prince for a while."

"Don't even joke about that, your Highness." Paul was cleaning up after the morning meal of dried fish and toasted bread. "I wouldn't know the first thing about being royalty. They'd know I weren't you and toss me in the dungeon for sure."

Aster laughed. "Well at least you wouldn't go hungry. The cooks use the dungeons to store vegetables for winter. That's why they won't let us play down there."

Aster finished rolling up his bedroll and tied it off. He stood up, grabbed his haversack and headed for the already saddled horses.

"Why do they keep vegetables in the dungeon? Where do they put the prisoners?" Paul finished stuffing the cook pot and several bags of food into his own pack and joined the prince.

"It's cool down there all summer and warm in the winter. Mandoline says it's not even magic, that's just how dungeons are. We've never had anyone do anything serious enough to throw them in the dungeon, so I don't know what we'd do. Toss them off the sea wall I guess."

"Well, I don't want to be tossed off any walls, especially the sea wall."

"You really don't like high places, do you?"

"No, your Highness, I surely don't." Paul hoisted the packs onto Wendy's back and started to tie them down. "Why I'm following you into the mountains is anybody's guess."

Aster looked at the mountain looming above them, shrouded in its perpetual mist of thick heavy fog. It was hard to believe this was all the result of magic. The occasional glimpses of the mountain itself certainly looked real enough, but then an illusion that didn't look real wouldn't fool anybody.

"I don't think you have anything to worry about. We won't be climbing the mountain itself and from the look of that fog bank, we'll be lucky if we can see the trail in front of us, much less how high up we are."

"There won't be any cliffs to fall off of, will there?"

Aster looked around, while they had climbed pretty high in the last couple of days, the land to either side was still mostly rolling hills. "I doubt it and if I'm right this used to be a trade route a thousand years ago. What's left of the road should be wide and flat. We'll be fine."

They finished loading the horses and walked them up the hill to the edge of the fog bank. Any doubts Aster may have harbored about the mist being the result of magic were dashed the moment he saw the wall of swirling white vapor. In spite of the blazing mid-summer sun the fog clung to the ground like a thick blanket of snow. When he thrust an arm into the vapor his hand all but disappeared.

"We're going into that?" Paul looked as skittish as the horses.

"It's just fog. Really thick fog, sure, but nothing to be afraid of." Aster mounted his horse and with some difficulty got Troy pointed up hill and into the fog.

"What if we lose track of each other. I been in bad fog before and it's real easy to lose track of things."

"Good point." Aster looked around a bit, then stared into the fog. "Got any rope?"

"Sure, we always put rope in the hunter's packs." Paul mounted his own horse and started rummaging in one of the packs. In a few moments he pulled out a coil of light rope.

"We'll tie the saddles together. As long as we stay with the horses we can't get lost."

The boys each tied one end of the rope to the horn of their saddles, then with a great deal of urging the horses moved into the fog. They were instantly plunged into a grey world where nothing seemed to be in the right place. Aster thought he'd be able to follow the trail, but he soon lost track of it and just tried to keep them moving in a straight line uphill towards the base of the mountain.

Nearly an hour later the mists began to thin before Aster. He urged Troy forward and they broke out into the sunshine. A few moments later Paul emerged right beside him.

"Um...Your Highness?"

Aster looked around expectantly only to discover they'd come out of the fog bank not twenty yards from where they'd entered it. They'd been traveling in circles the whole time.

"Okay, new plan. This time we walk and the horses follow. That way we'll be able to see when we leave the trail."

They dismounted and led their horses back to the trail. They hadn't gone more than ten yards into the fog again when Aster had to get down on his hands and knees, searching for signs of the trail. Even on his knees the mist was so thick he could barely make out details right in front of his face.

"What are we going to do now? Maybe we should go back before we get turned around again." Paul's nervous voice only angered the prince more.

"I'll crawl up this mountain if I have to. We are not going back!"

They moved forward, Aster alternately on his knees or crouching as he walked. He found their tracks from before as they crossed and re-crossed the path. Then the trail simply disappeared. The hard packed stone-free surface gave way to dusty earth littered with large stones. The horses slipped on the uneven footing and pulled at the reins so many times Aster finally had to stop so Paul could calm them down.

"It's okay, we'll get through this." Paul's voice came to Aster from somewhere in the grayness. "We will get through this, right?"

"We'll make it. At least we're still going uphill. That's something."

Aster tried to sound confident, but wasn't quite so sure of it himself. He crouched down again and looked closely at the area around their feet. They must have come several hundred yards from where the trail ended and the ground was getting rockier. Loose stones were everywhere.

"I just hope Troy doesn't pick up another stone."

The horse whinnied at the sound of his name and Paul reined him in. Then surprisingly, Paul laughed. "Well, at least we have a hoof pick with us this time."

Aster chuckled too, remembering the trader girl who'd sold it to him. He took out his belt knife and looked at it closely. She was right about the layering; if you looked really closely you could see the tiny lines running along the honed edge of the blade. He was beginning to doubt there were a thousand folds in the steel, however. He reasoned that many folds should be nearly invisible.

He blinked and focused his gaze past the knife edge to an odd shape in the mist, a shape just barely visible on the ground in front of him. He put away the knife and edged towards the unusual object. Three flat stones, each a little smaller than the one below it, were stacked one atop the other.

"Paul, come here."

A few moments later a dark mass appeared out of the fog and resolved itself into his friend. "What is it?"

"Could that be a marker of some kind?" Aster pointed at the little pile of stones.

Paul leaned forward for a better look, pulling the reins and the horses with him. The horses pulled back. "Looks like a pile of stones to me, but it's too small to be a trail marker."

Aster crawled forward and crouched over the little pile for a closer look. Bits of dirt were caked on the stones, as if rainstorms coming from different directions had once splattered them with mud. He brushed away some of the dirt and felt resistance from the rocks.

"They're stuck together."

"Mud?"

"Maybe."

He tried to lift the top rock off of the other two, but it wouldn't budge. He felt the tingle of magic in his fingertips as he strained to lift the tiny stone, which appeared to weigh more than a boulder. Finally he gave up and turned back to face his friend with a satisfied grin.

"It's a marker all right. A magical marker. And a magical marker in the midst of a magical cloud ought to lead us along a magical path don't you think?"

"Don't ask me, you're the one with a sorcerer for a teacher." Paul may have sounded skeptical, but his grin was as wide as Aster's.

"Get me that hoof pick thing, I've got an idea."

Paul disappeared into the fog, following the reins back to the horses. He reappeared a few minutes later and handed Aster the tool.

"What're you going to do with that?"

"Go fishing."

He knelt over the pile of stones again and began scratching at the dirt around them with the pick. After a little work he'd found what he was looking for. Two sections of dirt the pick was unable to break through extended out from the stones. One pointed back the way they had come and the other was pointing uphill.

"Ley lines! I don't know if they're part of the spell making this fog or something else, but I bet they'll lead us right to the mountain."

"What are ley lines?"

"Conduits for magical power. They channel it from one place to another, and can occur naturally or be created by a wizard to feed a spell. I'm guessing either the mountain or the fog needs a lot of power and there wasn't a natural source of it up here. So they built these ley lines from somewhere down in the foothills."

"Couldn't we just turn the fog off by breaking the line?"

"No, it doesn't work that way. Watch." Aster dragged the hoof pick across the line several times. No matter how hard he dug at the soil, it wouldn't budge. "The power holds the dirt together, not the other way around. Only another sorcerer can break this. Maybe a whole lot of sorcerers."

"So what are the stones for?"

"I think they mark a change of course. Ley lines are perfectly straight, so the spell holding the stones together acts like a hinge that connects two lines together at an angle."

"And you want to follow this thing?"

"Well, it's got to be better than what we've been doing."

They began slowly following the ley line uphill as it wove its way from one little pile of stones to the next. Aster crouched from time to time to scratch at the earth with the hoof pick and make sure they were still on course. Paul followed along with the horses in tow.

And then the path just stopped. The ley line ran right up to a vertical wall of grey stone and disappeared into it.

"Well that's it then. We've found the mountain, now what do we do?" Paul crossed his arms and waited for an answer.

Aster gazed at the wall of stone. He ran his hand up and down it a few times and then crouched to examine the ley line once more. "I'm not so sure. I don't think this rock was here when the ley line was formed. The line keeps going right into the rock."

Aster stood back up. He handed Paul the hoof pick and dusted off his hands.

"Have you noticed there's been a lot more big rocks along the path? I think there was an avalanche and that's just a great big rock that fell on the road." He pointed at the wall of stone.

Paul looked up into the grey mist. "So the road's blocked by a big rock that fell from somewhere up there. We're still stuck, right?"

"Maybe, and maybe we can just walk around it." Aster reached for Troy's reins. "I'll go around to the left, you go to the right. Keep looking for the ley line and call out when you find it. Head back here if the way is blocked and wait, otherwise we'll meet up again on the other side."

Paul looked nervously into the fog to their right. "What if there's something out there? A mountain lion or something?"

"Are you kidding? We haven't seen so much as a mouse all day. Nothing could hunt in this fog and even if they did there's nothing to hunt for."

"Except us."

Aster punched his friend in the shoulder. "Look, we could both go the same way, but then it might take twice as long to find the ley line again. This way if the path is blocked, only one of us has to backtrack.

You can't get lost if you stay within reach of that big rock."

"That makes sense, I guess." Paul pulled on Wendy's reins and approached the rock. Cautiously he reached out and tapped it with the hoof pick. The metal rang out ominously in the dense air. "You won't go running off without me, will you, your Highness?"

"Don't be silly and don't call me your Highness. You're the one wearing the royal coat of supreme justice."

"The what? No, the royal coat of what?" Paul began frantically pulling at the silk coat's buttons.

Aster laughed. "Stop, it's just a coat. I made that up so you wouldn't start crying on me."

"You're mean. You know that?" Paul wasn't exactly smiling.

"Look, we'll only be separated for a little while and then we can push on to the mountain together. There's nothing to be afraid of, really. Still friends?"

Paul stared at the ground where the ley line disappeared into the rock wall. He scuffed his foot at the dirt, which only moved when it wasn't on top of the line. Finally he looked up with a real smile. "First one to find the line on the other side gets the last apple."

Aster grinned and held out his hand. "Deal?"

Instead of shaking hands, Paul held up the hoof pick. "But I get to use this." He stuck out his tongue and turned to disappear into the fog, leaving Aster stunned and alone.

"Now, that's how a prince should act!" Aster laughed and turned to follow the rock to his left.

"I have a good teacher!"

Paul's voice was already becoming muffled by the fog and Aster wondered if they'd really be able to hear one another if they called out. He was sure they'd meet up soon on the other side, but he was worried about Paul losing his nerve.

He began feeling his way along the rock face and to his delight it quickly began curving away from him. Soon it became apparent that the rock, while quite large, was not going to block the entire trail. Then Aster ran into the pile of rubble.

Large boulders and loose rocks blocked his way, forcing him to move further to the left and away from the big rock. Not being able to see more than a few inches in either direction made navigating around the obstructions that much harder. Eventually he found a place where he and Troy could scramble up the pile and come down on the other side.

"Paul! I'm on the other side!"

He listened for a few moments and then heard a muffled reply. He couldn't make out what his friend was saying, but he sounded excited. Aster knew he was in a race now. He worked his way back to the big rock and pulled out his belt knife.

He started by dragging his boot heel in the dirt as he walked backwards around the base of the rock. Whenever the ground seemed not to give way, he would bend down and dig at the area with his knife. He'd gone only a few yards when he heard a noise.

It sounded like it might have been Paul. It was muffled, but not the same as before. This was a sharp sound, like a scream or a bird's cry and was followed by something else that sounded like a horse whinny. Aster stood up and listened carefully, but the sound was not repeated.

"Paul? Was that you?"

He listened, but heard nothing.

"Paul? Have you found the ley line yet?"

Still nothing. After another minute he shrugged his shoulders and continued his digging. Only a few yards further on his heel dragged over something very hard. A few pokes with his knife and he knew he'd found the ley line again.

"I found it! I found the ley line, you can stop looking now!"

This time, when he called out, his voice echoed oddly. The reverberations made him wonder if Paul had responded or not.

"Paul?"

No answer.

"Did you hear me?"

Still no answer.

He looked at his horse.

"I better go find him. You stay here and guard the line."

He felt around and found a sizable rock sitting nearby. He slipped Troy's reins under it, then patted the horse on the nose.

"I won't be long. He's got to be at least half way round by now."

He left the horse grunting behind him and began working his way around the rock. At first he moved quickly, but then remembered Paul had that hoof pick thing with him. It wouldn't do to bump into each other with that big sharp hook in the way.

He slowed down and squinted ahead, staring into the swirling mists looking for any movement. Then he heard Troy nicker behind him. He turned to look back, a futile effort as he could barely see the rock wall an arm's length away, but it saved his life.

As he turned, his weight shifted back to his left foot, letting his right foot come down lightly on a crumbling ledge of dirt. The ledge gave way and his right foot shot out into empty space. He folded down onto his left leg and instinctively sprang backwards, landing spread eagle on the rocky ground. He rose up slowly onto his knees, brushing dirt off his chest with a scraped hand.

"What in the name of..."

He turned around and crawled cautiously forward, feeling ahead with his hands before putting any weight on them. When he found the ledge, part of it crumbled away in his hand. He lay flat and edged forwards until his head was hanging over the edge.

Aster had no way of knowing how far the drop was. It could be a few inches or a few yards. His hand felt around for a rock, then held it close to his face and dropped it over the edge. He watched the rock fall through the swirling grey mist and then, just for a moment, caught a glimpse of clear air as the rock dropped out of the fog.

What he saw in that split second made his heart nearly stop. A sheer cliff fell away below him. Trees, hundreds of yards away, defined a small horseshoe shaped canyon far below. The rock he'd been edging his way along stuck out from the cliff and ended only a few yards below the mist. His eyes darted and searched the trees, but even before he knew what he was looking for the mists closed in and hid the scene from view.

Aster scrambled back from the ledge, coming up on all fours, panting. He was shaking from head to toe. Normally fearless, the prince was more frightened by what had almost just happened than he'd ever been while climbing the sea wall back home. The drop here was probably less, but still...A chill ran down Aster's spine.

"Paul?"

The Misty Mountain

Aster scrambled to his feet and raced back the way he'd come. He ran past Troy so fast the horse rose up and nearly kicked him in the head. He paid the startled horse no mind and kept on running until he reached the pile of rubble at the far end of the big boulder.

He clawed his way up the pile of loose gravel, half expecting Paul to be waiting for him on the far side, half dreading that he wouldn't be. At the top he called out again, this time screaming as loudly as he could. His friend's name echoed off the mountainside, but only silence answered him.

He slid down the far side and felt his way back to the big rock at a half run. He quickly found the place where they'd parted, the place where the ley line disappeared into the rock, but there was no sign of Paul or his horse.

"Paul? Where are you?"

He started to run in the direction his friend had gone, but stopped himself. He had no idea how far away the cliff edge might be on this side. He got down on his hands and knees and began crawling ahead as quickly as he dared.

All too soon he found the place where Paul and his horse had fallen. There were hoof marks all over the place. It seemed as though Wendy had frantically tried to keep her young master from going over the edge, but their combined weight had been too much for the crumbling hillside. The marks ended where a huge chunk of ledge had given way, sending horse and rider towards the canyon far below.

Aster flattened himself to the ground, looking down through the broken earth, and screamed.

"Paul? Can you hear me? You found something to hang on to, right? There's always a vine or something to grab on to. Hang on! I'll go find a rope or something to pull you back up with."

Aster sat up, he was all ready to run back to his horse until he remembered that the only rope was in a pack Wendy was carrying. He turned back to the ledge and strained to hear his friend calling out. All he could hear was the wind in the trees far below.

"Paul? Answer me. Do you hear me? I'm your prince and I demand you answer me this instant. Answer me, damn you! You can't do this to me. I'm your prince."

Aster tried to think. People fell off of cliffs all the time in his books. If they didn't grab onto something they usually fell into a deep pool of water or onto a tree. He hadn't seen any water when the mists parted, but there had been trees. He tried shouting even louder.

"Shout if you can hear me. Stop playing games, this is serious. I'm sorry I made you go off on your own. You can take off that stupid coat now. I'll let you have the last stupid apple. Just get your stupid butt back up here. Do you hear me?"

He sat up again. He was getting lightheaded from all the shouting. This was getting him nowhere. Paul would have answered by now, if he could. Aster had to do something. He had to find his friend, help him if he could. That's what royalty did, they protected their people. They risked their lives to protect their people, but what had he done to protect Paul?

"Nothing. I sent you off on your own, that's what I did. I sent you off when you didn't want to go, and now you're..."

Aster grabbed a rock that was sitting next to his boot and turned back to the ledge. He threw the rock over the edge and watched it disappear into the mist. He found another and tossed it too, but the rock simply disappeared and the fog didn't open up as it had before. Five rocks later he lay on his belly and wept.

"How could I have been so stupid? He was afraid of heights, I knew he was afraid of heights. I knew the mountainside was the other way, I should have let him go to the left. Then he would have found the ley line and I'd have jumped out of the way like before. Or maybe I'd be dead now."

Aster pounded on the ground as hard as he could, again and again, until bits of the remaining ledge began to fall off into the mists below. He stopped and watched them fall, parting the fog at last and giving him one final fleeting glimpse of the canyon beyond.

"I'm so sorry, Paul. I'm just so, so sorry."

Aster sat there for a while longer as the silence and the fog closed in on him. When he couldn't stand it any longer he got up and began working his way back around the boulder to where he'd left Troy.

He expected to have a hard time finding his horse. After spooking Troy by rushing past him in the fog, he expected the horse to be half way up the mountain, but Troy was standing there waiting for him right where he'd left him. He hugged the horse's neck and thanked him for being there.

"Paul and Wendy won't be going to the Misty Mountain with us, boy. They...they headed back down. You know how afraid they were of heights."

He took the reins, pulled out his belt knife, and began the long slow trek up the trail following the ley lines as best he could. More than once he said something out loud as though Paul were still somewhere nearby in the mist and each time the silence made him feel like crying all over again.

The day wore on and just when he was beginning to think the lines were leading him nowhere, the fog began to thin and they emerged onto a wide flat shelf at the base of the mountain. Directly ahead at the center of the shelf stood a tall pyramid made out of large uncut boulders. He wasn't surprised to find the ley line running right up to it.

As they walked past the structure Aster reached out and touched it warily. The stone was cold and damp, but he could feel no magical power emanating from it. "I don't think it's a sentinel. It must have something to do with either the mist or the mountain."

He looked past the pyramid to where the mountain rose in a sheer rock wall out of the shelf. As far as he could see in either direction, the wall continued unmarred by any crack or opening that might provide a passageway to the other side. Then he spotted a bush.

They had climbed to an altitude where neither grass nor trees grew. The only living things he'd seen for the last several hours were a few scrawny bushes clinging tenaciously to small pockets of dirt scattered among the rocks. One of those bushes appeared to be growing right out of the base of the mountainside, but the more he looked at it the more it seemed to be growing right out of the rock face itself.

He led Troy to the spot and bent down to examine the bush. Sure enough, there was no trunk sticking in the ground that he could see and some of the branches looked as though they were anchored to the very rock itself. Then he looked more closely at the wall. It seemed solid enough, but when he tried to press on it his finger passed through like it wasn't there at all.

He stood up. Looking back at the pyramid of rocks he noticed for the first time the similarity between it and the shape of the mountain top he'd glimpsed from the valley below. It must be the source of the illusion, with the ley lines providing the magical energy from somewhere down in the foothills.

"I was right. It's nothing but an illusion. Come on."

But Troy would have none of it. As Aster was about to pass into the wall the reins went taut in his hand and he was dragged backwards by the startled horse. Troy shook his head and snorted fiercely every time Aster tried to enter the wall. At last he led the skittish horse back to the stone pyramid, well away from the illusion that was spooking him.

"I really hate to do this, but it's the only way we're getting to the other side." Aster untied the extra blanket he'd brought and tossed it over Troy's head. The horse bucked and thrashed about for a few minutes, but finally settled down. Aster led him in a wide circle around the pyramid before heading straight for the rock wall again.

The passage through the illusion was not as quick as he'd hoped. It felt something like passing through the fog they'd been walking in all morning, which probably kept Troy from getting spooked again. But it was ten times thicker and Aster was walking completely blind.

Unlike the fog, which thinned out gradually, the illusionary rock ended abruptly and Aster discovered that what he'd thought to be a shelf was in fact a small plateau. He looked up at the false mountain looming above him. On this side it was a mirror image, curving out in front of them as it rose into the clouds. The effect was disorienting to say the least and he decided to walk Troy a bit farther before removing the blanket.

There was no concealing fog on this side of the mountain and Aster could see all the way to the end of the plateau. It was bordered on both sides by the legs of the neighboring ridges and narrowed in the distance to a point where they met. To either side the mountains rose higher, but there was an obvious pass between them.

He rode the rest of the afternoon in the shadow of the hollow mountain. He turned for one last look at it before going into the pass and the mountains beyond. It was a truly impressive illusion and it must have taken several wizards years to construct, but the answer as to why they went to all this trouble in the first place lay somewhere deeper in the mountains.

By the time light was beginning to fade from the sky, Aster was already high into the pass. He'd long since lost sight of the inside-out mountain and with the trail ahead looking pretty much the same as the one behind, he thought it was time to start looking for someplace to set camp for the night.

At this altitude the air was cold and thick with fog—a real fog, this time. Gusts of icy wind whipped around him from both directions and he hunkered down in the saddle trying to stay warm. He needed to find some kind of shelter, a cave or an outcropping of rock, but the trail was bordered on both sides by sheer rock walls. Just when he was about to give up hope, and set camp in the open, he rounded a bend in the trail.

There, nestled by a natural gap in the rock wall, sat a small stone cabin. It wasn't very large and looked deserted, but compared to the damp windswept ground it was as welcoming as any inn. Just visible behind the cabin was another building that looked like a stable.

"Well, it looks like we're sleeping under a roof tonight."

Aster dismounted and started leading Troy around the cabin to the stable. He was surprised to see the wooden doors on both buildings were still intact. If the history books were right, no one had traveled this pass for nearly a thousand years. In the damp air of the pass any wood should have rotted away by now. However the doors to the stable seemed quite solid as he pulled one open.

"I don't think this place is abandoned at all."

He'd expected to find everything covered in dust and full of cobwebs, but other than a slight musty smell the place looked clean and untouched by time. There were bales of fresh straw in the stalls and hay in the loft. He pulled his saddle off Troy's back and brushed him down with a currycomb he found hanging on the wall. He filled the manger in the stall with hay and added some oats from his supplies.

He approached the cabin a little more cautiously. It seemed less likely now that the place had been deserted for long.

"Hello? Is anyone there?"

He rapped on the door before pushing it open and stepping inside. There was only a bit of dust on the floors, solid wooden furniture sat everywhere and there were even curtains on the windows. Everything was neat and tidy, as though someone had cleaned the place before leaving. Even the straw mattresses on the bunk beds were turned down and made. Someone had used this cabin not so long ago, and from the looks of it, intended to return.

He'd worry about that tomorrow. The light was fading fast and the curtains on the unglazed windows did little to keep out the cold wind. He lit a fire in the fireplace using the sap wood the huntsman had suggested he bring, but soon realized there wouldn't be enough of it to last the night.

He went looking for something else to put on the fire. If someone went to all the trouble of bringing fresh hay up here, it stood to reason they might also bring wood for the fire. Sure enough he found a small woodpile next to the stable and brought in a few good sized logs. He threw one on the fire and sat down to eat.

There wasn't much in his pack; Paul had all the cooking supplies with him on Wendy. Aster found some trail food and the last of the goat crackers. It wasn't much, but it would hold him over until he could find something to hunt.

He stared at the fire, munching on dried raisins and nuts, waiting for the log to catch. And waiting... And waiting... But the log stubbornly resisted the flames. Aster picked out another log, making sure this one was good and dry before throwing it on the fire. It too just sat there, as impervious to the flames as the first.

Aster added more of the sapwood and it blazed to life almost instantly. He tried everything he could think of, but nothing would make the logs from the cabin's woodpile burn. In the end he used up all of the wood he'd brought with him, but it wasn't enough to keep the fire going for more than a few minutes.

He sat through the rest of the night, in the dark, wrapped in two blankets and shivering against the cold until the sky began to lighten the next morning. When he dozed off, dreams of Paul falling from the cliff, screaming as he fell, awakened him. He tried not to cry again. He tried to remember only the good things about his friend. He tried not to blame himself for something that was so obviously an accident. However, he didn't succeed at any of those things and eventually cried himself to sleep.

In the morning he examined the logs in the now cold fireplace. They seemed completely untouched by the heat and flames. Even the soot and ashes wouldn't stick to them.

"Magic!" Aster tossed the log back into the fireplace, kicking up a cloud of ashes. "Someone must have cast a preservation spell on the woodpile. There's no way of telling how long it's been sitting out there."

He took up his bedroll and haversack then went to get Troy. He wasn't too surprised to find all the oats he'd put out eaten, but the hay completely untouched.

"Not very appetizing, huh?"

The horse shook his head and snorted. Aster tried to snap a piece of the hay in two, but it just sprang back into shape as fresh looking as ever. "Sorry about that. Hopefully we'll run into something a bit easier to chew on later."

He took time to clean out the stall. It was something he'd never done himself and had always been told was a dirty nasty job, but whoever said that probably hadn't cleaned up magically preserved straw before. He soon had Troy saddled and heading down the trail towards the brightening sky in the east.

He rode for less than an hour before the trail began to widen and pitch downhill. Rock walls soon gave way to rolling foothills. Almost before he knew it they emerged into a lush green valley stretching as far as he could see into the east.

To either side of the valley, mountains of sheer rock rose to the clouds. The trail soon became a paved road. To either side of the road tall grasses grew green and lush, trees flourished in small thickets and birds could be heard chirping in them. He saw game moving in the distance and there was an abundance of life everywhere he looked.

Except on the road itself. There, not a single blade of grass grew up between the old cobblestones. It cut a grey, lifeless path through the valley, leading to a larger grey mass in the distance. It might have been an outcropping of stone, but Aster somehow knew it was a city and guessed it was his final destination.

The Next Attack

Mandrake crashed through the trees, landing hard on the forest floor, just missing the deer by inches. He reached out his neck and tried to catch the fleeing animal in his teeth, something that almost never worked, and got a mouthful of leaves for his trouble. As he sat there spitting them out, he watched the white tail of his prey disappearing into the underbrush.

This, at least, he couldn't blame on the humans. If it were merely food he was looking for, he could just plunder a nice plump cow from some farmer's field. It wasn't hunger that had him crashing through the forest. He'd attacked a village yesterday and his gas sack was empty.

The larger game animals were the best prey for making gas. A deer or an elk, which was mostly lean meat, would give off more gas for its size than any pig or cow. They were also very hard to catch when he felt so heavy.

He needed to remember not to empty the sack every time he attacked a village. He'd been planning his attacks more carefully this season. When he first began attacking the humans, he'd been lucky to burn a single farm in a week. His first attack on a village had nearly sent him swimming when the gas ran out while he was trying to burn a boat. He'd learned a lot over the years.

When he'd attacked the port city of Ensenor the day before, he'd known better than to try setting the water-soaked hulls ablaze. Instead he set fire to their sails and let falling cinders do the rest. That left him plenty of gas for the wharves and warehouses, but he'd gotten into trouble fighting a group of archers atop the city walls.

"Burn the walls, Mandrake, not the archers. The humans aren't worth the fire you waste on them."

It wasn't that he couldn't fly without the gas. If that were the case he would have starved to death long ago. Flying without gas was just different, it put more strain on his back muscles for one thing, and limited how high he could fly. Trying to transition from flying with gas to without, while actually still in flight, was awkward at best. And, more often than not, painful.

He remembered one farm he'd attacked in that first year, where he wasted an entire sack full of gas trying to set fire to a stone barn with a sod roof. Mandrake chuckled. "Your sire never taught you how to burn buildings, fool. You had to learn that all by yourself."

Something else he was learning was how to talk to himself when he was alone—and he was always alone. He would surely remain alone until the humans were gone and he could awaken the others. As a pup he'd spent hours talking to humans. He remembered having several human friends. Even some of his teachers had been human. Now, whenever he tried to talk with them, they either ran away or tried to kill him.

Mandrake looked up through the canopy of trees. Flying through all of that to reach open sky was going to be difficult and he didn't fancy picking twigs from under his scales for the rest of the day. Standing up on his hind legs, he stretched his neck and scanned the surrounding woods. Ahead, in the same direction the deer had disappeared, he saw a small clearing.

He carefully picked his way through the trees and underbrush, trying not to make too much noise as he went. There was always a chance he might still catch the deer grazing. However, as he broke through the brush at the edge of the clearing he froze. Before him the deer lay dead with an arrow in its chest. Standing over it was a tiny human—a male child, Mandrake thought.

The human had a rather large looking knife in its hand and was busily trying to cut open the deer. So intent was it on doing this that Mandrake was able to enter the clearing and cross to within a few yards of the child before it noticed him. Even then all it did was look up at him and smile.

"They just keep getting bigger and bigger." The child shook its head as it looked Mandrake up and down. Then resumed cutting into the deer.

Mandrake tried not to chuckle. "I'm as big they come."

That at least got the child's complete attention. It spun around, dropping the knife, and expertly pulled a bow from its back. It was fumbling for an arrow when Mandrake took another step forward. The child froze then.

Mandrake expected it to run away, but it just stood there staring up at him with an odd expression on its face. It looked for all the world as if it were about to ask him a question.

"What is it, child?"

"Are you some kind of moose?"

"A moose?" Mandrake had difficulty stifling a belly laugh. "Have you ever seen a moose before?"

"No sir, that's why I'm asking."

"Well, I am not a moose. A moose would not have wings." He unfolded his a bit to let the child see them.

"Then you're the biggest eagle I ever seen."

Mandrake lost his battle and laughed out loud. "I'm not an eagle, I'm a dragon. Haven't you ever seen a dragon before?"

"No sir, Daddy says there's only one dragon hereabouts and he's never seen it, either."

Mandrake thought about that. He'd been at war with the humans for ten years now. Could there really be anyone in Caledon who had not seen him at least once? "Where do you come from?"

"We live on Derry. We came here in a boat. I never got sick once!"

Mandrake had no idea where Derry was. It might be one of the little islands off the western coast. He'd all but ignored those because trying to get humans to abandon an island seemed doomed from the start.

"You did a good job bringing down that deer. A single shot?" Mandrake nodded to indicate the deer lying at the child's feet.

"Uh huh, I'm really good with a bow. Daddy says I'll be a huntsman someday. You want to see me shoot something?"

Mandrake tilted his head to one side. "All right, as long as it isn't me."

The child giggled. "No silly, I mean something else like..." The child spun around looking for something. Finally he pointed at a tree on the far side of the clearing. "See the knot in that tree. Bet you I can hit that."

"That's a mighty small target." And from the child's perspective it probably was.

"Naw, that's easy! Watch me." The child put an arrow to the string of the bow and raised it to his cheek. Without hesitation he aimed and loosed the arrow. It struck the tree at the very center of the knot.

Mandrake was actually impressed. "Well done. Someday you will indeed be a formidable hunter."

"Thanks, but I gots to grow up first." The child looked down at the deer and waved his hand. "I bagged me this whole deer and I can't even carry it back to camp." He suddenly looked embarrassed. "You was chasing this deer, weren't you, Mr. Dragon?"

"Well, yes, but I wasn't having much luck catching it."

"I'm sorry. Daddy says I should always ask before shooting at someone else's game."

"That's all right. It was your shot to take; I'd already given up on it anyway. What are you going to do now?"

"I was just going to cut out Daddy's favorite parts and take them... Hey, why don't you take the rest? I can't carry it and it'd be a shame to leave all this for the birds."

"Do you know what dragons do with such meat?" Mandrake had

intended to take the carcass all along, but now the child was giving it to him. That shouldn't make any difference, but it did.

"Eat it, I suppose. What else would you do with it?"

"Well, dragons have two ways of eating things. One is for food, the other is to make fire. If I eat this deer, it will be to make fire."

"That's all right. Everyone needs to make fire. How else are you going to cook stuff?"

Mandrake decided not to go into the details of what he intended to "cook" with the fire he made. "Just so. Thank you. I shall make good use of your gift, I promise."

The boy smiled and knelt down to begin cutting on the carcass again. In short order he had his pack full of meat. He stood up, cleaned and sheathed his knife, shouldered his bow and was turning to leave.

"It was nice meeting you, Mr. Dragon. Maybe we can go hunting again some time."

"Maybe." Mandrake didn't expect to see the boy again. In fact, he hoped he never would. He hoped the boy would go back to wherever he came from, grow into a man, and never set foot in Caledon again. He dreaded the thought of facing the child's bow and doing what he always did to survive.

"Goodbye!" The boy darted off into the bushes and disappeared.

"Farewell, child."

He waited until the boy was long gone before making short work of the deer. He was airborne shortly afterwards and rose sluggishly into the morning air. In a few days the meat would begin to decompose and make gas to fill the sack in his chest. Then he would be ready for another attack.

He'd been thinking that another coastal town would send an explicit message to the king: that Mandrake controlled every possible route into Castlekeep. He hoped that would finally drive the humans south. There was the perfect little fishing village not far from here, but now he was reluctant to attack it.

What if the boat the boy had used to get here was moored there?

That would be a most dishonorable way to return the favor of the child's largesse. To use the gas from his own deer to destroy the lad's only way home was not something Mandrake wanted to consider. He needed a new target, something worthy of such a gift.

He rose above the tree tops and turned east. In the distance the sun was finally peeking above the Eastern Ridge. He watched the bright disk rise and overwhelm the peaks one by one, until only one remained. The Misty Mountain.

Suddenly Mandrake knew where his next attack would take place. It had been years since he'd raided a village that far east, but what better place to put the boy's gift to good use? To finally give the people of that hated village a taste of his fire.

It would take a week or more to collect enough gas for a full out attack, but he didn't want to wait that long. News of such an attack would be slow making its way to Castlekeep and he wanted the king to continue feeling pressured. In a few days he would have just enough gas to burn a couple of fields and destroy a few key buildings. That would have to do for now.

With a renewed sense of purpose he began making his way back to the cave. He would wait there and make his plans, then in four or five days he would attack Traders Run.

The Palace

The ride across the valley was filled with wonder and strangeness; wonder at the abundance of life, and strangeness that none of it intruded upon the road itself. Troy would have preferred walking in the green meadows, but Aster was in a hurry to reach whatever lay at the end of the road.

His heart rose when they came upon the first farm. From a distance it looked quite normal. The farmhouse and barn were no different than the hundreds he'd seen on his journey. However, as he drew closer it became obvious that whatever malady afflicted the road, also held the farmstead in its grip.

The wild green fields, so lush and teaming with life, ended as though a line had been drawn in the dirt. Within that boundary it seemed as if every green blade and brown stalk had been plucked from the earth and replaced with barren grey soil.

The farm house and barn lay empty but not quite abandoned. As with the cabin in the mountains, everything was neat and tidy and showed no signs of having been abandoned in haste. He was too anxious to find the city to tarry long and investigate, but he could well imagine white lace curtains still hanging on all the windows and clean plates stacked neatly in the kitchen.

Aster was growing more frightened as he passed farm after farm, each one preserved in the same deathlike stasis. He wasn't sure

94

what terrified him more, the thought that these farms lay perfectly preserved after one thousand years or that just beyond their borders the valley teemed with so much life.

Then he came upon the first small town. Like the farms before it, all was quiet and grey within its borders. However, as he rode through the little hamlet, losing sight of the surrounding valley, the lifelessness of the place closed in on him. He hunkered down in the saddle, trying to get closer to the only life he could see, his horse. He quickened his pace then and fled the town in a near panic.

After that there were more farms, another little town, and then he decided to make camp. He found a nice little pond of clear sweet water next to a meadow. He let Troy have his way with the meadow—the horse feasted on the grass ravenously—while Aster did some hunting. It took no time at all for him to snag a hare and collect some apples from what must have once been an orchard.

He set a fire to roast the rabbit and then went exploring. After a thousand years there was little in the wild fields to suggest the tilled farmlands that had once covered the valley. He discovered the remains of a single stone corner post in a copse of trees, but nothing remained of the fence it once supported. He followed the fence line until he came upon a farm house well away from the road.

Within the grey ring that encircled the house and barn sat the mate to the stone corner post in the wood. It stood tall, with not a stone out of place, and wooden rails extended from it in three directions. Where the fence line left the circle of preservation the rails had been cleaved as cleanly as if by an axe, but on closer inspection he found the ends rotted away.

This was truly frightening magic. Aster imagined the fate of any animal or human caught with one foot inside and one foot outside that line. The image stuck in his mind and he was reluctant to explore the farm any further. He left the farmhouse undisturbed and returned to his roasting hare.

He sat by the fire, chewing bits of roast rabbit, and watched the sun set behind the peak of the Misty Mountain just visible in the west. He thought of the friend he'd lost there and became even more determined to find the Empress Sword and use it to rid Caledon of the dragon.

The following day was much the same. More farms, another small town, and the growing sense that his destination lay not far ahead. Perhaps it was the utter sameness of the surroundings that first led him to notice the caves.

The valley was bounded to the north and south by shear walls of rock. It was as if the valley had been gouged from the heart of the mountains by the Gods and the walls left smooth to prevent all the life within from escaping.

However, as he rode east he began to notice that the walls were occasionally pockmarked with dark holes. The further he rode, the more of the strange openings there were along both walls. Most were quite high up and there would have been no way to climb to them. And yet, some of the holes showed signs of having once been mined. Unnaturally straight lines and signs of stonework abounded.

By the time he found another meadow with a pond nearby to set camp in, the walls to either side of the valley resembled a grey honeycomb. In the distance the grey line had risen to become a great wall, stretching completely across the valley from north to south.

The pond was large enough to swim in, so he took advantage and cleaned himself up. When he went to put on his clothes, he thought about the silk coat he'd brought along just for this occasion. Remembering where it was now made the night seem chillier than it was, and he built the fire into a roaring blaze, hoping to chase away the ghosts that haunted his thoughts.

In the morning Aster mounted up for the short ride to the city. The outer wall did indeed stretch all the way across the valley, which was easily three to four leagues wide at this point. If the city extended that far from east to west then it was huge, making Castlekeep look small by comparison.

He found the giant wooden gates of the city not only intact, but standing wide open as though the city beyond were still alive and teeming with activity, rather than abandoned and silent. He rode through grey empty streets for hours, marveling at the strange mix of architectures.

The familiar two and three story beam and stucco houses of his own Caledon stood side by side with the low thatched roofed long houses of Greylands. Influences from the other Kingdoms could be seen as well, but the predominant building style was completely unknown to him.

Buildings with steeply pitched four sided roofs covered in clay tiles stood two and sometimes three stories tall. Ornate carvings adorned most of the exposed wood surfaces, but the walls themselves appeared to be made of little more than paper glued to wooden frames. Some appeared to be homes, others shops or storage houses, but they were all empty and lifeless.

Finally he came to a hill and found a long stone staircase leading up to an inner wall. The gates of this wall were painted red and even more ornate than the city gates had been. They stood slightly ajar and led to a long tunnel with another pair of heavy gates at the far end.

The tunnel was wide enough for two wagons to pass easily and twice as high as it needed to be. He noticed there were no arrow slits in the walls. An entranceway this long would make the perfect final defense against invaders, but it was as if the builders never expected it to be used that way.

Instead the walls were covered in elaborate murals. With the gates at both ends nearly closed, it was too dark to appreciate them entirely, but Aster was able to pick out the likenesses of dragons, oddly armored troops, strange animals and, surprisingly, a lot of trader's wagons.

Beyond the inner gates the tunnel opened up onto a vast courtyard. Massive multi-tiered stone fountains stood to either side surrounded by tall stone benches. Across the wide courtyard more stone steps rose up to a huge building with a peaked roof like those he'd seen throughout the city.

"Well, I think we've found the palace." Aster smiled as he dismounted his horse. "Not that it looks like any palace I've ever seen before, but then who's to say what imperial palaces looked like a thousand years ago, eh Troy?"

He tied the horse to one of the stone benches near the easternmost fountain. While it was obviously a fountain, there was not even a drop of water pooled in its basin. The bench was oddly shaped, with a curved top and standing taller than a man could comfortably sit on without his legs dangling off the ground.

"You wait here while I go inside and find the sword. I should be back by nightfall."

At the top of the staircase was a wide veranda that extended to either side of the building. The view of the city was partially obscured by the inner wall, but Aster could see the main gate off to the west and the road heading back towards the pass. When he looked the other way he saw another gate, this one closed, and beyond that the valley extended as far as he could see into the east.

The palace was huge. Massive round beams, as wide as an oak tree and tall as a fir, supported the blue tiled roof. The beams were covered from top to bottom with intricate carvings of animals. Among them, Aster saw quite a few dragons. Between these columns were stucco walls painted bright red and decorated with gold leaf.

Two massive doors were set into the center of the front façade, also painted red and decorated with gold to match the walls. One of the doors stood slightly ajar and Aster stepped through the gap into a large dimly lit chamber.

The room beyond was as big as the grand ballroom back home and completely empty. After exploring for a few minutes he found furnished rooms to either side separated from the main space by sliding panels.

While he might explore those later, the Empress Sword wasn't likely to be kept so close to the entrance. He set his sights on the long dark corridor stretching into the distance at the back of the chamber. He crossed the room, his footfalls echoing far too loudly on the polished stone floor.

He crept forward, hugging the corridor wall, as his eyes grew accustomed to the darkness. He'd only gone a few paces when he banged his knee on a heavy bench sitting against the wall. It was large, backless and made out of a heavy dark wood. He scooted around the bench and continued along the wall until he bumped into another one just ten paces from the first.

Moving out into the center of the hallway he could see more dark benches lining the length of the corridor on both sides. His eyes were adjusting now and he could also make out the dark shape of a tapestry hanging above each bench.

After a hundred paces or so there was a gap in the line of benches. Two more corridors, narrower than the first, ran off to the left and right. Aster stood at the intersection and peered down the side passages. Both were shrouded in darkness.

"Now what? This could be the beginning of a labyrinth."

It wouldn't do to get lost so soon after entering the palace. While the idea of a labyrinth was appealing, it didn't make a lot of sense. If these passages had been lit, his destination would probably be obvious.

He cursed his lack of foresight in not bringing a torch. He might find a torch in one of the side chambers near the entrance, but so far nothing he'd found in this enchanted land would burn. Wondering if something he'd brought with him from the outside could be used to make a torch, he glanced back at the entrance, at the bright sliver of light in the gap between the doors.

"Oh, bloody hell."

Aster forgot all about being stealthy as he stalked back to the big entrance doors. With very little effort he pushed them all the way open, letting in sunlight and illuminating the previously dark corridor all the way to the end.

It ended in a pair of massive bronze doors. They stretched all the way to the ceiling and were as broad as ten men standing shoulder to shoulder. A very realistic casting of a dragon in flight dominated the doors about half way up, its outstretched wings spanning them both.

Where the dragon's claws stretched down towards him, life-sized images of two robed maidens stood facing one another. Each held one hand up to the dragon as if beckoning it to land on their upturned palms. In their other hand each held the hilt of a broadsword. These swords stood out from the casting, cleverly providing door pulls.

After assuring himself that the swords weren't honed, Aster tugged on one and the door opened silently. Light poured into the hallway from the room beyond. One look inside told him exactly where he was.

Throne rooms were universally designed to intimidate those entering from the outside and this one was no different. The massive entry doors, polished black stone floors, vaulted ceilings painted to look like a star-filled sky, and the enormous columns—smaller at the top than at the bottom to make the ceiling look even higher—were all intended to make a petitioner feel small and insignificant.

The effect was completely lost on Aster who had grown up in such rooms. On the contrary, he felt more at home here than anywhere else he'd been in this strange city.

He strolled casually through pools of dappled sunlight streaming down from windows set high into the walls on either side of the room. He gazed in wonder at the huge and brightly colored tapestries hanging in each alcove, which were finer than any of the ones hanging back home. Like everything else he'd seen, only a fine coating of dust on everything gave any hint to the hundreds of years since a monarch last held court here.

Thirteen wide steps led to a raised platform at the far end of the room. Centered on the platform all by itself was a single immense throne. Made from the same strange black wood he'd seen throughout the palace, it was upholstered in red and gold silks. The back was round and embroidered with a huge green dragon, rampant in flight and breathing golden fire at the sky.

He mounted the steps warily. This was the point in all the stories where the hero encountered booby traps. He knew for a fact that, aside from a spell to keep anyone from slipping on the polished floors, no such traps existed in his father's throne room. Of course, it never hurt to be careful.

As he placed his foot on the top step a cold breeze caressed his cheek. He hesitated, looking around for something he might have brushed against, but seeing nothing he carefully stepped up to the throne. Lying on the seat, as though it had just been tossed there moments before, was a magnificent sword.

The blade was highly polished, but otherwise unadorned. The golden hilt guard was in the form of two feathered wings. Where the wings joined the haft a large green jewel was mounted. Smaller stones of all sorts were set around it. The haft was wrapped in red silk and the pommel shaped like a flower. It was obviously made for a girl, but Aster had to admire the sword for its beauty.

Then a voice boomed out of nowhere, echoing through the room and scaring Aster half to death. "Who dares come before the Throne of the Four Winds? Make known yourself and prepare for judgment."

The Empress

Aster nearly fell down the stairs when the disembodied voice boomed through the great hall. He looked everywhere for the source of the ancient-sounding voice, but as far as he could tell he was alone. Still, he had been asked a question.

"It is I, Prince Aster of Caledon. I come seeking the great sword of power that once belonged to the Empress of the Eastern Mountains."

His voice echoed through the hall for a long time. He waited until all was silent and then shrugged. "Who might you be?"

Aster jumped when an old woman popped her head out from behind the throne. "I'm Afanasia. What was your name again?"

She had grey hair piled high on top of her head in a fashion he'd never seen before. The skin around her sparkling dark eyes and heart shaped mouth was wrinkled, but not so much that it detracted from the woman's beauty. Her smile was impish and he could tell she was enjoying his startled reaction.

"A-Aster, ma'am, at your service. Was that you speaking a moment ago?"

"Oh yes! That was me." The tiny woman stepped from behind the throne and stood beside it, her hand resting on its arm. She was dressed in a long gown of brightly colored silk with a wide belt of red silk wrapped several times around her waist. In her hand she held a folded fan, which she waved around a lot, and used to point at things.

"I always enjoyed doing that myself, but not for official functions of course. You can just imagine what it sounds like with a herald's voice echoing off the walls. Very impressive, I can assure you. It's the shape of the room, you see. Old Chin designed it for me. When you sit on the throne you can hear people whispering all the way over by the big doors. I'll let you try it sometime. If you survive, of course."

"Excuse me." Aster's mind was reeling. He hadn't expected to find anyone here, much less a chatty old woman. "Did you just say *if* I survive?"

"That's right. You did say you wanted the sword, so whether you walk out of here alive or not really depends on who you brought with you."

"I didn't bring anyone with me. I came alone."

"You what?" The old woman bent forward squinting at him. "Just how old are you?"

"I'm thirteen. That's old enough to come here by myself, and old enough to be called a man."

"Thirteen, eh? Well unless your mother comes looking for you you'll never make it to fourteen. I suggest you turn around right now and go home. Next time, bring your sister with you."

The old woman turned and started walking away. Aster blinked and shook his head. "I don't have any brothers or sisters. Look, it took me two weeks to find my way here. I'm not just going to turn around and go home without the Empress Sword."

"Two weeks?" The old lady turned on him again, this time with fire in her eyes. "I spent two months wandering through these mountains just searching for this valley, then seven more to find the Chiho Empire. I was separated from my family for two whole years and you want *my* sword after only two *weeks*? Go ahead then, take it and die for all I care, stupid boy."

"Two years?" Suddenly the pieces fell together in Aster's head. "Did you say your name was Afanasia, as in Empress Afanasia, in the flesh?"

The old woman grinned at that. "I haven't had flesh or bone for a very long time, young man, but yes, I'm Empress Afanasia."

Aster's eyes grew wide. The woman standing before him had not only ruled this valley, but all four of the great kingdoms—Caledon included. Alive or not, she was almost certainly the key to his getting the Empress Sword. He dropped to one knee and bowed his head. "Your Majesty!"

Afanasia stepped up and placed her hand on his shoulder. It felt as solid and real as anyone's. "Stand up. You said you were just a prince and I only demand that kings bow before me. So, for the time being at least, you're exempt."

He stood up and gazed at the apparently real person standing before him. "You... You're not a ghost, are you?"

She smiled sweetly and held up her hands, wiggling her fingers at him. "Boo! Did you really think I was a one-thousand-year-old woman? I know I'm not as young as I used to be, but really!" She turned and walked over to stand, not beside the throne, but in it.

Aster wondered why he wasn't more frightened by this apparition, but then the Empress wasn't exactly a frightening person. A little scary, in an odd sort of way, but he found himself liking her for that.

"Your Majesty, about the sword..."

"Oh please, don't make me keep repeating myself. You're a boy... I'm sorry, you're a man. The sword will not tolerate a man's touch. Only a woman may take it up and wield it in battle. I don't wish to stand here and watch you die a torturous death, so please, just go home."

"But your sword is the only thing that can save my people. A dragon has awakened and come down from the north to destroy their villages and burn their crops. Those it does not kill outright face starvation and hardship. The army can barely keep up with all the refugees. We've withstood these attacks for ten years, but now my father is becoming desperate. All of his bravest knights have lost their lives trying to defeat the dragon. If your sword truly has the power to slay the beast, I dare not leave here without it. Please, your Majesty, I would gladly sacrifice my life to save my people."

"Do not speak so lightly of sacrificing your life." The Empress glared at him, her fists firmly planted on her hips.

"I do not take it lightly, your Majesty. My mother taught me the value of each and every life. Time and time again she showed me that even the lowliest of our subjects is a treasure worth more than gold itself. My father taught me that anything of great value is worth fighting for. So if I can trade my life for that of even one of my people, I would consider it a price well paid."

Afanasia stared at him balefully, dismay evident on her face. She shook her head and turned away, gazing down at the sword upon the throne. "It wasn't supposed to be like this! I expected the first one to be a man. Some brave handsome fellow all armored up and full of himself, but ten years passes from the first awakening and not one single knight comes looking for us. Then fate sends me a boy with a pure heart and a true sense of purpose."

She nodded and then turned back to Aster, frowning with her eyebrows arched high onto her wrinkled brow. "What am I supposed to do with you, young prince? You possess all the qualities I ever wished for in a successor, save one. Are you aware that powerful magic often demands dire sacrifices from those who would use it?"

"Yes. My teacher, Mandoline, did not wish to send any of our remaining knights here for that very reason."

"And you believe yourself to be expendable? Didn't you just say you have no brothers?"

"It's true, I'm sole heir to my father's throne, but if the dragon continues to destroy our land there will be no kingdom for me to inherit. My father can always choose another successor and I'm prepared to sacrifice anything to rid my people of this menace."

"Anything? Are you sure? There are things more precious than your life, you know. You must believe it in your heart. If you falter in your resolve, even the slightest, she will know it and you will die."

Aster suddenly realized the Empress intended to give him the sword. He fought the desire to jump up and cheer. She was all but telling him this would cost him his life, but even if he died along with the dragon, his people would be saved and his parents proud of him. He'd been raised to expect nothing less from his life.

He straightened up, squared his shoulders and stuck out his chest. "I am certain of it. I put my life in your hands."

"Very well then." The Empress stood aside and waved her fan at the throne. "I give you my sword, but take her at your own peril. She may ask you to sacrifice something more precious than you ever dreamed possible, and you may live to regret your decision. Assuming she lets you live at all."

Aster approached the throne again and reached for the sword. His fingers hovered over the hilt briefly. Was he really risking only his life? Something in the way the Empress had offered him the sword made him think there might be more to it than a deadly battle with the dragon. What else did he have to give? Just how powerful was the Empress Sword?

This was the moment of truth he knew would come, the point in every story where the hero risks his life to obtain some object of power. It was also the point where some character you thought was dead suddenly reappeared to help the hero. Aster looked over his shoulder, half expecting to see Paul come running through the great entrance doors, but all he saw was the Empress nodding back at him.

One thing she'd made abundantly clear was that if the sword rejected him he would die right here, right now, alone in this strange lifeless city. With Paul lying dead somewhere below the Misty Mountain, no one would know where he'd gone. No one would be coming to look for him, no one would ever know the sacrifice he'd made and he would never see his parents again.

He turned back to face the sword, tears welling up in his eyes and his hands trembling. As he did so his fingers lightly brushed against the Empress Sword and he felt an itching in his fingertips as the sword came suddenly to life.

The blade began to glow with a white hot intensity and a humming noise filled the air. Aster's hand was drawn to the hilt like a lodestone to a chunk of iron and his fingers wrapped around it of their own accord. Power surged into his arm and quickly enveloped him from head to toe.

Light brighter than the sun filled the throne room and turned Aster's world white. A huge clap of thunder shook the whole palace and he lost his footing. Falling backwards, he briefly glimpsed the face of the Empress scowling down at him just before everything else went black.

12

The Magic Sword

Aster remembered his eighth birthday. A traveling circus troupe was passing through Castlekeep that summer and the king invited them into the palace for a party in his son's honor. He'd sat curled up on the step in front of his father's throne all afternoon watching the acrobats, jugglers, wild animals and fools perform.

After a couple of hours, his urge to pee overcame his fascination with the performers. He tried to stand up, but discovered his left foot had fallen asleep. He could still remember the strange pain, as if thousands of needles were poking him in the ankle.

He hopped around, trying to escape the unfamiliar sensation, until he was about ready to cry. Then he noticed the circus fools mimicking him with a little dance of their own. He laughed so hard he wet himself, but after that day he'd always been careful not to let his foot fall asleep again.

He awoke now with that same prickly sensation covering every inch of his body. He felt like getting up and dancing around as he had back then to avoid the thousands of tiny needles torturing him, but he couldn't move. It was as if every last bit of energy had been drained from him.

He was laying on his back, the hard marble floor working in concert with the prickling to torture his backside. Cautiously he opened his eyes. Everything was bright and blurry, but far above the sky was filled with twinkling stars. He closed his eyes again.

How long had he been out? Was it nighttime already? That didn't quite make sense. It was much too bright for the stars to be out and wasn't he still in the throne room? Who could have dragged him outside? Then he remembered that gold stars were painted on the ceiling of the throne room and opened his eyes again.

The gilt stars glittered in the sunlight, red-gold with the colors of late afternoon, streaming in from the high windows on the west wall. Bright dust motes danced in the air above him as his eyes slowly began to focus. Everything was quiet except for the ringing in his ears, which was beginning to fade away.

With some difficulty he sat up and took stock of his situation. He was alive, which was more than he'd been expecting; he was in one piece, as far as he could tell; and the numbness was beginning to give way to a dull ache. He was sitting on the floor at the bottom of the steps leading up to the throne, apparently having just fallen down them backwards. Beyond all belief, the Empress Sword was in his hand.

He held it up, turning it this way and that. Its mirror bright finish gleamed in the sunlight and he marveled at the many exotic jewels encrusting its hilt. The history books claimed the sword was made smaller and lighter than a normal broadsword, but it felt heavy and perfectly balanced to his hand.

With some difficulty he managed to stand up. He felt dizzy at first and oddly off-balance. His chain mail shirt weighed more heavily on his shoulders than usual. The Empress Sword felt like a bar of lead in his hand. Even his ponytail pulled heavily at the back of his head.

He looked around for the Empress. He wanted to thank her for trusting him and also maybe to gloat a little about the sword accepting a boy as its new owner. She'd been scowling at him when he'd last seen her, so she might not be happy about all this. Whatever the case, there was no sign of her now.

He hoisted the Empress Sword up to an on guard position. It was beautiful, but there was something not right about the way his thumb lay across the red silk wrapping of the hilt. For just a second he could have sworn it wasn't his thumb. He twitched and watched it move, but it still bothered him.

Shaking it off, Aster took a cautious swipe at the air. The sword sang as it sliced through the dust motes. It was indeed well balanced and not at all the fancy trifle it appeared to be at first glance.

When he took a step forward, thrusting the Empress Sword out before him in a practice lunge, several things happened all at once.

First his head snapped back, as if something had snagged his hair. Then the short sword he was wearing made a loud tapping noise as it clattered across the marble floor. His chain mail shirt, which had been pinching at him for weeks, suddenly shifted, falling loosely off his left shoulder. And finally his trousers slipped through his belt, fell past his knees and bunched up around his ankles, nearly tripping him.

What had the Empress told him? That the sword might ask him to sacrifice something more precious than he ever dreamed possible? As he stood frozen in place, shaking from head to toe, feeling the cool air on his bottom and realizing that he wasn't feeling something else that ought to be there, awareness of what the old woman had been trying to say crept over him.

He slowly stood upright, afraid of moving too fast. He looked at the Empress Sword again, this time with fear and rising panic. He wanted to drop it, throw it away and run, get as far from this place as he could and hope it was all just a bad dream.

Aster tried to calm down and think about what to do next. He needed to do something with the sword and quickly, if for no other reason than he needed to pull up his pants before he could run away.

"Looking for this?"

Aster shrieked, tried to jump back, tripped over his trousers and fell to the floor. At the top of the stairs, standing next to the throne, was the Empress. In her hands she held a bejeweled scabbard that matched the decorations on the Empress Sword.

"Oh, my. You know, one of the reasons girls wear skirts is to keep things like that from happening."

The Empress laughed as Aster scrambled to his feet.

"What did you do to me?"

The old woman's eyes gleamed mischievously. "You strike me as a clever child. I'm surprised you haven't figured that out for yourself. I told you the sword wouldn't tolerate being touched by a man, and yet there you are holding it. Therefore it stands to reason you must be a woman now. You certainly look like one."

"I look like a..." Aster's eyes widened as the words sank in. He'd expected as much, but hearing it from the Empress made it seem all too real. He panicked. "I'm a... That can't be! I'm the crown prince of Caledon, the sole heir to my father's throne. I can't be a... I demand you change me back immediately!"

"Now, now. If I did that, you wouldn't be able to take the sword with you. Then what would happen to the good people of Caledon? Didn't you just finish telling me you were willing to sacrifice *anything* for them? Was that for real or was it all just talk?"

"I meant every word. I'd give my life to save my people, but how am I supposed to fight a dragon looking like some prissy little girl?"

The Empress began walking slowly down the steps towards Aster. The look in her eyes was no longer bemused. "Did you happen to notice the fine tapestries hanging all around this hall? They really are quite exquisite. Some of the finest artisans of my time spent years making them.

"Each one depicts a single dragon in desperate battle for its very life against a solitary knight. No two tapestries portray the same dragon, but in every single one of them the knight is the same. I, Princess Afanasia of Caledon, Empress of Kafu, defeated every dragon I ever faced. And, like you are now, my young friend, I was nothing more than a prissy little girl!"

The Empress was now standing toe to toe with Aster, her hard old eyes boring into him like augers. She was so close that, had she been alive, he would have felt her breath on his face. She thrust the scabbard into his hands and he involuntarily took a step back. He bowed his head, staring at the floor, afraid to look up.

Then he took a deep breath and let it out slowly. He couldn't run away from this. The sword meant salvation for his people. He really had been prepared to sacrifice anything and he could have been turned into something much worse than a girl. Whatever had just happened, it would be worth it in the end if the sword allowed him to defeat the dragon.

"I meant no disrespect, your Majesty. I just don't see how I can defeat a dragon like this."

The Empress's expression softened a bit. "Have more faith in yourself. You're not so different than I was at your age. We both came to these mountains on a whim looking for magic that might save our people. I persevered and forged an empire in the process. You may accomplish something equally as implausible."

"But making me look like a girl? Isn't there some other way?"

The Empress shook her head. "The magic of the sword is fixed and can't be altered. If you truly wish to help your people, you must play by its rules. Is being a girl really so hard?"

"I wouldn't know, I've never been one before, but I guess it can't be that tough. Girls do it all the time, right?"

The old woman laughed. "You may be surprised at what girls can do. Now, pull up your trousers, get on your horse and go find your dragon. Don't worry about what you'll do when you find him, the sword will take care of that. All you need to do is remain brave."

Aster slipped the Empress Sword into its scabbard. He pulled the short sword from his belt as well and held them both together. The Empress Sword was just a little bit longer.

"I can do brave." He bent down to pull up his pants and nearly toppled over. His balance was way off and he ached from head to toe. "I'm just not so sure about walking."

13

The New Girl in Town

Aster walked through the halls of the palace in a daze. He'd achieved his goal, he'd gotten a magic sword with enough power to slay a dragon and free his people, but at what cost? He'd been turned into a girl.

Or maybe he'd just been made to look like one. Maybe nobody would notice. He'd read stories where girls pretended to be boys and nobody realized it until she fell in love with the hero. That wouldn't happen in his case because he was the hero.

It might work out. After all he was still the prince. Who would dare question his being a little shorter or his voice a little higher? As long as he continued to act like a man nobody should be the wiser.

He stepped out of the palace onto the great veranda. The sun was peeking out from behind the clouds in the west and he guessed there were only a couple more hours before sunset. He looked down the long staircase and spotted Troy nosing around inside the big fountain.

He needed to leave the city and find some clear water before nightfall. Troy obviously needed it and Aster doubted he could find food for either of them inside the city. He wondered if he could reach the glade where they'd camped the night before. It had a pond large enough to swim in and Troy liked the grass there.

He walked down the stairs slowly, being careful not to trip over his baggy pants, then crossed the courtyard to where his horse stood.

He reached for the reins, but Troy backed away. When he reached for them again, Troy actually snapped at him.

"Hey, stop that! This isn't some kind of a game. I'm tired and I want to get out of here."

But the horse simply would not let Aster get near him. Even after he managed to grab the reins, Troy still would not let him get into the saddle.

"What's wrong with you? You're acting like you don't know me. I'm Aster, you idiot, I rode you all the way here from home. Remember?"

Then it came to him. Maybe Troy didn't remember who he was or more accurately didn't remember the girl who was standing here now. Animals were supposed to be more sensitive to these things, but maybe Troy just couldn't see through the spell the Empress had cast on him.

"All right, I know you think I'm someone else, but we can't just stand here until it gets dark. Let's just walk together for a while until you figure out who I really am, okay?"

Aster was exhausted, but he couldn't see any other way of getting out of the city. He tugged hard on the reins and Troy reluctantly followed him across the courtyard and out the gates.

They wove their way through the twisting streets in silence until they eventually came to the main gate. Beyond it were the lush green fields of the valley where Troy could eat and he could rest. He took one last look at the empty city before passing through the gates and heading west, toward home and a confrontation with the dragon.

He wasn't certain just when or where he collapsed, but he awoke to darkness, lying in the tall grass at the side of the road. He wondered if he'd dreamed it all; the sword, the Empress, and what she'd done to him. The dull ache from the transformation remained and he quickly felt between his legs. No, it had not been a dream.

He sat up and looked around. Troy was nowhere in sight. He wasn't getting out of this valley without his horse, so he stood up and began searching the dark field. The moon, only occasionally peeking out through the passing clouds, was half full. Once, when it lit up the field, he saw a dark shape moving in the distance.

"Troy? Is that you?"

A whinny confirmed it and Aster headed towards the sound. He found the horse happily munching on grass at the edge of a large pond. Aster smiled; maybe his luck was finally changing. He approached the horse slowly and it didn't shy away from him this time.

He found some fallen tree limbs and set a small fire. By its light he tried to get a good look at himself. He was shorter than before, that much he could tell from walking beside Troy, but his clothes seemed to be oversized in every way. Even the chain mail shirt he'd made to fit himself at age eleven. He tried to pull it over his head, but his hair caught in the links.

After a few minutes work he managed to free himself and was surprised to find his ponytail had turned from yellowish blond to jet black. He was also very surprised by how much more of it there was. He let go and it fell almost to his knees.

Then he stripped off the rest of his clothes and took a long look at what he'd become. His arms and legs were thin, but good strong muscle still lay beneath a layer of pale skin. His body looked very whitish by the light of the fire and was smoother and rounder than he remembered.

His weight was oddly distributed. There seemed to be more fat than muscle on his chest now and his waist seemed too thin. He tried not to look between his legs; he didn't want to think about what was missing or where it might have gone.

As he stood there shivering in the firelight, a glint of light from the Empress Sword caught his eye. He picked it up and held the mirror-bright blade to the light. He searched its surface for runes or decorations of some kind.

Instead he saw his own eyes reflected back at him. Not the light blue orbs that had greeted him in the mirror each morning, but strange dark eyes. They were oddly shaped and seemed to have no lids until he winked at himself. He tried to get a look at his whole face, but the blade was just too narrow.

It didn't seem possible, but he looked just like a girl now. He didn't feel any different. He had no desire to dress in frilly clothes or gossip about his friends. He seemed to be thinner and shorter than before, but still had enough strength to lift Troy's saddle into place.

As he slipped into the icy cold water of the pond, he tried to remember all he could about magical transformation. Mandoline had once explained to him why lead could not be changed into gold. The old man said the two metals were too different from one another and the power needed to transform even a tiny amount was greater than that possessed by all the sorcerers in the kingdom combined.

On the other hand, he'd seen all sorts of things made to look like gold by magic. Sometimes it was a thin layer of real gold taken from some other object. Still others had been purely illusionary, like the Misty Mountain. Aster couldn't think of two things more dissimilar from each other than boys and girls, so the spell must be an illusion.

He waded out deeper, the cold water at last giving him some relief from the constant aching. The one thing he knew for sure about illusions was that they were always temporary. All illusions would deteriorate over time unless they emanated from an object with strong magical power.

The Misty Mountain had stood for a thousand years only because that rock pyramid had been constructed and a source of magical energy supplied to it through the ley lines. The spell making him look like a girl must similarly be tied to an object of power, like the Empress Sword. It made sense for the Empress to place the spell on the sword, as Aster wasn't about to let it out of his sight.

He smiled as he swam across the pond. If the sword was the source of the illusion, then all he had to do was return the sword to the Empress. Once he was far enough away from the thing, he'd turn back into himself.

Elated by this realization, Aster plunged his head under the water. He swam back toward the campfire and when he'd reached the shallows he surfaced. As he stood up his head snapped back violently. It felt like twenty horseshoes had been tied to his hair. He fell backwards, landing with a huge splash that startled Troy.

Sitting waist deep in the icy water, Aster began gathering up handfuls of thick sopping wet hair. As he sat wringing out the water he realized it was becoming hopelessly tangled and he hadn't brought a brush with him. He'd be combing out the tangles with his fingers for hours. Being a girl, even an illusionary one, wasn't going to be easy.

Aster rode down out of the hills after three days crossing the valley, the mountain pass, and the magical fog bank surrounding the Misty Mountain. Troy's skittishness faded to the point where he finally let Aster ride him again, but leading him through the illusionary mountain and the fog had been even more difficult than the first time. Getting around the giant boulder where Paul had disappeared was both arduous and emotionally draining.

Aster heaved a sigh of relief when the rooftops of Traders Run appeared over the next hill. He was looking forward to a night or two in the soft beds of the Five Crowns Inn, so he quickened his pace. Since he was coming from the east this time, it didn't make sense to try and find the same stable. Any reasonably clean looking one would do for a night or two.

He found a decent looking one near the edge of town. The stable master was standing by the gate and reached for Troy's reins even before Aster dismounted.

"Afternoon, Miss. Is there something I can help you with?"

Aster dropped out of the stirrups and tightened his belt. None of his clothing fit properly now and it was often a struggle just to keep his pants up.

"Do you have room for my horse?"

"Certainly, Miss. How many horses are there in your party?"

"Just Troy here. I need to board him for a couple of nights."

"I'm sorry, but it's customary to board all the horses in a party at the same stable. Are you traveling with retainers?"

"I'm not traveling with anyone. Look, I just want to stable my horse long enough to pick up some supplies and then move on."

The man chuckled. "Even if something like that were true, Miss, I can't accept a horse for boarding without someone responsible present. If you bring one of your men with you, I'll see what I can do."

"What are you talking about? I boarded this horse on the west side of town just last week. They seemed to think I was responsible enough."

"I find that hard to believe. It's against the law. The stable masters on the west side might have been willing to make an exception, but I'm not risking my warrant on a little girl's foolish whim."

"Foolish whim?" Aster squared his shoulders and planted his fists on his hips. "I'll have you know, sir, I've been on the road for over a month and I'm quite capable of taking care of myself. I can pay you beforehand, in gold if you wish. Now, will you please board my horse for the night or I shall take my trade elsewhere?"

The stable master chuckled. "You're a feisty little thing, aren't you? I'm sorry, but come back with your father and I'll be happy to take your gold. Otherwise, I suggest you go find that fool on the west side and try talking him into breaking the law for you again."

Aster was dumbfounded. The man handed him the reins and just turned away. No one had ever brushed off the prince of Caledon in such a fashion. "Wait just one minute! Do you have any idea who I am?"

The man turned and looked down at Aster with a stern glare. "Yes I do. You're an annoying little girl and if you don't leave now I'm going to take a switch to you. Now git!"

The man seemed genuinely angry and Aster took a step back without thinking. He bumped into Troy who snorted and danced away, pulling Aster after him. As he led Troy away from the stable, with the stable master's eyes following them the whole way, he felt his anger rise.

"I suppose I'm not going to be treated like a prince as long as I look like this. Still, that's no reason to talk down to me like I'm a child. I may look like a girl, but I'm still thirteen. Maybe he's just a rude person by nature."

If that were the case, then only rude people were qualified to be stable masters in Traders Run. Aster was turned down everywhere he went and everyone he met treated him like a petulant child in need of an escort. After an hour of these frustrating confrontations he decided to check in at the Five Crowns and try again in the afternoon.

He tied Troy's reins to a post outside the inn and then straightened his clothing. He took a deep breath and strode into the inn with as much casual confidence as he could muster. As before, Mr. Harrison was standing behind his desk, but this time he was speaking to a man in dusty riding clothes.

Aster walked up to the desk and waited patiently. From time to time, Mr. Harrison would glance at Aster, smile politely, and then turn back to the other man. As the minutes stretched on Aster began to realize the innkeeper had no intention of interrupting his conversation to help him.

He cleared his throat and tried to make his voice sound deeper. "Excuse me, I'd like a room, please."

Both men turned to look down at him. Mr. Harrison glanced towards the door and then back at Aster with a questioning look on his face. "Of course, milady. Just as soon as..."

"There is no one coming after me!" Aster took a deep breath and tried not to shout. "I require a room for the next two nights. I will pay you in advance if I may have room number three." Aster stalked up to the desk and slapped down two gold sovereigns.

Both men looked from Aster to the coins and back again. After an awkward silence the innkeeper finally shook his head. "See what I mean, Hector?"

The burly man took one of the coins and held it up, turning it back and forth to look at both sides. "Seems real enough to me, and you think they're the same as the others? Where'd the boy say he got them?"

"Said he picked them up in Castlekeep. Said all the coins there look like this." Mr. Harrison fingered the coin still lying on the desk.

"Not likely. These sovereigns were hard struck and polished." The big man lowered the coin from his face and thrust it towards Aster. "Girl, where'd you get this?"

Aster'd had just about enough of this for one day. He was tired, frustrated, and now a stranger was challenging a coin of the realm with his own likeness on it. "I beg your pardon, but I'm attempting to secure lodging from this innkeeper. He's the one I wish to speak with, not you."

The man raised an eyebrow. "Well, beg pardon, your ladyship. I don't mean to hold you up none, but we don't see sovereigns like this in Traders Run every day. How'd you come by such pretty coins?"

"You have me at a disadvantage, sir. I don't know who you are or why I should answer such a question."

The man's look went from playful to serious in the blink of an eye. "I'm the sheriff of this prefecture and it's my job to know such things. Now, do you mind telling me where you got these coins?"

Aster's shoulders drooped. Of course the town sheriff would want to know where a stranger had acquired freshly minted coins. The follow-up questions were equally obvious, and all the better if he could avoid them being asked in the first place. There was no time to make something up, so the truth would just have to fit the situation.

"I got them from my aunts and uncles. They were gifts for my birthday."

"And where are these aunts and uncles?"

"In Castlekeep."

The sheriff and the innkeeper smiled at one another. Then the sheriff scooped up the other sovereign from the desk and held them both out to Aster.

"In that case, I think they'd want you to keep these. You come back with your father, and William here will settle up with him when you leave." The tone in the sheriff's voice was condescending in a way Aster had never experienced before. It was humiliating.

"I'll make sure you get room number three all to yourself, Miss." Mr. Harrison spoke slowly, as though he were talking to a small child. "When you get back to Castlekeep, thank your little friend for recommending my inn."

That puzzled Aster until he realized the innkeeper was actually talking about Aster himself. The man obviously didn't recognize him at all, hadn't even seemed to consider he might be a boy. Were all girls treated like this, or just odd looking ones dressed up in dirty, oversized armor?

"Thank you, I'm sorry to have interrupted your conversation." Aster sighed and accepted the coins from the sheriff, what else could he do?

The sheriff smiled, showing off the few yellowed teeth he had left. "That's all right, missy. I know you was just anxious to get into your room and change out of them clothes. Now, put them coins away before you go walking about, or someone might pinch them from you."

As Aster trudged towards the door he could hear the two men chuckling to one another. He hurried outside and walked over to Troy, who was tugging at some grass growing up between the cobbles. He leaned heavily against the horse's shoulder.

"This just isn't turning out the way an adventure should. What am I supposed to do if no one lets me stay at their inn?"

Troy snorted and Aster grinned.

"Or let you stay in their stable? We'd be better off out on the road; assuming anyone will sell us supplies. We better head for the marketplace."

14

The Blue Dress

Aster walked toward the market square. People continued
to stare as he and Troy passed through the busy streets.
The men seemed amused, their eyes laughing even when
their mouths remained shut. It was humiliating, but he couldn't
really say why.

The women he passed weren't laughing. They scowled
disapprovingly at him, pointing their fingers and shaking their
heads. Whenever he'd gone shopping with his mother, women
would always smile and fawn over the "little prince," but now they
whispered to one another and ushered little children back into the
shops as he passed.

What was so strange about a girl coming into town alone anyway?
And what was so wrong with a girl wearing chain mail and riding
clothes? He'd obviously just ridden in on a horse! Why did everyone
assume he was a girl? Perhaps these women were frightened because
they knew he wasn't. Perhaps the illusion was incomplete?

He stopped at the entrance to the market and scanned it
apprehensively. He thought about what he needed for his journey
and wished he'd gone with Paul to find such things the week
before. He wasn't about to find them standing here staring into the
marketplace, so he set off with Troy in tow.

The first wagon he passed appeared to be that of a garment maker.

Under the awning a table was set out and covered with bolts of cloth. A tailor's dummy stood behind the table displaying a brocade waistcoat with a plain black doublet draped over it. At the far end of the table stood a full-length mirror with a crack running across the middle. Aster caught a glimpse of himself in it as he passed by and stopped. He walked up to it and found a total stranger staring back at him.

The eyes, which he'd glimpsed only briefly before, were indeed unlike anything he'd ever seen—almond-shaped, with brown pupils so dark they appeared black. The nose didn't appear to be as flat as it felt, just small and perched high above a tiny bud shaped mouth with lips a remarkable shade of red. The skin surrounding those lips was a pale ivory color.

It was the face of a porcelain doll and with a groan he realized no one would ever mistake it for that of a boy. He looked tiny and silly in the rumbled oversized clothes and wondered how anyone had been able to keep from laughing out loud at the sight of him.

He stared at the reflection for a long time, until he noticed a squat little man glaring at him from the back of the wagon. Aster backed away from the mirror and tugged on Troy's reins.

"Come on. I don't think we'll be buying any supplies around here."

He felt certain now that the traders would give him the same sort of response he'd gotten from all the stable masters. He might be able to buy a frilly dress or some fresh vegetables to take home for supper, but no one was likely to sell him oats for his horse or dried meat for the road. Then out of his gloom a bright thought came to him.

"There could be one merchant in this market who'll help us out."

He found the stall with the orange striped canopy. The same girl was standing in front of it with her hands on her hips as if she'd been waiting there for him all along. He walked up to her and smiled.

"Excuse me, could you help me please?"

Maggie turned on him. "And just what do you think you're doing?"

Her familiar tone took Aster by surprise. Did she recognize him? "Uh...well that's kind of a long story."

"I'll bet it is. But what are you doing with that horse here in the middle of town? Don't you know horses aren't allowed on the paved streets in daylight?"

He didn't know that, and it probably explained most of the disapproving looks he'd been getting. "Well, no. I tried to put him up at a stable, but they wouldn't let me."

"Well no wonder, with you dressed in that get-up. People around here don't take to girls wearing clothes like that. You should have changed into your skirts before heading into town. Just who are you traveling with, anyway?"

Aster's hopes fell. Maggie hadn't recognized him after all. "I'm not traveling with anyone, and I don't have any skirts to change into. Like I said, it's a long story, but I could really use your help."

Maggie seemed to consider that for a moment, then her expression changed. "It was bandits, wasn't it? Those murdering thieves are everywhere nowadays. You must have barely escaped with your life. Tell me, are those the rogue's own clothes you've got on?"

Aster blinked in confusion. What in the world was she talking about? "No, no, that's not what happened. I wasn't robbed by bandits."

"Then what happened to your clothes? How come you're wandering around all by yourself with a man's horse and kit?"

She'd given him the perfect cover story and he blew it. He realized his mistake and blurted out the next thing that came to mind. "It was the dragon, you see..."

The girl stared at him blankly. He'd never told many lies except to Mandoline, and the old man saw through every one of them. He supposed blaming the dragon for his troubles was just too preposterous for anyone to believe, even if it was true in a way, but he'd said it already and now he had to keep going.

"The monster attacked us. My...uh...uncle was killed and...uh...all my clothes were burned up and this was the only horse left... And..."

Maggie threw herself at him, wrapping her arms around him and hugging him tightly. "Oh, you poor dear thing! You must have been terrified out of your wits. No wonder you're as pale as a ghost."

Aster didn't know what to do. Other than his mother and nanny, no girls had ever hugged him before. He wondered if it would be too forward to hug her back. Would she get the wrong idea about him? Then he realized that Maggie probably thought he was a girl.

He wrapped his arms gently around her waist and leaned into the hug. Maggie responded by reaching up and pushing his head against her shoulder. With a start, Aster realized she was now taller than he was. He stifle a laugh, but not before his shoulders shook.

"There, there," Maggie crooned softly into his ear. "You go ahead and cry all you want to. After what you've been through, any girl would need a good cry. And don't you be worrying about one single thing. Do you have a place to stay tonight?"

Aster breathed in the delicate scent of vanilla and lilac coming from the soft hair at the back of Maggie's neck. He could definitely get used to this, but he shook his head at such a thought. Girls fall in love with princes, not with other girls.

"No? Well then you can stay with us. I know Daddy won't mind once he's heard what happened. My name's Maggie, by the way."

"I know. I'm Aster." His face was still buried in the girl's shoulder, so the sound was somewhat muffled, but being this close to her ear there was no way Maggie could have missed what he'd just said.

Her hug relaxed and Aster let go of her. Maggie kept her hands on his shoulders, holding him at arm's length. "Did you say Astrid? That's an unusual name. But then, you're not from around here, are you?"

Aster blew out the breath he'd been holding. "No, I've just come from a place you've probably never heard of before. Thank you for your kind offer. I really didn't know what I was going to do next."

Maggie smiled. "Well, the first thing we need to do is get you out of those ridiculous clothes and into a proper dress. Unfortunately, the only ones I have in the wagon are fancy dresses."

"Oh, I can pay you for it. The dragon didn't take my money."

"Nonsense, this isn't the kind of town where you can sell fancy dresses anyway. You'd be doing me a favor by wearing the things around a bit. Just tell everyone where you got them, okay?"

Maggie winked and Aster smiled. They tied Troy to the back of the wagon and then climbed inside. It was a large affair with paneled sides and a roof, but it wasn't what you would call spacious. Every square inch was piled high with all manner of dry goods.

Maggie set about searching through a large wicker basket in one corner. After a few minutes of foraging she came up with a bundle wrapped in white linen.

"This ought to fit you, but it's back laced so I'll have to help you into it. After that, we can take your horse over to Daddy so he can get it stabled for you. You're not wearing a corset yet, are you? It's hard to tell with you wearing all that lot."

"A corset?" Aster wasn't even sure what that was, but he knew he didn't want to wear one just from the look on Maggie's face. "No, I don't wear one of those."

Maggie looked relieved. "Good, 'cause I don't have any in stock. Well, go on. Take everything off and let's have a look at you."

Aster tried to convince himself it was okay to get undressed in front of Maggie. For all intents and purposes he was a girl now, and there wasn't anything wrong with another girl seeing him without his clothes on, right?

He tried, but he just couldn't do it. He managed to get through undoing all the toggles on his jerkin before humiliation made him stop and look up at Maggie. He was just going to have to tell her everything and take a chance she that might believe him. "Maggie..."

"Maggie!" The loud voice came from outside the wagon. "Are you in there, lass?"

"What is it, Otis?" Maggie turned and stuck her head out the back of the wagon.

"You got a customer out here. Fellow wants some buckle fittings and I remembered you had those nice silver ones."

"I'll be right out!" Maggie turned back to Aster with a big grin on her face and whispered, "I've been trying to get rid of those fittings for months. You go ahead and get undressed, I'll be back to lace you up in a few minutes."

Maggie handed him the bundle and then jumped out the back of the wagon. Aster sat on a crate and sighed in relief. He looked over the bundle. The outer wrapping was a linen undershirt and the dress within was a pale blue. He chuckled. The dress would have matched his eyes perfectly, if they'd still been blue.

He quickly took off his riding clothes and slipped on the undershirt. It was plain linen with sleeves that came to just past his elbows and a squared front opening. It was too way long, dropping well below his knees, and he began to wonder how he might stuff all the extra material into his trousers. Then he remembered that girls didn't wear trousers under their dresses.

He held up the dress and stared at it. They looked completely different when they were actually on a girl. He couldn't tell if he was supposed to put it on over his head like a shirt or step into it like a pair of pants. In his mind he could almost hear his valet clucking his tongue and saying, "Please hurry, your highness. It's not as if you've never worn a dress before."

15

The Trader

By the time Maggie returned, Aster had found his way into the dress. She fussed with the strings behind his back as she rattled on about how good the dress looked on him. He tuned out what she was saying after a while; it sounded like a well rehearsed sales pitch and he really didn't care how nice he looked. It was much too formal a dress for wearing around town and he didn't plan on wearing it all that long.

He'd hoped to get the supplies he needed and be back on the road before nightfall. He wasn't quite sure what to do after that, but the sooner he found the dragon, killed it and returned the sword to the Empress, the sooner he could turn back into a boy.

He became aware that Maggie had stopped talking. He glanced over his shoulder and she was just standing there staring at him.

"What?"

"I asked if you were hungry. It's getting late, so I thought I would just close up shop and we can walk your horse over to the inn. Daddy's meeting me there for dinner and I asked you if you wanted to join us."

"Dinner at the inn? You want to take me to dinner at the Five Crowns Inn?" The irony was almost too much for him.

"The Five Crowns? Hardly. We always eat dinner at the Pig's Snout. It don't look like much, but the food's good and the innkeeper likes to barter with traders."

"Oh, I see. I really should just get the supplies I need and move on."

"That'll have to wait for tomorrow. Most of the traders pack up for the night around this time. You'd best come along with me. I'll get you fed and bedded down, then you can do all your shopping in the morning."

Maggie's grin told him he really didn't have a choice, so he nodded and followed her out of the wagon...where he promptly tripped over the long skirt gathered about his ankles and fell flat on his face.

After Maggie helped him to his feet and brushed the dust off him, Aster helped her move all of the trade goods from the table into the wagon. Moving around in the dress was awkward and uncomfortable. It pulled at him in strange ways and he tripped on the skirt a few more times. He tried to remember how the girls at court moved. They seemed to glide effortlessly around, their feet hidden from view, and he wondered just how they did that.

After buttoning up the wagon, he and Maggie walked south out of the marketplace with Troy in tow. It irked him that the horse took to Maggie right away, even though he was still somewhat leery of Aster. They'd only gone a short distance when Maggie stopped in front of a shabby building with blue shutters. Above the door a plank with a huge pig's face painted in garish colors swung back and forth in the light afternoon breeze.

"I'll go tie up your horse. You go inside and find us a place to sit."

Aster retrieved the Empress Sword from Troy's saddle and slung it across his back.

Maggie's eyes widened. "Here now, you won't be needing that thing. This place looks worse than it really is."

"I...I can't risk losing this sword. It...it was a gift."

Maggie looked skeptical, but nodded anyway. "All right then, but don't go waving that thing around. You're likely to hurt yourself and anyone near you."

She disappeared around the corner of the building, leaving Aster alone in the street. He took a deep breath, gripped the sword strap lying across his chest and walked through the tiny doorway.

Inside, the tavern was a single large room much bigger than Aster expected. Most of the room was filled with long tables arranged in rows running front to back. On one side wall a large hearth stood cold, allowing to the summer heat.

On the opposite wall two large barrels sat on racks. Several smaller casks sat next to them and all had wooden taps. A small serving bar stood before the barrels, its top stacked with earthenware mugs. A door near the bar lead back into what Aster imagined must be the kitchens.

The room was about half filled with an interesting mix of people. From the condition of their clothes he guessed most were laborers of one sort or another. There were also a few well dressed men and women. None of them would pass for courtiers of course, but several of the women were dressed in outfits at least as fancy as the one Aster was wearing.

He wondered why those women in particular seemed to be the only ones standing; the men sitting nearby and talking to them should have offered them seats.

The sound of knives against crockery, good natured laughter and the undertone of earnest conversation reminded him of meals at the castle garrison, when he would sit and eat with the men of the Royal Guard. The meals there had always tasted so good. Only later did he discover that whenever he was there the guards ate from the royal kitchens rather than their own stewpots.

Aster found an empty spot at the end of one of the tables. There were no chairs, just long benches to either side. All Aster had to do now was figure out how to sit down on one of them in the dress. There were benches just like them at the garrison house, but he'd never seen a woman actually sit down there.

He thought about lifting one leg over the seat the way a boy would, but could only imagine himself tripping on the skirts again. Finally he sat down backwards and swiveled around lifting both feet up to clear the bench at the same time. He was just about to congratulate himself when he saw another woman slip gracefully onto a bench from one end and glide along it into place.

"Or you could do it that way," he grumbled. Pretending to be a girl wasn't going to be as easy as he'd hoped. At least court life had taught him better manners than most of the common men he knew, but there seemed to be things girls shared only among themselves. Of course he wasn't really a girl; he only looked like one.

"Pardon me, Miss."

If Aster hadn't felt the man's presence behind him, he probably wouldn't have known someone was speaking to him. He turned and saw a short man wearing a mushroom shaped velvet hat staring down at him. The man's clothes seemed to sag on him, like they'd been intended for someone much larger, but the fabric looked expensive and new.

Aster was instantly wary of the little man, but greeted him politely enough. "May I help you?"

"Perhaps, Miss. That's a very pretty sword you have draped across your shoulders. Is it yours or are you carrying it for someone?"

Aster shifted uncomfortably on the bench. He was trying to turn and confront the man properly, but the dress kept binding his legs.

"I can assure you, sir, the sword is mine."

The man held up his hands as if warding off an attack. "I meant no accusation, Miss. I merely wished to know if the sword was yours to sell."

"To sell?" Aster gave up his attempt at turning around and instead slid further down the bench putting some distance between the little man and himself. "It's not for sale, and who are you to be asking such a thing?"

"Oh dear, I haven't properly introduced myself, have I?" The man bowed and removed his floppy hat, revealing a bald head surrounded by curly black ringlets.

"I am Thaddeus Markham, purveyor of fine jewelry and trinkets to delight the eye and entrance the heart. I sometimes also deal in weapons of a decorative nature and your small display piece there caught my discerning eye. I know of a collector in Castlekeep who's been looking for just such a blade to give his daughter. I could make it well worth your while, should you be willing to part with it, young lady."

Aster was getting really tired of being called young lady and Miss. "For your information, sir, this is not a display sword—something I would be more than happy to demonstrate if you continue to pursue the matter. Now, which part of 'not for sale' did you not understand?"

"Oh no, Miss. I understand that you don't *want* to sell such a beautiful thing. But if I may say so, a lady of your obvious upbringing in an establishment such as this, wearing that sort of clothing, suggests a fall from grace, as it were. You may not yet realize the importance of a full purse, but I warrant that you may before the night is out."

That gave Aster a moment's pause. He hadn't brought more than a handful of coins with him and it might take weeks to find and kill the dragon. Before too long, he'd need some source of money; looking like this, he couldn't just walk into any garrison post demanding a tribute for the prince.

"Wise words, and I shall take them to heart, but the sword is not for sale. Not now or at any time in the future."

"As you say. But should you change your mind, please come and see me first. I can offer you much more than the local shopkeepers. In fact I'll prove it to you."

The little man began digging around inside a large satchel he had slung over one shoulder. A moment later he pulled out a silver circlet. He polished it on his sleeve a few times and looked it over carefully before handing it to Aster.

"Oh no, I couldn't take anything..."

"Please do, Miss. It's not worth very much and I want you to have it, as a gift of good faith. All I ask is should you ever decide to part with the sword, you'll come see me first."

Thaddeus dropped the circlet into Aster's lap. He picked it up and looked it over quickly. It was made of a thin strip of silver metal that curled up at the ends to form the horns of a small ram's head. A small gold ring was threaded through the ram's snout and from it hung a teardrop shaped white crystal about the size of a grape. It looked to be well made, even though Aster was certain it was worthless. He handed it back to the man.

"I'm sorry, but I simply can't accept this."

"Please, Miss. It's a gift. At least try it on."

"Oh, all right." Aster slipped the circlet over his head. The little ram's head came to rest comfortably over the center of his forehead while the crystal dangled annoyingly across the bridge of his nose.

"Oh, I say, that is charming. I could never take it back now that I've seen how lovely it looks on you."

"Really? You think it looks all right?" It did fit nicely and if Aster had to play at being a girl he might as well look good while doing it.

"It does indeed. Now, should you ever need to find me, my wagon is located at the north end of the market square. Don't hesitate to come by day or night. I'll treat you right, Miss. You can always count on Thaddeus Markham."

The little man turned and disappeared into the crowd surrounding the bar. Aster shook his head and the crystal tickled his nose. He removed the circlet and examined it again.

"What have you got there?" Maggie walked up and set a large tray down on the table. "Oh, you bought something from that trader? Let me see."

"Well, sort of." Aster handed Maggie the circlet and she began eying it closely. "Do you know that man?"

"Not really. He showed up in the market about a week ago. We get his kind from time to time. Rolls into town, never really sets up shop, stays just long enough to do some trading, and then moves on. This is very nice, what did he charge you for it?"

"Nothing, he gave it to me." In answer to Maggie's dumfounded stare, he explained. "He wanted to buy my sword. When I told him it wasn't for sale, he gave me that circlet so I wouldn't sell it to someone else first. It's not like it's worth anything."

"Oh no, this is worth quite a lot! This band is made of fine silver. So is the ram's head. I don't recognize the stone, but the fastenings are real gold. This should sell for twenty florins at least."

"But he said himself it wasn't worth anything. Why would he give me something expensive?"

"I don't know, but I imagine you'll see him again soon enough. He either really wants your sword or he'll be wanting this back." Maggie smiled and passed the circlet to Aster. "Well, go ahead and put it on. I want to see how it looks."

Aster thought he'd much rather see Maggie wearing it, but slipped it over his own head with a sigh. "It looks silly, doesn't it?"

"No, it's perfect for you! Later we can brush your hair out over top of it, then it'll look like it was made for you." Maggie giggled as Aster's expression paled. "You really are a tomboy, aren't you?"

The Dinner Guest

gainst all reason, Aster was irked at being called a tomboy. He thought of Maggie as a tomboy and liked her all the more for it, but somehow being called one himself seemed improper. He was royalty after all! His cheeks felt warm and he worried he was blushing, so he turned to look at the tray of food rather than face Maggie. "Why are there three plates?"

"One's for Daddy of course." Maggie took a seat on the other side of the table. "He should be finishing up at the blacksmith's shop soon and we always meet here for dinner."

"So your father's a blacksmith, not a trader?"

"No, he's just helping out the blacksmith. Mr. Fenrick got a big order for battle axes from the local garrison and asked Daddy for help. Daddy's not a blacksmith by trade, but nobody knows more about weapons. He was a captain in the royal guard, before..." Maggie's voice trailed off as her normally exuberant expression grew dark.

"Before what?"

"Before Mama died. Daddy left the guard to take care of me. I know it's been hard on him and he misses it terribly. He's always talking about military things, so whenever an opportunity comes along for him to work with weapons or armor, I always tell him we need the money and encourage him to take the job."

"How long has it been since..." What Aster really wanted to

know was how long ago Maggie's father had been a captain in the royal guard. There was a good chance he'd been there when Aster was pestering the guardsmen for fencing lessons. However, he could tell from the way Maggie blanched at the question that he was treading on thin ice. "I mean, how long have you and your father been trading?"

"About ten years. I was really quite small when Mama died."

The dragon had first appeared about ten years ago. It must have been extremely hard for Maggie's father to leave the service of the king at such a time. Aster was dying to know more, but decided to change the subject rather than make Maggie more uncomfortable. "What's for dinner? I don't think I've ever had this before."

Maggie wiped away a tear and chuckled. "The same thing they serve here every night—and every day, too! It's trader stew. Be careful though, it can be a bit spicy for the uninitiated."

Aster examined one of the plates closely. Next to a sizable mound of dark rice was a glob of thick brown sauce. The stew seemed to consist mostly of root vegetables and the smell coming off it was quite pungent.

Maggie leaned across the table, glancing to the right and to the left to be sure she wasn't overheard. "I made sure the cook gave us extra meat."

If there was any meat at all on these plates, Aster wasn't sure he wanted to know what animal it had come from. Tentatively he dipped a spoon into the stew and lifted out a sloppy mouthful. It was sweetly spicy, but no more so than some of the Iggalian dishes the cooks at the castle sometimes served. More importantly, it was warm and filling and Aster ate another spoonful with relish.

"It's good. Better than what I've been living off of since..."

He was going to say since he'd bought pack rations here about a week ago, but stopped himself just in time. He really didn't want to go into the whole story of how he'd lost those rations when Paul fell off the mountain or about the spell making him look like a girl. That was embarrassing enough, but he also didn't want Maggie to know he was the same obnoxious boy she'd sold a belt knife to the week before. He needed to come up with some sort of story to explain himself, but he'd already forgotten half of what he'd told her at the market.

Maggie reached across the table and patted Aster's hand. "You poor thing! I'll wager you haven't had a well cooked meal in weeks. You're nothing but skin and bones. Why..."

"Maggie, who's your little friend?"

A man's voice cut through the noise of the tavern like a court herald announcing the arrival of an invading army. Aster twisted around to find a mountain of a man standing right behind him. The broad shoulders, square jaw and steel grey hair falling about his shoulders were impressive enough, but what made this man stand out was his bearing. The way he stood rigid and erect while in a pose of casual rest marked him for the soldier he most assuredly was—or had once been.

"Daddy, this is Astrid. You won't believe what happened to her. She was attacked by the dragon. Her uncle was killed. Everyone in her party was killed. She barely escaped with her life! Her clothes were all burned up so she had to dress in the rags of a hired killer..."

Aster looked aghast at Maggie. *Where does she come up with these things? How am I supposed to keep all of that straight? A hired killer?*

"Calm down. Let the girl speak for herself." The big man rounded the table and set one large hand on Maggie's shoulder. She blushed and went quiet.

"Allow me to introduce myself, lass. I'm Marcus Griffin, trader, at your service. I take it my talkative daughter has invited you to dinner. How's the stew?"

No doubt about it, this man had been a soldier long before he took up trading. The signs were unmistakable to someone like Aster who'd been raised around guardsmen. Aster's first impulse was to rise to his feet and prepare to return the man's salute.

However, when he tried to stand up, his foot caught on the skirt again and he slipped, flopping down on the bench with a thud. Embarrassed, he tried not to look at Mr. Griffin.

"It's a pleasure to meet you, sir. The stew is just fine, but a little spicy, just as Maggie said it would be. My situation is not as grave as she paints it, but nonetheless I'm grateful for your hospitality."

Mr. Griffin seemed to straighten up a bit. He stared at Aster for a long moment and then took a step back from the table. Aster was sure now that the former captain was about to salute his prince, but instead the man bowed formally at the waist in courtly fashion.

"You're most welcome, young lady. Please excuse me for one moment while I go to the bar for a tankard of ale."

He bowed again, not as formally, and then headed across the room. Maggie giggled as she pulled the remaining plates off the tray, setting one to her right and the other in front of her. "I think Daddy likes you. He barely speaks to any of my other friends."

"Friends?" Aster was confused as to exactly when, in the last hour or so, they'd become friends. Not that he didn't want to be friends with Maggie, but this all seemed to be happening very fast. Did common people do everything this quickly?

Maggie nodded as she shoveled a spoonful of stew into her mouth. She chewed, swallowed and took a sip of water before answering. "Daddy doesn't really pay much attention to my friends, unless they're boys. I'm surprised he bowed to you like that. He doesn't even do that for grown women. Of course, you're special."

"I am?" Of course he was special, he was the prince, but Maggie had no way of knowing that. So, what did she mean? Aster had to wait for Maggie to finish chewing another mouthful of stew before she explained that while foreigners were rather common in Traders Run, she'd never seen anyone quite like him before.

"It's your eyes. They're so beautiful, but different from most folks. I'll bet Daddy already knows where you come from. If anyone can find a way to get you home, he will."

Mr. Griffin returned to the table then. He set a large tankard next to his plate and then plopped down next to Maggie on the bench.

"How did things go at the blacksmith shop today? Are you about finished?"

"Almost, Pumpkin. Jack wants me to rework the tempering on about half of the halberds. Doesn't think they're up to the king's standard and I agree with him. Shouldn't be more than another day or two."

"When you're done, do you think we can help Astrid get home?"

Mr. Griffin looked hard at Aster then. He rubbed his chin as if he were in the habit of having a beard. "So, did the dragon really set upon you and kill your whole traveling party?"

Aster swallowed. This was maybe his last chance to tell the truth, but when it came right down to it, what was easier to believe? That the Crown Prince of Caledon had been turned into a foreign looking girl by an old empress who died a thousand years ago? Or a lie?

"Yes, sir. My uncle and...um...four others were...uh..."

"Never mind the details, lass. I know this must be hard. But won't someone come looking for you? Where were you headed? For that matter, where were you coming from? It's plain to see that you're not from any of the Four Kingdoms."

"I...I can't really tell you any of that, I'm sorry. I can't go home yet either." He looked at Maggie and smiled. "I have something very important that I must do first."

"It has something to do with that sword, doesn't it?"

Aster looked up and met Mr. Griffin's eyes for the first time. "Yes, sir. How did you know?"

"Girls don't walk about town with a ceremonial sword strapped to their back without some good reason. I won't ask you again where you came from or why you're in Caledon. I'm guessing it has something to do with the dragon, since he attacked you. If that's the case, your best course of action now is to head for Castlekeep."

"Well, west anyway." Aster wasn't eager to return to Castlekeep in his present condition, but the dragon's attacks so far this summer had all been in that part of the country. "I just need some help getting supplies and then I'll be on my way."

"All by yourself? I don't think so, lass. I'll be done with the blacksmith in a day or two, then Maggie and I will pack up the wagon and take you there. I've been wanting to do some trading along the coast before winter sets in and Castlekeep is a fine place to start. You and Maggie can ride the wagon and I'll hire a horse."

"But Astrid already has a horse. It's tied up out back. She didn't know the rules about horses in town."

Mr. Griffin stared at Aster again. "Well, if it's a pony, you may have to ride it alongside while I drive the wagon. I'll walk your horse over to Samuel's stable after we eat. Do you have somewhere to sleep tonight?"

Aster felt his face reddening again. "No one would let me hire a room. They wouldn't board my horse either."

"Of course they wouldn't. Don't be silly. You're just a girl."

Mr. Griffin dove into his stew and said little else for the remainder of the meal. Aster had been raised to lead such men, but now he felt overwhelmed by this man's presence. Physically Aster wasn't that much smaller than he'd been a year ago, but right now he felt tiny and powerless.

They finished the meal in silence, then went out to where Troy was tied to a small watering trough. Mr. Griffin looked the horse over very thoroughly and Aster was worried he might recognize something from the royal stables, but in the end the big man smiled and patted Troy playfully on the rump.

"Fine looking animal you've got here, but I'm afraid he's a hand too short to carry me. You'll have to ride him or let him tag along behind the wagon." Then he unhitched the reins and disappeared down the alley with Aster's only means of leaving town—and everything he owned except for the Empress Sword on Aster's back.

"You see, I told you he likes you."

Aster gave Maggie a puzzled look. "I'd hate to see how he treats people he doesn't like."

Maggie giggled. "Come on, the boarding house is just down at the end of the street."

They walked to the end of the alley—in the opposite direction from the way Mr. Griffin had taken Troy—and turned a corner. Across the street was an old two-story building with many tiny windows. They went up a flight of narrow stairs on the side of the building and entered the second floor. Half way down the hall, Maggie opened an unlocked door and held it for Aster.

"It isn't much, but its home."

Aster stepped into the small room and looked around. There was a cot next to the door, its blanket folded with military precision. Another slightly larger bed spread across the back wall. A simple commode cabinet sat next to the bed with a washbasin on top.

A rope had been stretched across the room from which two blankets hung. He guessed this was used to partition the room into separate sleeping areas for father and daughter. That was all there was, and yet this meager collection of furniture completely filled the small room.

Aster stood in the middle of the room and looked apprehensively at what little floor space was left. "I don't think this is going to work out. There's no room for my bedroll."

"Bedroll? Don't be silly." Maggie laughed as she slipped past Aster and knelt beside the bed. She pulled a spare pillow from underneath it, fluffed it up and tossed it next to the other one. "You're sleeping in the bed with me tonight!"

17
The Thief

Aster lay awake listening to the muted growls coming from the other side of the drawn curtain just a few feet away. Mr. Griffin's snores were loud and regular, but they were not responsible for Aster's inability to fall asleep. What thundered more loudly in his ears and kept him lying rigidly awake was the sound of Maggie's soft breathing coming from inches away in the bed right next to him.

He'd lost the argument over sleeping arrangements when Mr. Griffin returned from the stable with Aster's haversack, but not his bedroll. Then the big man went back to the tavern, leaving Aster alone with his daughter for the next few hours.

Maggie almost immediately started undressing him, a procedure nearly as complicated as getting the dress on in the first place. Then to his distress she'd asked him to undress her as well.

With both of them finally down to their undershirts, Maggie suggested they braid each other's hair. Someday he'd have to thank the captain of the guard for showing him how to plait Troy's tail. Otherwise he'd have been completely clueless.

Even so, Maggie's long brown braid wasn't nearly as neat and even as the black one draped over his own shoulder. Maggie had also insisted he wear the circlet, which was now impossible to remove without completely undoing the braid first.

There hadn't been anywhere in the sparsely furnished room to hide the Empress Sword. He didn't feel comfortable just leaving it out in the open, so it had ended up laying between them on the bed. From time to time he'd reach out and touch the hilt just to make sure it was still there.

He wasn't quite sure what might happen if he got too far away from the thing. It was making him look like a girl, at least on the outside, and he wondered what would happen if he was separated from the sword entirely. Would he turn back into a boy right away? What if that happened now, while he lay here in the same bed with Maggie? She'd roll over expecting to find a black-haired girl, only to see a blond prince lying next to her.

She'd probably scream. Girls always screamed in stories. Her father would wake up and throw back the curtain. Sword already in hand, he'd accuse Aster of defiling his precious daughter and chase him from the room. Terrified, Aster would race out into the street with Captain Griffin, now fully armored, in hot pursuit.

Aster was suddenly running naked through the streets being chased by an enraged ogre as people gawked at him from windows and doorways along the way. In one of the windows he saw his mother. She was crying and his father stood at her shoulder looking down at him with a disapproving scowl on his face.

The dark streets of the village soon gave way to an even darker tunnel. In the distance he could see a flicker of light and he charged towards it as the monster behind him closed in for the kill.

The light became a huge brightly lit cavern and at its center, sitting atop a pile of gold, was a monstrous dragon. The beast reared up on its hind legs and breathed out a column of white hot fire. It engulfed Aster, burning his flesh and roaring in his ears.

Aster sat bolt upright panting and sweating. For a moment he couldn't tell what was really happening and what had been part of his dream. His ears rang, but there was also a strange humming noise he could feel in his bones.

The room smelled energized, like the air after a summer storm.

Even though it was still dark, his vision had the red afterglow he would sometimes see when he'd looked at the sun too long. He reached for the Empress Sword, but it was no longer on the bed beside him.

He glanced over his shoulder and saw Maggie, already awake, crouching at the head of the bed trying to light the lantern. Looking around the room, he spotted a dark shape on the floor next to the bed which he was certain hadn't been there before. The persistent hum seemed to be coming from that direction as well.

He jumped out of bed and crouched cautiously over the dark figure. It was a man, lying on the floor with his back propped against the wall. He was twitching all over, his arms and legs jerking in spasms. Aster couldn't see the man's face in the dark, but clenched in his right fist and glowing faintly was the Empress Sword.

Aster pulled at the man's stiff fingers, trying to pry them one by one from the hilt of the sword. Light filled the little room as Maggie got the lantern lit and Aster saw a face contorted into a mask of pain and fear—the face of Thaddeus Markham.

He pried the last of the trader's fingers away from the sword and it dropped into his own hand. The humming stopped immediately and Thaddeus's body slumped to the floor. Aster located the sword's scabbard from where it had fallen and slung it over his shoulder. Standing up, he expertly flipped the sword over the back of his hand, reversing his grip, before sheathing it in one fluid motion.

"So you do know how to handle that thing." Mr. Griffin's deep voice startled Aster. The big man pushed past him then and bent over the unconscious thief. "That's quite a protection spell someone's placed on your sword. They certainly don't want you losing it. Are you girls all right?"

"Isn't that the man who tried to buy the sword from you earlier?" Maggie was now kneeling at the foot of the bed, holding up the lantern.

Mr. Griffin shot Aster a stern look. "You know this man?"

"Yes sir...Well, no sir. He came up to me in the tavern and asked if I wanted to sell my sword. When I told him no, he gave me this circlet." Aster pointed to his forehead. "But I've never seen him before tonight."

"Did you tell him you were staying here with us?" Marcus bent over the trader and began to pry something from his left fist.

"No. At the time I didn't have any idea where I was staying."

Maggie's father stood up and held something to the light. It was a pendant with a large white crystal in the center similar to the one on Aster's circlet. Surrounding the crystal was a ring of silver with little marks engraved at regular intervals around the perimeter like a compass.

"I'll be damned!" Mr. Griffin scratched at the back of his neck. "I've never seen one this fancy before. Maggie, shade the lamp."

Maggie picked up a pillow and used it to block the light from the lantern. The room grew dark again and the pendant in Mr. Griffin's hand began to glow. He moved it towards Aster and it glowed more brightly. When he held it away again it dimmed. When he put it right next to the crystal dangling over Aster's nose it blazed as bright as a candle flame.

"It's a tracking stone. The army uses these on night raids. A scout goes out ahead of the main force to find the enemy with the target stone. Then the rest of the assault team follows using the tracker. This man gave you the target stone as part of that headpiece knowing he could find you later using this."

"He was planning to steal my sword all along!" Aster was truly shocked. No one had ever dared to steal anything from him before.

"Even if you'd sold him the sword, he'd have used this to track you down and steal back the money." Mr. Griffin poked at the little man's leg with his bare toes, but Thaddeus didn't move. "He got more than he bargained for, I'll warrant. What exactly did that spell do to him?"

"I'm not sure." Aster knew very little about what the Empress Sword could do. The Empress had somehow used it to make Aster look like a girl, and it was supposed to have the power to defeat dragons, but he had no idea what other magic it possessed. *"The sword will not tolerate a man's touch,"* was all the Empress had told him. Thaddeus was in horrible pain by the look of him, but otherwise he appeared unchanged. "This is the first time anything like this has happened."

"Well, he's out cold. I'll just take him down to the sheriff. Hector's bound to be up and wondering what's going on. That blast was loud enough to wake half the town." Mr. Griffin dropped the pendant into Maggie's hand and then bent down to pick up the unconscious man.

"What about the tracker?" Aster touched the white stone attached to his circlet. "Won't the sheriff need these as evidence?"

"I think it's best we keep them both for now. He told you the circlet was a gift, so it's yours to keep, and if we turn over the pendant he'll just get it back when they let him out of the stocks. Then he'll turn right around and do the same thing to some other foolish little girl."

Maggie's father pulled the little man up off the floor and slung the limp body over his shoulder. After stepping into his boots, he marched out into the hallway where a crowd of curious nightgown-clad guests quickly made a path for him.

Aster stood there, stunned by Mr. Griffin's words. "Is that all I am now? A foolish little girl?"

He certainly felt foolish. What did he really know of the real world outside the castle walls? He'd probably just been lucky not to have been beaten up and robbed before now.

"Oh, don't mind Daddy, he didn't mean it that way. In fact, I think you impressed him with that little sword trick of yours."

Aster blinked and turned to look at Maggie. "Sword trick?"

"You know, when you twirled it around and put it away really fast. Daddy likes that kind of stuff." Maggie demonstrated what she meant by waving her hand wildly above her head and slapping herself on the back.

Aster grinned. Maggie was so sweet. She started laughing, but then stopped and frowned.

"What's wrong?"

"I have a confession. While you were getting dressed this afternoon, I looked at your sword. I had it in my hands for a couple of minutes, but nothing happened. Maybe the spell's not working right."

Aster smiled sadly. "No, it's working. It didn't hurt you because you're just a foolish little girl—like me."

The Knight

In the morning Aster went back to the tavern with Maggie and Mr. Griffin for breakfast. Everyone there already seemed to know about the attempted theft and the strange clap of thunder that had awakened them in the middle of the night. To Aster's relief, no one seemed to connect him with the strange happenings.

No one seemed to know anything about Thaddeus Markham either, except that he'd been mixed up in a few shady deals elsewhere in town. After a quick meal of sausages and eggs, Mr. Griffin went off to the blacksmith shop while Aster and Maggie headed to the marketplace.

When they got to the Griffins' stall, Maggie opened the wagon and they began to fill the tables out front. Then Maggie turned to leave. "If we're going to Castlekeep in a few days, I need to make the rounds. I'm sure lots of folks will want to unload some goods for trade there. Would you mind watching the stall for me?"

The prince of Caledon had suddenly become a common shop merchant. Running the stall mostly involved standing around watching the other merchants move things around inside their own stalls. He felt guilty that he wasn't as busy as they seemed to be, so he began moving things from the tabletop to the boxes underneath to the wagon and back again. He soon realized the other merchants were doing basically the same thing.

He was putting a box of sewing needles and brightly colored threads into the wagon and looking for another box of similar things to put out when he was startled by a voice coming from right behind him.

"Where's Maggie?"

Aster straightened up and took a deep breath, something he'd been doing quite a lot since Maggie had laced him into the dress again that morning. How did the girls at court stay in these things all day long and not collapse from lack of air?

He turned around and found a tall young man standing quite close and gazing down at him. It was the same young man he'd met the week before at the stable, the one who was looking for a princess in distress.

"Oh, it's you."

"You know who I am?" The young man looked very full of himself then. "Of course, most people around here do. I'm the best huntsman in the east country after all. Are you waiting for Maggie, too? You really shouldn't be moving boxes around while she's not here."

"I'm a friend of Maggie's. She asked me to watch the stall for her while she ran some errands. Would you like to buy something?"

"You're a friend of Maggie's?" Aster was beginning to remember why he'd found the young man so annoying. "She probably told you all about me. She likes me, you know. A lot of girls like me..."

Eric's voice trailed off and Aster realized the boy was waiting for a response. Did he actually expect Aster to say that he liked him too?

"I'm sorry, have we been introduced?" Aster slipped past the boy and walked quickly to the table out front.

"We need to be introduced?" The boy seemed shocked by the very idea, but he recovered quickly enough. "Well of course we do, how silly of me. I'm Eric Buckingham, huntsman, at your service."

Eric bowed so low his forehead nearly touched the ground. It was the sort of bow pompous new town officials made the first time they were presented to the king. Aster nearly laughed out loud, but managed to clear his throat instead.

"I'm Astrid, of the...um...Eastern Empire. Very pleased to meet you."

Eric tried to grab Aster's hand, but it wasn't there to grab for long. "Of the Eastern Empire? That's nothing but a legend."

"Um...well...no..."

Aster was getting nervous, Eric took another step closer and was looking to grab for his hand again. Thankfully a commotion out in the marketplace interrupted the huntsman's advance.

The general din of the market had quieted down and merchants were beginning to rush about, removing wares from their tables and replacing them with others. Eric leapt deftly over the table and stood in front of it, gazing off into the distance.

Aster considered following him, but didn't dare jump over the table wearing the dress. Instead he leaned across the table and tried to get a look at what all the fuss was about, but even on tiptoe he couldn't see past the next wagon.

"What's going on?"

"What's going on? It looks like the garrison's escorting some important person through the market, only I don't recognize any of the soldiers."

Aster gave up trying to see anything from behind the table and walked around it to stand next to Eric. Across the marketplace he saw two lines of armored soldiers marching down the row of wagons towards them.

"That's not the local garrison. Those are the colors of the royal guard."

"The royal guard? Don't be silly, what would the royal guard be doing here in Traders Run? Besides, that's Henry, the stable master, walking with the old man."

Between the lines of soldiers walked two men. Aster recognized one as the master of the stable where he'd first met Eric. The other man was taller and bearded, and had a shock of grey white hair. With a sinking feeling in the pit of his stomach, Aster recognized the old man.

"Mandoline!" He grabbed Eric by the sleeve and dragged him behind the table. "Quickly!"

Frantically Aster began looking for someplace to hide. He'd come to believe most people wouldn't recognize him as the prince, but Mandoline had always been able to see through Aster's deceptions.

Not only that, but the old man was a sorcerer—one of the greatest wizards in the Four Kingdoms. He could probably spot a transformation spell a league away.

"What's wrong? You have nothing to fear, milady. I will protect you."

"Good. Then pretend you're watching the stall for Maggie and don't let that old man find out I'm here."

With that Aster spun the boy around, pushing him towards the table before diving under it himself. Aster heard the sound of marching feet passing just inches away from where he crouched behind some boxes. The footfalls of the guardsmen grew louder until they abruptly stopped right in front of the stall.

Softer footsteps approached the table and Aster held his breath. He was pretty good at holding his breath from all the times he'd snuck into his father's council chamber. The worst punishment he'd faced then was a stern lecture, but now he was afraid Mandoline would tell his father what had happened—or, worse, make Aster return home looking like a girl.

"This is the young man I was telling you about, my Lord. Eric, what are you doing here?" The voice sounded like the stable master's.

"Doing here?" Eric sounded nervous. Aster guessed he was getting his first dose of Mandoline's icy stare.

"Yes, where's Maggie?"

"Maggie?" Eric paused. Aster reached out and punched Eric's knee; it was like hitting an oak tree. "Oh yes, I'm watching the stall for Maggie."

"I can see that, but where is she? We must talk to her right away."

"You need to talk to her?"

"Enough of this! Ask the boy if he knows where the prince is." Mandoline was using his annoyed commanding voice; one that Aster knew all too well.

"Yes, of course, my Lord. Eric, do you remember a young boy who stabled his horse at my place last week? Blond hair, kind of short for his age and..."

Mandoline interrupted the stable master. "The boy we're looking for is Prince Aster. You spoke to him at this man's stable last week. Where did he say he was going?"

"That boy was the prince? I thought he was just some noble's brat out to bring back a trophy to prove his manhood. We get a lot of those coming through here and since I'm the town's best huntsman..."

The table shook as someone slammed a hand down on top of it. Aster hugged his knees and Eric took a half step backwards.

"Where—is—the prince?"

"The prince?" Eric swallowed audibly. "He...He didn't say exactly. He wanted to do some hunting up in the mountains. Bag an elk or a..."

"Did he mention the Misty Mountain?" Mandoline had moved from his annoyed voice to his calm, really angry voice.

"The Misty Mountain? There aren't any elk near the Misty Mountain. He wouldn't have gone there. Maybe a mountain goat or two, but nothing worth trophy hunting."

"Bah! This fool knows nothing. Stable Master, where is the girl you mentioned?"

"She was supposed to be here, my Lord. This is her father's wagon." The stable master was beginning to sound nervous as well.

"Find her, and bring her to me at the inn. I'm tired of this cat and mouse game. Captain, pay them and then go find that fool of a sheriff. Tell him I want positive results this time."

"Yes, Lord Sorcerer!" Aster thought he recognized Captain Landings's voice.

The table moved again as Mandoline backed off. The old man's soft footsteps were quickly replaced by the louder sounds of an armored guardsman.

"This is for your trouble, lad."

Eric took a long breath before speaking—he'd probably been holding it until the old sorcerer left. "My trouble? But he never let me finish answering his questions. I wouldn't feel right taking..."

"Just take the sovereign and be glad the Lord Sorcerer didn't demand anything else from you. Stable Master, here's something for your time and efforts as well. When the girl returns, please escort her to the Five Crowns Inn. Assure her that she will also be compensated for her trouble."

"Certainly, Captain. Thank you." Henry sounded very thankful indeed, and Aster wondered just how much gold Captain Landings was handing out trying to find him.

The captain shouted to his men and Aster heard their heavy footsteps fade into the market sounds before the stable master spoke again. "Do you know who that was? The king's own sorcerer, right here in Traders Run! And did you hear that? The prince has gone missing. To think Prince Aster himself brought his horse to *my* stable. Maybe I should change the name to something more princely?"

Eric sounded puzzled. "Change the name? Your stable doesn't even have a name. Why do they want to talk to Maggie?"

"She sold something to the prince. The sheriff came around looking for polished coins like the prince gave me, and found one in her money box. Listen, when she gets back, you take her over to the Five Crowns. There'll be another sovereign in it for you, I'll warrant. Meanwhile I'll go see if I can find Hector before they do."

"You're looking for the sheriff? He should be over at the Pig's Snout eating his lunch about now."

The stable master sighed. "No, he's out looking for some girl who came into town yesterday with more of them shiny coins. He thinks the prince gave her them coins and she might know where he is now."

Eric edged closer to the table, discreetly pushing Aster further underneath. "Some girl?"

"Hector said she looked foreign. I'd better find him quick and tell him that sorcerer is looking for him. Don't forget to tell Maggie they're looking for her. As long as the king's men are handing out sovereigns, you two should get as many as you can."

Aster held his breath as the stable master's footsteps faded into the distance, then he let out a long sigh. Things had just become a lot more complicated. A hand appeared before him and he looked up to find Eric bending over him. The older boy had a strange look on his face.

"Are you all right, milady?"

"Uh...I'm fine." Aster took Eric's hand and let himself be pulled to his feet. When Eric seemed reluctant to let go, he added, "Thank you."

"It's you, isn't it? The sheriff and that sorcerer are looking for you, because you know where the prince is."

The young huntsman might be annoying, but he certainly wasn't stupid. Aster couldn't tell him the truth, it was just too weird, so the lie needed to be a convincing one.

"You may have noticed that I'm foreign."

Eric looked down at him and smiled. "Foreign? Well yes, but you're still quite beautiful."

"Huh? Oh, thank you." Aster thought he might be blushing, but he couldn't fathom why.

"Anyway, I came to Caledon...with my uncle, to help the king...your king, to kill the dragon. We were to meet with your prince, but..."

"Were you going to marry the prince in return for the aid of your country?"

"What?" Aster paused, unable to process that thought for a few moments. "No! How could I marry my—the prince? I mean...that wasn't the plan. We met secretly and he gave my uncle these coins." Aster reached into his coin pouch and pulled out a handful of the bright sovereigns.

Eric whistled. It was probably more gold than the young man had ever seen in one place before. "Are these the coins Henry was talking about? They'd sure stand out around here, all right. So the prince gave you this gold to buy your kingdom's allegiance. Where is he now? Where's your uncle?"

"They're...well, the dragon attacked us before I was ready. It killed my uncle and...um...took the prince. I don't know what happened after that. No one must find out that I'm here. If they capture me and take me to Castlekeep before I can find the dragon and kill it, your prince may never return."

"Kill the dragon?" Eric looked skeptical. "You expect to kill the dragon? You, milady?"

"Yes! With this..." Aster reached under the table where he'd stashed the Empress Sword earlier. Drawing it from the scabbard he lofted it between them in one swift motion.

Eric stared at the sword for several seconds before smiling. "You're going to kill the dragon with this sword? But this is just a toy. The only way something like this could possibly harm a dragon..."

"It's a magic sword! An ancient magic strong enough to defeat any dragon, and only I can wield it. Will you help me?"

"Will I help you?" Eric's features contorted one way and then another. He seemed to be struggling with what to do next. Then his eyes hardened and he took a step toward Aster.

Aster was afraid the young man might try to seize the sword. He didn't wish the fate of last night's intruder on anyone, much less Eric, but the young man surprised him even more by grasping Aster's other hand, the one clutching the coins, and dropping to one knee.

"What must I do? I'm yours to command, my lady. I will lead you to the very gates of hell if that be your wish." Then he twisted Aster's wrist around and kissed the back of his hand lightly.

Stunned, Aster let the coins drop from his hand. He remembered this exact scene from dozens of books he'd read, the brave young woodsman swearing fealty to the princess in distress. He also knew what usually came next in all of those stories.

He stared at the sword in his hand. He'd watched his father elevate many knights and never once had the king laid his sword on their shoulder. Instead he would hand them a rolled up parchment bearing the man's new arms, slap him on the back and then everyone, including his father, would retire to the banquet hall to get very drunk.

Aster didn't think a drinking party was going to satisfy the young man who now seemed unwilling to ever let go of his hand. Feeling quite uncomfortable, and more than a little embarrassed, Aster lowered the Empress Sword onto Eric's left shoulder.

"I dub thee Sir Eric. Arise and take your place in my service."

The Damsel in Distress

Aster was beginning to wonder if Eric was all right. The young man remained kneeling even after Aster told him to get up, and he wouldn't let go of Aster's hand. The table prevented Aster from backing away and it might have been bad form to smash the pommel of his sword down on the wrist of someone he'd just knighted. Still, he wanted Eric to let go. Having his hand held like that was really embarrassing.

"Eric...Sir Eric, I need to leave town as quickly as possible. I can't let Mandoline find me here."

Eric looked up at last, his eyes wide and sporting a grin that looked unsettlingly like a leer. "You wish to leave town? I know many places in the surrounding hills where we can hide undetected for weeks."

Aster frowned at the *we* part. "All right, but I'll need my horse."

Eric stood up, but continued to hold Aster's hand in his.

"Your horse? No problem, I'll go fetch it and then we can ride out together. Where is your horse stabled?"

Aster finally managed to extract his hand from Eric's. He quickly hid it behind his back lest Eric reach for it again.

"That's the thing, I don't know where he is. Maggie's father took him somewhere last night."

"Captain Griffin? Still not a problem, I'm known at all the stables in town. What does your horse look like?"

Aster was surprised to hear Eric use Maggie's father's rank title. He'd gotten the impression Mr. Griffin didn't use it anymore.

"It's a chestnut colt with white fetlocks and a small patch of white on his forehead."

"Chestnut colt? Sounds like the horse that boy... I'm sorry, the one the prince was riding."

"Oh... I guess it could be the prince's horse. It was the only one left after the dragon roasted all the others."

"Roasted the others?" Eric paled a little at that. "Well, all the better if it is the prince's horse. I wouldn't soon forget such a fine bred animal. I'll find him and then we can leave town under the cover of darkness. It might not be safe for you to wait here, though. The sheriff's likely to pass through the market again, if only to ask Maggie and the other traders if they've seen you."

"We can't just leave Maggie's stall unattended."

"Leave the stall unattended? Of course not, we'll ask Mr. Applesmith next door to watch it until Maggie gets back. Traders take care of their own, you know. I have the perfect place for you to hide out until nightfall. No one will think of looking for you there."

Aster was impressed with the way Eric had suddenly taken charge. He really was quite a talented young man and probably would make some noble an excellent huntsmaster one day. Aster began moving things from atop the table to an empty box below it while Eric went to talk to the man in the next stall.

Aster retrieved his haversack from the wagon before they closed it up. Eric insisted on carrying the pack for him, but Aster just as insistently refused to let him touch the Empress Sword.

Images of that thief lying on the floor, his face a mask of pain, made him overly cautious. He slung the scabbard across his back and followed Eric out of the marketplace.

"Exactly where are you taking me?"

The huntsman stopped and turned around.

"Where am I taking you? Why, someplace safe of course." He turned away and took another step, but then looked back over his shoulder. "You're not afraid of the dark, are you?"

Eric led him from the marketplace into the back alleys of Traders Run. The young man was remarkably stealthy; even burdened with Aster's pack, he slipped to and fro without a sound.

For his part, Aster seemed to be a constant source of noise. The unfamiliar skirt liked to catch on everything they passed and more than once Eric was forced to stop and free him from the clutches of one protrusion or another. Every time it happened, Aster felt a little more embarrassed.

Eventually they worked their way to the back of a tavern near the west end of town. Carefully avoiding the open kitchen door, Eric directed him instead to a rough wooden opening set in an angled box off the back of the structure. Under the door, crude stone steps led down into a cellar.

Eric explained that Traders Run had once been a mining town. When the deposits of precious metals ran out, the town continued to flourish as a trading hub between the important north-south routes and the main road to Castlekeep. The only reminder of its past were the myriad tunnels buried just below the streets.

A few of those tunnels had been turned into root cellars and wine vaults by enterprising innkeepers. The moment they stepped into the dimly lit basement, Aster understood why. The room was much cooler than the street outside and a chilly breeze from somewhere at the back of the long narrow room touched his cheek.

They walked past crates of dry goods, then barrels and casks of various sizes, until they came to the far end where racks of dark wine bottles stood out from a flat masonry wall. Eric pointed to a small wooden louver set low into the wall. The cool breeze seemed to be coming from it.

"See this? The temperature stays the same down in the mines whether it's summer or winter. Behind this wall is one of the old vent shafts, so they left this opening here to keep the stores from spoiling."

"I see. Very clever." Aster was genuinely impressed. Like the royal cooks back home, the local tavern owners had taken advantage of underground storage to keep things cool, but had eliminated the long flights of stairs that led to the castle's dungeon.

Eric pulled on the louver and it slipped easily out of the wall. He set it aside, then produced a candle from his jacket and handed it to Aster. "Do you see that lantern by the door? Use it to light this and then follow me."

Aster watched the young huntsman crawl through the small hole in the wall and finally realized what Eric had in mind. With a wide grin he ran back and lit the candle. By the time he returned, Eric had already pulled his haversack inside and was holding a hand out to Aster.

Reluctantly he took the offered hand, which actually came in handy—his skirt, once again, caught on a protrusion and he went tumbling through the hole. Eric lifted him to his feet and Aster got the uncomfortable feeling the older boy didn't want to let him go. After a few awkward moments, Eric finally released him and pointed down the dark tunnel.

"Have you ever been in a mine before? This one leads down to several vent shafts that go even deeper into the ground. Don't worry, they're all boarded over now. Beyond that point, the tunnel continues on to the basement of a bakery on the south side of town."

"Is that where I should meet up with you, at the bakery?"

Eric looked puzzled. "Are you hungry? I meant for you to wait here until I return with our horses, but if you desire cakes I shall lead you there."

"No, no, What I meant was...Oh, never mind. I'll wait for you here."

"Are you certain about the cakes? It would be no trouble."

Aster shook his head vigorously. "No, I don't want cake."

"Very well. You should be quite safe here, but try to make as little noise as possible. The tavern's directly above us and should be quiet this time of day. I'll return for you soon."

With a grin the young man bounded through the opening like a rabbit going to ground. After Eric replaced the louver, leaving Aster alone in the dark, his footsteps receded into the distance.

Aster spent some time exploring a little deeper into the tunnel, but there wasn't much to see except rock, dirt and the occasional wooden support beam. He ended up back at the louvered opening, sitting on an old empty wine cask, bored out of his skull.

He pulled a book from his haversack and tried to read, but there was no place to set the candle down except on the floor. He soon gave up and put the book away. He lost track of time and even dozed off for a bit.

He was sitting on the cask, idly flicking the white jewel off his nose, when he heard noises coming from the other side of the wall. Thinking Eric had returned with the horses, he picked up the candle and stood. However, when he heard two distinct voices, and neither one sounded like Eric's, he panicked.

The male voices were rough sounding, and they laughed like drunken guardsmen. He thought if they came to the back of the storage room they might see the light from the candle through the louver, so he blew it out. The cave was plunged into darkness.

The voices grew louder and he distinctly heard one of the men mention wine bottles. Fearing they might hear his breathing or the rustling of the stupid dress, he hurried deeper into the cave.

Aster backed away slowly. He watched the tiny slivers of light splaying across the floor from the louver for any sign that the men might be coming through to look for him. Just when he thought they'd gone, he heard a creak from the darkness behind him.

The next thing he knew, the floor gave way and he was falling. His hand brushed the side of the vent shaft and he grabbed for it, coming away with nothing more than a handful of dirt. The wall angled towards him and he hit it hard. He slid down the wall for what seemed like an eternity, scrambling for a foothold. Then he hit bottom and crumpled into a heap.

Aster had never been afraid of the dark, but he was quickly becoming aware that he'd never really experienced true darkness before. This wasn't the inky blackness of a moonless overcast night, where everything was without color and shadows seemed to hold all manner of potential danger.

No, this was the complete and total absence of light. Where a hand held before his nose did not exist, and every sound sent his mind reeling into a frantic scramble for identification.

He'd been sitting in that terrible darkness for several hours, as best he could reckon. Miraculously, he'd not broken any bones during the fall, but he was bruised and he thought there might be a nasty gash on his left elbow. It was hard to tell for sure in the pitch blackness.

He'd tried climbing back up the wall of the shaft, but without being able to see handholds he hadn't gotten very far. Now he just sat there, alone in the darkness, wondering what to do next.

As it turned out, he wasn't completely alone. From time to time he could hear the scurrying of little feet nearby. And once, something had actually tugged at his skirt.

He assumed they were rats, and entertained the idea of catching one. Not to eat—he'd have to be down here a long time before he was that desperate—but he thought he might be able to tie a string around it and let the little creature lead him out of the cave. He gave up on the idea when he realized he didn't have any string.

Aster didn't think the darkness was fair. Never, in any of the books he'd read, had the hero been stuck in a cave unable to move because it was too dark to see. Even when they mentioned it being dark, there always seemed to be just enough light for them to find a secret passage or some bit of useful treasure. The only treasure he had was the Empress Sword and it stubbornly refused to be any help at all.

He drew the sword out again and held it up in front of his face. He still couldn't see it, couldn't see anything, but he knew it was there because the annoying little jewel hanging between his eyes would always bang against it just before his nose touched its surface.

"Why can't you light up or something? You lit up like the sun when that thief grabbed you last night. I'm not asking for sunshine, just a little magical fire, a glow, anything!"

He sighed and let his forehead rest against the cold metal. After the inevitable chorus of white gem against steel died away, the silence settled in again. Only, this time he heard something more than the scurrying of tiny feet or the dripping of water. Aster heard whispering.

Could the sword talk? It didn't seem possible, but where else could the whispers be coming from?

"What? What did you say? I can't hear you."

He strained to hear. It was a little louder now, but he still couldn't make out the words. He shook the sword, hoping to wake it out of whatever mumbling dreams it might be having.

"Come on, speak up, you stupid sword."

Then he noticed a faint glimmer coming from the blade. To his light-starved senses it was like a blazing torch, even though it was little more than a yellow flicker. The whispering was becoming more distinct as well. He could almost make out the words...

"I heard something down this way."

"Are you sure that thing's right? We're way deeper than the level of the wine cellar. Maybe we should go back and start looking from the other end of the tunnel."

The light on the blade grew stronger and then Aster heard the sound of footsteps. Not the running of little paws, but the footfalls of people. Two people, in fact, and his heart nearly leapt out of his chest when he realized who they were.

"Maggie! Eric! I'm down here!"

The Call to Arms

Aster assumed they were somewhere above him, up where he'd fallen down the mine shaft in the first place. He stood and stared up into the darkness, straining to see a glimmer of the light he'd seen reflecting off the Empress Sword.

"I'm down here! Maggie? Eric?"

"Who are you shouting at, my lady? We're both right here."

Aster whipped around and was blinded by the lamp Eric held towards him. He threw up his arms to block the light and through them saw Maggie standing with her hands on her hips, shaking her head.

"There you are! We've been worried sick about you."

"I...I fell through the floor and ended up down here. How in the world did you find me?"

Maggie held up a glowing jewel mounted in a circular frame attached to a silver chain. "I knew this tracker thing might come in handy. Good thing I wove that circlet into your hair. Like Daddy said, it led us right to you."

"Are you harmed, my lady?"

"No, I'm fine. Just a little bruised and dirty, is all."

"I'll say." Maggie examined Aster's elbow by the light of the lamp. "You've scraped up your arm a bit and just about ruined that poor dress."

"I'm sorry. I can pay for the dress..."

"Don't you go worrying about that. The important thing is that you're all right. Now, why in heaven's name were you down here in the first place?"

Aster looked up at Eric, who was gazing down at the trench he was digging with the toe of his boot.

Aster cleared his throat. "Well, I didn't mention this to you before, because it's supposed to be a secret, and it could be dangerous. I came here to meet with your prince. That's why the dragon attacked us. Now there's someone in town looking for the prince..."

"Maggie, did you know that boy you were mooning over last week was actually the prince of Caledon? He was traveling in disguise to meet secretly with Lady Astrid. Her kingdom is uniting with ours to destroy the dragon. Great armies are massing at the borders, just waiting for her signal to march against the beast. I brought her down here to protect her from discovery and the ruination of our fragile alliance."

Aster stared at Eric, dumbfounded by the tall tale he was weaving. Did everyone in this town simply make up wild stories on the fly? He had trouble trying to think up a convincing reason for why he'd blown out the candle, much less all of that.

Slack-jawed, Maggie looked from Eric to Aster. "Is all that true?"

"Well, something like that. The point is, if Mandoline finds me I may never get a chance to kill the dragon." Aster realized he was still holding the Empress Sword in his hand. He raised it up to show Maggie. "With this sword I can defeat it, but that old man will probably want to take it away and send me home."

Maggie shook her head. "If you're talking about the king's sorcerer, then you can stop worrying. They mounted up and rode out of town nearly two hours ago. He headed off east towards the mountains with the sheriff and the whole garrison."

Eric grunted. "Why did they take Hector with them? I'm twice the tracker he is!"

Aster almost laughed out loud with relief. He sheathed the Empress Sword and touched Eric's arm. "Sir Eric, this is our chance to escape. With the sheriff and the garrison both out of town, there'll be no one to follow us. Perhaps we should leave before they return."

Eric straightened his shoulders. "You fear they'll see their mistake and return for me? You may be right. Very well, follow me!"

With that, Eric turned and began marching down the tunnel. Maggie leaned in close to Aster and whispered in his ear, "*Sir* Eric?"

Aster chuckled, although it came out sounding more like a giggle. "I'll tell you later. We'd better follow him before he gets too far ahead with the light. It's really dark down here."

Aster felt silly for having thought the sword was talking to him, when in fact it was just Eric and Maggie. He felt even more foolish when they rounded a corner no more than a hundred paces from where he'd been sitting and found the tunnel sloping upward.

Stone steps were even set into the floor of the steep incline to make it easier to climb. If he'd felt his way along the wall for half an hour he might have found his way out on his own. As he trudged up the tunnel after Maggie and Eric, he tugged on Maggie's sleeve.

"What made you think to use the tracking stone to find me?"

"I went to the stable to check on our horse. If we're leaving in a few days, I wanted to get him new shoes and such. So I walk in, and Mr. Gardener isn't there, just Peter. And Peter says, Mr. Gardener's gone to the market to look for some new spices. Mrs. Gardener is one of the best cooks in town and Mr. Gardener brings her all these strange spices from the market. She cooks them into the most amazing things and Peter gets the leftovers sometimes. So Peter's telling me all about…"

"Maggie?" Aster had to say her name several times before the girl stopped talking and looked quizzically down at him. "You were telling me about the tracking stone?"

"Exactly. So I'm standing there talking to Peter about spices when Eric runs in all excited, looking for a chestnut colt for this girl he's just met. I ask him what he's going on about and he tells me some nonsense about a damsel in distress, who has a magic sword, and needs his help. Well, that's when I knew he was talking about you."

Aster grinned. "I guess there aren't that many magic swords around, huh?"

Maggie winked at him. "Or damsels in distress, for that matter. Not in Traders Run, anyway. So, then I went with Eric to get you from the wine cellar, but you weren't there. We looked further back in the cave and that's when Eric noticed the pendant glowing. We found the place where the floorboards were broken and the pendant pointed us down the hole. We had no way to climb down after you, but I remembered this old mine entrance right across the street from Mr. Gardener's stable, so we went back there, and then we found you down here."

Aster fingered the little jewel at his forehead. "I'm glad I didn't rip this annoying thing off and throw it away. It's been driving me crazy."

"Well if you plan on wandering off like this all the time, you'd best keep it on." Maggie giggled.

"No way. From now on I'm sticking to you like glue."

They reached the top of the stairs and Eric pushed aside a creaky old door. He stood outside holding it open for them as Maggie stepped through ahead of Aster. Before he could follow her lead he heard whispering from the tunnel below. He turned and listened intently, but couldn't hear anything. Then the Empress Sword began to vibrate in its scabbard. Aster drew it out and held it up.

"The First is come. Be ready."

The voice was strange, soft and melodic, but with a hard edge that made him think immediately of danger. The accent was unfamiliar, but it was definitely female and it was definitely coming from the sword. Aster brought the sword closer to his face and whispered back to it.

"What did you say?"

"A dragon has come. I am ready for him. Are you?"

Aster heard a commotion outside. He paused, waiting for the sword to say something else, then he turned and raced through the doorway. Maggie and Eric were standing in the middle of the street while dozens of frightened townspeople ran past them.

"What's happening?" he shouted as he ran towards his friends, dodging fleeing people as he went.

"What's happening? There appears to be something going on in the west end of town." Eric pointed down the street at the crowd of people running towards them.

Maggie pointed across the street at what appeared to be a stable. "There's Peter. Peter! Peter, over here!"

A boy appeared at the stable gate. He had a small pack on his shoulder and looked as frightened as everyone else. He saw Maggie waving and ran over.

"Maggie! Eric! You must flee! The dragon is upon us! The dragon!"

Eric grabbed the boy by the shoulders. "How do you know it's the dragon? Calm down and tell me what's happening."

The boy was shaking all over, but he took a deep breath and did as the huntsman asked. "Mr. Griffin came in while I was getting that chestnut yearling ready for you. He was all excited. Told me to saddle up a stallion for him while he got into his armor. He rode out to meet the dragon. It's finally come for us. Traders Run is doomed!"

"Daddy? No!" Maggie screamed and turned to run down the street.

Eric let go of the stable boy and blocked Maggie with an arm. "What's wrong? Your father knows what he's doing. He just wants to slow the beast down until the town can be cleared. He'll be fine..."

Aster pushed between them and grabbed the stable boy by the shirt. "The other horse you were grooming, is he ready to ride?"

"Y-yes, Miss. All saddled up and ready to go, but..."

"Sir Eric, with me!"

Aster raced towards the stable, heedless of whether Eric was following him or not. He'd been raised to lead armies, after all, and the thought that one of his commands might not be followed to the letter never even occurred to him.

Inside the building he found Troy saddled and ready as promised. He took the horse's bridle in both hands and pulled the large brown head down far enough that they were looking at one another eye to eye.

"We're going into battle. This is serious. No hesitation, no complaint, do what I say and do it now." He released the horse, which whinnied and tossed his head, but did not back away. Aster turned to find Eric only just entering the stable.

"You're going into battle, my lady? I really don't think..."

"Get over here right now and put me on this horse. You are my knight and I have given you an order. Now do it!"

Eric's jaw dropped. He looked ready to protest, but he broke into a run anyway. Snatching Aster off his feet, the young man tossed him over the saddle like a sack of potatoes. Aster righted himself and then stretched for the reins, but they were just out of reach. Eric grabbed the reins and handed them to Aster.

"Please wait for me to get Nightstorm so that I may ride with you, my lady!"

Aster stopped and stared down at the young huntsman, his brows knitting together as his head tilted slightly to one side.

"You didn't ask me a question first."

"What question should I have asked?"

Aster shook his head and kicked Troy in the sides. Horse and rider bolted through the half-open doors at a trot. Troy leapt the fence at Aster's urging and pounded up the street to the astonishment of Maggie and the stable boy.

The streets were choked with people fleeing for their lives, but Aster urged his mount on. Troy broke into a full gallop as terrified people dove out of their way. Aster's hair came loose from its braid, fluttering out behind him like a black cape.

One thought consumed him and drove him to ride faster and faster. *I must find the dragon! I must find it and kill it before it kills Maggie's father!*

21

The Dragon Attack

andrake had been looking forward to this for a very long time. The village wasn't that large and the farms supporting it were few, but it stood within sight of the abomination. Whoever had conjured a mountain across the pass leading home must have lived for a time in this village.

With his keen eyesight he picked out the thatched roofs of the town from many leagues away. He would burn a few fields and then wreak havoc on the town itself. With his gas sack nearly full, he could almost guarantee complete destruction.

Dense forest gave way to cultivated fields below him. Humans seemed especially fond of tearing down trees to grow their food on barren soil. Every dragon knew the best way to renew a forest was to begin with scorched earth. Human farms he'd burned years ago were already covered with new saplings.

He lined up on a field of dry yellow grass furthest from the stream. He'd made that particular mistake early on, watching his handiwork easily put out by the pesky humans. He'd also learned not to bother with the hilltops. He only needed to start the fires on the upwind side, and the wind would blow the fire up and over the top, setting the whole hill ablaze.

He carefully opened his throat, letting a small measured amount of gas leak from the sack in his chest into the back of his mouth.

Breathing in through his nostrils, he added air and pressure to the mix. At the precise moment when he was lined up with the base of the hillock he opened his mouth. His rock-hard back teeth ground across one another, producing a tiny spark.

As a young pup he'd burned his mouth many times learning to do this properly. The trick was to already have the gas moving outward when the spark ignited it. But not too fast or the whole thing would come out in a smelly cloud, filling his nostrils and making him cough and sneeze embarrassingly.

Fire roared from his throat as he let more gas bleed slowly from the sack. Experience taught him this would last for about twenty wing beats before the air in his lungs gave out and he began eating his own fire.

He swung his head from side to side, laying down the flames in a jagged line that would avoid creating a natural firebreak. If he did this just right, the blaze would be all but impossible for the humans to put out.

As he approached the far end of the field he closed off his throat and blew out the last of the burning gas, then shut his mouth. He pulled up, banking just enough to glance over his shoulder at the wildfire he'd created.

He fired two more fields before he saw the first humans. They were running, panicked, toward their burning fields from a small, ramshackle house. The silly fools had no chance of saving their farm. They should have been packing up and heading south—out of the county and out of his way.

The town was closer now. Just a few low hills separated him from the first small clusters of buildings at its edge. He would save the destruction of the town until he'd set a few more crops ablaze. He needed the extra lift the gas gave him for maneuvering through these low hills. When it began to run low, he'd use the last of it to burn as many buildings as he could.

He was lining up on a fourth field when he spotted the horse and rider galloping towards him. He sighed and proceeded setting the crop ablaze anyway. The number of knights sent against him had been dwindling in the last couple of years and their skills had been diminishing as well. The last one he'd faced hadn't even survived the first charge.

The knight rode to the top of a nearby hill, jumped from his horse and struck a challenging pose. Mandrake considered just ignoring the fool and going about his business burning the fields, but there was an etiquette about these things. The pride of all the dragons rested solely on his shoulders until he awakened the others. He banked hard, came around and flew straight toward the bothersome human.

The man had chosen his position well. The hillock he stood upon was too small for both of them to stand together. The man would begin with the advantage of higher ground, but for all the good it would do he was welcome to it. Mandrake settled on the hillside and rose up on his hind legs, his head at the same level as the man atop the hill.

"Hold dragon! I cannot allow you to do further harm."

Mandrake waited for him to say more, regarding the man as one might a butterfly emerging from its cocoon. "Is that it? No proclamation from the king, no declaration of divine rights, not even an invocation of holy sanction? Be careful, knight, your mantle of fealty may be slipping."

"I need no authority other than the safety of these people. Go away. You shall not destroy this village."

"I shall do whatever I please, and it pleases me to see all humans leave this place. You're a desecration of the land and an abomination to all nature."

The man faltered momentarily and Mandrake wondered if he might actually be considering his claim. The knights he had fought before had all been the "attack first, ask questions later" sort. So far, none of them had lived long enough to ask him any questions.

"Be that as it may, I cannot allow you to pass. Prepare to do battle."

"I'm ready, good knight." Mandrake chuckled at the pun. It was a shame to kill this fellow; at least he was fun to talk to. "Do your best, human."

The man wasted no time in making his charge. Mandrake was taken off guard and barely dodged the attack. Dragons fought on all fours; sitting here on his hind legs, he was an easy target. He side-stepped the charge and the man's blade slid ineffectually across the scales of his hind leg. If he hadn't moved, the blow would have struck his less well protected belly.

Mandrake dropped to the ground and regained his balance, but the man was behind him now. He swung his tail blindly and was pleased to hear a grunt and the sound of scales crashing against metal. He turned to the right and put some distance between himself and his attacker. Then he turned on the human.

The man was already running at him again, sword held low in preparation for an upward thrust. He was hoping to get under Mandrake's scales and sink his weapon into the soft flesh underneath, but Mandrake would have none of that. He feinted right and then swiped at the man with a foreclaw. The man managed to dodge out of the way and once again tried to run past Mandrake.

This time the dragon was ready for it. When the sword raked across the scales of his hind leg, he brought up his tail and crushed the man between it and his rump. The man staggered away as Mandrake spun around, letting the momentum build up before catching the man across the chest with his tail again. This sent the man sailing down the hill where he crashed into a clump of trees.

Barely winded, Mandrake trotted down the hill to where the man lay motionless. Along the way he passed various pieces of armor that had fallen off the human during his short flight. A helm, a leg guard, an entire arm piece and—most notably—the man's sword lay in the grass. Mandrake walked up and placed a foot on the man's chest. The human still breathed, but Mandrake couldn't imagine why.

He looked down and noticed that the man's hair was grey and his face lined with years. Were they done sending him warriors and pups? Had the king nothing left but old men? Yet, this one had fought well. It seemed a shame to simply crush the life out of such a fighter.

The man stirred and then opened his eyes. Mandrake bent his head low, staring the man in the eye. "Yes, old man, you live. And I think that you shall live a bit longer. I like you. When I'm done, gather your people together and leave this place. Take them south and never return."

He pressed down on the man's chest just hard enough to get his point across. The man winced and made no move to get up when Mandrake released him. Convinced the battle was over, Mandrake turned and strode back to the hilltop. He began jogging down the other side, building up some speed. Then unfolded his wings and leapt into the air.

He banked left, making a wide sweeping turn to the south. The fields were all ablaze now and would burn for hours until there was nothing left. With that old knight out of the way, he could now make quick work of the town. He'd just enough gas left to set fire to a few buildings and still have an easy flight home.

He leveled out, lining up on a church steeple in the distance, and beat his wings harder to increase his speed. One quick pass over the town to panic the humans would minimize the risk of some archer getting off a lucky shot and spoiling his good mood.

When he first saw the tiny figure on the hilltop directly ahead, he wasn't sure exactly what it was. It looked human enough, but the white hot light it emitted was brighter than anything he'd ever seen. As he raced towards it he made out the figure of a young girl in a tattered blue dress, her black hair billowing in the breeze. The light was coming from a sword she held before her like a shield.

He laughed at the absurdity. He'd just defeated a very worthy knight in fair combat and now they were sending a child against him? This was hardly worthy of his time. He brought up a mouthful of gas from his chest bladder and with a mighty exhale sent a flaming ball of fire straight at the tiny human.

Suddenly the sky before him lit up and the girl's sword flared brighter than the sun. He watched in disbelief as the ball of fire split in two and went flying off in opposite directions, missing the child completely.

"That's not possible!" He roared and again opened his throat to the gas, this time holding it for a long, sustained blast. Fire spewed from his mouth as he closed in on the girl, but again the flames parted and she remained untouched. He banked to the left and came around for another pass. Once more he belched fire at her, again to no avail.

Then suddenly he dropped from the sky, his belly crashing through treetops as he struggled to stay airborne. He was a fool! He'd emptied his gas sack and lost all the extra lift it gave him. His body felt heavy and his muscles screamed in protest, but he managed to clear the hilltop just beyond the reach of the girl and her blazing sword.

He hit the ground hard on the far side and skidded down the hill, stopping just in time to avoid crashing into a stand of trees. He struggled to his feet and turned to stare back up the hill at the girl. Her sword flashed brightly as she juggled it from one hand to the other. When it finally stopped moving, it was high above her right shoulder and pointed at him.

He repositioned himself as the girl began her charge. He had no fire left, but he outweighed his opponent a hundred to one. If he could avoid the sword or sidestep her charge altogether it would be a simple matter of smashing her to the ground and ripping her to pieces.

The girl was halfway down the slope when the sword flared again. Brighter than before, the white heat stretched out towards him. A wall of immense magical power slammed into him like a mountain of rock. It knocked the wind out of him and made his heart skip a beat. The force enveloped him, wrapping itself around him so completely he was covered by it from nose to tail.

He waited for the magic to do something—to tear him limb from limb or simply snuff out his life. But nothing happened. The girl continued her charge down the hill head on, without even trying to evade a counter attack. He tensed his muscles, gauged the distance between them, and pounced.

Nothing happened. Not that he was paralyzed, all his muscles still worked, he simply couldn't move. He strained as hard as he could, but the magic held him rooted in place. As unthinkable as it seemed, he stood frozen and defenseless in the face of a single human child. With a terrible sinking feeling, he realized he was about to die.

Fear gripped him for the first time in his long life. He was the first to awaken, the chosen one, destined to become the leader of his clan. He'd wanted to prepare the way for the others by ridding this land of these wretched humans. Now he was going to die by the hand of one without ever seeing another dragon awaken or feeling the touch of a female or hearing a hatchling break free of its shell and knowing it was his own.

Pain the likes of nothing he'd ever imagined exploded in his left shoulder as the sword passed effortlessly through his scales and sank deep into his flesh. He felt the sword sink deeper and deeper, cutting and burning its way through muscle and sinew on an unerring course, he was certain, for his heart.

His left foreleg went numb and collapsed under him. Unable to move, he was helpless to do anything but fall to the ground in a heap. His head hit so hard his vision blurred. Waves of nausea flooded over him and he thought he might pass out. When his sight returned a few seconds later, he wished he had.

The girl stood before him, the blazing white sword in her hand dripping with his own blood. She raised the sword above her head with both hands, the tip pointing down at his neck. She meant to finish him off, and there was nothing he could do about it. He stared in horror as she advanced slowly across the blood soaked grass, and then he did the unthinkable. He begged for his life.

The Oath

"What did you just say?"

In all the times Aster snuck into his father's court to eavesdrop on official councils about the dragon, not once had anyone mentioned that the animal could talk. He'd always heard the dragon referred to as a wild beast, a savage creature, a soulless thing bent on destruction and wholly without intelligence aside from cunning or malice. Now it was talking to him?

"I asked you to spare my life."

"You can talk?"

"Yes, of course I can talk. I learned the language of humans from my dam a long time ago and I've not forgotten it. For all the good it's done me."

"Why haven't you spoken before this?" The Empress Sword, light as it was, grew heavy in Aster's hand. The last thing it had whispered to him was, *"Finish this now or listen, as you choose."* The sword's tip, hanging in the air between him and the paralyzed dragon, began to wobble, so he lowered it to his side and continued listening.

The dragon chuckled as best he could without moving his head. "I have spoken many times, but has your kind ever listened? Don't you think I asked the elders of this very village why the path to my homeland had been blocked? Don't you think I begged them to let me pass? Did they listen? Did they ever once answer me with the truth? No! Not even once."

"Wait, you know about the valley beyond the Misty Mountain? Why didn't you just fly over it?"

The sigh escaping the dragon's mouth smelled of sulfur and rotting things. "Dragons cannot fly that high. Even the lesser mountains are beyond us, but that great wall of stone is more than any drake could hope to surmount. Do not think I haven't tried."

"I don't suppose you ever tried flying through the mountain, did you?"

"Do not mock me in my final moments. Are you going to kill me or let me go?"

Aster suddenly remembered why he was there. "No. Why should I let you go? You've killed hundreds of my people, destroyed dozens of villages. You've thrown my father's kingdom into near ruin. What possible reason could I have for sparing your life?"

"I've killed no one who did not first try to kill me. I destroyed their villages to drive them off, not to kill them."

"What about all the people you've eaten? Were they trying to eat you first?"

"Eat humans?" The dragon closed his eyes for a moment. "What an interesting idea. No, I've never tasted human flesh and I don't think I care to start. You see, I was raised with humans, called them my friends at one time, but they've betrayed me. Even so, it would not be honorable to treat them as cattle."

"Then why cause all of this death and destruction? You make this sound like a war."

"It is a war! I need this land for my people. It's the only place we can live and thrive. The lands to the south are too warm. To the north is the sea and beyond that is the land of frozen wastes and long slumbers. You humans can live anywhere. You do not have to be *here*, but we do."

Aster wanted to say that wasn't true, that Caledon was big enough for the dragons to settle in amongst the humans, but he knew it would never happen. Everyone, everywhere, hated this dragon and wished him and his kind dead. How had the Empress done it? How had she brought humans and dragons together? Aster thought of the remote valley, and the mountainsides filled with caves.

"What if I could show you the way back to the hidden valley? Would you stay there and leave Caledon alone?"

The dragon paused. "You've been to the Valley of Wind?"

Aster smiled and held up the Empress Sword. "Indeed! And I can take you there. It's not that far, just a few days ride. Probably a lot closer for you because you can fly."

The dragon glanced at the blood-soaked ground. "It may not be possible for me to fly right now, but if you speak truthfully, if you know the way to the Valley, I will follow you. I swear it."

The sword vibrated in Aster's hand. *"The Oath!"*

"The oath?" Aster gaped at the sword. Why did it seem capable of only speaking enigmatic phrases? An actual sentence every now and then might be nice.

Mandrake managed to raise an eye ridge. "You wish me to swear the Dragon's Oath? Very well, but I shall have to get up in order to do so properly."

Aster shook the sword. He wasn't entirely sure how to make it stop doing whatever had frozen the dragon in the first place. So far, it seemed to have a mind of its own when it came to magic. "I'm not really sure..."

Just then the sword started humming again. It vibrated Aster's whole arm and when it stopped, the dragon seemed to slump even flatter to the ground than before.

The dragon groaned painfully as he slowly, carefully rolled over. "You might have warned me first. That hurt."

"I don't really know how to...I'm sorry, are you going to be all right?"

"I've been wounded before, but never like this. I usually heal rather quickly." The dragon grunted and pushed himself up on his hind legs. His left foreleg, held close to his chest, was not moving. "Do magical wounds heal differently?"

The dragon towered above Aster now, making him feel very

small. The gash in its chest seemed larger than something he could have made with such a small blade. "I'm not sure. I haven't had this sword for very long."

The dragon cocked his head to one side, wincing from the movement. "Then you're not the Empress, or one of her children?"

"Well, no. Actually I'm Prince Aster of Caledon. I went looking for the Empress and she sort of gave me her sword."

"No offense, but you don't look like the *prince* of anything. And how does someone 'sort of' give you the Sword of Kai?"

"It's a long story. Does my not being the Empress mean you won't swear to leave Caledon?"

"It means nothing of the sort. I was just curious as to whom I am about to swear my lifelong allegiance. You hold the sword that once claimed the loyalty of my sire. That is enough. Shall we get on with it?"

"Yes, of course." Aster wasn't quite sure how one took an oath of fealty from a dragon. "What's your name?"

"I am called Mandrake."

"No titles or anything?"

"I was chosen to be the First. That is, the first of my clan to awaken. It's not so much a title as a responsibility I earned through competition."

"That will do." Aster placed the tip of the Empress Sword on the ground before him. He held the pommel in one hand and gestured with the other. "Mandrake, First of the Dragons, come forward and declare your Oath."

With some difficulty Mandrake knelt down, using only his right leg. For a moment he looked as if he might change his mind, but then lowered his head and closed his eyes. When he opened them again Aster thought he held his head a little higher. "I swear to follow the Sword of Kai wherever its bearer shall direct me. As my sire before me, I shall pledge my loyalty and my life to its protection. This I swear on the bones of my ancestors."

There was a long silence before Aster cleared his throat. "That's it?"

"You want more?" Mandrake cocked his head to one side and glared at him.

"No..." Aster wasn't sure what he was expecting, but these things usually lasted for hours in his father's court. "No, that's just fine."

"Good, because if there ever was more to it, I can't remember. Now, where would you have me go?"

Aster paused and thought about that. "Well, east into the mountains of course, but Traders Run is that way. It might not be a good idea for you to go near the town just now." They both glanced at the black smoke rising from the fields to the south. "Come to think of it, you probably shouldn't stay around here at all. To the northwest is a dry riverbed. If you can make it that far, rest there and I'll come for you tomorrow."

"All right, I shall try and fly there. You should stand back in case I fall. I wouldn't want to crush my new liege on her first day."

He wasn't sure, but Aster thought the dragon might have smiled then. He pulled the sword from the ground and backed away up the hill. At the top he stopped and watched Mandrake flex his wings. A terrible thought suddenly came to him, that he was being very naive. "Mandrake! You won't go burning any more fields or killing any people, will you?"

The dragon looked up at him sullenly. "Not unless it is by your command, young Empress. I serve you now."

Young Empress? The impact of what he'd just done finally sank in. The dragon he so recently swore to kill, that his kingdom wanted and expected dead, was alive and had sworn his loyalty to Aster. But Aster looked like a girl, he carried the sword of a woman and now this dragon, sworn to follow him, had called him Empress. This was moving too fast and seemed very wrong. He'd let the situation get out of control.

He shouted for the dragon to stop, but his words were lost on the wind kicked up as Mandrake lifted unsteadily into the air. The dragon hung for a few moments, his foreleg dangling lifelessly, then turned to the northwest and disappeared over the trees.

"What have I done?" Aster looked at the sword in his hand. It was quiet now and cold. "Was all this your doing? What are you? *Who* are you?"

The sword remained silent. He turned back to the south, looking at the burning fields, and sighed. Then he glanced down at the bottom of the hill and saw a horse standing near the tree line. At its feet lay a man in armor.

"Captain Griffin?" Aster ran down the hill. He'd just managed to sheath the sword when he tripped over the skirt and went tumbling. He rolled the rest of the way down. The captain's horse nickered and threatened to buck as he slid to a stop at the animal's feet. Aster held up his hands and shushed the animal, fearing more that it would trample the captain than himself.

Before Aster could get to his feet, he heard another horse whinny in the distance. He looked around and spotted two horses trotting towards him. One was Troy. The other was a black stallion with two riders. "Eric? Maggie?"

As soon as they stopped, Maggie jumped down from the horse and went running to her father. Eric dismounted and ran to Aster, lifting him to his feet and making him blush again.

"Daddy?" There were tears in Maggie's voice as she dropped to her knees next to her father. Aster struggled free of Eric's grip and raced to join her. Captain Griffin lay very still and his eyes were closed. "Oh Daddy, please, no!"

"Don't shout, Pumpkin. I'm injured, not deaf."

Maggie swayed backwards, falling against Aster. He held her steady as she regained her composure, which she did with typical feistiness. "Deaf? I thought you were dead!"

"No, I'm not dead, not quite. You can thank Astrid here for that. Well done, lass."

"You saw what happened?" Aster wasn't sure whether to be proud of what he'd done or embarrassed.

"Most of it." Captain Griffin tried to sit up, but winced in pain and then lay back down. "Didn't hear much, but I saw what you can do with that sword of yours. Don't ever let me call that thing a toy again."

Aster smiled, then Eric leaned over them. "Captain, do you mean to say that Lady Astrid actually scared the dragon away with her sword?"

Maggie nodded. "We saw it fly off to the north. It flew away from town."

"You'd best tell them, lass. I only know what I saw. Only you know what you did." Captain Griffin looked him in the eye and Aster stopped smiling.

Maggie looked up at him over her shoulder. "Astrid?"

Eric touched his shoulder and Aster stood up, backing away from the little group. "The dragon...He didn't run away, I...I sent him away."

"You *sent* it away?" Maggie's mouth remained open.

"The sword...I wounded him. He begged me. He swore an oath. It all happened so fast!"

"Easy, lass. It's all right. You stopped the beast from attacking Traders Run. That's enough." Captain Griffin tried to sit up again, this time groaning loudly before falling back to the ground.

"Are you hurt?" Maggie turned back to her father.

Captain Griffin laughed. "Yes, Maggie my love. When an old man challenges a dragon, he's most likely to get hurt. I think I might have cracked a rib or two by getting in the way of its tail. Eric, be a good lad and ride back into town. Find the doctor and have him bring a cart."

Eric didn't move. He stood between Aster and Captain Griffin, looking back and forth between them. Finally he nodded to the captain and then stared at Aster. The look on his face was unreadable.

"Where did you send it?"

23

The Right Thing to Do

Aster paced the hallway of the boarding house with Eric. He'd finally managed to convince the huntsman that it was too narrow for them to pace side by side, so now they walked in opposite directions and only met at the door to Maggie's room. At one such meeting, the door opened and the doctor stepped out.

"How's Captain Griffin? Will he be all right?"

The doctor looked over his glasses at Aster and only nodded. When Eric joined them a moment later, he turned and spoke to the huntsman. "Ah, Eric. Marcus is pretty badly injured. He should not be moved for several days at least. Could you arrange to have his meals brought here?"

"He can't be moved? I'll have Mary over at the Pig's Snout bring him some stew."

The doctor winced. "The Snout's stew might be a bit much for him right now. Have one of the other taverns do it."

Aster tapped the doctor on the shoulder. "Is there anything I can do?"

The doctor turned and smiled at him. "Haven't you done enough, young lady?"

Word spread quickly through the town that Aster had ridden out and faced the dragon. However, it was generally assumed Captain Griffin had finally driven off the beast and prevented the town from being burned. No one seemed to consider that Aster had done anything more than get in the good captain's way.

"You two take good care of our hero." The doctor patted Aster on the head, shook Eric's hand, and then walked to the end of the hallway where he disappeared down the staircase.

"Are you all right?" Eric was getting good at reading Aster's bad moods.

"I'm fine. I just wish someone around here would take me seriously."

"Take you seriously? My lady, I would take you..."

The door opened again and Maggie stepped out. Her eyes were red and swollen, but there was a wan smile on her face when she looked at Aster. However, when she spoke, it was to Eric first.

"Be a love and run down to the Rutting Bull. Get Daddy something to eat. One of their morning plates would be good. He'd also love a bit of ale."

"Breakfast and ale? Sounds about right for the captain." Eric gave Maggie a mock salute and then bowed to Aster before running down the hall.

Maggie giggled. "He's so sweet. You certainly seem to have him wrapped around your finger. Whatever did you do to the lad?"

Aster shrugged. "All I did was knight him."

"Can you really do that?" Maggie's tone seemed serious.

Aster hung his head. While technically the crown prince could knight someone, it usually required the consent of the king. In his present condition, Aster wasn't sure his father would consent to anything he did.

"Never mind, come on in. Daddy wants to see you, alone." She pushed open the door and stepped aside. He walked sheepishly past her and Maggie closed the door behind him. Inside, Captain Griffin was lying on Maggie's bed. His bare chest was wrapped in bandages, as was his head. He didn't look up when Aster approached.

"Is Maggie outside?"

Aster turned to make sure the door was shut. "Yes, sir."

"Why didn't you kill it?"

"I...I don't really know, sir."

"But you could have, with that sword, couldn't you?"

Aster backed away from the bed. When he bumped into the cot, he automatically sat down. "I suppose so. Mandrake was frozen, unable to move. The sword went through his hide like it was parchment."

"Then *why* didn't you kill him?" There was anger in Captain Griffin's voice, and something else. Something frail and hopeless that one would not expect from such a man. It sent a chill down Aster's spine.

"It just didn't seem like the right thing to do. He said something about humans keeping him from his homeland. I think he's talking about the Misty Mountain. I know all about that, and the Valley of Wind, too. I thought if I could just take him back there, Caledon could be saved and no one else needed to die. Isn't it better to have a living ally than a dead enemy?"

Captain Griffin looked at him then. An odd expression passed over the man's face and he started to say something, but stopped and looked back up at the ceiling again. "All right. What do you propose to do next?"

"I suppose, when Mandrake is ready to fly again, I'll take him to the valley like I promised."

"Will you be coming back?"

Aster thought about that. Once he'd shown Mandrake the way home, Aster would be free to return the sword to the Empress. He fully expected her to take the spell off of him then. When he returned, it would not be like this. "No, sir. In all likelihood you'll never see me again."

Captain Griffin sighed. "That's what I thought. Have you considered what this means to the people of Caledon, to King Cosmos? Don't you think he deserves to learn firsthand what happened with the dragon?"

"Maybe you could tell him. Maggie says you were in the royal guard once. I'm sure the king would believe you."

"That's not the point, lass. The king and the people deserve to hear this news from the person who actually did it—from you. If I were to go to Castlekeep and tell the king that a mere slip of a girl fought the dragon, made him swear allegiance to her, and then walked off into the mountains never to return, what do you think he'd say?"

Aster stared at his feet. He had a pretty good idea what his father would say, and Captain Griffin had a point. "I'm just not sure Mandrake will wait that long."

"You wounded him pretty good, lass. The way he was flying off, he won't be going very far and he won't be following you into the mountains anytime soon. Give him a few weeks to recover, and in that time go see the king. He might reward you with something to make the trip home a little easier."

"I don't want a reward. The only reward I want will come when I take Mandrake home."

"Then do it for Maggie. She's grown fond of you, you know? Before you disappear from her life forever, give her a couple of weeks and a bit of adventure. She doesn't realize yet that you let the dragon live—the same dragon that killed her mother. Show her it was all worth it."

Aster drew in a long deep breath. He stood up and straightened his shoulders, the Empress Sword settling all too comfortably across his back. "All right, I'll go to Castlekeep, but not until you're well enough to come with us. I should go find Mandrake and tell him what we're planning. He might need food or something."

"Get Eric to hunt up a deer or two for the dragon." Captain Griffin smiled. "That boy's sweet on you, you know?"

"Yes." Aster closed his eyes and balled up his fists. "I know."

The streets of Traders Run were dark and gloomy at this early hour. Not as dark as the tunnels Aster knew were just below his feet, but still dark enough to make him pause now and then to get his bearings. He'd never walked through a sleeping town before, let alone with a skittish horse in tow.

He'd not really intended to lie to Captain Griffin, but the more he thought about it the more he was convinced it would be better for everyone if he waited and returned to Castlekeep as himself. He could always straighten things out with his friends later. They would understand once they knew the whole story.

It felt good to be wearing pants again, and his chain mail shirt too. He'd found where Maggie stowed them in her wagon and changed into them before going to the stable for Troy. He put several gold coins into the Griffins' money box to pay for the ruined dress and to help with Captain Griffin's recovery.

Now he was making his way to the east side of town. He'd told Mandrake to meet him there and hoped they'd be well into the mountains by sunrise. His plan was to hide in the foothills until the dragon was healed enough to fly through the Misty Mountain. Then he'd fulfill his promise to Mandrake, return the sword to the Empress, become a boy again and go home to tell his mother and father the whole complicated story.

He rounded the corner of a small storehouse and found his way blocked by a team and wagon. Standing beside it was another horse with a rider. In the dark it was difficult to make out the faces, but Aster could never mistake their voices.

"Didn't I tell you she'd come this way? I'm not called the best huntsman in the east country for nothing."

"And just where do you think you'll be going at this early hour?" Maggie's irritation was obvious even without seeing her face.

"Oh, just out for a walk."

"With your horse?"

"Well, after all the excitement, he couldn't sleep either. How did you know I'd be here?"

Maggie laughed. "You might be good at sneaking out quietly, but you make enough racket in your sleep to wake the dead. I missed your dear little snoring last night and had a pretty good idea where you'd gone. After that, finding you was the easy part." She held up the glowing white tracker medallion.

Aster flicked at the little jewel dangling above his nose. "I really need to get rid of this thing. All right, you caught me, now why are you both here?"

"We're going with you, of course."

"Did you know the dragon thought you were taking him into the mountains?" Eric shifted in the saddle as Nightstorm nickered impatiently. "He wasn't at the old riverbed where you told me he'd be, either. He was way off to the east of town when I found him. I gave him the deer you asked me to…"

"You fed Mandrake already? I only just asked you to do that at dinner? It's been dark the whole time." Aster was beginning to suspect Eric's boast about being the best huntsman in the east country might just be true.

"Daddy asked Eric to go feed your dragon after he got back from the Rutting Bull. Daddy was convinced you were up to something and it looks like he was right. You promised to go to Castlekeep, remember?"

"And I will, right after I've taken Mandrake home."

"You told Daddy you weren't coming back from there, that we'd never see you again." There was more pain in her voice now.

Aster's chain mail shirt suddenly felt very heavy. His knees buckled and his shoulders bent. He didn't want to go home like this, but he also didn't want to disappoint his friends.

"So we're just going to leave your father behind and head for Castlekeep?"

"Well, Daddy won't be *that* far behind. He's asleep in the wagon." Maggie giggled and Aster wondered if she could see him blushing in the dark.

"I'm not asleep!" Captain Griffin's voice, coming from the back of the wagon, wasn't exactly angry, but it wasn't happy either. "We can talk about all this in the morning, but can we please get moving before we wake up the whole town?"

"Yes, Daddy!" Maggie paused and Aster could sense her peering down at him. "Well, your ladyship? Are we going east or west?"

Aster looked up at the stars. The sky around them was already turning indigo. He sighed and walked Troy over to join his uninvited chaperones. "I suppose we'll have to go east for a just bit. I need to let Mandrake know."

"Let the dragon know what?" Aster could practically hear the smile on the huntsman's face. "I've already told him we're going to Castlekeep and he said he'd catch up with us in a few days, when his leg feels better. He's already getting around on it a bit and it certainly hasn't affected his appetite. I've never seen anything eat so much venison so fast before."

"Can we please start moving for the King's Road?" Captain Griffin's voice sounded more irritated than before.

As they marched west through the quite streets of Traders Run, Aster tried to remember if he'd ever read a book where the hero was as useless as he felt now. He knew his friends meant well, they just didn't understand how important it was for him to return the Empress Sword before going home. If only they knew he wasn't really a girl!

24

The Secret

The wagon and two riders moved slowly down the King's Road. Aster would have preferred the back roads and byways he and Paul had used on their way out, but that really wasn't possible with the wagon and the need to keep Captain Griffin from jostling around too much inside of it.

They passed through a couple of small villages. News of Aster's encounter with the dragon had spread quickly. However, each village had a slightly different account of how the brave former Captain of the Royal Guard had driven off the dragon—a dragon who, apparently, had decided to eat a little foreign girl before burning Traders Run to the ground. Eric and Maggie did their best to straighten things out, but usually just managed to confuse the story even more.

The sun was getting low on the third day when they finally rode out of the hills and into the forests east of Maybrook. Eric found a large clearing just off the road and they pulled the wagon into it for the night. Maggie assigned Aster to collect some firewood while Eric went to hunt up something for dinner.

In short order, Aster returned with an armload of sticks and dropped them next to the fire pit Maggie had already dug at the center of the clearing. He looked around approvingly. The wagon sat off to one side, with the horses tied up behind it. A few bedrolls had already been spread out on the ground next to the fire. In just a few minutes, Maggie had swiftly and expertly turned the empty clearing into an encampment.

Aster heard Maggie humming on the far side of the wagon and found her there fiddling with Troy's saddle. He walked up and she looked over her shoulder at him. "Where's Eric?"

He was a bit disappointed by the question, but shrugged it off. "I haven't seen him. I suppose he's still hunting for dinner."

"I hope he doesn't bring back anything too large. We don't want to be cooking all night, do we?" She looked over her shoulder again and winked at him.

Aster wasn't sure what she meant by that. He'd never learned much about cooking, so he decided the best tactic was just to go along. "Yeah, that wouldn't be much fun."

Maggie stopped undoing the saddle strap and started laughing. She looked at him with a playful grin. "Have you ever actually butchered and cooked anything the size of a wild boar? I didn't think so. You'd better hope he brings back something a lot smaller."

She turned around and started loosening the fittings on Aster's haversack.

"What do you think you're doing?"

Maggie finished untying the haversack and it slipped off Troy's back into her waiting arms. "Well, a noble lady such as yourself can't be bothered with such things, even if you are dressed like a common highwayman."

"What makes you think I'm a noble lady all of a sudden? Here, let me take that." Aster reached for the haversack, but Maggie jerked it away from him.

"Oh, no you don't. You can barely dress yourself without help and it's obvious someone else has always done your hair for you. I'm guessing someone's always picked out your clothes for you, too. You'll be needing a lady in waiting on this trip and I'm the only one here with the basic qualifications." Maggie turned and marched around the wagon.

"In spite of what you think, I can take care of myself." Aster picked up his bedroll and trailed behind her like a puppy.

"Is that so, your Highness?" Maggie raised an eyebrow when Aster stopped dead in his tracks. "Don't give me that look. It's what Daddy keeps wanting to call you, until he catches himself. Maybe he knows something about you I don't?" Maggie dropped the haversack on the ground next to her own bedroll and knelt beside it.

"Uh...No, I don't think he'd have any reason to call me something like that. Your Highness is a royal title and I couldn't possibly be of the royal bloodline."

"Would you listen to yourself? 'Of the royal bloodline,' indeed. Any common girl would know I'm only joking. You're a lady all... right..." Maggie's voice trailed off. She'd just opened Aster's haversack and was looking inside.

"I can pretty much guarantee you I'm not any sort of lady. ...Maggie?"

Maggie reached into the haversack and pulled out the belt knife he'd bought from her. She drew it slowly from the sheath, her face a grim mask of growing recognition.

"Um...I can explain that." Aster fidgeted with the bedroll in his hands as Maggie got to her feet.

"How could you?" Maggie shifted the knife to an underhand grip and pointed it at Aster. "I knew I'd seen those clothes before. Did you kill that nice boy or just leave him lying naked somewhere in the mountains so he could freeze to death?"

Aster took a step back. He had nothing but the bedroll to defend himself with. "It's not what you think. Let me explain. It was the sword..."

"The sword? So you killed him with that thing? Or did you just let him pick it up? Then while he was struck dumb and wracked with pain you stole his horse and all his clothes?"

"It wasn't like that at all. The boy you remember went looking for the sword, but it won't tolerate a man's touch. When it chose me..."

"So you were his rival, then? You got the sword, but you have more compassion for a murdering dragon than you do for a sweet boy who was naive enough to trust any pretty girl that came along. Even you."

"You thought he was sweet?" Aster probably should have been paying more attention to the business end of the knife pointed at his belly, but Maggie had just called him sweet *and* pretty in the same sentence!

"That dragon murdered my mother and almost murdered my father, too, but you're so power-hungry you let it live to become your slave. You'd kill anyone who gets in your way, just like you killed that poor boy..."

"Maggie, I *am* that boy! The Empress cast a spell on me to make me look like a girl so I could use the sword against the dragon."

"What kind of a fool do you take me for? I've seen you without your clothes on and you ain't no boy!"

"I can't explain that. It's magic! But I'm the same person you sold the knife to. You told me it came from somewhere in the south. You told me it was folded a thousand times. You even showed me the layering along the edge."

Maggie glanced at the knife in her hand and snickered. "And he was just green enough to believe all that drivel. That just proves he bragged to you about it before he died."

"I invited you to dinner at the Five Crowns Inn. You made me think you were married. Then the last thing you said to me was your father would be happy to have another satisfied customer. I'm telling you the truth. Maggie, please believe me."

Maggie's expression faltered for a moment, then her eyes grew hard once more. "He could have told you that, too. It don't prove you're him."

"If you don't believe me, then ask your father. I think he's figured it out somehow."

"No," Mr. Griffin's deep voice was close behind Aster. "I had my suspicions, but until this moment I didn't think such a thing was possible. Maggie, put down the knife before you hurt yourself."

"But Daddy, she's a murderer!"

"No, Pumpkin, she didn't murder anyone. This is his Royal Highness, Prince Aster."

"No..." Maggie began to shake her head slowly back and forth. "She can't be..." The knife slipped from her shaky hand and fell to the ground. "No!" With a scream she burst into tears and ran off into the woods.

Aster started to follow her, but Mr. Griffin put a hand on his shoulder. "She'll be all right, your Highness. She's probably more upset about you not killing the dragon than being the prince."

Aster noticed the big man was leaning very heavily on his shoulder. "Should you be up walking around? The doctor said you needed to rest. Let me help you back into the wagon."

"Thank you, your Highness, but I can make it on my own."

"Don't be foolish. You're injured." Aster put his shoulder under the big man's arm and walked him slowly back to the wagon.

As Aster settled Mr. Griffin on the pallet in the wagon, he smiled and shook his head. "Just like your father. King Cosmos always thinks of his troops first and his own well-being second."

Aster pulled a blanket over the injured man. "How did you know who I was?"

Mr. Griffin took a deep breath and then closed his eyes. "I'll never forget the day Maggie's mother died. Abigail was a wonderful woman, and the love my life. She ran a tavern in Moonhaven. That's where she and Maggie were when the dragon struck the first time."

"Moonhaven's just up the coast from Castlekeep, only a few leagues to the south where the river runs into the sea, but there's no town there."

"It never was very big, just a place for the fishing boats to moor up at night. Abby's tavern was the only place you could go to get a meal. I met her when the army bivouacked outside the town once. After we were married she stayed on to run the tavern while I pulled my duty at Drakenshold, going home to her loving arms just once a month."

"So you were at the castle when the dragon attacked Moonhaven?"

"Yes. It was an average day. I was due to go home in two more, so I was biding my time, really. Then the young prince showed up with his nanny in tow. He couldn't have been more than three or four, but he stormed in, demanding to be taught how to fight with a sword."

Mr. Griffin shifted into a more comfortable position, then smiled and closed his eyes. "All the fellows knew I had a little girl at home about that age and they all thought I was disappointed because she wasn't a boy. So they sent the little prince to me. We made a wooden sword together and I started showing him how to parry and thrust, but he wasn't so steady on his feet yet. What impressed me the most was, no matter how many times he fell down, he always got up and came at me again.

"Finally I taught him how to hold his sword boldly above his right shoulder and charge head long at his enemies." Mr. Griffin opened his eyes and smiled at Aster. "When I saw you charging down that hill, lass, my first thought was why I hadn't taught you to never do such a foolish thing unless you've got an entire army at your back."

Aster grinned, but also felt his face growing red. "It was the only thing I could think of. No one ever taught me how to attack a dragon. I couldn't even remember where I'd learned to charge like that."

"Well you need some practice at it. You couldn't even hit a motionless dragon squarely in the chest!"

"At the time, I didn't know he couldn't move. I was more worried about not tripping over the stupid dress than where the sword was going to end up."

"Always go into battle prepared, your Highness. Next time out, tuck your skirts up first and don't leave your back wide open."

"Oh, there won't be a next time. As soon as I get Mandrake settled into the Valley of Wind, I'm giving this sword back to the Empress, the spell will be broken and I'll never have to wear a dress again."

"Do you think it wise to just give the sword back? Such a weapon could become a powerful tool for a king."

"You've seen what this thing does to any man who touches it. That's why the Empress had to make me look like a girl just so I could pick it up. If I keep it, I'll never be a king."

"A queen, then. It's power that rules kingdoms, lass, not just men."

Aster looked off in the direction Maggie had gone. "I'm learning that some things in life are more important than power."

"Ah, I see now." Mr. Griffin leaned back on his pallet and stared at the roof of the wagon. "She likes you, too. Last week she wouldn't stop going on about this boy she'd sold a knife to, but I think she likes you even better now. Be careful with her. She's more delicate than she puts on."

"I'll be careful, sir. Maggie's my best friend. I never want to hurt her."

"Good. And just who do you think you're calling sir, your Highness? Your father always called his captains by their first names. I'd be honored if you'd call me Marcus."

"That might be a little awkward, me looking like a girl and all, but I'd like to call you Captain Griffin, if you wouldn't mind. I don't think calling me your Highness is appropriate, either. Until I'm rid of this spell, you'd better keep calling me Astrid."

"It's a deal, then. Now, go bring back that headstrong daughter of mine before she goes and gets herself lost in the woods."

"Aye, Captain Griffin!" Aster stood at attention, saluted, and then laughed. It felt good having someone else know his secret. Now all he needed to do was find a way to explain it to Maggie. Assuming he could even find her in the growing twilight.

25

The Love Triangle

Aster crashed through the underbrush, trying to follow whatever path Maggie had taken out of the clearing. He wasn't sure just what he was going to tell her—there were so many things he wasn't even sure about himself—but he wanted her to know that he liked her. Liked her a whole lot.

He stumbled upon a large apple tree with some clear space beneath it and stopped to get his bearings. He thought he was near the stream, but couldn't yet hear the sound of flowing water. He was straining to listen for it, or maybe even Maggie's crying, when a noise from the bushes startled him.

"Are you lost, my lady? I'm heading back to the clearing if you'd like me to show you the way."

Eric was standing behind him with a brace of rabbits flung over one shoulder. Aster wondered how he'd gotten two of them so quickly.

"No, I'm not lost, I'm looking for something."

"Looking for firewood? Apple doesn't make good firewood. It's difficult to light and burns too hot for cooking meat."

"I'm not looking for firewood. I'm looking for Maggie. She ran off this way."

"Maggie ran off? But I just saw her kneeling by the stream over there." Eric pointed in the general direction Aster had been heading before he stopped. "She didn't look like she was running anywhere."

Aster glanced over his shoulder and smiled. "That's good. Captain Griffin was worried she might get lost out in these woods."

"And he asked you to look for her?"

"Yes, he asked me to look for her. Why does everyone think I can't take care of myself? I'm thirteen, I've been going on hunts my whole life, I've been fencing with a real sword since I was six years old. I know how to take care of myself!"

"You've been hunting and fencing before? But you're a girl, a very beautiful girl."

"No, I'm not. You don't understand. My father is the king and..."

Suddenly Eric dropped to his knees and grabbed Aster's hand. "Have I offended your Highness? I knew you were a princess all along, but I assumed you were traveling in disguise. Does Maggie know the truth?"

When Eric wouldn't let go of his hand, again, Aster rolled his eyes skyward. "Yes, Maggie knows. She just found out, that's why she ran off. I need to find her and explain everything."

"Do you wish me to take you to her, your Highness?"

While it was nice having people call him your Highness again, it was a little disconcerting to have a boy older than himself say it while looking up at him with adoring puppy dog eyes.

"I..." Aster blew out his breath and took another before answering. "I would like you to go back to the encampment and see if Captain Griffin needs anything. I'll go talk to Maggie and we'll both return before nightfall. Is that all right?"

Rather than answer, Eric rose up. He held Aster lightly by the shoulders and leaned in closely. "Is that all you want from me, your Highness?"

"Um...Yes, for now." Aster swallowed uncomfortably. There was something unnerving about Eric's closeness, but also something oddly exciting about it. "Eric, I..."

Eric bent down and kissed him on the lips. Aster went stiff all over and his eyes grew wide. After a few seconds Eric straightened up again. The smile on his face was nearly ear to ear. "I am yours to command."

With a wink, the older boy released Aster and turned towards camp, disappearing quickly and silently into the undergrowth. Aster felt himself wobble. His knees were a little weak and he thought he might be losing his balance. Then he blinked twice, turned away, and quickly wiped his mouth on the sleeve of his shirt. "Ewwww!"

Maggie was kneeling by the stream just where Eric said she would be. She seemed to be drawing figures on the surface of the water with her finger. Aster cleared his throat to let her know he was there, but she didn't look up.

"Are you really the prince?"

"Yes." He was afraid to say more—he didn't want her to burst into tears again—but when she remained silent he felt he had to say something. "It's sort of a long story."

"I've got time."

Aster swallowed and then took a deep breath. "I heard about the Empress Sword, how it could defeat the dragon, and decided to go looking for it. We've lost so many good men already that Mandoline—he's the old sorcerer who came to Traders Run looking for me—he said we shouldn't send good knights chasing after fables. So I came alone."

Maggie laughed a quick short laugh that sounded as though it might have been half sob. Aster winced and wrung his hands.

"I found an old abandoned city in a valley beyond the Misty Mountain. The ghost of the Empress still lives there and she gave me the sword."

"The ghost of an empress gave you a magic sword, just like that?"

Aster wished Maggie would at least turn around. This story was embarrassing enough without telling it to someone's back. "Well, the Empress doesn't really look like a ghost or anything, and it's more like she let me borrow it, but you've seen what it does to men who touch it. She had to cast a spell on me, to make me look like a girl, just so I could pick it up."

Maggie looked over her shoulder at him then. Her eyes were red and her face was wet as though she'd been trying to wash away her tears in the stream. She looked vulnerable and beautiful.

"Why did she make you so strange looking? Shouldn't you look like a girl version of the prince?"

"I think, maybe, this is what the people who lived in that old city used to look like. There were lots of tapestries at the palace with black haired women in them. I don't really know for sure."

Maggie stood up, brushing at the front of her skirt before turning to face him. "Why didn't you tell me all this before?"

"Would you honestly have believed me? You didn't even know I was the prince when you sold me that knife. How was I supposed to tell you who I really am, looking like this?"

Maggie smiled and Aster felt a great weight lift from his chest.

"You're probably right. It's hard to believe even now." Then she frowned again. "But you didn't have to make up such a wild story! Telling me the dragon killed your uncle and that you have whole armies waiting to invade Caledon. Really?"

"Me? You and Eric thought up all that stuff on your own!"

"You didn't try and tell us otherwise, now did you?"

"Well, no." Aster stared at his feet. "I'm not really good at lying and you guys almost had me convinced I was a princess from a foreign land."

Maggie giggled. "You even knighted poor Eric. He's going to be so disappointed."

"Well, technically under the right circumstances I can..." He realized she was teasing him. "I'm sorry, please forgive me. Can we still be friends?"

"Of course we can still be friends. It doesn't matter if you're a boy or a girl, a prince or a pauper, it's what's in your heart that counts. You're a good person."

She stepped up in front of him. He really wished he were still taller than Maggie. He remembered how easily Eric had bent down and kissed him. He wanted to kiss her that way right now. When she bent down instead and gave him a quick peck on the cheek he felt his face flush.

"We should probably head back to camp soon. It's starting to get dark..." Maggie paused and looked down at Aster inquiringly.

"What is it?" He imagined his pale face red with embarrassment.

Maggie cocked her head to one side. "I guess I should start calling you your Highness."

"I'd rather you didn't. It's not like anyone's going to recognize me."

"Oh, I'll bet your parents will recognize you. You're their only child, after all."

"Do you think so?" He'd been avoiding the whole idea of going back to Castlekeep because he didn't want to face his parents. The thought of them not recognizing him was too painful.

"I'm sure of it." Maggie gave him a little reassuring hug. "Now, let's get back before Eric messes up my fire pit."

"Stop right there!"

When they reached the clearing, Eric was bent over the fire pit, about to set fire to a huge pile of sticks. Maggie marched over and pulled some of the wood from the stack as she lectured poor Eric on how to set a proper cooking fire.

Aster went to the back of the wagon and looked in on Captain Griffin, who was sound asleep. He finished rolling out his own bedroll and picked up his belt knife from where Maggie had dropped it. He started to put it back into his haversack, but stopped to think about the odd chain of events that had led him to buy it from Maggie in the first place. It all started when Troy picked up a stone in his shoe.

That reminded him the horses were still saddled, so he walked around to the far side of the wagon and began removing them. He'd just hoisted Eric's very heavy saddle off of Nightstorm when he felt the Empress Sword vibrating on his back. He set the saddle down and drew the sword.

"He is come for you."

"All right, enough of that. We need to talk. If you think you can just rattle your scabbard any time you like, say a few cryptic words that are going to get me into trouble and then fall silent again, you've got another think coming. Now, tell me, exactly *who* is coming?"

"Mandrake."

"There, now that wasn't so hard, was it? What's your name?"

"Kai."

Aster grinned. "What's your favorite color?"

"Do not patronize me, former-boy. The dragon waits for you by the stream."

Aster decided not to push his luck. Getting the sword to talk to him was a big step forward. For one thing, he now knew he wasn't crazy and that the sword was capable of holding a conversation when it felt like it. He sheathed the sword and turned back to Eric's horse.

"Sorry, Nightstorm, you're going to have to wait a little while longer for your brushdown." He patted the horse's neck and then walked around the wagon. Eric and Maggie had gotten the fire started and were still kneeling by the fire pit arguing over how to build it up. Aster grabbed a water bucket from the side of the wagon before approaching them.

"I'm going down to the stream to get some water. I'll be back in a little while."

"You're going to the stream for water? I'll come help you carry the bucket." Eric was already half way to his feet.

"I can carry a bucket by myself. Besides, I want to wash up."

Eric's eyes lit up. "Wash up? I can escort you to the stream and..."

"And do just what?" Maggie rocked back on her knees, her hands planted on her hips. "Astrid just said she's going to go wash up, so you'll be going nowhere near that stream until she gets back!"

"It's all right, Maggie. Eric, I know where the stream is now and I can manage just fine. Besides, Maggie needs your help here with the fire."

Maggie made a face and stuck out her tongue, then she slapped Eric's hand as he tried to slip a piece of wood onto the flames. Aster chuckled to himself and headed off into the woods. He'd managed to patch things up with Maggie all right, and with her father, but Eric was going to be a problem. He didn't think the young man wanted to know Aster was a boy. That might be all right, as long as Eric didn't start kissing him again.

He got to the stream and looked around. The forest undergrowth was thicker near the water and it was hard to pick out the big green dragon against the trees in the failing light. When he finally spotted Mandrake on the other side of the stream, he worked his way along the bank until he was opposite the dragon.

"Hello, Mandrake. How are you feeling?"

The dragon stared at him for a long time before responding with a confused looking grimace on his face. "What do you mean, how am I feeling?"

"Just that, how's your shoulder? Does it hurt much? Does it seem to be healing?"

"It hurts, a little. I cannot put my full weight on it yet, but at least I can stand on all fours for short periods of time."

"Any trouble flying?"

"Flying is easy, it's landings I'm having trouble with."

"Good. Are you hungry? Did Eric bring you enough to eat yesterday?"

"Why are you asking me all of these questions?"

"Because I'm worried about you. You're my responsibility now."

Mandrake had been leaning further and further out over the stream towards Aster, but now he sat up straight again. "In what way are you responsible for me?"

"Well, you swore the Dragon's Oath to me. You agreed to go wherever I tell you to go, and that places you under my care. It's what we humans call fealty."

"I know what the word means, child. What I don't understand is why you should care about what happens to me."

"Look, my father's the king. When someone swears fealty to a king, he's placing himself in the service of the crown with the expectation of certain things in return: land for instance, like the Valley of Wind; or sustenance, like the deer Eric caught for you; and they always expect protection. Well, there isn't much I can do about that right now, but as long as you're in my service I shall defend you with my life. I've spent years learning how to serve my people. Right now, you're the only people I've got."

The dragon slumped a little while Aster was talking and refused to look at him. When Mandrake did meet his eyes again, he didn't seem quite so angry. "You're not like the other humans I've met since awakening. You're more like the ones I remember growing up with. What would you have me do?"

"Well, rumors about us are already spreading to the little towns we're passing through, but they all seem to have gotten it wrong one way or the other. They don't understand that you're not a threat any more. Who knows what the story will be like by the time it gets to Castlekeep.

"I think you need to come with us and meet the king. I'm willing to speak with him on your behalf, but at some point you need to meet face to face, if only to prove I'm not lying."

The dragon jerked his head up and glared at Aster. "You want me to fly into a castle filled with soldiers and sorcerers when I'm already injured? Are you mad?"

"No, I'll be there to protect you. No one will be able to attack you without first attacking me. I can't speak for Captain Griffin or Eric, but I'm almost certain they'll protect you too."

"The old man and the boy traveling with you?" Aster nodded and Mandrake sighed. "I like that old man, he fought well and bravely, but I find it hard to imagine him defending me."

"He probably wouldn't on his own, but I think he'd defend me and I'm pretty sure Eric will jump at any chance to do something brave and foolish for me." Aster grinned just thinking about that.

"What about the girl?"

"Maggie? Oh, well she's a different story. Girls don't usually take part in battles and besides, she's not exactly happy about all this. You killed her mother in Moonhaven long ago, so it may take a while for her to forgive you."

"That was before I knew most humans would run away if I just flew over the town once or twice before setting fire to everything. I'm sorry for that mistake. I'll try and make it up to her somehow. I think you're mistaken about girls not taking part in battles, though. In my experience it's the females who fight longest and fiercest. You yourself didn't falter in the least against me."

"Well that's because I'm not...Really? Girls fight longer and fiercer?"

"Yes. That's why I've had to killed so many more of them than men. They won't give up and run away from their homes."

That puzzled Aster for a moment, until he remembered his own mother drilling the castle staff on where the house arms were stored and how to arrange for the final defense of Drakenshold. He was quite certain she would never give up the castle to any invader.

"So, you'll follow us to Castlekeep?"

"Yes, if that is your wish."

"All right then, but don't follow too closely. If people see us coming down the road with a dragon, they might panic."

Mandrake chuckled. "You may have a point there. I shall remain unseen. You need but call for me if I'm needed."

Aster wasn't sure what the dragon meant by that. "Call for you? How can I call for you?"

Mandrake returned the prince's confused look. "Why, the same way you summoned me here tonight, I suppose."

"I didn't summon you."

"Well someone told me to be here, at this time and place, to meet with you. It spoke human and had a female voice. I assumed it was you."

Aster reached back and touched the pommel of the Empress Sword. He had a pretty good idea who'd summoned Mandrake, but he had no idea how to make Kai do it again.

The Homecoming

Aster sat astride Troy, looking down at the city of Castlekeep. It had been nearly two months since the night he and Paul snuck away together using the old baker's cart for a disguise. He wondered what sort of reception his people would give their returning prince. He didn't think he was likely to find out any time soon.

Last night's camp had been in a large meadow, beside a lake he knew well. It was part of the royal hunting reserve and for the first time in his life he'd felt out of place there.

For three weeks they'd traveled the King's Road, passing through forest and field, village and hamlet, and never once did anyone recognize their prince. Everywhere they went, tales of the dragon's defeat had spread before them. Never was Prince Aster even mentioned and only rarely was the strange foreign girl or her magical sword included in the story.

Captain Griffin called out to him. He was sitting next to Maggie, at the reins of the wagon, dressed in his slightly dented armor. "Are you ready for this, lass?"

"No, but that's hardly reason to put it off."

"Are you *sure* you don't want to change into a dress first?" Maggie had been harping on him all morning about his riding clothes. He wasn't happy about marching up to the castle and perhaps being presented to his father wearing dirty oversized clothes. He was even more afraid of his father recognizing him if he were in one of Maggie's fancy party dresses.

He wished he had his dress armor. He'd briefly flirted with the idea of sneaking back into the castle at night and getting it from his room, but Captain Griffin would hear nothing of the sort. He reasoned the king would understand they had come fresh from doing battle with the dragon. The news of the beast's defeat would far outweigh their less than courtly appearance.

"Won't you reconsider? You'd look most beautiful in that red dress Maggie picked out for you." Eric's adoration had only intensified over the last couple of weeks. It was all Aster could do to keep the young man out of kissing and hugging range.

"I'm not entering the castle wearing a dress. This is embarrassing enough as it is. Let's just get on with it before I lose my nerve."

He nudged Troy forward and the others followed. Somehow, over the weeks, he'd gone from riding sullenly at the rear of their little caravan to leading it. That position of leadership had felt good out on the road, but right now Aster wished he were hiding inside the wagon.

They rode into Castlekeep largely unnoticed. There were no restrictions on horses or wagons here and the streets were teeming with them and lots of people too. No one paid much attention to them until they came to the small market square at the south end of Castle Lane where the Griffins were quickly recognized.

"Marcus! You're on the road early this year." A large woman with a scarf over her head and a long apron over her skirts ran up to the wagon smiling. "And just look at you, Maggie! My, you've grown."

A man in a leather apron joined her. "What are you all dressed up for, Marcus? Has the king called up the reserves?"

Captain Griffin laughed along with the man and then shook his head. "No Thomas, he hasn't called me up, but I am bound for the castle. I have important news for him from Traders Run."

The crowd around the wagon was growing quickly and now they all fell silent. Someone on the far side of the wagon from Aster called out.

"Is it about the dragon? I heard the beast ate a little girl."

"I heard it ran off after burning all the fields."

"I heard the whole town drove it off with crossbows."

"I heard the lord sorcerer went there and killed it."

Captain Griffin raised his hand. "Wait, wait, none of that is entirely true..."

"Was it you that bested the beast?" The man in the leather apron looked around and everyone began nodding in agreement.

"No, but I did fight the beast. All I got for my trouble was a belly full of cracked ribs. Over there's the one who bested the dragon." Captain Griffin rose up in the wagon seat and pointed to Aster. "If you're looking for a hero, my friends, there she is. Her name's Astrid and she wields a magical sword. The dragon answers to her now, and she plans to take it and all its kind far away from Caledon."

Every eye in the square turned on Aster. He scanned the stunned faces of the merchants and traders. Most looked as if they'd just been told the sea was made of cheese. Some looked curious. Some looked perplexed. Still others just looked as though they couldn't even see him.

There was dead silence as Aster tried to figure out what he should say. Then the laughter began. It started slowly, but spread quickly as, one after another, everyone in the square thought they'd gotten the joke.

Captain Griffin looked angry. "Quiet down, you fools. Listen to me! Astrid defeated the dragon. That's what we're here to tell the king."

"You tell that one to the king and he'll make you the court jester!"

Eric edged Nightstorm forward until he stood between Aster and the crowd. "Are all these people mad? Can't they see who you are? Pay no attention to them, your Highness. They're just a bunch of simpletons."

"No they're not." Aster reined Troy in and turned him towards the castle. "They're good people and welcome to their opinions. I just hope they can still laugh about anything an hour from now."

He moved up the street and away from the jeering crowds. Eric followed along just behind him, fending off anyone who tried to get too close. By the time they reached the gates of the castle, Captain Griffin and Maggie had caught up to them with the wagon.

"I'm sorry, lass, I thought that would go better. We expected as much after the reception you got in Maybrook, but I was hoping for better out of this lot. What really matters now is the king's reaction, and I'm guessing he'll be mighty happy to hear what you have to tell him."

"I hope so. This is going to be tough enough as it is. Maybe I should let you do all the talking, Captain."

"Only up to a point, lass. Once I've introduced you, I need to step back and let you speak for yourself."

Aster started to protest, but Maggie stopped him with a smile. "You can do this. I know you can."

"Thanks, Maggie." He swallowed the lump in his throat and tried to think positively, but inside he was remembering every court introduction he'd seen go terribly wrong. His father was neither tolerant nor kind to outsiders who came before the crown to negotiate on another's behalf.

As they approached the gates of Drakenshold, two guards approached them holding up their hands. They stopped and waited for the men to get closer.

One of the guards lowered his hands to his hips and laughed. "Well as I live and breathe. If it isn't Marcus Griffin."

The other guard smiled broadly and held out his hand. "How's it going, Captain? What brings you back for a visit all suited up?"

Captain Griffin reached down and shook the man's hand, wrist on wrist, in the fashion of the royal guards. "I've just come from Traders Run and I have news for the king."

The guardsmen shared a glance with one another. "We've been hearing some odd rumors out of Traders Run lately. I think the king might welcome a reliable source of news. Tell me, is the dragon really dead?"

Captain Griffin glanced briefly at Aster and then smiled. "That's news I believe the king will wish to hear firsthand."

The guard chuckled. "You're probably right. I'll send word inside that you're coming. Your young friends can wait out here."

"No, the news I bring involves them."

The guard looked them over, his eyes narrowing as he came to Aster. "Very well then, but you'll need to leave your wagon and horses out here. We have orders to keep the courtyard clean tonight. They're expecting guests."

The way the man said it Aster could only assume that some sort of social affair or court function was planned. It seemed odd that his parents would schedule something with their son still missing, but for all he knew, they might be holding his wake.

They took the wagon and horses to the small stable beside the castle entrance. Aster had no sooner dismounted than Maggie was fussing over his hair, straightening the circlet on his forehead and picking at his clothes again.

"Maggie! I'll be all right. I'm not going to a fancy dress ball, I'm probably not even going to court."

"You're going to meet the king and you look a right mess. Won't you at least put on a skirt under the chain mail? Do you want to look like a boy in front of his Majesty?"

His sense of decorum warred with his embarrassment one last time, and the later won out again. "I wish to heaven I did look like a boy right now, but I don't, so his Majesty will just have to deal with me the way I am. Now stop fussing over me and get yourself ready. You're about to meet the king too, you know."

"Do you really think so?" Maggie began priming and pulling at her own clothes. She'd braided up her hair and picked out her best outfit that morning: a green skirt and bodice over a lace-trimmed white underdress that made her look like a maiden from a fairy story.

"I wouldn't be surprised."

Aster turned to see Captain Griffin lecturing Eric again. They'd been at it for days, the older man telling the younger one what he could and could not say in front of the king, teaching him how to comport himself as a soldier instead of a common huntsman. After all, he was Aster's one and only knight. That thought, at least, made the prince smile.

Finally they were all ready, and headed for the gate with Captain Griffin in the lead. A crowd had already gathered there, drawn by rumors both good and bad, no doubt. Aster wondered if the guards would let the crowd follow them into the castle. He didn't want too many people in there; he wasn't exactly sure what was about to happen.

At the gate, the guards waved them through. They passed below the portcullis and into the courtyard. A large group of people were already pouring out of the palace's grand entrance. Aster picked out a few familiar faces before the flow stopped and a squad of guardsmen marched out, moving the crowd aside and taking up positions along the staircase.

The crowd fell silent, turning as one towards the doorway, and Aster held his breath. The king, his father, emerged from the palace with a big smile on his face. He'd expected to be presented to the king in the council chambers—or at best, in the foyer—but to have his father come all the way outside to greet a stranger was unusual.

Could someone have recognized Aster and told the king his son had returned? Did his father just somehow know he was there? Aster fought down the urge to charge up the stairs and give his father a big hug. He suddenly felt very happy to be home.

27

The Reunion

Following Captain Griffin's lead, Aster approached the stairs where King Cosmos was descending to meet them. More people were pouring out of the palace now, filling the stairway and spilling over into the courtyard. The crowd closed in behind them as they reached the stairs.

The king stood on the bottom step beaming down at them. "Marcus! I might have known it would take a man of your caliber to bring down the dragon. How did you do it, man?"

Captain Griffin bowed to the king. "Your Majesty, I wish I could claim the honor of having defeated the dragon in your name, but alas I cannot. Although I did pit my blade against the beast first, it was someone much younger than I who actually bested him."

The king's eyes swept over the small group of travelers and settled at last on Eric. "So this is the young man we have to thank for our salvation. You've earned the gratitude of all Caledon, my boy. Come forward and let my people meet their liberator."

Eric paused momentarily, looking from Aster to the king and back again, then with a shrug he started forward. Captain Griffin stopped him with a hand on his arm and stepped forward, himself.

"Your Majesty, Eric is not the young—person—who faced the dragon. Allow me to present..." He turned and looked at Aster.

Captain Griffin must have seen the confusion in his face. His father had just looked right at him, more than once, and not recognized his own son. This would be awkward no matter how he was introduced now. He lowered his eyes and shook his head.

Captain Griffin swallowed and nodded in return. He turned back to the king and straightened his shoulders. "Allow me to present Princess Astrid of the Great Eastern Empire, bearer of the Empress Sword, who defeated the dragon."

"Princess?" The king's eyes grew wide and those gathered around Aster began to back away.

Aster shuffled his feet uncomfortably. Finally he looked up at his father, his eyes filled with the tears he dare not shed. Then a smile broke across the king's face and Aster's heart leapt.

The king laughed. It was a hearty good natured laugh and he turned once more to Captain Griffin. "Marcus you old goat, I'd forgotten what a fine sense of humor you have. Only you would dress your daughter up in that ridiculous outfit and pass her off as a knight in shining armor. A good one, old friend, but come now, tell me truthfully, who really slew the dragon."

"Your Majesty..." Marcus looked very uncomfortable. The king had just accused him of making a joke out of a situation that had claimed the lives of countless innocent people, including his own wife. Aster thought that would deeply wound a man like the captain.

Silently Marcus reached for Maggie's shoulder and pulled her to his side. "Your Majesty, *this* is my daughter."

Aster drew in a sharp breath and let it out slowly. He was done asking his friends to do what was rightfully his responsibility. The sound of ringing steel filled the air as he unsheathed the Empress Sword, and everyone around him froze.

He strode forward and in a quick motion buried the tip of the sword into the dirt at the base of the stairs near his father's feet. He knelt on one knee and rested his head against the hilt, the little white jewel on the circlet tapping loudly against the steel in the silence.

"Your Majesty." The words caught in his throat and made his voice sound even higher pitched than usual. "I am indeed the one who fought and defeated the dragon. If you doubt Captain Griffin's word, I can prove it to you."

The king looked down at him, a little shocked and probably even more annoyed that a girl had drawn a blade in his presence. "If you can prove that absurd claim, young woman, you may name your reward. However, I warn you, I've had just about enough of this foolishness. Do whatever you came here to do and be quick about it."

His father's tone was the same one he often used when banishing local magistrates for embezzling tax money. With a sigh, Aster stood and looked his father in the eye. He still saw no hint of recognition there.

"As you wish, your Majesty."

Aster pulled the Empress Sword from the ground and turned away from his father. He walked purposefully through the crowd towards the empty courtyard near the gates. The faces he passed were mostly bemused, some on the verge of open laughter. He must look like a fool; a little girl dressed up in a boy's idea of battle gear and carrying a shiny little sword while a knee-length braid of jet black hair bounced along behind him.

He reached the center of the courtyard and lifted the Empress Sword high above his head. He turned it slowly, letting the afternoon sun glint off its mirrored surface.

"Now."

He just stood there for several awkward moments gazing up at the clear blue sky dotted with fluffy white clouds. Somewhere in the distance he heard a cry like that of an angry hawk and he lowered the blade. The crowd behind him began to titter.

Then a dark shape appeared to drop from one of the clouds. As it descended towards the ground, alarms could be heard rising from all around the castle and out in the city beyond the walls. The crowd in the courtyard stopped laughing and began to panic. The dragon they'd all thought dead was now diving out of the sky toward them.

Mandrake swooped low over the castle, making a quick pass. He looped around the southeastern tower and approached the courtyard. The massive dragon back-winged to a halt, hovering momentarily, before setting down lightly on his hind legs right in front of Aster.

Aster looked up at the dragon with some concern. Mandrake still held his left foreleg close to his chest and although the wound in his shoulder was healing, it looked painfully inflamed. Mandrake didn't seem to notice the pain, but grunted angrily as he glared at the crowd of humans cowering before him.

The sound of iron-shod feet running on stone filled the courtyard. Dozens of castle guards poured onto the battlements, crossbows at the ready. Alarmed, Aster whirled around to face the frightened crowd. He shouted at them as loudly as he could. He only wished his voice sounded more commanding and less like the protests of a petulant little girl.

"Hold! He won't hurt anyone unless he's attacked first!"

The king pushed through the wall of bodyguards who'd jumped in front of him when the dragon appeared and held up his hand. The guards on the battlements lowered their bows, but kept them cocked and ready.

"What is the meaning of this?"

Aster approached the staircase again. This time the crowd made a wide path for him, the fear in their faces being quite evident. The only person smiling now was Maggie and he grinned at her before addressing the king.

"Your Majesty, I present to you Mandrake, First of the race of dragons. He comes seeking the forgiveness of the crown and would petition the throne for a truce between his kind and the good people of Caledon. The war which has been developing for the last ten years stems from a grave misunderstanding on his part. He wishes to end the conflict and leave your kingdom in peace."

Mandrake bowed his head and spoke in a low rumbling voice that made Aster's speech sound like the squeaking of a mouse. "I am at your mercy, your Majesty."

The king straightened his shoulders and looked from the dragon to Aster. The anger faded from his cool blue eyes, replaced with a look of surprise. Then he glanced at Captain Griffin. "The wound in the beast's shoulder—is that your doing, or did this child do that?"

"Astrid is the only one who could have wounded the dragon, your Majesty. She carries a sword of immense magical power. I saw her wield it myself, and the dragon had little choice but to beg for his life."

The king addressed Mandrake next. "Dragon..."

"Mandrake," Aster interrupted. "His name is Mandrake, Majesty."

"Yes, of course. Mandrake, this girl claims to have defeated you in battle. Is this true?"

Mandrake hissed as he came up to his full height again. Aster could tell the dragon wasn't impressed with his father's handling of the situation so far.

"It's true, and you would do well to pay her more respect."

The king looked down at Aster again, but the look in his eyes was more like frustration than respect.

"Indeed. She seems willing to speak on your behalf. If that is acceptable to you, I would have her tell me more of this 'misunderstanding' between us."

Mandrake snorted. "I go where she tells me to go. I do what she tells me to do. That is the oath I have sworn."

"Very well, then." The king dismissed the dragon and then turned on Aster, speaking in a low voice through clenched teeth. "Listen to me, girl, the longer that dragon sits in this courtyard the more likely someone's fear will overcome his better judgment. I do not wish to see my palace turned into a bloodbath. Make it go away and we will continue this discussion in private."

Aster was heartstricken by his father's tone. Even as a small child he'd never been talked down to like this. He tried not to let the disappointment and hurt sound in his voice.

"I must be assured that Mandrake will not be harmed. There's a small lake some ten leagues to the east of Castlekeep beside a large clover meadow. If I send him there, will you keep your people away from him?"

"My army will have the area cordoned off by nightfall. No one will come near the beast, I assure you."

Aster nodded solemnly and took a step backward. As he turned, to go speak with Mandrake again, he caught sight of Maggie. There were tears on her cheeks and she looked every bit as devastated as he felt inside. He smiled weakly for her benefit and she buried her face in her father's shoulder.

"Oh, Daddy, do something, please."

"Quiet, Pumpkin."

Aster walked back to where Mandrake waited impatiently. Looking up at the enormous dragon, he put on his best fake smile. "Well, I think it's going rather well so far, don't you?"

Mandrake lowered his head nearly to the ground and spoke as quietly as he could. "I think you should let me step on that man before he makes you cook his dinner."

Aster winced. He was certain everyone in the courtyard had been able to hear the dragon's deep booming voice—including the king.

"Easy, that's my father you're talking about. He's just not used to dealing with, you know...girls. I want you to fly out to that nice lake where we camped last night and wait there for me. If you so much as see another human, get out of there and fly east. I'll catch up to you when I can."

"All right, but do not tarry here too long. I do not trust these humans, and father or no, I do not like the way their king treats you."

"I'll be fine. Now go, before one of these guardsmen takes a potshot at you and it ricochets off and hits me."

Aster backed away while Mandrake spread his wings and lifted off in a cloud of dust. As the dragon disappeared into the blue sky to the east, Aster turned and walked back to where his father waited.

"Your Majesty, Mandrake is grateful for the opportunity to make peace with Caledon. Shall we continue the negotiations now?"

"Grateful, is he?" The king looked as though he'd caught most of what Mandrake had just said. "We shall reconvene these talks at court in one hour. See that she is appropriately dressed, Marcus."

With that, the king turned on his heel and stalked off up the staircase. He disappeared into the palace and the crowd began to disperse. Everyone stared at Aster as they passed him. Some with fear in their eyes, others suspicion or distrust, but not one of them recognized their prince.

Captain Griffin put his hand on Aster's shoulder. "I'm sorry, your Highness. That could have gone better."

Maggie sniffled and wiped her eyes. "Oh, Astrid, are you all right?"

"I'm fine. I'm just a little disappointed, that's all." He tried to smile for Maggie's sake and nearly broke into tears. Instead he looked at Captain Griffin. "So I'm a princess now, am I?"

"Well it seemed fitting under the circumstances. You're going to need all the standing of a princess just to get King Cosmos to listen to you. We've got some time to prepare. What do you think we should do?"

Aster sighed. "The first thing we'd better do is head back to the wagon." He closed his eyes and gritted his teeth. "We need to find a dress I can wear at court."

28

The Negotiations

So you see, your Majesty, Mandrake believed the mountain was as real as everyone else does. However, he remembers a time when it wasn't there at all. He assumed someone had conjured the mountain into being to keep the dragons from reaching their homeland. A war of misunderstanding has been growing ever since."

Aster stood nervously at the center of the throne room, not in the council chambers as he'd hoped. Rather than discussing this with his father face to face across a large table, he was forced to gaze up at the king sitting on his throne. The comfortable feeling he'd always had for this room was gone. Now he was the poor soul all alone before the power of the crown with the weight of the room bearing down on him.

It didn't help that the wine colored dress Maggie had picked out for him looked ridiculously out of place here. The short puffy sleeves, the layer upon layer of skirts and the delicate lacework across the front did nothing to reinforce his position as a warrior princess who'd just conquered a mighty dragon.

The king cleared his throat and the unusually large crowd of nobles in attendance stopped murmuring. There were clearly three times the required number and Aster wondered where they'd all come from. Most of the king's advisers were nowhere in sight, and the nobles present weren't the sort his father would turn to for council anyway.

"So tell me, who did conjure up this imaginary mountain of yours?"

"It's not imaginary, it's an illusion. I have no idea who built it or why. It might have been put there by the Empress to keep outsiders from finding the Valley of Wind. Or it might have been built by the ancient rulers of the Four Kingdoms to keep the Eastern Empire at bay."

"And you propose to do what? If, as you say, the dragon can't fly over the mountain, then he is still stuck here, correct?"

"But he doesn't need to fly over it. He can fly right through it. Or he can land and walk through it with me if he prefers. Either way, once he's on the other side he can easily fly through the pass and into the Valley of Wind."

"And once the dragon is on the other side of the Misty Mountain, will he be trapped there?"

"I don't see why he would be. I had no more trouble passing out of the mountain than I did going in. Mandrake should be able to fly into and out of the Valley as he pleases."

"Then what is to prevent him from flying back into Caledon and resuming his attacks?"

"Well, the Oath, your Majesty." Aster couldn't understand why his father was acting so imperceptive. He knew why Mandoline wasn't here, but none of the king's other important advisors were here, either. Could they all be out looking for him?

The king beckoned to an aid who scurried forward with a parchment. "Yes, this so-called Dragon's Oath. The information we have says the dragon has bound himself to your will. Is this correct?"

"I wouldn't put it that way. It was more like an oath of fealty. He agreed to stop his attacks on Caledon if I led him to the Valley of Wind."

"In the courtyard this morning, your dragon said he goes where you tell him to go and does what you tell him to do. Is this true?"

Aster didn't see where he was going with this. "I suppose so, yes."

"Then what is to prevent you from ordering him to resume his attacks on Caledon in your name?"

"Your Majesty, I..." Aster was shocked speechless. How could his father even think he would do such a thing? He would be betraying his people, betraying the kingdom he was heir to, betraying everything he had ever been brought up to believe. Why would his father, of all people, think him capable of such heinous behavior?

Because he doesn't know you're his son, Aster thought sullenly. *Because to him you're nothing more than some upstart little girl who refuses to say where she comes from and demands the king submit to her every whim.*

"Your Majesty, I know that I'm asking you to blindly place your trust in me when you have no good reason to do so. I know that I'm asking you to have faith in a stranger from a strange land, but I swear to you that I would no sooner see Mandrake attack your people again than would your own son." Aster choked back a sob. "If what you fear were true, I could have simply taken Mandrake into the mountains and unleashed him upon your people without ever coming here to explain myself. My only desire is to bring peace to Caledon and to secure for Mandrake the homeland he desires."

The king stared down at him silently for a long while. He handed the parchment back to the aid who withdrew quickly. When he spoke again, the king's voice held none of its former harshness.

"Well said, princess. You must understand that my people have suffered greatly from these dragon attacks. Before I would have them believe they are over, I would..."

The doors of the throne room opened with a loud thump, followed by the noisy footfalls of a page running across the stone floor. The boy skidded to a stop before the court herald, who bent to listen to the lad's urgent whispers. The herald's eyes grew wide and he pushed the boy aside as he crossed to the throne and knelt beside the king.

He whispered into the king's ear for only a second before being interrupted. "When did he arrive?" In answer, the herald glanced towards Aster and then resumed his whispering. At last, the king dismissed the herald and looked down at Aster.

"I need time to think about all that you've said. I also need to confer with my advisers on the best course of action to implement this treaty between the dragons and Caledon. We shall resume these negotiations later. Until then, please accept the hospitality of my castle."

The king rose abruptly and exited through a side door. The sudden end to the audience confused and worried Aster. It wasn't like his father to just walk away from a petitioner like that. He turned to leave the throne room himself and spotted Captain Griffin waiting for him by the main doorway.

"That went very well, lass. I believe you've persuaded the king to agree to the treaty."

"Maybe, but I'm worried about what just happened. Do you think the army might have attacked Mandrake?"

Captain Griffin pulled at his chin. "Something like that might happen if a soldier let his fear override his orders, but I think the king would have reacted differently to such news. I believe he was hurrying off to meet with someone. Someone he wishes to discuss all this with. Have you noticed that none of the royal advisers are present?"

"Yes, I noticed that right away. I'm afraid they may all be out looking for me, just like Mandoline."

"Then my guess would be that one or more of them have failed to find you, and returned."

Aster grinned. "They probably weren't looking for a prince in a red dress."

Captain Griffin chuckled. "Aye, Prince Aster always favored white. But you look very nice in that color."

"Why thank you, Captain." Aster was actually feeling optimistic now. If the king agreed to make peace with Mandrake, then they could be on their way to the Misty Mountain within a day or two. "But if it's all the same with you, I think I'll take it off for now. I might start liking these frilly things."

He laughed, and then he and the captain walked out the doors and into the reception hall. They were passing the grand staircase when Aster heard a voice that stopped him dead in his tracks.

"Princess Astrid, may I have a moment of your time?"

Aster turned to face his mother, the queen. He wanted to race to her side, wrap his arms around her and not let go until she knew it was really him, but Captain Griffin's firm hand on his shoulder prevented that. He started to bow, then caught himself—he wasn't really sure how to curtsy. "Your Majesty?"

His voice was shaky and frail, but the queen didn't seem to notice. "I know that you're here in Caledon on a very important mission, but I would beg a boon from you."

"A-anything, your Majesty."

"A ball is being held here at the castle this evening. I'd hoped my son would have returned by now, but seeing as how he's still away, I was wondering if you would agree to be the guest of honor. I know the people of Caledon would enjoy the opportunity to get to know you better."

"I-I don't know..." Aster felt dizzy. His mother hadn't recognized him either.

"There will be plenty of young gentlemen your age in attendance and I'm certain we can fill up your dance card satisfactorily. Your traveling companions are, of course, invited as well. Captain Griffin has been long missed at court."

"I would be honored, your Majesty." Captain Griffin bowed low. When he straightened up, he poked Aster in the small of his back.

"I...It would be my pleasure to attend your party. However, I'm afraid that I'm traveling without benefit of a wardrobe."

"Oh no, my dear, what you are wearing is just fine. It suits you well."

"T-thank you, your Majesty."

"I've arranged rooms for you and your lady in waiting on the second floor. Captain Griffin, can I lure you away from the guardhouse? I have a room set aside for you and your squire, as well."

"How could I refuse such a gracious offer, your Majesty? My squire and I accept with gratitude." Marcus bowed once more and then poked Aster in the back again.

He tried to curtsy, but had no idea what he was doing. He felt awkward and foolish. "Yes, thank you for your kindness, your Majesty."

The queen smiled and then walked away, her attendants trailing behind her. Aster followed her with his eyes, willing himself not to call out, knowing he must not make a scene no matter how torn he felt inside.

Captain Griffin cleared his throat. "You handled that well, lass."

"I thought maybe she, of all people, would at least...I guess there just isn't anything left to recognize." He shook his head and looked up at Captain Griffin. "And since when do you have a squire? Eric?"

The big man grinned. "Since my daughter became your lady in waiting, I assume. Shall we go tell them both about their new lives of servitude?"

"Somehow I think they'll be more excited about spending the night in the castle, and going to the ball." They resumed their course toward the courtyard, but Aster suddenly stopped short. "Captain? What's a 'dance card'?"

The Waiting Dragon

Mandrake sat curled up on the sandy shore of a small lake, staring at the line of soldiers along the hilltop in the distance. They'd been there for more than an hour now and every time he so much as twitched they went into a panic. His shoulder hurt like mad and he'd have liked to get up and walk around a bit, but he was afraid of starting a war he could not win.

What was the little Empress thinking? He didn't need an army to protect him from humans; he'd been doing that quite well on his own for ten years. And why send him here, to this empty field next to this tiny lake where he was completely exposed? It was madness and he should have refused, but he couldn't.

His sire once tried to explain the Dragon's Oath to him. As a pup he wasn't required to swear the Oath to the Empress, but his sire wanted him to understand what it meant. They sat together for hours as the old dragon tried to put into words something dragons could really only feel deep within their being.

Mandrake didn't understand it then, but now he could see all too well why his sire had difficulty explaining it. The very moment he'd completed the Oath, short as it was, something inside him changed. His fury and hatred of the humans faded, only to be replaced by a singular devotion to just one of their kind. He could no more disobey the little Empress now than he could stop breathing.

He still distrusted the humans, still felt they had wronged him in the past and he deserved retribution for what they'd done, but he could no longer feel the anger. Whenever he tried to tap into that rage he saw the image of the girl looming over him, white death blazing in her hands, listening to him, believing him, and forgiving him.

She talked to him as if he were one of her own. She felt no distress in being near him and somehow she made others feel the same way. The boy, Eric, had been bringing him meat for weeks, apparently happy to be doing favors for another of her followers. Mandrake suspected the boy had also sworn himself to Astrid, for he addressed her with the same awe and devotion Mandrake felt.

And yet there was more to Mandrake's devotion, something that transcended fear and respect—something about her sword. It had changed him. He was not the angry young dragon he had once been. The change was nothing as dramatic as the girl claimed to have undergone—she would have him believe she'd once been the Crown Prince of this kingdom—but something had definitely changed within him. He felt, in some ways, more mature.

There was movement on the hilltop. A large number of men were pushing some sort of wooden contraption into place. It had a large triangular frame with a long pole swinging vertically in the middle, all mounted to a base with wheels on it like a wagon, but for some reason the men were pushing it into place without the use of horses.

Mandrake didn't know what to make of the thing. It was big enough to be a watchtower, but there was no place atop the pole for a man to stand. And even if there were, the way the pole swung back and forth would force them to hang on for dear life. He supposed it could be a weapon of some sort. If so, they were aiming it right at him.

More and more, the humans appeared to be readying for a massive assault, with Mandrake as their only target. This was not good. If he obeyed Astrid's command, as he felt he must, the army would have to attack him first before he could do anything.

He was in a poor position here on the lakeshore, the lowest

ground in the wide open meadow. He was surrounded on three sides—on two by hills now teeming with soldiers and on one by the forest that might conceal any number of additional troops. While he had a reasonable amount of gas in his sack, it wasn't nearly enough to burn more than a few acres of the meadow. He would be better off reserving the gas for a high, swift flight over the lake and away from this death trap.

Mandrake heard the two men walking toward him before he actually saw them. The one wearing armor was making enough noise to awaken a hibernating bear. The huge white flag the other one carried sounded like it was caught up in a hurricane rather than just flapping in the breeze. He tried not to move too much as they approached. Neither one seemed to be armed, but he tensed himself for a quick takeoff nonetheless.

"Ahoy, dragon!" The one in armor was obviously laboring under the delusion that Mandrake was a boat. "We come under this flag of truce to speak with you."

"Is that what that is? I thought you were bringing me a napkin."

The armored man paused, head tilted sideways, with a perplexed look on his face. Finally he shook his head as if to clear it of something disagreeable. "Um, no, the king has ordered us to stand guard over the game reserve and let no man enter. We have also been tasked with seeing to your needs."

"My needs? Just what do you think I need?"

"Well, uh, something to eat perhaps? We can get you anything you like."

"Anything I like?" Mandrake had thought to dismiss these fools, but this promised to at least be entertaining. "You know, I'm craving a nice oryx."

"What is that?"

"You don't know what an oryx is? The swift-running deer of the northern Iggalian plains? The ones with the really long thin horns that are perfect for picking your teeth after dinner?"

To illustrate, Mandrake extended one long fore-claw and raised it to his lips. Sticking it into the corner of his mouth he moved it around against his hard back teeth, making a most awful screeching noise.

The man carrying the flag nearly dropped it, he was shaking so hard. The man in armor stood his ground, but began fidgeting uncomfortably. "Begging the dragon's pardon, but this is Caledon. We have no such creatures here."

"Oh, I see. Only creatures that live in Caledon, then?" The man nodded. Mandrake extracted the claw from his mouth and began scratching his chin. After a moment he raised the claw high into the air. "I know! I'll have an ibex. I'd love a good ibex."

"An ibex?" The armored man frowned. "You want a mountain goat? We're nowhere near the mountains."

"So? You said I could have anything I wanted as long as it comes from Caledon."

"Yes, but we can only get you animals that are here on the reserve, or perhaps from a nearby farm. It would take us weeks to bring an ibex here from the mountains."

"So, basically you're offering to bring me only the food I could simply get up and catch myself?"

The armored man paused. He looked like he was sweating far more than the warm afternoon called for. "Well, yes. I suppose you could look at it that way."

"Oh, well then. I wasn't all that hungry to begin with."

"Something to drink perhaps?" The man's eyes nervously followed Mandrake's claw as it swung down to point at the lake not two steps away. "Oh, yes, of course. Anything, then? Anything we can do for you?"

"Now that you mention it, Captain..."

"Um, I'm just a lieutenant."

"Really?" Mandrake raised an eye ridge dramatically. "A lieutenant in charge of so many men? Impressive."

"No, my captain sent me to speak with you."

"Your captain doesn't strike me as a very brave man. Now listen, Lieutenant, I need only one thing. My shoulder hurts and it would feel so much better if I could get up and move around. I'd like to be able to walk over to the lake for a drink, or be able to go into the woods and find a place to relieve myself. However, I can't do any of those things with that army of yours going into a panic every time I so much as stretch a muscle."

While he spoke, Mandrake swept his extended claw over the men's heads, indicating the line of soldiers on the distant ridge. His claw caught on the white flag and he casually wrapped it around his paw, letting it slip slowly free as the breeze tugged on it.

"What I want you to do for me, is to not panic. I was directed to wait at this place by the little Empress, and I was told not to attack any humans—unless they attack me first. Do you understand, Lieutenant?"

"Y-yes, my lord dragon." The man stood stock still, his voice cracking as if there were not a drop of moisture left in his throat.

"My suggestion to you would be to move all those men to the other side of the hill, where they cannot see me and I cannot see them."

The lieutenant nodded vigorously. "B-begging the dragon's pardon, could we keep a few men on the hilltop? Just as sentries in case you should need something after all."

"That would be fine. Just remember to tell them that I might walk around or even take to the air a few times as the mood strikes me."

"I will inform my captain of your wishes. Would there be anything else?"

"Yes. That device you rolled into place just now."

"The trebuchet?"

"Whatever it is, if you don't wish it turned into a bonfire within the hour, I suggest you remove it from my sight. And if there are any sorcerers over there, they should leave with it. Is that clear, Lieutenant?"

"Crystal clear, my lord dragon."

"One last thing?"

The lieutenant didn't look like he wanted to hear more, but he nodded anyway.

"You did very well here. You're a brave man, and any time you'd like me to arrange a field promotion, just send over that cowardly captain of yours."

Not all humans can appreciate a dragon's grin, so Mandrake threw in a wink for good measure. Both men finally smiled, and the lieutenant even blushed a little.

"Thank you, I'll take that under advisement, and I'll have all but two of the soldiers removed to the far side of the hill within the hour. Have a pleasant evening, my lord dragon."

The lieutenant bowed and Mandrake returned the gesture by lowering his head. He watched the two men walk back out over the meadow towards the hill. He thought they were walking a bit more assuredly going than they had coming.

True to the lieutenant's word, the soldiers began disappearing from the hilltop less than an hour later and the odd wooden device was rolled away shortly afterwards. Mandrake stood up stiffly and tried putting his full weight on the sore leg. It began to buckle, so instead he limped over to the lake and took a long drink.

He felt better after walking around a bit and decided not to tempt fate with the scouting flight he'd been planning. He settled in for the night on the far side of the lake where he had a good view of the two guards standing on the far hill and the sun setting in the west. He found himself wondering if the little Empress might be enjoying this beautiful sunset, as well.

The Grand Ball

Aster stood at the window staring out at the setting sun. The sea was calm, as it usually was this time of year, but he had the sense a storm was brewing out there somewhere. Occasionally he glanced at the decorative little card tied to his wrist with a ribbon. A page had delivered it to the room about an hour ago.

It wasn't that he'd never seen the little cards before. He'd seen them dangling from the wrists of all those girls he'd been forced to dance with. He just never thought to ask what they were. Now he understood why the girls always seemed to know exactly when it was their turn to dance with him.

Captain Griffin had explained how the dance cards worked. How the queen's social aides would decide which boys danced with which girls, matching social statuses to ensure only the right sort of pairings took place. But actually seeing the list of boys' names inside the card had driven home the truth. In agreeing to attend the queen's ball, Aster had agreed to spend the night dancing with sixteen boys, most of whom he already knew.

"Penny for your thoughts?"

Aster turned to look at Maggie. She'd changed into one of her own "fancy dresses," a beautiful green gown with white lace trim. Neither it nor the one Aster was wearing were the sort of outfits he was used to seeing at royal gatherings. The fabrics weren't all that rich and the styles were simple by comparison. He was certain there would be plenty of gossip about them at the ball. However, right now he thought Maggie looked more beautiful than ever.

"You look amazing."

"Do you really think so? Do I look like a lady in waiting?" She giggled, and it just added to her beauty.

"No, you look like a lady. No one's going to pay any attention to me while you're in the room."

"Go on! Stop your joking." Maggie blushed. She glanced at the dance card in Aster's hand and then lifted her own wrist to look at the one they'd given her. "Who do you suppose all these boys are?"

"Very likely, the pages and squires of all the boys on this one." He waved his own dance card dismissively.

Maggie examined her card more closely. "You may be right. Eric's name is on here, and he's supposed to be Daddy's squire." She giggled again. "Poor boy, he's gone from huntsman to knight to lowly squire all in the span of a few weeks."

Aster smiled. He half wished Eric's name was on his dance card. At least he'd already been in that young man's arms once before. What was he going to say when all these other boys, some of them his cousins, danced with him?

There was a knock at the door and Maggie went to open it. Captain Griffin stood in the doorway resplendent in formal, if somewhat outdated, court attire. Standing behind him was a rather uncomfortable looking Eric.

"Daddy, you look great! I told you they'd still fit."

"Just barely. My old clothes fit Eric much better than they fit me."

Eric stepped in, looking quite handsome in a long coat and leggings. What seemed to be bothering him most were all the ruffles on the shirt. He kept pulling at the collar, trying to smooth them out. Aster could sympathize with him.

"You look very dashing." Aster smiled at the huntsman and it brightened the young man's mood immediately.

"Do you really think so? I've never worn anything this fancy before. They're not as comfortable as regular clothes, but if your Highness likes it, I'm sure I can get used to them."

Maggie chuckled. "I wouldn't worry about it too much if I were you. It's only for one night. You'll be back in your greens, hunting food for the tavern keepers in Traders Run before long."

"What if I don't go back to Traders Run? Some noble lady might take a fancy to me tonight and want me to stay on at her estate. You know, I..." Eric stopped short when he caught Aster's eye. "Oh, your Highness! I didn't mean—I mean I didn't mean—I mean I'm still your loyal knight."

"That's quite all right, and Maggie's correct. It's just a party. Go and have fun. With the prince absent, I'm sure there'll be lots of girls from noble families looking to dance with a handsome young man like you." Aster grinned wolfishly. *Better you than me, my friend.*

"We should probably be going, your Highness."

Captain Griffin held out his arm. Aster stared at it dumbly and didn't move. The big man cleared his throat. "It's still customary for the guest of honor to be escorted, is it not, your Highness?"

Aster nodded. "Yes, of course. It's just...shouldn't you be on my left?"

Maggie giggled and shook her head. "Tomboy!"

"Her Royal Highness, Princess Astrid of the Eastern Empire, and Captain Marcus Griffin."

It was the shortest introduction Aster had ever been forced to endure. The court herald, a man named Alowishus, seemed very put out that he was expected to announce a royal entrance with but a single breath.

Aster was also surprised by the reaction of the assembled guests. Usually everyone in the room bowed quietly to their prince, but tonight they all began to clap their hands as if rewarding a performance of some kind. Dressed as he was, with the addition of several underskirts from Maggie's stores, Aster felt as though he were afloat in some strange aquatic play.

Eric and Maggie, for their part, seemed to be floating as well once they were introduced. Captain Griffin seemed undisturbed by it all. In spite of the applause, Aster sensed an air of reservation in the room. It was as if everyone present was only playing their part and each was anxiously waiting for someone else to make a mistake. He scanned the room for familiar faces and noted it was also a more mature cast than usual.

Whether they genuinely meant it or not, everyone did have a smile on their face. Except, he noted, a group of brightly clad young women on the far side of the room. They looked considerably put out, probably because this ball had originally been planned to give them an opportunity to dance with the prince. Aster wondered if their faces would brighten any if they knew the object of their desire was actually here.

With a gentle tug on his arm Captain Griffin started them walking across the dance floor toward the queen. The king was not present. Aster knew his father hated these things almost as much as he did, but the king usually forced himself to attend any function held for foreign dignitaries. His absence from a ball honoring visiting royalty was rather odd.

This time, Aster remembered to curtsy. It hadn't been as hard or mysterious as he'd thought. Once Maggie hiked up her skirts to show him what to do with his feet, he found it wasn't that much harder than a proper bow.

The queen actually arose to greet Aster, the first real concession anyone had made to his claim of being a princess. In an odd way, it made him feel guilty. "Welcome, Princess Astrid. Are your rooms to your liking?"

"Indeed yes, your Majesty. The view from the window is quite spectacular. Maggie wouldn't stop going on about it all afternoon."

"The view is what Drakenshold is best known for. Hopefully you'll give me the opportunity to show you some of its other fine points."

"Like the rose gardens?" Aster blurted it out without thinking.

The queen tilted her head, but smiled nonetheless. "You've heard of my roses?"

"Yes, Captain Griffin told me all about them. He says they're quite exquisite and not to be missed." Aster was getting better at making things up on the fly, but he was still a long way from reaching Maggie or Eric's level of fabrication.

The queen smiled at the captain. "Why thank you, Marcus. The gardens have grown quite a bit since you last saw them. Perhaps you'd join us for a tour?"

"Indeed, your Majesty. I would consider it a great honor."

"Be sure to bring your daughter along as well. Isn't she about the same age as Aster?"

"That she is, your Majesty, just a few months older."

Why is every girl I know older than me?

"And you, Princess, if I may be so bold as to ask, how old are you?"

Aster knew he looked a good deal younger than Maggie, but he simply couldn't lie to his mother. "My thirteenth birthday was on the equinox this past spring."

"Really? How extraordinary. My son was born on the same day. I'm terribly sorry he's not here to meet you. Aster ran off with a little friend of his to go hunting and hasn't returned yet. Perhaps you'll still be with us when he does?"

"I doubt I'll be here that long, but I'd love to see him someday soon."

Captain Griffin coughed into his hand. Aster thought it was to cover up a laugh, but the slight tug on his arm reminded him not to get too deeply into conversation with his mother.

"I should take my leave now. This is a ball, after all, and I believe there should be music and dancing. Neither will likely occur if I stand here all night talking to your Majesty."

His mother laughed, a sweet sound he never knew how much he could miss. "You're quite right. I see you already have your dance card. Please do enjoy yourself."

"I shall try." Aster curtsied again and the queen motioned for the music to resume. As they were walking away, Aster leaned on Captain Griffin's arm for support. "This is very hard, Captain."

"I know, but you're doing fine so far. Try to relax and have some fun, like the queen said."

"If you want me to have some fun, take me over to the garrison house and let me do some fencing. I'd sooner be crossing practice swords with the boys on this list than dancing with them! At least they won't spend the whole night gossiping about other boys..." Aster suddenly looked up. "Boys don't do that, do they? Gossip about other boys?"

Captain Griffin chuckled. "No, lass, the hard part is getting most boys to talk at all. The art of social conversation is one of the first things we have to teach them when they join the royal guard."

"Oh, good. I wasn't sure about that. I've never danced with a boy."

Aster stopped walking, his feet suddenly rooted to the floor. His eyes grew wide and his heart began to pound in his chest.

"What's wrong, lass? You're looking paler than usual."

"I've never danced with a boy before." He looked anxiously around the room at all the young men gazing at him. Until now he'd considered dancing with boys to be about the same as dancing with girls. He didn't like dancing anyway, but now the prospect of being held by all these tall, broad shouldered young men seemed more frightening than displeasing.

He spun around and spotted Eric walking arm-in-arm with Maggie. The huntsman still looked woefully out of place and very nervous, but right now he was the one boy Aster knew would not make fun of him if he messed up the dance. He dropped Captain Griffin's arm and ran to Eric, thrusting his hand at the older boy's chest. "Dance with me."

"Dance with you? Your Highness, I don't think I can."

"Why not? Don't you want to dance with me? Do I have to make it an order, *Sir* Eric?"

"Make it an order? Please don't make it an order. I-I don't know how to dance." Eric looked mortified at the admission.

"Not a problem." Aster grabbed the young man's free hand and dragged him away from Maggie and towards the center of the hall. "Just do everything I do and I'll take care of the rest."

"*You'll* take care of the rest?"

"Don't start that with me again, just do as I say."

Aster held Eric's right hand in his left and then grabbed the young man's left hand and put it on his own shoulder. The court musicians were always attentive and, seeing the guest of honor on the dance floor with a partner, they immediately began to play. Eric looked confused, but Aster raised their clasped hands and began pushing the taller boy around in time to the music.

"Relax, you're doing fine."

Aster noticed other couples gathering around them, moving in circles. Aster steered them into the nearest circle and joined the traditional round. Eric was a bit unsteady and they kept getting out of sync with the other couples, but Aster didn't care. He was into the rhythm of the dance and his panic over dancing with other boys forgotten for the moment.

When the dance ended he even remembered to curtsy to Eric rather than bow. This might work out after all. As the other couples mingled about, Aster held steady to Eric's hand and when the musicians started to play an introduction to the next dance he moved to begin again.

"I beg your Highness's pardon, but I believe this young gentleman is my partner for the next dance."

Aster froze at the familiar sounding voice. He hadn't seen Penelope mingling about. He'd been hoping that with the prince absent, she might not have come. He turned to find his cousin nearly prostrate in a curtsy so low it seemed physically impossible.

Penelope rose slowly and smoothly to her full height. She'd been taller than Aster before, but now she towered over him. Her green eyes sparkled in the way they only did when she was planning mischief.

"I am Lady Penelope Kathryn Augustine Winthrop, at your service." Penelope nodded to Eric and then glanced at the dance card hanging from her own wrist. "And this is Esquire Eric Buckingham, is it not?"

Aster nodded politely in response, but gripped Eric's hand so tightly the boy winced. "Lady Penelope, you take me by surprise. I would have thought your card filled with the sons of noble families, not the squire of a former guardsman."

Penelope looked confused. "Your Highness has me at a disadvantage. Have we met before?"

Aster's glee at having flustered Penelope was tempered by almost giving away his secret. "Why no, I don't believe we've met. I merely assumed that someone with so many names must certainly be of high noble rank. Of course you may dance with Eric."

"Thank you, your Highness. I'll try not to break him. Is your Highness absolutely certain that we've not met somewhere before?" Penelope was staring at Aster, looking him up and down, but never quite finding anything to identify him with.

"Quite certain, Lady Penelope." Aster reluctantly released Eric's hand and stepped away. He retreated from his cousin's icy stare. Penelope was the last person Aster wanted to have recognizing him.

The dance started up then, another round where the couples did not change partners. He watched Penelope and Eric wheel about the dance floor together. Eric seemed more at ease this time and less like the fish out of water he'd been while dancing with Aster.

Penelope, for her part, was all smiles. As usual, she never seemed to stop talking. Aster found himself worrying about what Eric might say to her. The huntsman still hadn't realized Aster was a boy enchanted to look like a girl, but he might say something Penelope would recognize nonetheless.

As he watched them, an odd feeling began to grow in the pit of his stomach. He wasn't prone to tummy aches, and this wasn't quite the same thing, anyway. Eric seemed to be having such a good time now, and that made the swirling sensation in Aster's gut even worse. When Eric actually began to smile at Penelope, Aster tasted acid rising in his throat.

He turned away from the dance floor. He needed fresh air and he meant to make for one of the small balconies that flanked the ballroom on the seaward side. However, standing right behind him blocking his way, was a handsome boy Aster recognized immediately. It was his eleven-year-old cousin Kevin, from his father's side of the family.

Kevin bowed low with a flourish. "Princess Astrid, I believe that I have the honor of the next dance."

"You do?" Aster looked at the boy dumbfounded. His stomach was still churning and the thought of dancing with anyone right now made him feel like throwing up.

"Yes, I believe your Highness will find my name at the top of her dance card." He smiled proudly. Aster's Uncle Garrett must have called in quite a few favors to get his son on the top of the list.

Aster stared down at the little card tied to his wrist. He pulled on the ribbon, untying the bow, and handed the card to Kevin. "Here, be a good lad and hang on to this for me."

Leaving his cousin looking dumbly at the little card, Aster raced through the crowd and disappeared onto the balcony.

31

The Future and The Past

Aster sat in the familiar center recess of the library window, looking out at the moonlit sea and trying not to think about all the crazy things running through his head.

There was a quiet tapping on the window behind him and he sighed. He turned slowly, expecting to see the annoyed face of the librarian, but found the worried face of Maggie staring out at him instead. He scooted to one side and she pushed open the other half of the window.

"How did you find me?"

Maggie held up the glowing tracker pendant and smiled. "This thing comes in handy whenever you decide to disappear. How'd you get out there? These windows are all locked from the inside."

"I climbed up from the ballroom." Aster hugged his knees to his chin and stared back out at the black sea.

Maggie leaned out the window, gazing down the rough stone wall towards the rocky breakers far below. "You're crazy! Why didn't you just use the door. It's open, you know..."

"I never use the doors to get into the library." Aster buried his face in his knees and laughed. "I've been climbing this wall since I was a little boy. I guess I just wanted to see if I could still do it."

Maggie carefully hopped up on the windowsill, her legs remaining safely inside. "If you're worried about Eric and that Lady Penelope person, you can stop. She dropped him like a sack of warm horse apples the minute you left the room."

Aster looked up with a weak smile. That shouldn't have made him so happy, but it did. The tightness in his gut returned as he looked at Maggie's profile in the moonlight.

Maggie turned ever so slightly to face him, leaning her back against the far side of the niche. "You know, I'd be careful of that Penelope woman. She wants something mighty bad, and she strikes me as the sort who's willing to do almost anything to get it."

Aster chuckled. "Up until a couple of months ago, what she wanted was me!"

Maggie raised an eyebrow. "You must have been quite a catch. What were you like when you were a prince?"

Aster pulled his knees closer to his chest. As far as he was concerned, he hadn't changed at all. "Well, I was blond, like everyone else in the family, and had blue eyes like my father. I was taller and a little stronger. My voice changed last year, but it still wasn't as deep as I'd hoped it would be."

"That comes to a man with age. Go on, what's it like being royalty?" Maggie leaned forward, resting her hand on the ledge next to Aster's feet.

"I had to attend a lot of dances and parties like that one. They're all pretty boring, though. What I really enjoyed was going to the garrison house and training with the guardsmen. Other than that, I spent most of my time reading. My room's filled with books, mostly tales of brave knights and heroic adventures."

"Like the adventure you've been on, right?"

Aster laughed. "No, none of the heroes in my books ever had this happen to them." He held out his arms, presenting himself for her inspection. "In fact very little of what's happened to me was in my books. I'm beginning to think whoever writes those things never went on a real adventure themselves."

"Probably not. Most people are too caught up in the everyday adventure of living to be going off on treasure hunts. And the reality of fighting a dragon seems anything but heroic once you've seen it up close."

"I'm sorry about that..."

Maggie held up her hand. "Don't say you're sorry again. I understand now why you let the beast live. He seems an honorable sort of dragon, after all. You gave him the chance to wipe out the whole kingdom today and instead he acted more like a gentleman than the king. I guess if you trust him, I can too."

"Thanks, Maggie."

They stared out at the setting moon in silence for a long time. Then Maggie turned to look at him again.

"So, you like Eric, right?"

Aster smiled sheepishly before he realized exactly what Maggie was asking. "What? Eric? Well, sure I like him. He's a great guy. We're buddies, you know?"

"But you got mad when Lady Penelope started to dance with him, didn't you?"

"Well, yeah. I'd hate to see that black widow sink her fangs into any of my friends."

"What if Eric was dancing with me? Would that make you mad?"

The thought of anyone else dancing with Maggie made his blood boil, but he knew she wasn't asking if he was jealous of her. Maggie liked Eric, that much he knew already, but Eric had set his sights on Aster. Or more precisely, on Princess Astrid.

"Maybe I should tell Eric who I really am."

Maggie leaned back against the stone wall again and laughed. "Do you think he'd believe you?"

"No, probably not. Nobody believes anything I say anymore, except you and your father. I never lied to anyone when I was a boy. Well, not about important things, anyway. I can't figure out why nobody recognizes me, either. Not my father or Penelope or even..." His voice trailed off.

"Maybe you should talk to your mother. I can see it in her eyes. She misses her little boy and everyone around her seems to think you're dead already. It can't be easy on her."

"What could I possibly say?"

"You might start with the truth. If anyone here's going to believe you, it'll be your mother. Then you might just tell her how much you love her."

Aster pinched his nose and tried not to cry. "Do you remember your mother?"

Maggie stared out into the darkness, her smile fading into something not quite a frown. "She died when I was three. Mostly I remember how much happier Daddy was when she was alive. Sometimes when I smell vanilla and cinnamon I think about her, but I don't really know why."

Aster sniffed at the warm night air, but all be could smell was the sea. "My mother always smells of roses. Even in the middle of winter. Isn't that strange?"

"It's not strange, that's her perfume. And a right expensive one, I'd guess." Maggie chuckled. "You really don't know the first thing about being a lady, do you?"

"Is it so obvious?" Aster grinned sheepishly. "Look, once I've taken Mandrake back into the mountains and given the sword back to the Empress, will you..."

"Will I, what?"

He couldn't finish the question because he really didn't know what he hoped she'd say. He wanted Maggie to be a part of his life somehow, but when he turned back into the prince that might not be possible. Surely he'd be forced into marriage with someone like Penelope and where would a guardsman's daughter fit into the life of a king?

Aster shrugged his shoulders and then stretched out his legs, letting them dangle over the edge. "I should probably get back to the party."

"Ah no, the party's over. After you left, the queen was called away too. The only one still down there, trying to run the show, is Lady Penelope."

"That sounds like Penny. Maybe I'll go see my mother." He leaned forward and glanced up the wall. "I'd better do it before the moon sets though. This gets harder to climb when you can't see the cracks."

Maggie leaned forward and looked down the sheer wall again. She shuddered. "Do me a favor and just come inside. Try taking the stairs like everyone else, for a change. It's more ladylike, you know?"

"Is that a fact?" Aster grinned at her. "Are there any other pearls of wisdom you'd like to share with a poor foreign girl unaccustomed to polite society?"

Maggie hopped down from the windowsill, back into the library, and then stuck her head out to answer him. "Well, for one thing, the next time you dance with a boy? You might let him lead."

"No! I didn't...did I?" Aster was mortified. No wonder Eric had looked so confused.

"Oh, yes you did. And you did a fine job of it, too, but from now on let the boy hold *your* waist and just try doing everything backwards."

As he stood up, Aster stared down at the waves crashing on the rocks far below. He'd never before considered what it would be like to fall all the way to the bottom of the cliff, but he reasoned it might be a kinder end. Facing his mother right now would be nothing compared to facing Eric later.

Aster left Maggie at the main staircase. She was heading down to the ballroom to rescue her father and Eric from Penelope's clutches. Meanwhile, Aster headed up. When he reached the level just below the royal chambers, he glanced down the hallway where the doors of his room sat dark and silent.

He longed to just go in there, light a candle and sit curled up on his bed reading his precious books until the wee hours of the morning. He supposed the doors were locked now, his mother's attempt to preserve everything for his eventual return—a return that should take place in another month or two if everything went right.

So far, nothing about this adventure had gone right. Not since the day his friend Paul fell off the cliff and was lost forever. The magic sword he'd been searching for had made him look like a girl. The dragon he'd planned to slay was still alive. From his dealings with the king to his first dance at the ball he'd managed to ruin for the queen, his triumphant return home had been a complete disaster. And to top it all off, the girl he was in love with loved a boy who was in love with him who he just might be in love with, too. He didn't think it could get much worse.

He mounted the last flight of stairs and walked slowly down the hallway, checking as he went that the red dress was still on straight and his hair wasn't too messed up from the wind out on the sea wall. He stopped in front of the door to his mother's sitting room and knocked lightly.

A few moments later he heard footsteps inside. Bridget, the queen's handmaiden, opened the door. There was surprise on her face until she recognized him. She smiled and curtsied, but then looked at Aster with a worried expression.

"Princess Astrid, the queen is indisposed to see anyone at the moment. Do you need some assistance in finding your rooms?"

Aster fought the urge to call the girl by name. "No. Could I perhaps speak with her Majesty? It won't take long and it's about her son."

"Prince Aster?" The look of shock on the woman's face was strangely over-exaggerated. "Perhaps her Majesty will wish to speak with you after all. Please come inside and wait just a moment while I announce you."

Aster stepped into the familiar antechamber and stood by the door as Bridget disappeared into the next room. He looked at the ring of plush chairs set against the wall and imagined them filled with his mother's ladies in waiting. They were always busily doing needlework whenever he came here on winter afternoons. One of them would usually have some sweets to give the little prince, which the queen would usually take away unless he hid them well.

Bridget reappeared and held the inner door open for him. "Your Highness, the queen will see you now."

Aster stepped through the door into his mother's bedchamber. As usual the air was filled with the light scent of roses. His mother stood by one of the tall windows. She was still dressed in her ball gown. As Aster approached he noticed the queen held a lace handkerchief clutched in one hand. Several others sat crumpled on the table beside her.

"Your Majesty." Aster curtsied as low as he could. There was no way he would ever match one of Penelope's performances, but he was willing to give it a try.

The queen turned to face him and Aster gasped. His mother's eyes were red and puffy. Tracks of tears smeared her makeup. The wan smile she gave him looked strained and fake.

"What is wrong, your Majesty?"

"I apologize for my appearance, Princess Astrid, and I'm sorry the ball ended so abruptly. I've received some very bad news this evening. My son..." The queen faltered and leaned back against the table, lowering her head.

Without thinking Aster stepped forward and took his mother's arm. He steadied her and, after dabbing her eyes with the handkerchief a few times, she stood on her own once more.

"I've just learned that my precious son is dead."

The blood drained from Aster's face. His knees went weak and he thought he too would need to be held up. Then, just as quickly, he stood bolt upright. *Wait just a minute, I'm not dead!*

"Your Majesty, what makes you think such a terrible thing has happened?"

The queen continued to dab at her eyes with the handkerchief. "Aster left Drakenshold about six weeks ago with a little friend of his—a stable boy, I think. That's not unusual, Aster loves to go on hunting trips by himself, but he usually returns after a week or two. The king sent out search parties three weeks ago and until tonight we'd had no word from them."

Aster was confused. Mandoline had been in Traders Run four weeks ago and he'd have had to leave Castlekeep at least a week before that. The queen wiped her nose and continued.

"One of the king's advisors returned earlier today with the sad news. My darling Aster loved to climb things. He was always up a tree or hanging off a wall somewhere. They think he fell trying to climb the Misty Mountain. They found his broken body in a ravine."

The queen wept openly now. Had Aster been himself he might have tried to comfort her, but as it was all he could do was present himself for her to wrap her arms around and let the queen cry into his hair.

"You must not cry so, your Majesty. The king's advisor could be mistaken. The body might not be your son's."

His mother shook her head and separated from him long enough to reach behind her and lift a box from the table. "No, when they found him, he was wearing this. My sister Winifred gave it to him for his birthday."

She opened the box and inside were the torn and bloodied remains of a silk coat. The same silk coat Aster had packed the night he left the castle. The one he made Paul wear when they first arrived in Traders Run. The one Paul was still wearing when he disappeared on their way to the Misty Mountain.

"P-perhaps it wasn't your son. Maybe someone else was wearing his coat when they fell. A bandit, maybe, or that stable boy?"

The queen shook her head. "No, I wish that were possible, but I've seen his body. His beautiful blond hair. His gorgeous blue eyes. His sweet face crushed..." She paused to sniff loudly, her body wracked by a sudden tremor, and then she slumped against the table once more. "It was my son. I would know him no matter what."

Aster choked back a sob of his own. He backed away from his mother just as the sound of loud knocking came from the sitting room. He heard Bridget opening the door and soft deep voices coming from beyond. He had to do something right now, before this farce went any further.

"I have something very important to tell you, your Majesty. Your son is not dead, he's right here in..."

The door behind him opened and he turned to see Captain Landings of the royal guard stepping into the room, followed by Captain Griffin. Behind them he could also see Maggie standing in the middle of the sitting room with a perplexed look on her face.

Captain Landings dropped to one knee. "Your Majesty, the king has ordered Princess Astrid be brought to his council chambers at once."

Aster looked at the queen and shook his head. He'd been so close to telling her the truth, he had to finish telling her who he really was.

The queen took a deep breath and let it out slowly. "May we have a moment longer, Captain?"

"The king was quite insistent, your Majesty. He wants to see the princess right now."

The queen looked from Aster to the guardsman to Captain Griffin and back again, a jumble of conflicting emotions flashing across her face. When her eyes finally settled on Aster, there were still tears in them, but also a glint of hope. "You should go now. We can talk again later."

Aster curtsied, gave his mother one last wan smile, then turned and followed the two men out of his mother's room. As he passed Maggie he silently asked her what was going on, but she just shrugged and walked with him out into the hallway.

32

The Reward

Aster stood before the door of his father's council chambers and for the first time in his life waited to be announced before entering. There seemed to be a larger number of guardsmen milling about the castle and an entire squad of them flanked this door alone. He didn't understand what was going on, but all the answers were probably waiting for him on the other side of that door.

The door opened and Aster walked into the council chamber, followed by Captain Griffin. Captain Landings had led Maggie off to their room directly from the queen's chambers. The council room was empty except for his father, sitting alone at the far end of the long table, and the guard who closed the door behind them, but remained just inside as if to block the exit.

The king looked up from the papers he was reading, but did not rise. "Please forgive the lateness of the hour, Princess. I thought you might still be at the ball. Did you enjoy yourself?"

"I didn't stay very long. I'm not fond of dancing."

"So I was informed. I was also told you were just with the queen in her chambers. She must have told you what a sad day this is for our family and for the Kingdom of Caledon."

"She told me the prince had been found dead. It must have come as quite a shock." It had certainly been a shock to Aster.

248

"Indeed, but we shall all mourn his passing tomorrow. This evening I wish to speak to you of something more sanguine. I've had the opportunity to discuss your proposal for a peace treaty with one of my most trusted advisors. We're just waiting for him to return now with the details. I believe you'll be most excited by what we have to propose."

"Your Majesty?" Aster bowed his head to the king, but he was confused as to what details needed to be worked out. If the crown agreed not to attack Mandrake, he would leave Caledon. It was that simple. Then Aster could return home, as himself this time, and put an end to this silly rumor that he was dead.

There was a knock at the door and the guard opened it. Aster turned in time to see Mandoline march through the door. The old sorcerer didn't even glance at Aster as he headed around the table. He laid a parchment before the king and then took up his usual position behind the king's left shoulder.

Mandoline crossed his arms over his chest and then looked at Aster for the first time. Their gazes locked and Aster knew in that instant that, whatever the sorcerer and his father had cooked up, he wasn't going to like it.

The king read through the document the old wizard had brought him. "Excellent, this will do nicely. Princess Astrid, I would like you to meet my chief adviser and court sorcerer, Mandoline."

"Charmed, your Highness." Mandoline did little more than bow his head. "We nearly met in Traders Run. Had I not been in such a hurry that day, I might have actually witnessed your amazing defeat of the dragon."

"Indeed, Lord Sorcerer? That would have been a treat."

Did Mandoline find Paul's body? Surely he'd be able to tell it wasn't me. So why'd he tell my mother I was dead? And why is my father smiling?

"So, after conferring with Mandoline, I have decided to formally make peace with your dragon."

"That's wonderful news, your Majesty. Thank you. Mandrake will be excited to know that I can take him home now without any interference."

Mandoline raised an eyebrow. "The trip into the Eastern Mountains is a long and arduous one, is it not, your Highness? Our recent tragedy also shows just how dangerous it can be."

"Yes, it can be dangerous, but I've made it safely through before and I'm not afraid to do it again."

"Of course you're not afraid." The king chuckled. "But what if you didn't have to make the trip at all?"

"Your Majesty, I don't believe Mandrake would fly through the Misty Mountain unless I first showed him the way." Aster had other reasons for wanting to return to the Valley of Wind, but he didn't think it wise to share those reasons with his father while Mandoline was in the room.

"Yes, but what if he didn't need to fly through the mountains at all? What if his home were right here in Caledon?"

"Your Majesty?"

The king lifted the parchment from the table. "This day I have decreed that Mandrake, the Dragon Lord, has been made a subject of this Kingdom. He is to be granted arms and given such lands from the royal hunting reserve as to provide for his needs. How does that sound?"

"That's a very generous offer, your Majesty, but impractical. While I'm sure Mandrake will give it a great deal of consideration, he's sworn to follow me back to the Eastern Empire. He may not have a choice in the matter." Aster actually thought the dragon would snort and laugh at the idea of living in Caledon, but didn't say as much.

The king glanced over his shoulder, deferring to Mandoline. "We considered this, which is why the decree has a second provision."

The king nodded. "With the sad news that my son will not be returning to us, the Kingdom has lost some of its hope for the future. The queen and I would certainly find Drakenshold an emptier and colder place without his youthful exuberance. However, from this tragedy springs both hope for Caledon and a solution to this problem."

Aster felt Captain Griffin's muscles tighten as the big man discretely touched his back. He obviously didn't like the direction this was going any more than Aster did.

"Therefore, my dear, it is with much joy that I decree your adoption into the royal family of Caledon. From this day forward you shall be my daughter. Of course, being a woman, you would not be in line to inherit the throne, but I'm quite certain Constance will find a suitable young man for you to marry right away. One day he'll rule the Four Kingdoms by your side."

"I-I'm stunned, your Majesty. Such an offer...I'll need some time to think about it before I can give you my answer."

Mandoline coughed into his hand. "That will not be necessary, your Highness. The king has already signed the decree and I have ordered the proclamation be heralded throughout the kingdom. Your elevation ceremony will take place tomorrow."

Aster stared blankly at Mandoline. This was all his doing, surely, but to what end? His father had said he would rule the Four Kingdoms. What exactly did they have in mind?

"So you see, you have nothing to worry about. Both you and the dragon will live here in peace for the rest of your lives. You'll instruct the dragon on when and where to go, and together we will share our newfound peace with the other kingdoms."

"But surely, I have some say in this. I'm honored that you wish to make me your daughter, but I really must return to the Eastern Empire. I have the right to make my own decisions."

Mandoline smiled for the first time, and it was not a pleasant smile. "Do not be so naive, your Highness. You're a woman and you have no such right. Only your father has the right to deny the king's decree. Tell us where to find him and we shall summon him forth. Otherwise, consider yourself lucky to be spending the rest of your life inside this castle."

Aster knew in an instant that this was exactly what they had in mind. He was a prisoner. They would keep him here, use him to control Mandrake, and then use Mandrake to attack and subjugate the other Kingdoms. He also knew exactly what he must do next. He smiled as sweetly as he knew how.

"Then I accept your Majesty's kind offer. What would you have me do, *Father?*"

The king smiled broadly and for an instant Aster saw in his eyes the love he'd not seen there since returning home. "You must be tired from all this excitement. Go back to your rooms and get a good night's sleep. Tomorrow will be a very busy day."

Aster curtsied and with one last calculated glance at Mandoline he turned and walked through the door with Captain Griffin at his side. As they passed, the squad of guardsmen outside the door fell into step behind them.

Captain Griffin spoke in a low tone, never looking down at Aster. "The king no more believes you are dead than I do."

"What makes you say that?"

"No man, even though he may hate and despise him, would dismiss the news of his only son's death so callously."

"Do you think he knows who I am?"

"That I cannot say, but they intend never to let you or the Empress Sword out of this castle again."

Aster lowered his head and stared at the floor as they walked. "Yes, I know."

"What are your orders, your Highness?"

"Orders, Captain? Are you not still in the service of my father?"

Marcus finally looked down, his face a mask of grim determination. "I left the king's service ten years ago, but I entered your service the day the dragon, who had just bested me, bowed at your feet. What would you have me do?"

Aster smiled up at the captain. He'd been hoping the big man would say something to that effect. "What I would have you do, Marcus, is gather up your daughter and your belongings and return them to your trader's wagon. Prepare to leave Castlekeep as quickly as you can."

Captain Griffin nodded. "And what would you have me tell Eric?"

"Tell my trusty knight that I release him from my service, just long enough for him to take up a new trade."

"A new trade? Just what might that be, lass?"

Aster smiled. "I think Eric would make a splendid horse thief, don't you?"

Aster stared down into the blackness. The moon had set several hours before and the great sea wall of Drakenshold was all but invisible below him. The darkness was going to turn an otherwise easy climb into something far more dangerous.

When he and Captain Griffin returned to the guest rooms, they filled in Maggie on what they wanted her to do. She'd gone with her father to help pack their things and returned with a pair of Eric's pants. Maggie quickly shortened them for Aster. She also cutoff an underdress to shirt length and removed the skirts from the bodice of the red dress he was wearing.

He helped her pack her own things and then said goodbye to her in the hallway as though he never expected to see his lady in waiting again. As he expected, the guards outside the room locked the doors behind him and he could still hear them pacing outside an hour later.

He swung his legs out the window and turned around, searching for a foothold with his toes. He immediately wished he had on a good fitting pair of boots rather than the linen slippers he'd been wearing all day. He found a toehold and then let go of the windowsill.

He worked his way north along the wall, hoping to cross the familiar pathway leading down from his own room one story up. When he found it, he flirted with the notion of climbing up to his room, but he couldn't risk the chance that Mandoline had stationed guards there as well.

He also couldn't risk using the same way out he'd taken before. There were bound to be more guards about the castle, looking for just such an escape attempt. Instead he was going to try and find his way to the northwest battlement. He'd once found a way down to the cliff face there.

It took nearly an hour, but as soon as he was off the wall he worked his way along the cliff to a place where the castle diverged from it. There he was able to climb back up onto level ground. Brushing himself off, he glanced up into the darkness at the battlements. When he was certain no one was looking down at him, he moved away from the wall and into the small greenery overlooking the sea.

It didn't take long to find the path leading to the old oak tree that was the park's defining feature. How it had flourished for centuries in the shadow of Drakenshold no one could say, but it was the one landmark Aster was sure Eric could find.

There, he found Troy tied to a bench and grazing on the grass. He hugged his horse, then untied him and led him out to the street. He mounted up and rode first north and then east, taking the long way through the narrow side streets to avoid being seen from the castle. He caught up with the Griffins' wagon on the King's Road about an hour later.

"It's about time." Captain Griffin said, drawing the wagon to a stop. "I was beginning to worry you weren't going to join us after all."

Aster grinned, though he supposed it was too dark for his friends to see. "Drakenshold is supposed to be impossible to get into. That makes it just a little harder to get out of. Where's Eric?"

"I sent him on ahead to scout a place for us to leave the road. It won't take long for them to come looking for you once they realize you've gone. The sooner we get off the road, the harder it'll be for them to find us."

"Thank you, Marcus. It's good having you in charge."

"And what about the one who did all the packing, made you some clothes and lied our way out of the castle for you?"

"Thank you, Maggie. I just don't know what I would do without my lady in waiting." Aster sighed. If he were to tell the truth, he didn't know what he would do without any of them.

The Ambush

They met Eric less than a league down the road. He was standing by a gate set in an old wooden fence, holding a lantern, and grinning from ear to ear. The young huntsman opened the gate and directed them through. As Aster rode past, Eric reached out and touched his leg.

"Did I steal the right horse, your Highness?"

"You did indeed, Sir Eric. You may now add royal thief to your long list of accomplishments." Aster giggled, because he fully expected the young man to do just that.

They followed an old rutted path through the grassy field where sleeping cows paid them little attention. Finally they came to the edge of a forest where Eric had already removed the rails from one section of fence. Beyond it an overgrown path, just wide enough for the wagon, disappeared into the trees. Aster helped Eric replace the rails and then they set off, letting the dark forest swallow them up.

They stopped to rest the horses by a stream about an hour later.

"It won't be daylight for a few more hours." Captain Griffin was staring up at the sky through the canopy of leaves. "We shouldn't stop tonight or tomorrow either. Maggie, you and Astrid try to get some sleep in the wagon. Eric and I will switch with you in the morning."

Aster frowned. "I'm not tired."

The big man grinned. "Of course not, what could be tiring about climbing down the walls of Drakenshold in the middle of the night? We need you to be sharp and alert tomorrow, lass. You'll best know if we're being followed and you have enough hunting skills to keep us on the path."

Maggie giggled. "He's got a point. I can get lost in a garden."

"All right, but wake me right away if anything happens."

"Of course, your Highness."

Captain Griffin bowed and Aster got a good look at the big man's eyes. They were twinkling in the lamplight with a fire Aster had not seen there before. It was the kind of fire he remembered seeing in the eyes of guardsmen whenever they were exercising their skills. Captain Griffin was a born leader and now he had a company to lead once more.

They tethered Troy's reins to the back of the wagon, then Maggie crawled inside, followed by Aster. He was afraid he wouldn't be able to rest, being so close to Maggie, but within minutes the rocking motion of the wagon had put them both to sleep with Aster wrapped protectively in Maggie's arms.

They awoke to the sound of banging, as crates and boxes fell on them. The wagon was shaking and jumping from side to side. Maggie half crawled, half stumbled to the front and opened the little door behind the driver's seat.

"Daddy? What's going on?"

"We were followed, Pumpkin. Get back inside!"

Aster saw the captain crack the reins and the wagon lurched forward again, throwing Maggie to the floor. Aster stuck his head out the back and in the darkness could just see Troy trotting along to keep up. He freed the horse's reins and then whistled.

"To me!"

When the horse closed on the wagon Aster leapt, grabbing Troy around the neck and hauling himself into the saddle. Only as an afterthought did he think to make sure the Empress Sword was still on his back. It had become such a part of him that he only sensed it when it wasn't there.

He urged his horse past the wagon and caught up with Eric on Nightstorm.

"What's going on?"

"What's going on, your Highness? There's a patrol on the path behind us. I have no idea how they could have found us so quickly. We're making for the river. There's a shallow ford ahead and several different paths branch off on the other side. We'll lose them there for sure."

"Astrid!" Aster looked back at the wagon where Captain Griffin was waving and pointing ahead. "Ride on without us!"

"No! I won't leave you all behind!"

"They don't want us, lass! They only want you! Now go!"

It felt wrong, but it made good sense. Aster urged Troy forward into the darkness. They raced along, leaves and small branches slapping at their sides. Aster only hoped no low-hanging branches lay across the path. The rickety sound of the wagon fell away behind him and soon all he could hear were Troy's hoofbeats.

Then he heard horns. Somewhere in the distance a hunting horn blew. He couldn't tell if it was behind or in front of him, but almost immediately another sounded, and then another. Ahead, the path turned to the right and for just a second he thought he saw a light flare in that direction, but when he looked again he saw nothing.

Troy took the turn at a trot and broke out into a large clearing. Instantly fires flamed to life all around them and Troy reared up at the sudden blinding light. Aster tried to hold on, but his legs simply weren't long enough to hold him in place. He slipped from the saddle and landed hard on the ground.

He rolled with the fall and got to his feet as soon as he stopped. Small bonfires burned every few yards around the edge of the clearing. Standing next to each one was a royal guardsman holding a small torch. In the middle of the roadway, blocking his path, stood Mandoline.

"Welcome, your Highness. We've been waiting for you. As usual, your entrance was well worth the wait."

Aster squared his shoulders and dusted himself off. He noticed one of the guardsmen catching Troy's reins and drawing the horse quickly, if not easily, off into the surrounding woods. He took a few staggering steps towards Mandoline, then paused to let his head stop swimming.

"No, please, allow me." Mandoline walked slowly towards him. "You've come all this way, and it's long past your bedtime, you must be tired."

"What do you want? How did you find me?"

"Finding you was the easy part, and you know what I want. The Empress Sword must not leave Caledon."

"You want my sword?" Aster reached back and pulled Kai from her scabbard. Around the clearing, all the guardsmen drew their swords as well. He slowed his movements and then presented the sword, hilt first, to the sorcerer.

Mandoline looked down at it, then up at Aster, then he threw back his head and laughed. "Do you think I'm a complete fool, Aster? Oh yes, I know who you really are. I would have discovered it much sooner if that idiot of a sheriff in Traders Run had introduced me to this gentleman right away."

Mandoline motioned with his hand and a dark figure emerged from the shadows. Thaddeus Markham walked into the light of one of the fires grinning like a fool. In his outstretched hand he held a tracking medallion just like the one Captain Griffin had taken from him.

Aster crossed his eyes and stared at the tiny jewel dangling above his nose. *If I ever get out of this, I'm going to smash that thing into tiny pieces.*

"So, you had more than one medallion?"

"Quite so, Miss. I'm not always so lucky in getting them back and the Greylands wizard who makes them for me gives a quantity discount to his best customers. You should have sold me the sword when you had the chance."

Aster held up the Empress Sword and pointed it at the little man.

"That would have only brought her wrath upon you sooner. I trust you enjoyed your little encounter?"

Thaddeus paled noticeably and backed away from the sword. "I most certainly did not! That thing's pure evil. I never felt such pain in my whole life. Why, if the Lord Sorcerer here hadn't paid me to find you, I wouldn't a come within a league of that damned thing."

Mandoline chuckled. "A prime example of what I was telling you, Aster. Fooling around with such powerful magic can leave a lasting impression on a man, if it doesn't kill him outright. I told you that so you wouldn't do anything too foolish when you found it."

Aster remembered the queen telling him that search parties were sent out looking for him a week after he'd seen Mandoline in Traders Run. "Wait, you came looking for me right away. You asked Eric if I'd gone to the Misty Mountain. You must have known I was looking for the sword."

"Know it? My boy, I'm the one who sent you off to find it. Do you think I left ten years of my painstaking research laying out on that worktable just so you could find it by chance? Not only did I know you'd sneak into my study, I've spent years equipping you with all the knowledge necessary to puzzle out the mystery of the sword once you did. I also made certain you had all the skills and knowledge needed to find the lost empire and return the sword to me. Of course I never expected you to return looking like this."

Aster snorted "Your painstaking research failed to mention that the sword doesn't like men."

Mandoline raised an eyebrow. "No, you failed to read everything I left out for you. You've always been too impatient for your own good. It wasn't too hard to figure out what had happened once I got back to Traders Run and heard all about your exploits there. Then I met Mr. Markham here and he led me right back to Castlekeep."

"If you knew who I was, why did you tell my parents I was dead?"

"Because as the prince you were the perfect pawn to find the Empress Sword and bring it back, but I would no sooner entrust its use to you now than I would hand a butcher knife to a baby. You were the one who presented the king and queen with a princess, I just gave them a dead prince."

"You must have known that body wasn't mine. What possible reason could you have for pretending it was?"

"Your untimely death seemed the best way to persuade the queen to accept a foreign-born princess as her daughter. I would have found some other way to convince her you were dead, but finding the stable boy's body made it so much easier. Someday you'll have to tell me about the transformation spells on his hair and eyes. Potions? Never mind, the details are unimportant. What matters is your mother believed it."

"And my father? He believed it too?"

"No, silly boy, I told the king who you really were as soon as I found out what you were up to. A treaty with the dragon, how perfectly like you. I needed your father to understand the opportunity this opens up for us. It's so much better than what we had planned."

"Planned? What do you mean? How long has my father known about this?"

"Since the dragon first appeared in Caledon, of course. There was only so much I could do personally to mold your character. I convinced the king it was in the best interest of the kingdom for you grow into something a bit more like those storybook heroes of yours than a real prince. For example: what is the most important attribute of a good king?"

Aster didn't even need to think before answering. "A king must be willing to sacrifice his life for his people. Everyone knows that."

"No they don't. Real kings don't sacrifice themselves for anyone. That's what armies and knights are for. However, I had to make certain you would be willing to give up your life to bring back the Empress Sword. With my guidance—and some carefully selected reading material—your father's been filling your head with that nonsense since you were old enough to talk."

Aster felt dizzy, beads of sweat broke out on his brow, and his knees threatened to collapse beneath him, "I don't believe you! My father wouldn't do that!"

"Think what you like, but ask yourself this: just how much influence could even the Lord Sorcerer have over your upbringing without the king's consent? Mind you, at first he didn't like the idea, since there was a good chance you'd die trying to find the sword, but I managed to convince him it was an unfortunate necessity, if the kingdom were to survive."

Aster shook his head in disbelief. "This is nonsense! My father would never agree to something like that. For one thing, I'm his only heir."

Mandoline sneered at him. "I have to admit that it was unfortunate when Queen Constance failed to produce a second heir, but you do have plenty of cousins. Any one of them would happily take your place on the throne. That was actually a sore point between the king and I for many years, but when I discovered the sword's aversion to men, the answer became far simpler."

That took Aster by surprise; to his mind, Kai's aversion to men had cost him dearly. "How so?"

"As king, you would never be able to use the sword yourself. I figured you'd find some little commoner like that guardsman's daughter to carry it back for you. Frankly the notion of turning you into a girl never occurred to me—quite clever, that. No, I decided to groom a young noblewoman to use the sword in your stead. By marrying you off to her, we'd solve both problems."

After years of his schooling, Aster was familiar with how Mandoline's mind worked, and he could see where this leading. "So you were always planning to use the Empress Sword to subjugate the dragon—not to kill him. Then you intended to use Mandrake to conquer the other kingdoms just like the Empress did a thousand years ago. But when I showed up looking like this, you had to change your plans. You couldn't marry me off to this "princess" of yours, but you were all ready to marry me off to some boy and make him king."

"Yes, all I had to do was make a few minor changes to the marriage papers we already had drawn up. I threw in the lordship for the dragon and the adoption was the king's idea. He's a sentimental fool, but he can be quite useful at times. Now come along, Aster. If you're a good little girl I might even let you pick your own husband."

"I'm not going back with you, Mandoline. If you force me, I'll just escape again. And you said so yourself, you can't take the sword away from me."

"No, I can't, but I brought along someone who can."

Mandoline raised a hand and waved it forward. A short figure dressed in white stepped out from behind him. It appeared to be a young man, blond like most of the nobles in Caledon, and wrapped in a white cloak. The boy reached up and undid the clasp at his neck, shrugging his shoulders and allowing the cloak to drop to the ground.

Beneath the cloak he was clad in white leather armor with dark epaulettes. The bright gold fastenings and bejeweled buttons sparkled in the light from all the fires. At his hip was a full broadsword in a jewel-encrusted scabbard.

With a sinking feeling in his gut Aster recognized the armor as his own, and when the figure drew closer he recognized it too.

"Penelope."

34
The Sword Fight

enelope stepped towards Aster, stopping just out of reach, and looked him up and down with a disapproving scowl. "You've become such a scrawny little thing, haven't you, cousin? And not very pretty, either. What's with those eyes? They make you look so...common."

Aster watched with growing dread as Penelope drew her sword—his sword—in one smooth, practiced motion. Unlike the Empress Sword, Aster's ceremonial sword was a full length broadsword and Penelope was tall enough to draw it from her hip.

"Why are you wearing my armor, Penny?"

"You have no use for it anymore. As far as Aunt Constance is concerned, her son is dead. Since I'm the next in line for the throne, this lovely ensemble would have come to me eventually anyway. Mandoline simply thought I might like to have it a bit sooner."

Aster snorted. "You're not in line for the throne. You're a girl!"

"Look who's talking? Under normal circumstances I would have to agree with you, but the situation is hardly normal. Once you give me the Empress Sword and I use it to slay the dragon you were too cowardly to kill, the king will surely forego normal protocol and name whoever I choose to marry as his successor."

"What makes you think I'm just going to give you the sword? If you want it, you're going to have to take it from me." Aster raised the Empress Sword into an *en garde* position and murmured to it, hoping Kai would respond. "If there's anything you can do to help me, now would be a good time."

A small burst of magical energy flared from the hilt of the sword. A dim blue white glow traveled up the length of the blade and then quietly dissipated into the air. Aster rolled his eyes and sighed. "Oh great! Thanks a bunch!"

Penelope laughed. "Very impressive. I shall have to remember that little parlor trick when I take the sword away from you. And I *will* take it from you, Aster. I'm a head taller and I have a longer reach than you."

Aster knew she was right. He studied her stance and realized she must have taken lessons from the same swordsmaster who taught him. Master Drayman had ground that same posture into him so often he felt he must sleep in it sometimes. But the old swordsmaster was not Aster's only teacher.

The things he'd learned from the guards at the garrison house didn't come from the world of polite fencing. He'd need every dirty trick he knew to keep this blonde harpy from running him through. Still, even if her swordsmanship wasn't up to his level, she had him at such a physical disadvantage it probably wouldn't matter in the end.

Penelope sneered gleefully. "It's not my reach that's going to let me win against you, though. Oh no, I'll beat you into the ground and you'll never even touch me. Do you want to know why? It's because you're nothing but a mama's boy. The goody-goody Prince of Caledon. Everyone knows you'd rather die than strike a girl."

It was true. He'd been taught never to raise his hand against a woman, any woman. But he'd also just been told that everything he'd ever learned might be a lie. Here he stood wearing the remnants of a dress, facing off against a girl wearing a young man's armor. His world had been turned upside down more than once lately, and so far he'd managed to adapt to every change.

Suddenly, Maggie's words popped into his head. *It doesn't matter if you're a boy or a girl. It's what's in your heart that counts.*

In his heart, he knew Penelope would misuse the sword's power. With it, she would kill every last dragon that crossed her path, destroying an entire race in the process. He couldn't allow that to happen.

He adjusted his grip, raised the Empress Sword above his right shoulder and, with a wicked grin of his own, he charged. "Don't bet on it, *Prince* Penny."

He charged at her the same way he'd charged Mandrake, but without the reckless abandon. This time, he had a plan. He hoped to take Penelope by surprise and get briefly inside her defenses. Rather than run her through, he'd try to bring the flat of his blade smashing down on her wrist, hopefully breaking her grip on the broadsword.

It might have worked against a boy, but Penelope's gut reaction to the attack was to bring her hands up to guard her face. The broadsword came up with them and she managed to parry his downward blow with it.

Aster rolled away from Penelope's counter strike and got behind her. With her blonde hair tied in a ponytail at the base of her neck she looked just like a boy in armor. It helped him to forget he was fighting a girl as he adjusted his grip for another attack.

Penelope rounded on him, her eyes ablaze with anger. "Why you little..." She lunged at him, her blade coming up and making contact with the tip of his sword. The force behind the thrust surprised him and the Empress Sword went sailing over his head. It was all he could do to hold onto it as he staggered backwards, away from Penelope's next thrust.

He danced back, constantly evading the flurry of crisscrossing slashes. Penelope seemed to be standing miles away from him and it was impossible to parry the blows raining down on him out of the dark. He began circling to the left, away from her more forceful blows, and that slowed Penelope's advance.

She stopped swinging and grinned at him, but he could see she was already winded. She taunted him in ragged short spurts. "I hope you—realize—there's no place—for you—to run."

"Who's running?" Aster charged at her again, parrying away her sword at the last minute and throwing his shoulder into her rib cage. He heard the wind blow out of her as he slipped past, but she didn't go down. Instead, Penelope spun around as he bounded away, and swung out at him.

Aster felt the tip of her blade rip easily through the brocade of his bodice and slice into his left shoulder. He staggered away and managed to come around, raising his sword. The pain tore through him like a ripsaw and he wanted to fall to his knees and scream, but Penelope was already charging at him again.

Sometimes the ground can be your best friend.

That advice hadn't made much sense when it had been taught to him at eight years of age, but he'd enjoyed tumbling around the practice field with the guardsmen that day. Now with his left arm out of commission and an enraged opponent coming at him with a broadsword held high above her head, he finally understood what it meant.

He gave in to the desire to fall down and dove right under Penelope's *coup de grâce*. He hit the ground rolling and barreled through the girl's legs. Penelope went flying and Aster curled into a ball from the pain of having dirt ground into his wound.

He recovered as quickly as he could, staggering to his feet and circling wildly trying to catch a glimpse of his cousin. He was crying uncontrollably now and his eyes were blurry from the tears, but he couldn't make them stop. They streamed down his cheeks and ran into the corners of his mouth where their saltiness mixed with the taste of dirt.

He saw a blurry white form rise up from the ground a few yards away and advanced on it. His left arm wasn't moving so he wiped at his face with the sleeve of his sword hand. As his vision cleared he discovered Penelope, standing unarmed and frantically looking around for her sword. He quickly followed her lead.

Both their eyes locked on the broadsword at the same moment. Penelope dove for it, but Aster got there first. He slammed his foot down on the blade just as her hand closed on the hilt. She screamed in pain as her fingertips were smashed into the hard soil. She rolled away and Aster slid the broadsword in the opposite direction with a flick of his toe.

As Penelope lay there, clutching her crushed fingers, he pointed the Empress Sword at her throat.

"Yield, Penelope. For heaven's sake, just yield and get this over with."

Penelope looked up at the blade hovering just above her chin and scowled. He tapped her cheek with the point just hard enough to remind her who was in charge now. Her glower faded and her eyes filled with fear. She was just about to open her mouth when the air rang with the sound of steel against steel and the Empress Sword went flying from Aster's hand.

Aster found himself staring down the dark blackened blade of an ancient broadsword pointing at his own neck. He followed its length upwards to gaze speechlessly into Mandoline's stern face.

The old sorcerer made a growling noise. "Enough of this foolishness! Don't move. Your mother already believes you dead. Don't make me bring her a second body."

The old man glanced down to where Penelope still lay on the ground, just as stunned as Aster by the sudden turn of events.

"You disappoint me, Lady Penelope. I'd hoped to give you this one moment of glory, but I'm beginning to lose patience with your incompetence. Now, stand up and stop sniveling."

Penelope got to her feet still rubbing at her sore fingers. She started to say something to Mandoline, but then looked away.

She turned instead to Aster, hate filling her eyes again. Self-consciously, she stopped rubbing her hand and looked him straight in the eye.

"You cheated. You wouldn't fight me properly, so you forfeit and I claim the match. The Empress Sword and Caledon are mine."

Aster shook his head. "Don't do this, Penny. Let me take the sword back where it belongs. You can have the throne for all I care, but..."

Penelope slapped him so hard across the cheek that he fell to the ground. Then she squared her shoulders, turned and marched dramatically to where the Empress Sword had fallen. She bent down and lifted it by the hilt, holding it aloft for everyone to see.

The clearing suddenly erupted in a swirling cloud of dust and Aster's ears were pierced by a harsh, high-pitched screech. Aster tried to cover his face with his good arm, but couldn't keep the dust from stinging his eyes. He looked up through the churning maelstrom and saw a massive shape looming in the air above them.

"Mandrake?" Aster shouted and was answered with another thundering cry from the dragon. "What are you doing here? Get away!"

Around the clearing, guardsmen began to fall back. Mandrake was circling in the air above them, shrieking and snapping at them fiercely. One by one they abandoned their posts and ran off into the woods. Penelope stood directly below the dragon, rooted in place with a look of shock and terror on her face.

Mandoline gazed up at the hovering dragon and then at the stunned girl. "Use the sword! Slay the dragon with it!"

Penelope came to her senses and raised the Empress Sword, pointing it at Mandrake. "Hold, foul dragon! I am Lady Penelope Winthrop of Caledon. Prepare to meet your doom!"

To Aster's horror, the sword blazed to life, glowing white hot in his cousin's hand. Mandrake fell back momentarily, but held his ground as the sword's power increased. A crack of thunder so strong it shook the ground ripped the air, and a bolt of pure white energy shot straight up from the sword into the sky.

Then the full power of the sword flared out, engulfing Mandrake from head to tail in its golden glow. The dragon screeched, arching his back and throwing his head into the air. Aster screamed and tried to run forward, but he couldn't move. And above it all, he could hear Penelope laughing.

The Final Battle

Aster watched in horror as the Empress Sword's magic engulfed Mandrake. The weapon channeled inconceivable amounts of power from the heavens above straight into the dragon, and Penelope continued laughing hysterically. At any moment, Aster expected to see Mandrake's wings stop moving. He wasn't sure what would happen after that. Either the magic would hold Mandrake suspended like a puppet above the clearing, or it would drop him crashing to the ground.

Aster still couldn't move. He seemed rooted in place while wave after wave of magical energy rippled out from the sword and passed through him. Oddly, the searing pain in his shoulder had all but stopped as his anxiety over Mandrake's situation grew.

It seemed to be taking a very long time. On the hill outside Traders Run, Mandrake had been stopped instantly after the sword flared in Aster's hand, but now the dragon's wings continued to beat. If anything, they were beating faster and more regularly than before.

Then Aster heard Mandoline shouting. "This is all wrong!"

The old man might be right. This doesn't feel the same as before.

The color, texture and sheer quantity of energy flowing into and out of the sword was different. Mandrake continued to hover above Penelope, apparently unaffected by it, and he was no longer favoring his left shoulder.

269

Then Aster noticed the wound in the dragon's chest beginning to fade. Where it had been swollen and inflamed just moments before, it now appeared to be healing right before his eyes. The damaged scales around the area closed in over the wound and appeared to mend themselves.

Mandrake suddenly extended his wings to their full breadth and raised his head high. He roared in a way Aster had never heard before, a low-pitched explosion of sound so full of power it shook the trees around him.

Then fire—not the pale blue dragon fire Aster had seen before, but a golden-colored fire—erupted from the dragon's mouth and shot high into the sky. Aster sucked in a breath. He suddenly remembered where he had seen this exact same thing before.

Embroidered into the back of the Empress's throne. A mighty dragon, filled with grace and power, proclaiming his mastery over all things by breathing golden fire into the sky.

She knew! The Empress knew this would happen!

"Mandrake!" Aster laughed and shouted as loud as he could.

In answer the dragon roared again. Below him, Penelope threw down the Empress Sword, but it did not stop channeling power. She turned and ran away from it, stumbling and falling. She curled into a fetal ball below the glowing dragon and didn't move.

"The sword, you stupid girl! Go back for the sword!"

Aster watched as an enraged Mandoline cast away his own sword and raised his hands above his head. Magic coursed up from the ground, flowing through the old wizard's body and making his robes billow about him. The magic collected in the space between his hands and formed a great ball of churning green energy.

Tendrils of the magic arced out over Aster's head and struck Mandrake. The dragon roared in anger, then turned on the sorcerer. Golden fire erupted from his mouth, this time directed down at Mandoline, who countered with another blast of green lightning.

Aster flattened himself against the ground. Massive bolts of writhing power stretched out from the sorcerer's lightning ball to meet the dragon's fire and they exploded together in the air above him. He held his breath, waiting for either the searing flames or the crackling magic to roast him alive.

Suddenly he felt the familiar enveloping force that had protected him from the flames outside Traders Run surround him again. The inferno raged harmlessly above him and he no longer felt the heat of it on his back. The bubble of magic also kept him from being crushed beneath the firestorm, but it did not shield him from the horrendous noise.

He crawled toward the place where Penelope had dropped the Empress Sword. He was careful never to raise his head too high, lest it rise above the sword's protection. Eventually he reached the spot and grasped the sword.

"It is about time, former-boy."

"Sorry, I didn't want to get my head blown off."

"You do not trust me to protect you while standing up?"

"Oh, well...Sure. That is..." Embarrassed, he stood and the envelope of magic swelled with him, pushing the raging green and gold forces aside as if they barely existed. "What now?"

"I am a sword. Do you know how to use a sword?"

Aster smiled as he turned towards Mandoline. "Indeed I do."

He charged the sorcerer. Green lightning and golden fire parted before him like waves before the prow of a ship. He swung upwards, rising on the tips of his toes, catching the ball of magical energy just above the old man's head. It exploded on contact, sending Mandoline flying and leveling trees in every direction.

The quiet that followed was almost as frightening as the roar of the battle. Aster stood at the center of the clearing panting and drained; it was all he could do to remain on his feet. He watched Mandrake settle to the ground nearby. The dragon looked almost as shocked and befuddled as Aster felt.

He held up the Empress Sword and smiled. "Thank you, Kai."

"Finally, a bit of gratitude from the whelp."

Aster grinned as he sheathed the sword. He staggered towards Mandrake, who seemed preoccupied with blowing tiny blue fireballs into the air.

"What's wrong?"

"The gold fire is all gone. The feeling of power is gone, too. Did you know this would happen when you summoned me?"

Aster chuckled. "No. Kai doesn't tell me much about what she's planning. In fact, it seems no one has ever told me what's really going on. This probably won't be the end of it, either. We still have to get you to the Misty Mountain as quickly as possible. I just hope the others aren't hurt."

"What about him?"

Mandrake raised his leg, apparently completely healed now, and pointed to the figure dressed in white leather curled up on the ground nearby.

"Oh, no." Aster rushed to his cousin's side and knelt down beside her. He touched the girl's shoulder. "Penny, are you hurt?"

Penelope pulled away from his touch, rolling into an even tighter ball. "Go away! Make it go away! Make it go away!"

His cousin began whimpering softly and refused all of Aster's attempts to rouse her. He shook his head and stood back up, looking around for the old sorcerer. He spotted Mandoline's body amidst a pile of broken trees. Bending over it was Captain Griffin.

"Marcus!" In spite of his weariness, Aster broke into a run. He threw his arms around the big man and hugged him tightly. "Are you all right?"

"Aye, lass, no harm done." Captain Griffin laughed as he returned the hug and patted Aster lightly on the back. "Maggie's fine too, she's just bringing up the wagon."

"Did they catch you? I heard horns."

"They stopped us and searched the wagon right after you rode off. When they didn't find you they began blowing those damned horns. I thought they were going to hold us there all night, but then that ungodly racket started up and a whole squad of royal guardsmen came running down the trail past us—hightailing it back to Castlekeep, no doubt. I'm going to have to have a long chat with the king about the training of his guard."

Aster laughed. "You do that, the very next time we're in Castlekeep. Where's Eric?"

"I'm not sure. When you disappeared down the trail, he turned off of it. Haven't seen him since. I expect he'll turn up any minute with breakfast in tow."

Aster nodded in agreement. Then he remembered Mandoline's unmoving body at their feet. "What about, him? Is he…"

Captain Griffin crouched down next to the old man again. "He's alive, but from the look of this lump on his head he'll have one demon of a headache for about a week. Is this your doing?"

"Not really. I think all I did was break the seal on Mandoline's spell. The energy he'd built up in it was released on him all at once." Aster looked at the devastation all around the clearing and shuddered.

"You humans love to fool with forces you don't fully understand." Mandrake had crossed the clearing and was now standing near them. "Magic belongs in the Earth and the Sky, not in the hands of foolish old men."

"You looked like you were having fun using just a little bit of that magic yourself." Aster grinned up at the dragon.

"That was your doing, little Empress, not mine." He looked away for a moment and shuffled his foreclaws. "But it was fun."

Captain Griffin roared in laughter. Aster joined in and soon even Mandrake was chuckling.

"What's so funny?" Aster looked up to find Maggie sitting at the reins of the wagon just inside the clearing. The wagon looked somewhat worse for its race through the forest, but it was still in one piece.

"You all look a right sight, standing here laughing your fool heads off, with daylight no more than an hour away. Have you forgotten these woods might still be crawling with the king's soldiers?"

"You're quite right, Pumpkin. We should be going as soon as Eric shows up."

There was a rustling from the forest on the far side of the clearing and a black stallion picked its way carefully through the fallen trees. Another horse followed it, this one with a rider, and from behind the second horse stepped Eric.

"Did you lose your horse, your Highness? This fellow says you gave it to him, but I didn't really think you would do that, seeing's how you just had me steal it for you and all." He reached up and pulled the limp form of Thaddeus Markham from Troy's saddle. The little man fell into a heap on the ground.

"You didn't kill him, did you?"

Eric looked down at the little man. "Kill him? I might have, but the fool dashed off and struck his head on a low-hanging branch before I had the chance. He's been out cold ever since."

Aster walked across the clearing to have a closer look at the thief. As he passed Maggie she called out to him. "Astrid, whatever have you gone and done to your bodice? I could have put the skirts back on that dress for you."

Aster stopped and felt his shoulder and the long tear in the fabric. "I'm sorry. Penelope caught me with my own broadsword. You might be a little more concerned about me though, she sliced me pretty deep." Even as he said this, Aster noticed that his left arm was no longer limp and the pain, which had almost done him in, was now gone.

Captain Griffin caught up to him and examined his shoulder closely. "This looks like a sword cut, lass, but there's no sign of a wound here. Just a tiny scar."

Aster started to protest, but then spotted Mandrake, who rolled his own shoulder suggestively. "Maybe I just imagined it."

Maggie climbed down from the wagon to have a good look for herself. She poked at Aster's shoulder through the hole. "Did you say Penelope did this to you with your own broadsword? Lady Penelope? From the party?"

"Yes, that's her over there." Aster pointed to the white clad figure still curled up on the ground. "Mandoline knew what would happen to any man who touched the Empress Sword, so he brought Penelope along to take it away from me."

"Well it's a good thing she didn't get her hands on it." Maggie strode over and bent down to examine the girl. "I'd hate for a conniving witch like this to get her hands on your dragon."

Mandrake snorted and Aster sighed. "Maggie, he's not *my* dragon. He's not a pet or a slave. He's sworn to my service, but that doesn't mean I own him."

"Maggie?" Mandrake's voice rumbled through the clearing like thunder. Maggie stood up and turned to face the dragon towering over her. She was trembling, but whether out of fear or anger Aster couldn't tell.

Mandrake bowed his head and spoke more softly. "Ten years, four months and sixteen days ago I attacked the harbor village of Moonhaven. During that attack I set fire to a tavern. At the time I did not think humans would stay inside a burning building and try to put out the fires I started. Apparently that is what your mother tried to do. She died and I was responsible. For that I apologize."

Mandrake lowered his head to the ground before Maggie and rolled over on his back. Maggie hesitated for a moment and then walked slowly towards the dragon. She put her hand on his massive scaly neck, running her fingers over the rough, hardened surface. Then she balled her hand into a fist and began pounding on the scales as hard as she could.

Captain Griffin took a step towards her, but Aster stuck out his hand to stop him. "Leave her be. She needs to let this out."

Maggie screamed and pounded on Mandrake's neck with both hands, keening the loss of her mother in the only way she knew how. The dragon lay motionless, obviously unaffected by the blows, but allowing this tiny human to do as she wished. After several minutes, Maggie was spent. She collapsed, weeping on the dragon's neck.

Aster let Captain Griffin go to her then. The big man gathered his daughter up in his arms and carried her back to the wagon. Aster approached Mandrake, who was still sprawled on his back, gazing up at the brightening sky.

"Thank you. That was a very noble thing you did for Maggie."

"I didn't do it for her or for you. I did it for myself. I have much to atone for before I go to awaken my kind. I don't wish them to make the same mistakes I've made. This was but a start." He rolled over and stood up. "Besides, she's a friend of yours. It would be easier for all of us if we were not enemies."

Aster smiled. "You know, for a terrifying monster, you've got a pretty soft heart."

"Please don't spread that around. I have a reputation to maintain."

Aster shook his head and chuckled. He walked back to the wagon where Maggie was washing her face. She smiled up at him and he knew she would be all right, but he wondered just how he'd known that all she needed was a good cry.

He turned to Eric and Captain Griffin. "We should get moving. The soldiers will have regrouped by now."

"What about those three?" Eric swept his arm around indicating Mandoline, Thaddeus and Penelope.

Captain Griffin pulled at his chin. "The sorcerer and the thief are out cold, but there's no telling how long that'll last or what they'll do when they awaken. I suggest we tie them up just in case."

Aster nodded. "I agree. That just leaves Penelope."

Maggie wiped her face with a dry rag and joined them. "She's asleep as best I can tell. She looks like she's had an awful fright. I doubt she'll be coming anywhere near Mandrake again." Maggie actually smiled up at the dragon.

Aster smiled too, but it faded quickly as he began to assess their situation. "All right then, we'll just leave her to sleep it off. Let's make sure there are no weapons left in the clearing and then we'll get out of here. I'd like to be across the river and heading east as soon as possible."

Captain Griffin and Eric headed to the wagon for some rope

while Maggie went about collecting Mandoline and Penelope's swords. Aster turned to Mandrake.

"I'd like you to fly back towards Castlekeep and see how many guardsmen are actually following us. Don't let yourself be attacked and whatever you do don't attack anyone by yourself. We'll face them together, if we have to face them at all."

Mandrake nodded and then took off in a cloud of dust, quickly disappearing beyond the trees. Aster watched his friends busily doing what he'd asked them to do, and sighed.

This felt so right! This little band of friends, working together to help him get Mandrake home. It was really a shame that it was all going to end soon.

The Return Home

etween Captain Griffin's leadership, Eric's hunting skills and
Mandrake's aerial reports, they managed to evade the king's
armies for the entire three-week journey back to the Misty
Mountain. They bypassed Traders Run altogether when Mandrake
spotted a brigade of archers camped just outside the village.

They rode up the ancient trail to within sight of the mists and
stopped. Mandrake circled high overhead for a few minutes and
then landed near the fog bank on the road ahead of them. Aster
went forward to meet him alone.

"All right. The pass is just beyond the mountain, the valley is at
the far end of the pass, and the city about twelve leagues beyond
that. Fly on ahead and we'll catch up to you in a day or two."

Mandrake looked down at Aster with an exasperated expression. "I
told you, the mountain is too high for me to fly over. Even with my
chest sack full and my stomach empty, I can only make it half way up."

"You don't have to fly over it, silly, just fly *through* it."

Now Mandrake looked annoyed. "What sort of fool do you take
me for? Do you really expect me to just fly straight into the side of
a mountain for you? If that's how you're planning to get rid of me,
it won't work."

Aster grinned. "I hadn't actually thought of that. It might have
made a good backup plan. But I'm serious. It's only an illusion. The

mountain's not really there. It feels like passing through a thick fog, and you'll be on the other side in no time."

Mandrake didn't look convinced. He regarded Aster with a dour look, but eventually he shook his head and snorted. "All right then, but mark my words. Even if I do smash into a wall of solid rock, I'll survive. Then I'm coming back here to eat your horse." He leaned over and placed his head close to Troy, making the horse buck backwards.

Aster patted the frightened animal. "Easy, Troy, it'll be fine. Nobody around here believes me, but we've been to the other side. At least you know I'm right."

Aster rode back to join the others as Mandrake lifted off. They watched him rise into the sky for a few minutes before Captain Griffin finally spoke. "That's going to be one angry dragon if the mountain turns out to be real."

"Why won't anyone believe me? I tell you, it's all an illusion. I walked right through the thing, twice, not more than a month ago."

"Yes, I believe that *you* walked through it, but what if the spell treats walking princes and flying dragons differently? What if the only place that isn't solid is right behind that pile of rocks you were telling us about?"

Aster's eyes grew wide. "I hadn't thought about it like that." He turned and looked anxiously up through the fog at the partially exposed mountainside. It suddenly looked all too real to him.

Mandrake circled higher and higher until he was above the level of the main fog bank. He looped around a few more times, his head craning towards the peak as if examining it for any hints to its true nature. Then he banked and headed straight for the mountain.

Aster held his breath as Mandrake disappeared momentarily behind the fog and then reappeared just moments before hitting the mountain. When the dragon's head slipped through the rock face as though it wasn't there, Aster breathed a sigh of relief. Mandrake's shoulders passed inside, and ripples began to spread out across the mountain.

It looked like the calm surface of a lake disturbed by a single drop of rain. Circular waves formed at the point of entry and swiftly moved outward, twisting and bending the image of the mountain in the sunlight.

As the dragon's hind legs passed through, a hole formed and began to grow rapidly. By the time Mandrake's tail was passing from view, the mountain, which had loomed over Caledon for a thousand years, was dissolving before their eyes.

Not only was the mountain disappearing, but the fog bank surrounding it was starting to dissipate as well. Within seconds it faded away to reveal a clear trail heading up into the hills toward the now-discernible pass between the northern and southern mountain ranges.

"What just happened?" Eric didn't try to mask the awe in his voice.

"I'm not sure." Aster felt a trembling across his back as the Empress Sword's scabbard began to vibrate. He unsheathed it and held Kai out before him.

"The First has come home. Now the Awakening begins."

Captain Griffin sat up in his saddle. "What is it, lass?"

Aster turned to them with a big smile on his face. "I think the Misty Mountain was just a fence, put up to protect the homeland of the dragons from us humans until one of them returned. Mandrake just opened the gate."

With the mists and the mountain gone, passage into the Valley of Wind was swift and uneventful. Aster stopped for a while at the place where the huge boulder had broken off one of the real mountains and fallen across the road. There was plenty of room to the left for the wagon and horses to pass. He stood near the cliff where he'd lost Paul. After saying goodbye to his old friend, he turned and rejoined his new friends.

They spent the night at the little cabin near the summit. This time the firewood burned easily and all three horses ate the hay, which they seemed to enjoy very much. Captain Griffin made sure they cleaned up the place in the morning; he suspected it was going to get more use.

Aster could tell the difference the moment he saw the valley. The road, which had before cut a grey winding path through the lush fields, now blended in and was hard to follow with the eye. The farmhouses they passed, while still mostly devoid of grass or living things, seemed more inviting than before, as if the farmers had just stepped out and would soon be returning home.

"You were right, lass." Captain Griffin had taken to walking alongside the wagon most of the time, the injuries he'd received battling Mandrake all but mended now. "These farms look as if they've been abandoned for a week, not a thousand years."

"The spell preserving them must have ended when the Misty Mountain went away. They didn't look this—alive—before."

"It's a shame there's no one coming back to work the fields." Maggie looked radiant in the clear mountain sunshine. "These hills look as if you could grow anything here."

"How about that, lass? Is there any chance the people of the Empire are hidden away somewhere, preserved as well?"

"I don't know. Everywhere I've been, it looked as if they packed up and left without ever planning to return. At this point, though, nothing about this place would surprise me."

Marcus stretched his arms over his head and drew in a deep breath. "Life could be good here."

Maggie pouted her lips and furrowed her brow. "Are you going to stay? Even after... You know."

The subject of Aster returning the Empress Sword and becoming himself again had cropped up from time to time since the battle in the woods.

Aster shrugged. "I really don't know, Maggie."

"I mean, they all think the prince is dead. If you were to waltz back into Castlekeep right now, they might burn you for being a ghost."

"We don't burn ghosts any more, but you might be right. I'd probably not be welcomed back there with open arms. My father might not even want me back at all, but I can't just let my mother go on thinking I'm dead."

Captain Griffin patted Troy on the neck as he stepped closer. "There are other ways to let the queen know you're still alive, lass."

Eric appeared on the side of the road ahead of them, emerging from the surrounding green fields with more stealth than a man on a large black horse ought to. He waited for them to catch up, then fell in step next to Aster.

Captain Griffin looked up at the young huntsman and wrinkled his brow. "What's the matter, no luck hunting?"

"Hunting? I wouldn't call this hunting. There's so much game here all you have to do is stand in one place long enough and wait for whatever you want to just wander by. These animals are almost tame. Even the wolves don't look very fierce."

"There are wolves?" Maggie sat up a little straighter on the wagon seat and looked around.

"Are you afraid of wolves, Maggie? You shouldn't be. These looked more like overgrown, overfed house dogs."

"Are those the only predators you've seen, lad—the wolves?"

"That I've actually seen? Yes, only the wolves. But I've also seen signs of bear higher up in the hills to the south."

Aster looked to the south and wondered how Eric had managed to go that far and come back again in the few short hours he'd been gone. He shifted uneasily in his saddle. Ahead, the walls of the city were coming into view. They should arrive at the palace by noon and then it would be time to confront the Empress again.

"Do bears frighten you, your Highness?" Aster looked up to find Eric staring down at him with a reassuring look on his face. He totally misunderstood the question.

"Yes, she's a little frightening, but I wouldn't call her a bear."

Captain Griffin stifled a laugh, Maggie giggled and poor Eric just stared at him with a bewildered look. Aster smiled up at the young man and shook his head. The Empress was a little hard to explain to people.

They didn't speak much after that, but rode on towards the city in silence, each one lost in their own thoughts. Well before noon they passed through the massive outer gates of the city. Captain Griffin remarked that the gates did not look as if they had been forced open, but rather left open for anyone to pass through.

Aster shrugged. "They probably thought the Misty Mountain was protection enough."

"Why haven't any of the animals come through the gate?" Maggie still sounded worried about the wolves and the bears.

Aster looked around. He hadn't seen so much as a mouse when he was here before. "I think it was the way the city was preserved. There was nothing living here at all. No food or water of any kind. It was also a lot—I don't know—greyer."

It was true—the city now seemed full of colors he'd not noticed before. He remembered all the houses being one uniform color, but now there were buildings painted red and green, blue and white, and colors he'd never seen on a house before.

They rode through the quiet streets, marveling at the odd assortment of architectures. Eric wanted to explore some of the larger buildings, but Captain Griffin wouldn't allow it.

"There'll be time for exploring later. Right now Astrid has business at the palace, and a strange business at that. I don't like the idea of you dealing with ghosties and ghoulies, lass."

Aster's eyebrows shot up. "You're not afraid of ghosts, are you?"

"No; the fact is, I don't believe they exist at all. Are you sure your Empress isn't just someone telling you that they're a ghost?"

"She's either a ghost or a spirit, or whatever you call someone from a thousand years ago. I'm pretty sure she's not alive. She was living in this place when nothing else could or would. That's pretty convincing, don't you think?"

"I think it would take an awful lot to convince Daddy of anything." Maggie smiled down at her father from the wagon. When he smiled back, she stuck out her tongue.

Captain Griffin laughed. "We'll see, Pumpkin. Just as soon as we get there."

Marcus pointed into the distance, where the peaked roof of the palace could just be seen through the rooftops of closer buildings. Aster swallowed a lump in his throat. It wouldn't be long now.

37

The Decision

By the time they reached the palace, the sun was high in the sky. When they passed through the tall gates into the great courtyard, Mandrake appeared in the sky above them.

The dragon circled the palace a few times and then landed on one of the long stone benches near the entrance. Aster could now see the railings were designed specifically for the dragons to perch upon. It was clear the courtyard was once as much a gathering place for dragons as it was for the city's human inhabitants. Maggie brought the wagon to a halt near one of the fountains while the others dismounted.

"Well, you weren't exaggerating about the size of the place, either." Captain Griffin said, looking about the courtyard. "This must have been a teeming market town at one time."

"What makes you say that?"

"Well, those paintings at the entrance for one thing. Also the number of shops and storage houses we passed along the way. If the old rumors of a passage to the far east are true, this city would have been the gateway to that passage. It must have been something in its day."

Aster was oddly pleased that his friends liked the ancient city so much. He felt a pride for it that he just couldn't explain. "You might be right about that. We can look around for more clues later. Right now, though, I should return the sword to the Empress."

Maggie finished unhitching the horse from the wagon and joined them on the steps. Aster watched her gracefully climb the stairs towards the palace entrance and wondered how she was going to react when he became himself again. He paused to clear his thoughts and was bumped into by Eric, who'd been following him too closely.

"Eric, you know I'm going to give the sword back to the Empress. I might not be the same once I come back from the throne room."

Eric smiled confidently. "Not the same, your Highness? I don't know much about magic, but you can count on me no matter what dire fate awaits you inside. Nothing will change the way I feel about you."

Aster sighed. However things went with the Empress, the next few hours weren't going to be easy ones. When they reached the top of the stairs, he walked over to where Mandrake perched proudly on the stone railing.

"So, did you find the cave you were looking for? The one you grew up in?"

"Yes, but I decided to take another. It's larger and has a better view of the city." Mandrake scanned the landscape in a long slow arc, ending up with his head facing away from Aster. "Are you really giving up the sword?"

"I have to. I can't stay like this. I have to go back and let my mother know I'm still alive. My place is on the throne of Caledon."

"Your place is here." Mandrake looked at the sky and closed his eyes. "I remember the first time I stood on this very chiang and faced the assembly. I'd just won the tournament that secured my place as the First. I was presented to the Empress that day. You remind me a lot of her; you always have."

Mandrake brought his head down even with Aster's and looked straight into his eyes. "I'm ready to lead the dragons, all of the dragons. That's what I was raised to do. You were similarly bred to lead the humans, all of the humans, and anything less would be an offense to your nature. We can rule the Four Kingdoms together. You know that in your heart."

Aster bowed his head. "Yes, I know, but I don't think I need to be the Empress here to do that. When I'm King of Caledon I can persuade the other kingdoms to form an alliance, and together we can live at peace with the dragons. It just might take a little longer, that's all."

"Do what you feel you must." Mandrake raised his head again and looked away. Aster felt a coldness growing between them and with a heavy heart he turned away from the dragon and rejoined his friends at the entrance to the palace.

Captain Griffin looked grim. "Are you sure this is what you really want?"

Aster nodded and then moved forward. "Let's go."

Their footsteps echoed through the empty corridor as they passed by the ornate chambers, gardens and hallways of the palace. When they reached the far end, they entered the throne room together. The others held back as Aster crossed to the dais and slowly climbed the stairs to stand before the dragon throne.

He pulled the Empress Sword and its scabbard from his back and held them up. He hadn't wished to admit until now just how reluctant he was to give her back. Kai felt good in his hands, as though she were made for him and not for some girl who lived and died a thousand years before he was born...but these weren't *his* hands.

Gently he placed Kai on the throne where he'd originally found her and stepped back. Then he turned and walked slowly down the steps without looking back.

When he reached the floor he raised his head to the vaulted ceiling and called out. "I've returned the sword, your Majesty! We defeated the dragon together and he won't bother my people again. I don't need Kai now, so you can have her back."

There was no answer. Aster listened for the old woman's voice or the sound of her footsteps, but only the distant moaning of the wind outside reached his straining ears. He heard Captain Griffin whisper to the others, followed by the sound of the great doors closing quietly behind him.

Aster waited a few more minutes, then his shoulders sagged; he suddenly felt defeated. "Please take back the sword, your Majesty! She belongs here with you. And if you would please, could you turn me back into a boy again?"

"I didn't turn you into a girl in the first place. Kai did."

Aster jumped a yard into the air at the sound of the Empress's voice coming from right behind him. He turned to see her standing there with a mischievous grin on her face. "You nearly scared the life out of me, your Majesty!"

"Isn't that what 'ghosties and ghoulies' are supposed to do?"

Aster looked embarrassed. "Oh, you heard that? I'm sorry. Captain Griffin wasn't trying to be insulting or anything. I just don't think he believes me all the time."

"You'd be surprised what that man does and does not believe." The Empress moved past Aster and mounted the steps to the throne. She looked down at the sword and then back to Aster. "I like him, and you'll need someone of his quality by your side in the coming years. Are you really sure you want to give this back to me?"

"Oh yes! She helped me defeat the dragon and now he won't be attacking my father's kingdom anymore."

"So, you *killed* the dragon?"

Aster stared at the floor, shuffling his feet. "Um, well no, but he swore to me that he'd never attack Caledon again."

"He swore to you?" The Empress knitted her eyebrows together. "To you or to the sword?"

"Well, to me, of course."

Aster thought about it for a minute. He remembered the day outside Traders Run when Mandrake, wounded and in fear for his life, knelt and swore the Dragon's Oath. Aster had been holding the Empress Sword before him. Mandrake could have been bowing to her instead of him. He frowned at the memory. Suddenly, he wasn't entirely sure what had actually transpired that day.

The Empress smiled again. "Never mind, it doesn't matter. Let's assume he'll keep his promise and never attack your father's kingdom again. What about the others?"

"The others?"

"The other dragons. Surely you didn't think there would be only one? You've seen the mountains surrounding this valley. Each one of those caves was home to a mating pair, in my time. I'm proud to say that every pair had at least one pup. Most had many more. All of those young dragons went north, and are now awaiting their time to arise and take on the world. Do you expect each of them to abide by a promise made to you by just one of their kind?"

"Mandrake seems to think most of them will. Can't someone else use the sword to deal with the rest? There must be plenty of real women in the Four Kingdoms who are better swordsmen than I am. Couldn't you let one of them use Kai to stop the dragons? Why does it have to be me? I'm tired of this crazy spell. I'm tired of looking like a girl. I just want to be myself again!"

The Empress frowned. She descended the steps slowly and stood in front of Aster. She put one hand on his shoulder and used the other to lift his chin. She spoke to him in a clear, gentle voice.

"Child, Kai did not cast a spell to make you look like a girl, she changed you into one. To tell the truth, I don't know if she would change you back into a boy again even if I asked her to."

"But I am a boy! I'm not a girl. I may look like a girl on the outside, but inside I haven't changed. I'm still a boy. I'm still me!"

"Kai chose you because of who you are on the inside. She didn't need to change your courageous and compassionate soul, only the physical shell that holds it. All great magic requires a sacrifice from those who would use it, and you agreed to that willingly. Only a woman may touch the sword, so for its sacrifice she took your manhood. In return she will serve you, and only you, for the rest of your days."

Aster saw sadness creep into the Empress's eyes. The sword must have demanded such a sacrifice from her, as well. "Did the sword change you into a girl as well?"

The old woman blinked and then laughed. "What? Oh my goodness no. I was never particularly good at womanly things, but

I was born a girl. No, the sword took something far dearer from me than my gender."

"Your Majesty?" Aster couldn't think of anything worse than what had happened to him, but he sensed he had a great deal to learn about the price of magic.

"I should be resting at peace with my ancestors right now, but I gave Kai my soul so she would bond with my sword. My body died long ago, but I continue on. When you are but a fond memory in the hearts of slumbering dragons, I shall still be here watching over her."

"The spell preserving the city and this palace—that was you, wasn't it?"

The Empress smiled again. "Yes. I couldn't just stand by and watch my beautiful home wither and turn to dust. So I spent my time keeping the place up and waiting for the next Empress to arrive. Imagine my surprise when she turned out to be a cocky young prince. Are you ready?"

Aster felt the crushing weight of destiny descending on his shoulders. He'd believed he knew what he wanted, but now he wasn't so sure. He thought of Caledon, his mother, his home, the king, Mandoline, and Penelope. Could he really go back to all of that if he became the prince again?

He thought of his new friends. Eric, who was more loyal to him than any retainer he'd ever had. Mandrake had sworn fealty to him, and so had Marcus, apparently. Would they continue to follow him as the Prince of Caledon?

And then there was Maggie. She was the best friend he'd ever had. He loved her and wanted to be with her forever. He thought she loved him as well, but would that love survive his becoming a boy again? She'd told Eric and her father that she *had* liked him as a boy, but she became friends with a girl.

Aster sighed and then nodded to the Empress. "What should I do? Do I just ask Kai to turn me back into a boy?"

Afanasia stepped to Aster's side and wrapped her arm around his shoulders. With a gentle nudge, she coaxed him to climb the steps with her and stand before the throne.

"If you truly want it in your heart, she already knows. You'll need to pick her up again. Don't worry, your friends are right outside waiting to help you."

Aster looked up at the old Empress. Her smile was kind and her eyes twinkled. He wrapped his other arm around her and she hugged him back. Then she moved aside and waved her fan at the Empress Sword. He reached for it, but stopped just before grasping the hilt.

"What exactly happens when a man touches the sword?"

The old woman chuckled in a way that made the hairs on the back of Aster's neck stand up. "Ah, I have no doubt it's uncomfortable for them, but it was actually meant to be enlightening. You see, when a man grasps Kai, he's granted a vision and experiences all the sensations a woman feels during childbirth."

Aster furrowed his brow. "Is that painful?"

"There's only one way to find out. Take up the sword, child, and good luck to you."

Aster held out his hand. He closed his eyes and, with the image of Maggie's face firmly in his mind, he lifted the Empress Sword from the throne.

The Awakening

The cave was large, airy and—Mandrake hoped—inviting. It was also well located and provided the kind of status the First male needed if he ever hoped to attract an outstanding female. Mandrake stood in the center of his new home and stretched. No matter how hard he tried, nothing touched stone but his feet.

He was ready, the valley was ready, even the few humans who had arrived in the last few weeks were ready. It was finally time to go and awaken the others.

Mandrake folded his wings and walked to the entrance. Looking out at the bright midday sun reflecting off the rooftops of the city, Mandrake tried to imagine the skies filled with his old friends. *And pups! There will be so many pups.*

He leapt into the air, extending his wings to catch the updraft, and sailed towards the city. Looking west, he saw a line of wagons heading his way along the road leading from the pass. There seemed to be more and more of them coming every day, and he turned toward them to have a closer look.

As he passed over the wagons, their occupants waved to him, as if a dragon flying overhead were the most natural thing in the world. He wondered at what sort of people would travel this far to settle an unknown land ruled by a once-feared beast. Then he saw a young boy jumping up and down on one of the wagons, waving frantically at him. The boy looked familiar, so Mandrake landed next to the wagon.

"Hello, Mr. Dragon!"

"Hello, boy. Have you come to hunt in my valley?" Mandrake recognized the young archer he'd met in the woods months before—the same boy whose generosity had led him to attack Traders Run and, by extension, had opened up this valley.

"You see, Daddy, I told you he could talk! Mr. Dragon, this is my father."

The man sitting next to the boy nervously removed his hat and nodded his head to Mandrake. "Begging your pardon, my Lord. Jake here goes on a bit. With your permission we'd like to go to that city yonder. I've heard tell there are jobs for men with metalworking skills. I used to be a blacksmith on Derry."

"I'm sure the Regent will welcome you with open arms. He tells me he needs all sorts of men to bring the city back to life. We also need our share of good hunters." Mandrake winked at the boy.

"I can handle that for you, Mr. Dragon!"

"My name's Mandrake, and I'd be honored if you'd call me by my name."

"Sure thing, Mr. Mandrake!"

The dragon threw back his head and laughed. He bid them both farewell and then took off, circling up into the cool mountain air. In the distance, he spotted a figure waving to him from the palace. He banked to the northeast and prepared to land on the terrace.

The figure turned out to be the Regent, looking very out of place in the ancient court robes he'd been wearing more often of late. The man was clearly more comfortable being a soldier than an administrator, but the fledging Empire was in need of both at the moment, and everyone was wearing several different hats.

"Mandrake!" Marcus called out to him as he settled on the stone chiang. "Is this the day?"

"That it is. I'll be gone for about a month, but when I return the skies will be full of dragons."

Marcus smiled a bit uncertainly. "That will be a sight to see, lad. How many will there be?"

Mandrake took a long deep breath. "I don't really know. I was never told the actual count. As the First, I flew north ahead of the rest. I was deep into my own slumber when they arrived. They may not all come back with me either, at least not right away."

"Oh?" Marcus looked suddenly concerned.

"It's been ten years, and that's far longer than it should have taken. Some may have already awakened and left the Slumberlands. Others, my rivals, may decide I'm unworthy of leading the clan now and go off on their own. However, most will come here, eager to begin new lives. I won't know how many, exactly, until the first assembly is held."

Marcus nodded. "I was afraid of something like that. Those others are likely to pose a problem. Will they fit in if we bring them here by force?"

"Yes, I believe so. Even the most hostile of dragons are still bound by their honor. If they swear the Dragon's Oath, they shouldn't be a problem."

"And if they won't swear the Oath?"

"In that event, the Empress will just have to decide what to do with them."

Marcus pulled at his chin. "Let's hope we don't face that problem too often. She has enough to worry about right here with the valley coming back to life."

"I noticed more wagons coming through the pass. There's a blacksmith and a capable hunter on the way."

Marcus looked to the west. "And more traders no doubt. The word's beginning to spread that the pass is open again. I'm sure this is only the beginning."

"Why would traders be coming here? Is there anything to trade for?"

"Not much as yet, but that'll change very soon."

Mandrake cocked his head sideways. "I don't follow you."

"Right now there's plenty of wild game in the valley, and for a time that'll provide food and a source of tradable furs. However, such a bounty won't last long. Eventually someone's going to have to raise cattle to feed all these dragons you're bringing home. Someone else is going to have to raise crops to feed the cattle. Those farmers are going to need tradespeople to keep their farms running and the tradesmen are going to need goods brought in from the other kingdoms. So the smart traders are getting their foot in the door early."

"You're starting to sound more like a royal advisor than a soldier."

"No, lad, I'm still just a soldier who spent enough time on the road to know that every trader's dream is to settle down and open up a shop somewhere he can call home. That's a hard thing to do in the Four Kingdoms these days. There's always someone whose family's been there for generations, telling you to move on. And it's not just traders having a hard time getting themselves established. We've already seen some farmers, and that blacksmith you mentioned, come looking for a new home."

"You make it sound as though we dragons can't survive without you humans."

Marcus grinned. "Hardly. But together we can make this valley a mighty Empire once again."

"Is that what you want, or what she wants?"

"I think it's what we all want. A home we can be proud of."

A rattling sound came from inside the palace and they both looked around to see what it was. A figure dressed in heavy metal armor came trudging out of the entrance doors. He seemed to be having trouble seeing out of the large ornate helmet and looked around by turning awkwardly at the waist.

As he shuffled over to them, clanking and jangling with every step, Mandrake recognized the huntsman inside the armor. Using both hands, Eric lifted the helm just enough to look at them through the eye slits.

"Captain Griffin, are you sure this is the right kind of armor? It's awfully heavy and it doesn't look like any drawings I've ever seen."

Marcus laughed. "You wanted to dress like a knight, lad. This might just be ceremonial armor from a thousand years ago, but it's all we've got for now."

Mandrake shook his head. "That's not ceremonial. It's the armor of the Palace Guard of Kafu. I remember seeing men dressed in such armor on this very terrace many times during my youth."

"The Palace Guard of what?" Eric swung around to face Mandrake.

"Kafu. That's the name of this city."

Eric rolled his arm up over his head and the armor clanked noisily. "Did the palace guard move around much? This is the most uncomfortable thing I've ever had on."

"It might be a bit more comfortable with the breastplate facing forwards, lad." Marcus chuckled again. "I'll show you how to wear it properly later. Have you seen Maggie?"

"I've got it on backwards? I knew something was wrong. Last time I saw Maggie she was back rummaging around the palace living quarters. Said the Empress asked her to find something."

Marcus grinned. "Then we might not see either of them again for quite some time."

"No, I think that's your daughter." Mandrake inclined his head towards the palace entrance and both men looked around.

Maggie walked out onto the terrace dressed in a long robe. It was made from black silk that had large white flowers woven into the shimmering fabric. A wide black sash wrapped around her waist several times and she walked awkwardly on a pair of wooden sandals.

"You look lovely, Pumpkin. Where'd you find that?"

"There's a whole room filled with these robes, Daddy, and they're all made of silk, the finest I've ever seen."

"That's called a ki, and you wear it very nicely."

"Thank you, Mandrake! Today's the day you leave to get the other dragons, isn't it?" Mandrake nodded. "Then you'll have to wait a bit. The Empress is having a little more trouble walking on these clogs than I am, but she was right behind me."

They all looked at the palace entrance again. There was movement just inside the doorway and then a tiny figure appeared. At the sight of her, Mandrake sucked in a breath and held it.

It was as if time had suddenly rolled back a thousand years. The Empress emerged into the light dressed in the red and gold ceremonial ki of her office. The ki was heavily embroidered with swans and lilies, mostly in threads of pure gold, but mixed in were all the colors of the rainbow. She looked resplendent, even if she was only wearing two of the traditional seven layers.

Her dark hair was piled high on her head and held with black onyx combs trimmed in sliver and set with pearls. Her delicate face was not covered in the traditional white makeup that had been in fashion when Mandrake was a pup. He smiled, remembering that the first Empress had not often worn the heavy makeup either.

Everything about the figure in the doorway was regal and elegant, except maybe the way she kept fidgeting with something inside her ki.

Mandrake stood erect, clutching the chiang tightly with his claws, and bowed. Beside him Marcus followed suit, and a clanking noise accompanied Eric's attempt at going down on one knee. The Empress approached them slowly and stopped fidgeting long enough to extend her hands to them.

"Oh no, please get up. I only demand that kings bow before me now." Astrid giggled, but Mandrake didn't see anything funny about that. "How do you like the clothes Maggie found? I finally have a dress I'm comfortable wearing. There's even a little pocket in here for a knife."

Maggie groaned. "Will you please stop fiddling with that stupid pocket. You're going to loosen the sash again."

"No, I'm not. The Empress said you tied it correctly this time."

"According to you! You're the only one can hear her."

"That's not my fault."

"Your Majesty?" Marcus held his hand between the two girls and they both looked up at him. "Mandrake is leaving today."

"Is that today?" Astrid walked over to Mandrake. "I'm sorry, I forgot all about it. Is there anything I can do before you go?"

"Nothing, your Majesty, until I return again with my kin. Then

I would have you preside over the first assembly. You might wish to think about what you'll say to them. You'll want to make a good first impression."

"Then how about I just say welcome home." Astrid smiled and Marcus cleared his throat. "Um... And maybe a few thousand more, carefully chosen words I'll be discussing with my Regent while you're gone."

"That should do quite nicely." Mandrake considered his next words very carefully. "If I may say so, your majesty, you look—happier. I'm glad you decided to stay."

Astrid paused with a frown on her face. She'd made a very difficult decision in becoming the Empress, and only she knew how much it had cost her. After a few moments her face brightened again.

"So am I. Good luck on your journey. Bring home as many as you can. Tell them the Empress of the Eastern Empire awaits their arrival with open arms. I can't wait to meet each and every one of them."

"I will tell them that."

"Goodbye, Mandrake. Do take care." Maggie waved, rocking unsteadily on the wooden clogs.

"Will you be bringing back any pretty girl dragons?" Eric clanked again as he raised his arm for a wave.

Then Marcus gave him a quick salute. "Safe journey, lad. Fly swift and avoid as much of Caledon as you can."

He stared for a moment at the unlikely group of humans who'd given him back his homeland. Now they were allies and perhaps one day soon, if Astrid had her way, they would be his countrymen. They were also something he had never expected, after ten long years of fighting the humans: they were his friends.

"Goodbye, my friends." He spread his wings, flexed his back muscles and lifted off the terrace. After hovering there for a moment longer he roared a farewell greeting and turned toward the west.

With the wind at his back, he raced through the valley. Flying just above the treetops, he climbed into the pass and wove his way through the mountains. It was an easy flight, one that would not trouble the adults, but one day soon it would become a trial of sorts for the older pups. As it had been in his youth, the day one managed to fly out of the valley was the day one became a dragon.

Beyond the pass, he raced across the plateau and into the foothills. The village of Traders Run came into view. Word had come from arriving traders that the king's army had finally left the town a few days before. Feeling safe and a bit elated, Mandrake decided to fly over it.

He did not risk too low a pass; he wasn't exactly sure what sort of reception he would get there. When he saw the humans running through the streets, he was at first disappointed. Then he noticed they were not running away from him, but toward him.

He circled down for a closer look and discovered that most of the humans running through the streets chasing him were children. They were waving and calling out to him, and most of them were laughing. He briefly considered landing and talking to them, but he wanted to be well north of Caledon's border by day's end. He made a mental note to visit Traders Run when he returned and bring with him some of the other dragons.

He banked north, leaving the children's joyful cries behind, and climbed into the clouds. He kept close to the mountains all day long until he was well into the Greylands. The air tasted cold here, a familiar tang that seemed wrong to him. His long sleep was over and he would not return this far north ever again.

He settled on a low mountaintop for the night, watching the sun dip spectacularly into the clouds, turning them red as the sky slowly darkened.

By this time tomorrow I'll be in the Slumberlands. I wonder what's waiting there for me.

As excited as he was by the prospect of awakening his kin, he was already looking forward to returning home. He wanted to introduce the other dragons to the young Empress—who had once been a prince—and tell them all about how she saved him with the Empress Sword.

About the Author

Paulette Jaxton began writing prose and poetry in high school, but was encouraged to focus on math and science instead by well meaning teachers. A world famous poet once praised a verse she wrote about butterflies, until the women noticed a spelling error and pronounced the poem "a piece of crap."

In the 1970s, Paulette left college to pursue a career in computer programming at NASA's Goddard Space Flight Center. Later she went on to work for Digital Equipment Corporation developing telecommunications software and advanced user interfaces. She currently works developing interactive kiosk technology for retail applications.

She kept her writings to herself until 2008 when she produced *Form Letter Rejection Theatre*, a podcast anthology of her short speculative fiction. *The Empress Sword* is her first novel.

www.ingramcontent.com/pod-product-compliance
Lightning Source LLC
Chambersburg PA
CBHW021956010726
47494CB00003B/756